THINGS WE SHOULDN'T DO

LINDSEY CACY

APARIGRAHA PRESS

For Delissa—

who helped carry this story in its making,
and who knows that choosing yourself
can be the hardest and bravest thing of all.
May you always trust the quiet voice that says,
keep going.

PROLOGUE

"The minute people fall in love, they become liars." –Harlan Ellison

Lies are greedy. They breed in silence, in shadows, in the places you refuse to look. Usually by the time you realize how far they have spread, it is too late. Someone always gets caught in the wreckage.

They never tell you how easy it is to live inside a lie. At first it feels like protection—like wrapping yourself in something warm so no one sees the cracks underneath. You start with little things: what you want, what you need, what you cannot bear to admit. Then the bigger lies come—the ones you tell to keep your marriage together, to keep yourself from shattering, to keep the truth from dragging you under.

When I think back, I cannot decide what ruined me first: the lies John told me or the lies I told myself. Maybe it does not matter. Maybe our story was always going to end this way.

Because once the truth clawed its way to the surface, everything I thought I knew about love and loyalty came undone, and what was left in its place was darker than I ever imagined.

And I was standing in the middle of it.

CHAPTER ONE

I know he's lying, just as surely as I know he fucked her two weeks ago.

If there's anything I've learned in my thirty-nine years on this earth, it's that men will lie to cover their asses every single time. It's instinct, like breathing. And as I look at him standing there, hands on his hips, staring at me as if I'm the problem, I feel disgust. Not surprise; disgust. The deceit rolls off his tongue like it's second nature, and his audacity is almost comical.

Nine and a half years.

For nearly *ten* years, I've given this man my love and loyalty. I gave him the best years of my life. I gave him my fucking thirties. And if you ask any woman over forty, she'll tell you the same thing: your thirties are when life finally starts to get good. You outgrow the dumb naivety of your twenties and step fully into yourself. I gave him that.

"Are you even listening to me?"

I return my gaze to my husband and realize he's still talking.

Oops.

"No," I admit. "I'm just trying to process everything."

He throws his hands in the air and sighs loudly, pure exasperation.

Men really are immature.

His words keep coming, explanation stacked on top of explanation, each one thinner than the last. I stand there listening, nodding when it feels expected, even though something inside me has already gone still. The truth isn't dramatic. It doesn't explode. It settles, heavy and unmistakable, right in the center of my chest.

This is it.

I feel the heartbreak first, a dull ache spreading outward, followed quickly by something sharper. Anger. Not loud. Not wild. *Clarifying.* Years of trust rearrange themselves in my mind in a matter of seconds, every instinct I talked myself out of suddenly snapping into place.

By the time he finishes speaking, whatever chance he had is already gone.

Here is this grown-ass man, five years older than me, standing in our bedroom like a child throwing a tantrum because he got caught.

Gross.

"I'm leaving," I say, matter-of-fact, turning to the desk to grab my purse. When I look back at him, I catch a flicker of fear in his eyes.

"Leaving? Like *leaving me* leaving? Aren't we going to talk about this?"

"Apparently we have nothing to talk about, since you claim you didn't do anything." I sling the purse strap over my shoulder. "I need space. Time to myself."

His caramel-colored face flushes red. "I don't know how many other ways I can tell you—Constance is just a lady at my job. We went to have drinks, and nothing else happened!"

I start tossing a few things into my oversized purse: leggings, a sweat-shirt. Then I move into the bathroom attached to our bedroom, scoop up my toothbrush and deodorant, and drop them into my little essentials bag from Forever Twenty-One.

When I walk back out, he's sitting on the edge of the bed, head in his hands, muttering to himself.

Pathetic.

"I saw the messages, John. Friends from work don't talk about 'how good you felt last Saturday,'" I say, calm but cold. My heart pounds in my temples as I watch him, waiting for the panic to surface on his face.

"This is crazy," he blurts, flustered. "She was talking about a conversation we'd had. She told me about some guys she was seeing, so I was just being a supportive friend. The conversation made her feel better, and I'm sure that's what she meant by that."

"I'm sure," I say, flat.

Something I learned long ago: when a man doesn't have an answer, he doesn't admit it. He buys time, ransacks his brain for an excuse, and hopes you'll back down first.

Not me.

I shake my head and walk out. The long hallway of our lavish Long Island home stretches ahead of me, and with each step I take, the air feels lighter. By the time I pull my phone out of my yoga pants, I'm already texting Jenna to say I'm coming over.

***

"Oh, yeah, he's definitely cheating," Jenna says as she takes my bag from me. "I can't believe he tried to say she was referring to a conversation."

I set my purse down on the small glass table next to Jenna's sand-colored couch, then flop onto the couch.

"I know, girl," is all I can manage. I lean my head back and close my eyes. I feel her sit next to me.

"Well, you know you can stay here as long as you need. I'll be at work most of the time anyway."

Jenna is a big-time criminal defense attorney who works upward of sixty hours a week. At least. Looking at her—with her petite stature, long blonde hair, and big blue doe eyes—you wouldn't know it. But she's a shark in the courtroom. If I ever became a criminal, she'd be the first person I'd call, not just because she's a good friend.

"Thanks, babe," I say with a weak smile. "I need some time to figure shit out. After all these years and everything we've been through together, I can't believe he could do this to me—and then have the audacity to lie in my face."

She's shaking her head, her big blue eyes dark and narrowed. "It's disrespectful! And gross—guys are just gross."

"Well, lucky for you, you only have to deal with them in a professional sense," I say.

She lets out a short bark of laughter. "Women can be just as scandalous in relationships, Lo. Trust me."

"People just suck in general, I guess," I mutter, suddenly feeling defeated and worn down.

Jenna slaps her hands on her knees and stands. She grabs my hand and pulls me up so I'm standing beside her.

"Let's stop going down this road and have some wine," she chirps. I listlessly follow her into the kitchen. I feel a little lighter as I sit on the barstool she gestures to at her kitchen's center island.

I take a large gulp of the cool, crisp liquid when she hands me my glass. Setting it down, I close my eyes. When I open them, I see Jenna staring at me with a concerned look.

"What?" I ask, reaching for my long-stemmed glass again.

"Nothing," she says quickly, playing with a long blonde lock of hair. Her eyes meet mine again, and she sighs. "I hate that you're dealing with this. You don't deserve it."

"Nobody deserves this, Jenna. It's the blatant lying in my face for me—the fact that he could look me in the eyes and tell me earnestly that what I saw wasn't real. It's disturbing."

"It's gaslighting," she says.

I look down at my hands, my vision blurring. I swallow hard, but my throat burns anyway, like my body is protesting the lie I keep telling myself. I've spent years learning how to stay composed, how to hold things together even when they're already fractured. This is just another version of that, I tell myself. Another moment where I choose dignity over devastation.

John doesn't deserve a tear.

The thought lands, then wobbles. Loving someone for this long doesn't shut off on command. It doesn't vanish just because I finally see the truth, or because I know—deep down—that I deserve more than half-truths and quiet betrayals. The ache spreads, slow and insistent, pressing against my chest, demanding to be felt.

I take another sip of wine, slower this time, letting myself feel the break for a breath before sealing it back up. Strength isn't the absence of pain. It's refusing to keep bleeding for someone who never learned how to hold what he was given.

"So," I say after a steadying breath. "Now what?"

"I'm going to get the guest room ready for you, then let's grab some food, maybe? If you're hungry."

I nod. "Thanks again for letting me crash here."

She waves her hand dismissively as she takes a sip from her glass. "I live alone and am looking forward to some company! Think of this as an extended sleepover."

I can't help but laugh. Jenna refills my glass and pecks me on the cheek before heading past me to the guest room.

I sigh and look around for my purse. Spotting it on the couch, I stand and walk over. I rummage until I feel my sleek plastic phone case. There are several notifications, and from what I can see on my lock screen, they're all from John. Rolling my eyes, I return to the kitchen island and, more importantly, my glass of wine.

I scroll through his nine text messages. They range from "Where are you?" to "Come on, babe, can't we just talk?" I decide to ignore them for now.

Good, I think. Let him squirm.

"Okay! The room is ready for the taking," Jenna says from behind me, and I almost jump off the barstool at her sudden presence.

She smiles sheepishly before giving me a quizzical look. "You okay? I'm not used to seeing you so jumpy."

"I'm okay. John sent some messages."

"Ew," she says, wrinkling her nose. "Saying what?"

"Oh, you know, the usual. I'm sorry, come home, where are you," I say with a dramatic eye roll.

Jenna shakes her head. "Well, fuck him. Let him wonder what you're up to for a change."

I nod, liking the sound of that. I'd spent countless hours waiting for him and wondering where he was. It felt rewarding to know he was at home, probably doing the same thing right now.

"That's a great idea," I say, flashing Jenna a wicked smile. "Now, where should we eat?"

She unlocks her phone and starts searching. "There's this little taco place that just opened downtown. It's supposed to be amazing, and they have margaritas."

"Perfect," I say, standing and stretching. "I'm going to get changed, then I'll be ready to go."

Chapter Two

We giggle, bumping shoulders and nearly tripping over each other as Jenna fumbles with her janitor-worthy set of keys. The entire ring jingles, and she mutters under her breath while trying to find the right one. The pitcher of margaritas we split over dinner has made its presence painfully clear in my system, sloshing in my stomach and pressing on my bladder until I feel like I might burst.

"Why do you have so many keys?" I whine, bouncing on the balls of my feet. My purse keeps slipping off my shoulder every time I shift, and I'm too busy squeezing my thighs together to care. I can't decide if I'm laughing or crying as I squirm behind her, practically dancing in place on the porch.

She snorts, squinting at the lock. "It's not my fault you didn't use the bathroom at the restaurant!" Her laugh bubbles out, full of amusement at my misery, and the keys jangle louder as she finally separates the one she wants. The metallic clink echoes in the stillness of the quiet street, and all I can think is that I'm one second away from peeing on her welcome mat if she doesn't get this damn door open.

At last, the lock clicks. She pushes the door wide, and I bolt past her with a strangled noise, tossing my purse onto the couch like it's on fire. I don't even glance around; I'm already sprinting down the hallway, making a beeline for the bathroom.

The door stays open behind me as I drop onto the toilet with no grace at all. Relief comes instantly, tearing out of me in a loud, almost comical rush. My whole body sags, and I let out an audible sigh as if I've been holding my breath for hours. From the kitchen, Jenna's laughter rings out, sharp and cackling.

"You weren't kidding when you said you had to pee like a racehorse," she calls over her shoulder. "Sounds like a goddamn fire hose in there!"

I laugh in spite of myself, shaking my head, mortified but too relieved to care. "*Shut up!*"

When I'm finally finished, I take my time washing my hands, splashing cool water over my flushed face. The sight of myself in the mirror—cheeks pink, curls slightly wild from the humid air, eyes glassy from tequila—makes me laugh quietly again. I pat my face dry and step back into the hallway, following the sound of Jenna's giggles.

She's already at the kitchen counter, pouring water into two giant glasses. She moves with the casual authority of someone who has hosted drunk friends before and knows the drill.

"Drink," she orders, thrusting one into my hands. "So you don't feel like death tomorrow."

The glass is cool against my palms. I raise it and drink greedily, gulp after gulp until I'm halfway through before I even lower it for air.

Jenna arches a brow, impressed. "Well damn."

I grin, wiping my mouth with the back of my hand and catching a stray drop at the corner of my lip. "Thank you. I can't believe we drank the whole pitcher between us."

Her laugh is low and warm. She shakes her head as though she expected nothing less. "Lightweights. Come on, let's get some sleep, woman."

I lean into her, hugging her tightly. The alcohol makes me all soft and sentimental, and I murmur another thank you for letting me stay. Her house smells faintly of vanilla candles and fabric softener, and that little mix of scents feels comforting and familiar. It's warm and inviting, the opposite of the cold, sharp tension that's waiting for me back at my own house.

The stairs creak under my weight as I climb, and upstairs I slip into the guest room. The bed is neatly made, the pillows plump—the kind of cozy setup that makes me feel instantly cared for. I sink onto the mattress, leaning back against the plush pillows, but comfort doesn't mean rest. My body is heavy with booze and exhaustion, but my mind won't settle.

The room hums with the quiet of central air, but inside my head, it's chaos. Thoughts spin restlessly, replaying the day on loop. John's face. His voice. The way his lies slid so easily off his tongue.

And then *Constance.*

The memory drops into me like a stone in still water, rippling out, unavoidable.

Constance Keller. His newest executive assistant. Young, blonde, tiny. The complete opposite of me with my five-eleven frame, my loose yet often unruly auburn curls, my body carved from years of discipline and Pilates. I'm approaching forty. She can't be more than twenty-five.

It wasn't her resumé that made my radar blare. It was the way she looked at him.

I remember watching her glide across the event space, balancing two glasses of champagne like she'd rehearsed. Her eyes locked on John's as though no one else existed. And when I glanced at him, expecting to find his gaze anywhere but on her, I caught him staring right back. That flicker of panic when he realized I'd noticed told me everything I needed to know.

"Hello, John," she'd said, her childlike voice laced with a familiarity that scraped every nerve raw in my body.

I'd raised an eyebrow, waiting for her to acknowledge me.

"Hi, Constance." John's hand shot to the back of his neck, rubbing like he always did when caught and uncomfortable. Then he gestured toward me. "This is my wife, Halo."

Her gaze slid to me, assessing. Thank God I'd worn the green velvet dress. Tight in all the right places, dipping low enough to show off my surgically enhanced cleavage, clinging to my thighs and ass like it had been made for me. Paired with red heels, I'd leaned into a look that screamed festive but dangerous. Santa's sexy little helper, if you will.

"Hello," I'd said, my smile polite but my eyes sharp, fixed on hers with a silent message: *I see you, bitch.*

She swallowed and glanced at her feet. "Hi, nice to meet you."

We stood in an awkward triangle, bodies suspended in the crowded hum of the event.

"Constance is my... uh, assistant," John offered. "She handles all the Student Services scheduling, keeps my meetings straight. She graduated from Shady Oaks a few semesters ago."

Why the life story? Why the nervous over-explaining?

"That's great," I'd said, eyes still locked on hers. "Sounds like you work very closely with my husband."

Her lips curved into a smirk that didn't match her words. "Yes, I do."

The words burned, and in my head a single word hissed back. *Cunt.*

John had tipped back his glass, swallowing what was left like it might save him.

"What do you do, Halo?" she'd asked in that syrupy voice, too sweet to be sincere.

I'd tilted my head, eyes narrowing. "Oh, my husband didn't tell you?"

Her smile faltered, eyes darting between us.

"I'm an English and Literature instructor," I'd continued smoothly, stepping closer so my height towered over her tiny frame. "I also work at Shady Oaks University."

Her eyes widened, darting back to John, then me. She stepped back, but I didn't move.

"So maybe I'll see you around on campus," I said evenly, holding her stare like a blade pressed to skin.

She mumbled something about finding a friend, her face struggling to rearrange into composure. But she still looked rattled when she slipped away into the crowd.

Good.

I exhale, bringing my awareness back to Jenna's guest bed. Sleep is nowhere close, though my body aches for it. I glance at my phone on the nightstand, the screen lighting up with a text from my brother, Paxton.

Yo what's up with John calling me and asking where you are? You good?

I type back: *I'm good. Long story, but I'm staying at Jenna's for a few days. Big fight with John.*

Silence follows. No more messages from John. Thank God. I plug in my phone, roll onto my side, and close my eyes. The margarita buzz softens the edges of everything, lulling me.

But I know the storm hasn't passed.

Not even close.

***

I check my phone to ensure I am not early, but it is indeed 10:15 a.m.

I'd agreed to meet my brother, Paxton, to get breakfast and coffee at 10 a.m. downtown. But true to form, he is late. I text him.

You coming?

I hear a phone chirp behind me and whirl around to see Paxton approaching. His hair is normally braided back in cornrows, but this morning it is pulled into a frizzy bun at the top of his head. His usually trimmed-up beard looks unkempt, and he's wearing a wrinkled Crenshaw hoodie and basketball shorts. Not his usual dapper look.

"Don't even say it," he says in a rough voice when he sees my face.

"I won't. Rough night?"

He raises his hand to his head in an attempt to smooth his messy hair. I stifle a giggle.

"Let's eat. We can talk inside, and I need coffee," he says, opening the cafe door and ushering me in.

We're seated at a little corner booth near the back, and I'm grateful for the privacy. I glance over the menu even though I know exactly what I'll order. Whenever we come here, I always get the house-made corned beef hash with two eggs over easy. But knowing my indecisive brother will be gazing at the menu, grappling with the too-many options, we'll be here for a while.

"So, what the hell happened with John?" he asks. "He called me five times and sent all these texts asking if I knew where you were. I was at the gym, so I didn't see all his calls and shit until after—and that's when I texted you."

The waitress arrives and hands us each a water. "Do we know what we're having?" she asks cheerfully.

I shoot Paxton a look, and he looks up, sheepish. "Gimme like five minutes?"

"You do this every time," I say as the waitress walks away.

He laughs and continues to search the menu. "So John. What's his problem?"

"He's mad because I left. Because he's having an affair. And I don't think he's worried if I'm okay as much as he's worried I'm out fucking one of my colleagues."

Paxton lowers his menu to reveal his widened eyes. "Wait, what? What do you mean, having an affair?"

"Pax, he's cheating on me... I mean, I think he is. I found texts on his phone about 'how good he felt' after a weekend he was supposedly only out with the team having drinks. He came home super late and slept in, and that's when I saw the text from his assistant."

Paxton stares at me, taking in what I've shared. After a second, his eyes narrow and he slams his fist on the table.

"Are you fucking serious? He's cheating on you? With his coworker?" His voice is low and controlled, but I can tell he's pissed.

"I think so. What else could explain that text?"

"Did you ask him about the message?"

"I did. He said it was because he comforted her when she was feeling sad and that the 'feeling good' was due to that—not about something physical." Even hearing myself say the words, it sounds stupid.

"What a dumbass," Paxton snorts. "That doesn't even sound right. And why would he be comforting another woman, especially someone he works with? That's sketchy as hell."

I nod, even though *sketchy* doesn't come close to covering it, and glance up as the waitress approaches, grateful for the pause. We order, exchange quick thank-yous, and I wait until she's gone before I keep going.

"I'm torn," I say, leaning back in my chair. "Because my gut says he's cheating. He's been coming home late and acting off, like his attention is already somewhere else. And maybe I don't have proof that it's phys-ical—maybe it hasn't crossed that line—but he's still choosing her." I shake my head, the words spilling out now. "He's talking to her, leaning on her, letting her in, and that still feels like a betrayal. Honestly, it almost hurts more."

Paxton stays quiet, so I keep going.

"We've been together for ten years, Pax. *Ten.* And somewhere along the way, he decided someone else could have parts of him that used to belong to us."

He nods, the edge of his anger easing as something more thoughtful takes its place. Paxton leans back in his chair, jaw tight, eyes fixed on the table for a second before he looks up at me again.

"Ten years is a long time, Lo," he says quietly. "That's not something you just throw away, and it's definitely not something someone gets to disrespect." He shakes his head. "I don't care what the excuse is. You don't deserve to be cheated on. Not physically. Not emotionally. None of it."

"I know," I say. "But I need to be sure. I need proof."

He exhales slowly, like he's choosing his next words. "I get wanting certainty," he says. "I do. But don't let needing proof turn into you gaslighting yourself. If something feels wrong, it probably is." His voice softens. "I just don't want you talking yourself into accepting less because you're afraid of what confirming it might mean."

We're quiet for a few moments, the silence between us filled by the steady hum of the cafe. The low murmur of conversations blends with the hiss of the espresso machine, the clatter of plates, the occasional burst of laughter from a nearby table. A waitress glides past, balancing a tray stacked with mugs, and the rich scent of coffee beans lingers in the air, mixing with the buttery sweetness of fresh pastries from the counter.

Our food arrives, plates sliding onto the table with a comforting clink. Steam curls upward, carrying the savory smell of corned beef hash, eggs, and toasted bread. My stomach growls, and Pax shoots me a look that makes me laugh despite myself.

Our eyes meet across the table, the swirl of cafe life moving around us like a blur, and we grin at each other the way we always have, like nothing outside this moment can touch us. It's small, but it's enough.

"Let's eat," he says, already reaching for his fork, as if feeding himself is his way of grounding us both.

Chapter Three

Jenna's silver BMW pulls up, and I smile. Still too full from breakfast, I told her I'd meet her for coffee instead since she was heading downtown to shop. Music spills out of her car, and I laugh when I see her belting the lyrics to whatever song she's got blasting. When she gets out and notices me grinning, she flashes a sheepish smile before walking to the pay-and-display machine.

"Taylor?" I tease as I approach her.

"Nope. Cardi," she answers with a smirk. She turns her attention back to the machine, slipping her card in and waiting for the printed tag.

"What stores are you hitting? I'm still stuffed from breakfast with Pax." I pat my belly for emphasis. I'd eaten every bite of my food and felt three months pregnant now.

"I need a dress for a date on Thursday."

"*Oooh,* a date?" I coo, wiggling my eyebrows. She laughs and punches me lightly in the arm.

"Chill out, Lo. It's just dinner after work."

"Where'd you meet her? I want all the details," I say as we walk down Main Street toward the mall.

Jenna gives me a side glance. "She recently got hired as a legal assistant at our firm."

"She's your assistant?" My voice betrays my shock.

"Not mine. Not directly anyway. She's the office assistant. Answers phones, schedules meetings. I hardly work with her. And it's only dinner."

I consider this as we step into the mall, the automatic doors sliding open and cool air hitting my face. Macy's perfume drifts faintly through the entrance.

"Well, please be careful," I say gently, not wanting to sound judgmental. "If it turns into something, you'll have to keep it quiet."

"Totally. And like I said, it's just dinner." She studies me, reading my face. "What are you thinking? I know that look."

I stop walking. "J, I'm happy you're even going on a date. It's been forever. I just want you to be careful."

She squeezes my shoulders, looking me square in the eyes. "I will be. And thank you for being supportive."

Inside Macy's, we split up. She heads to the dresses while I wander toward the women's shoes.

Oh, *hellooo.*

Shoes are the one thing I never feel guilty about. And if there's an unwritten rule for women, it's that retail therapy is mandatory when your husband cheats. I cringe at the thought but use it as permission to pick up the $119 hot pink Jessica Simpson pumps I don't need.

I slip off my sandal and slide into the shoe, hobbling over to the mirror. My long legs look leaner, sharper, more commanding in those heels. I tug it off reluctantly and start scanning other styles when my phone vibrates in my bag. I dig for it, fingers brushing the sleek case.

John.

My stomach drops. I frown, considering voicemail, but know he'll keep calling. I answer.

"Lo! Oh my God, baby, are you okay?"

I roll my eyes, shifting the shoebox under my arm. "I'm fine. I told you I needed space and would be gone a few days. Why are you calling Paxton and making him worry?" My anger flares the moment I hear his voice.

"When you didn't answer me, I panicked. Can you blame me? You've never disappeared in ten years of marriage. Jesus, Lo, can you blame me?"

I take a breath, grounding myself as I stare at my reflection in the store mirror. My phone buzzes again in my hand, a text from Jenna asking where I went.

"I gotta go," I say, clipped.

"But we just started talking. When are you coming home so we can work this out?"

"I don't know. Tomorrow, maybe. I need to think."

He sighs, defeated. "Okay. Please come home soon. I love you."

I end the call without responding. Let him sit with the worry. I open Jenna's text and reply that I'm by the shoes. Sliding my phone into my pocket, I crane my neck and spot her weaving through the racks. She reaches me, brow furrowed.

"What's wrong?" she asks.

"John called. I made the mistake of answering."

"Oh shit. What'd he say?"

"He says he's worried. About me, about where I am. It's bullshit." I shake my head hard, curls bouncing around my shoulders.

"Well, if he cared that much, he wouldn't have fucked his colleague."

"Exactly," I snap, exasperated. We move through the maze of heels and summer sandals. "So I didn't tell him where I'm staying. Said I'll come home when I feel like it."

"Good for you." Jenna drapes her arm around me. "Lucky for him, you're not out living your best life with some random guy."

I laugh. "That's not me. I don't do flings or randoms."

She shrugs, tossing her blonde hair, and I let out a long breath I didn't realize I'd been holding. It feels good to be validated. After months of lies and second-guessing, I know I was right. No one wants proof their husband is cheating, but relief comes with knowing you weren't crazy.

We linger for another fifteen minutes before heading out. Outside, the sky is a clear, brutal blue. Jenna unlocks her car, the metallic paint glinting in the sun.

"You want a ride to your car?" she asks.

I squint against the light. "I'm going to walk a bit. Clear my head. I'll meet you in an hour or so."

She waves and drives off, leaving me on the sidewalk with my thoughts. I turn and stroll down the street. It's quiet, the sidewalks mostly empty, and I'm grateful for the space.

Of course, my mind drifts to John and our ten-year marriage.

What happened to us?

We were the couple people envied. Friends teased us, saying they wished their marriages looked as solid as ours. Even with his demanding career, we made time for date nights. He'd surprise me with flowers at my office or meet me on lunch breaks for quickies in our Tahoe. The tinted windows and roomy seats made for perfect midday escapes.

But two years ago, everything shifted. He became more withdrawn, less attentive. At first, I blamed the workload. A new president had taken over at the college, and John was under pressure to boost enrollment numbers. I understood. I was patient.

But when enrollment stabilized, nothing changed. He still stayed late, came home stressed, snapped at me over small things. And when you rarely see your husband, it cuts deeper to feel like even that sliver of time isn't wanted.

I tried to plan dates, weekend getaways, anything to reset us. He brushed me off. Too tired. Too busy. Even in bed, he pulled away. Sex felt mechanical, obligatory. Once or twice, he couldn't even stay hard, something that had never been an issue.

And then came Constance.

I met her at the Christmas party. She was too familiar with him, and he looked rattled in a way I'd never seen. I asked about her later, trying to keep it light, but he brushed it off. Said he "barely knew her."

"Well, she seems to know you," I'd shot back, stepping out of my dress.

His whole body went tense. "What are you trying to say, Lo?" His brown eyes narrowed, fingers fumbling at his shirt buttons.

"Jesus, Lo. It's always something with you lately! Now you're jealous of my twenty-something assistant?"

"Always something?" I spat. "I barely see you. And when I do, you're short and irritated. We haven't connected in months, John. If you'd pull your head out of your ass, you'd notice how far we've drifted."

We fought until exhaustion silenced us.

When I woke, his hands were on me. He slipped my panties off, his mouth between my thighs, murmuring apologies against my skin. We made love for the first time in weeks, and he whispered "I'm sorry" over and over with every thrust.

At the time, I let myself believe he was apologizing for the distance, for neglecting me.

But now, walking under the harsh midday sun with everything unraveling around me, I wonder if he was apologizing for something else.

For *her*.

Chapter Four

It's early when I hear Jenna turn on the shower. Squinting, I look over at the digital clock on the nightstand. 6:35 a.m. I roll back over, burying my face in the pillow, then immediately change positions, remembering the advice I'd recently seen on my Botox lady's Instagram about how sleeping on your face leads to premature aging.

I stare up at Jenna's perfectly smooth white ceiling and think about my day. It's Sunday, and I need to work tomorrow. Luckily, I only have two classes to teach, both first-year English Literature, which I could teach in my sleep. And they're both after 1 p.m. I reach for my cell phone and disconnect it from the long white charger. Before I even unlock it, I see texts from John and Paxton. I open Pax's first.

Yo! Just wanted to say I love you, sis, and I'm here for u. Let me know if you need anything.

I smile despite my anxious mood. I love my brother so much. He's younger and a little more, shall I say, free-spirited than I am, but he loves me, and I know he'd do anything for me.

Thanks, brother, I reply, adding a heart emoji.

My phone pings almost immediately with a response from Pax. Two fist bump emojis.

What are you doing so early? It's Sunday, I type. This man is known for sleeping in, especially on the weekends. I watch the bubbles appear as he types his response.

Going to a farmers market thing with Grace, he replies.

Grace is Paxton's girlfriend, someone I haven't met yet but have heard plenty about. He's pretty private about who he's dating, so I'm grateful he shared anything. From the way he talks about her, she has him completely smitten, a softness in his voice I don't usually hear. It's strange, imagining my brother, who's always been guarded, sharp-edged, and quick to change the subject when it comes to relationships, finally letting someone in. Part of me is curious, maybe even a little protective, but mostly I'm just glad to see him happy. God knows he deserves it.

I'm staring at the new messages from John when my phone buzzes again. I hesitate, then open the thread anyway, my thumb moving before I can talk myself out of it.

Please just talk to me. I know things have been tense, but I miss you. I hate the idea of us like this.

My chest tightens. There's something almost convincing about it, the way he manages to sound sincere without actually saying anything at all. No apology. No accountability. Just enough tenderness to tug at the part of me that still wants to believe him.

I'm about to type a response when I hear a soft rap on the door.

"Come in," I call, forcing a sing-song brightness into my voice.

Jenna laughs as she pushes the door open. "I heard your phone going off, so I figured you might be awake."

I scoot over so she can sit beside me on the bed, quickly setting my phone facedown. She smells good, like baby powder and roses. Her long blonde hair is damp and twisted into a loose topknot, and she looks effortlessly beautiful in a white T-shirt and boxer shorts.

"You saved me from responding to John's messages," I say, rolling my eyes.

"Ugh," she says. "But honestly, part of me can't blame him. I'd be losing my shit too if I thought I was losing you."

I smile at my friend. "Thanks, lady. I was lying here thinking about what I should do. I teach tomorrow, so I'll need to go home at some point before then to grab some work clothes. But I'll probably do that in the morning when I know he's already at work. The thought of seeing John is still sickening."

"Yea, I don't blame you," she says softly. "Just know you can stay here as long as you need."

I lean my head onto her shoulder. "I appreciate you, girl. I don't know what I'd do without you." And it's true. I may not have a huge friend group, but the ones I have are rock solid.

She leans her head against mine. "I got you. Always."

We sit there like this for a moment, and despite the crumbling of my marriage, I feel calm, like things might be okay. If not now, then soon.

"What are you doing up so early?" I ask as I straighten up.

Jenna stands and faces me with a sly grin.

"Well, we're both off today, so I figured we could go to that new rooftop pool in the city! It's supposed to be in the 80s, and I already reserved our spots from 12 to 3. And this is the last week it's open before it closes for the colder months!" She's practically bouncing.

I can't help but grin back. "But I didn't bring a swimsuit," I protest. "And I'm not going back to the house today while he's there waiting."

"You can wear one of mine!"

I raise an eyebrow, giving her a skeptical look. "My tits are *not* gonna fit in your swimsuit, bitch."

She giggles and playfully touches my chest. "Oh yea, I always forget you have these big ol' fake titties."

I push her away, but now we're both cracking up. "I guess we're going shopping. *Again,*" I say through my laughter.

***

It takes us almost forty-five minutes to find parking for the pool, and when we do, we're a good three blocks from the building.

That's New York City for you.

It truly is a perfect early-Fall day, though, and the walk is beautiful, with tall buildings and leafy trees lining the sidewalks. Everyone is out, and everyone looks happy. Summer is probably my favorite time to be in the city.

I watch a couple walking toward us, holding hands and smiling. The man is looking at his partner the way John used to look at me, and I swallow hard. He's hanging on her every word, and she's glowing, speaking so freely it radiates off her. The comfort between them is palpable. I tear my eyes away and glance at Jenna, who's oblivious to my little gut punch. She catches me looking and beams.

"Aren't you so excited about the pool?" she asks, grabbing my hand.

I nod and force a thin smile. Jenna doesn't seem to notice, and I'm grateful. I wouldn't even know how to explain what I'm feeling.

We approach a tall apartment building, and I shield my eyes as I gaze up at the rocky facade. "Do we need to be residents here?"

"I have a connection," she says, wiggling her eyebrows. "One of my clients lives here and got me in for the whole summer. Anytime I wanna swim, I just let him know a day or two before, and I'm good."

"I love this for us," I say with a smile.

We sign in with the bored-looking doorman, who instructs us to take the elevator to the rooftop pool.

I have to hand it to Jenna, the pool is beautiful. And surprisingly not as crowded as I expected on a Sunday. We find two lounge chairs, stow our bags, and settle in. I glance around, taking in the scene. There's an outdoor bar across the deck. I nudge Jenna and point.

She looks up from slathering sunscreen on her legs. "Ooooh! Shall we?"

"Duh," I say, leaning back and slipping on my sunglasses. The sun is warm, the air just right, and I let myself sink into it.

"What do you want?" Jenna asks, wiping her greasy hands on an extra towel.

"Let's go see what they have."

We join the short line, squinting to make out the chalkboard menu. Strawberry margaritas, beer, wine. When it's our turn, a short, curvy Latina with glossy black hair greets us. Her eyes sweep over us and linger on Jenna. Not unusual. Jenna is hot, especially in her white bikini.

"What can I get you, ladies?" she asks, still looking at Jenna.

"I'll have a white wine, please," I say, forcing her to shift her gaze.

"Ok, I'll have that right up." Her eyes flick back to Jenna. "And for you?" Her tone softens noticeably.

Jenna leans forward, brushing her fingers against the girl's hair. "First of all, your hair is to die for. And I'll have a margarita, please, love." She flashes a smile that could melt steel.

"Coming right up," the girl says, nearly breathless.

We step aside, and I slap Jenna's arm. She widens her eyes innocently.

"Jesus, Jenna," I hiss. "Could you have laid it on any thicker? That poor girl was flustered."

Jenna shrugs, grinning. "What? I'm single and she was gorgeous. I'm in my hot girl summer era."

"Are you gonna get her number?"

"Nah. I'm just having fun, Lo."

I roll my eyes but laugh. Of course Jenna would turn a poolside drink order into a flirtation.

The bartender returns with our drinks, and Jenna nearly knocks me over to grab them. She hands me my plastic cup of wine before sinking into her chair.

"Thanks, big pimpin'," I say, taking a sip.

"She asked for my number," Jenna says, smirking.

"Of course she did."

We sip in silence, soaking up the sun. My new bikini is skimpier than I'd like, but I've been diligent with the gym and yoga, so I know I look good in it. Neon green and baby blue stripes pop against my honey-brown skin.

Halfway through my wine, I already feel it buzzing. Lightweight problems. I push up my sunglasses and scan the pool. Only two people are in the water. I tie my auburn curls into a messy bun.

"I'm gonna take a quick dip," I announce. "The wine is hittin."

"I'm coming too!" Jenna tilts back her glass, drains it, and hops up.

We wade in together, the water perfect against my skin.

"See? Best way to spend a Sunday," Jenna says, smiling.

"Most definitely," I agree.

I spot a float and climb on, letting the water carry me. My eyes close, the sun warm on my body. I drag my hands lazily through the pool and breathe deep. For the first time in days, I let myself relax.

Chapter Five

Pulling into the Faculty and Staff parking at Shady Oaks feels strangely comforting. I'm here much earlier than I need to be, but there are online tests waiting to be graded, and the thought of sitting in that house after showering and changing into work clothes was unbearable.

The lot is quiet in that way campus lots always are before the rush. Because it's fall semester, mornings stay light. Most students avoid early classes if they can. The air has that crisp edge that only September brings in New York, a mix of cool promise and faint dampness, like the ground still hasn't let go of summer. A few leaves scrape across the asphalt, tossed by the breeze, and I pause for a second to watch them tumble before gathering my things. Scanning the lot, I notice Sam's car parked one row over.

Nice, I think, already typing out a text as I walk toward Woodard Hall. *Coffee?*

Her reply comes almost instantly. *Yes! My first class doesn't start until 11:30.*

Yay! Meet you at the cafe\ by Woodard in 15?

She hearts the message. I smile, slip my phone into my bag, and keep walking.

Inside, Woodard Hall is cool, the blast of air conditioning chasing away the bite of fall air clinging to my skin. The hallways smell faintly of floor polish and chalk dust. When I unlock my office, the familiar creak of the door greets me. It's not much, but it's mine.

The walls are that same weird cream I've always hated, so I've nearly buried them in diplomas, art prints, and anything that makes the space less sterile. My favorite piece, the big Buddha painting, pulls my eyes every time—blues and teals and greens so vivid it feels like water, like breath. For a moment, I let it center me.

My desk, however, is a disaster. Stacks of essays, open books, three different coffee cups in varying stages of decay. I run my fingers along the edge, half laughing at myself. *I'll clean this later.* But not now. Right now, there's Sam.

When I step back outside, the sunlight hits me hard, forcing my eyes into a squint. "*Sheesh*," I mutter, shielding my face. The quad is waking up now. A group of students walk past, earbuds in, coffee in hand, all backpacks and sleepy faces. The cafe's big glass windows glint in the light, and inside I immediately spot Sam.

She sees me at the same time and cries out, "Lo!" Her voice cuts through the buzz, and she's in my arms before I can respond. She smells like coconut shampoo, her curls soft against my cheek. For the first time in days, my shoulders drop.

"Samaya Jones, aren't you a sight for sore eyes," I tease when we pull back. "Feels like forever."

She laughs, eyes glittering. "It's been two weeks. California was amazing—exactly what I needed."

I grin. "Oh shit, the trip. How was it? How's your sister?"

We shuffle into line, sunlight pouring through the windows and pooling on the café's wood floors. She tells me about Serenity and her baby, how big he's gotten, how she didn't want to leave. Her words spill with warmth, and I let them wash over me like balm. For a few minutes, I can pretend my life isn't unraveling.

We grab our drinks and sit by the window. Outside, students crisscross the campus lawn, tossing a frisbee, hugging friends, sipping pumpkin lattes. The ordinary hum of life moves on, even as my own feels frozen.

Sam leans in, finally asking, "So, how are things for you? What have I missed?"

The question stings. She doesn't know. Nobody really knows. Shame curls in my stomach, sharp and immediate, even though I know it shouldn't be there. I didn't do anything wrong. I know that, logically. Still, the feeling settles anyway, heavy and uninvited, like I've failed some invisible test I never agreed to take. I glance at her, at the sincerity in her face, and something inside me gives.

"Things have been... bad. At home." The words sound foreign even as I say them, like they belong to someone else's life. Admitting it feels like peeling back a layer I've worked hard to keep intact, exposing something tender I wasn't ready to name out loud.

Her smile falters. "What happened?"

And then I say it. "My perfect husband, Mr. Vice President himself, is having an affair. With his assistant."

Sam's gasp is loud enough that she slaps a hand over her mouth, eyes wide. "Wait. He's fucking *Constance Keller*?"

Her words slice the air, and for a moment I freeze, checking to see if anyone else heard. The cafe is nearly empty. I exhale slowly. "Yes. I'm pretty sure. I saw texts."

Her face twists, disbelief and anger mixing. "She's what, twenty?"

"Twenty-six," I answer flatly, sipping my latte to keep my hands from trembling.

She shakes her head, muttering. "Unbelievable. Has he admitted it?"

I let out a short, humorless breath. "Of course not. He hasn't admitted anything." I hesitate, then add, quieter, "If anything, he's doing that thing where he makes it sound like I'm exaggerating. Like I'm reading into things that aren't there. Like I'm the problem for even questioning it."

Sam's expression tightens.

"It almost hurts more," I continue, the words tumbling out now. "Not just that he's too close to her, but that he won't even own it—he looks at me like I'm crazy for noticing, like ten years together doesn't mean I know when something's off." I shake my head. "So I stayed with Jenna this weekend. I just needed space from him…"

Sam studies me for a long beat, then leans forward. "What are you going to do? Are you going to talk to Constance?"

The thought lands like a punch. It hadn't even occurred to me. Could I do that? Confront her? Would she even tell me the truth?

Sam doesn't let me off the hook. "She's fucking your husband. You're damn right you can ask her. What's more unprofessional—asking her or what she's already doing?"

I almost laugh. She's right. Still, my chest tightens at the thought. Damn near ten years of marriage. The life I thought I had. Gone.

Before I can answer, my phone buzzes with a reminder. "Shit, I've got quizzes to grade before my 1 pm."

We hug, her arms tight, her voice soft. "Hang in there. Call me if you need anything."

I nod, swallowing the lump in my throat.

***

My last class of the day ends in a blur. Students scrape chairs back, their chatter a mix of weekend plans and groans about homework. The fluorescent lights hum above me as I gather papers from the podium. When the door swings shut behind the last of them, silence takes over, heavy and too still. I exhale, ready to turn off the lights and retreat to my office, when movement catches at the edge of my vision.

John.

His broad frame fills the doorway. My heart drops into my stomach.

"Hey, Lo. Sorry, I didn't mean to scare you," he says, lips curving into that crooked smile I used to love. It doesn't land the way it once did. His eyes look tired, bloodshot even, and his suit jacket hangs carelessly from his shoulder like he couldn't be bothered.

I grip the edge of my desk to steady myself. "What are you doing here?" My voice is flat, sharp, nothing like the warmth I used to greet him with. For the first time in more than a decade, his presence feels wrong.

He steps further into the room, shoulders slumped. "I'm your husband. What do you mean, what am I doing here? I want you to come home." His tone wavers between frustration and pleading, like he can't decide which will work on me.

I laugh bitterly, the sound brittle in the empty classroom. "Now you want to play the role of loving husband?" The words scrape my throat. He reaches for me, and I jerk my arm back before his hand can touch me. My whole body recoils. "Why won't you tell me the truth about Constance?"

His mouth opens, then shuts. He shakes his head slowly. "There's nothing between us," he says, voice low, almost defeated.

I study him, every inch of him. The practiced way his jaw sets, the twitch in his brow, the faint stubble he normally would have shaved by now. He looks less like the man I married and more like a stranger wearing his skin. Still handsome, still commanding, but there's a hollowness in him that wasn't there before. The John I fell in love with was bold and electric, with a laugh that shook walls and a way of looking at me like I was the only person alive. That man is gone. In his place is someone slippery with excuses, brittle with secrets.

"What if I asked her?" I say, my voice steady even though my insides twist. "What do you think she'd say?"

For a split second, I see it in his eyes: panic. A flicker so fast most people would miss it, but I know him too well. My chest tightens. He knows I know.

"Why would you do that?" His voice pitches higher, strained. "Why would you even ask her something like that?" He shakes his head, already backing away from the moment. "Do you have any idea how humiliating that would be for me? For both of us?"

There it is. Not denial exactly. Deflection. The problem isn't what he's done, it's that I might expose it.

"There's nothing going on," he insists, too quickly, like saying it louder might make it true.

I don't answer. I don't have to. The silence between us thickens, heavy with everything he refuses to say. He can call it humiliation if he wants. I know what it really is.

He scrubs a hand over his face and exhales, shoulders sagging. "Please come home. You can have the bedroom. I'll sleep on the couch. Just... come back."

I stare at him, really stare. At the way his tie is loosened, his collar wrinkled, his hair out of place. He looks diminished, small even in his six-foot-four frame. Once, I would have rushed to him, reached up to smooth that hair, to tuck myself into the arms that used to feel like safety. Now, all I feel is exhaustion. Bone-deep and unshakable.

"Fine," I say quietly. "But I don't want to see you. I get the room."

His face brightens so quickly it almost makes me sick. Relief floods him like a dam has broken, and he nods, eager, desperate. "Ok. Whatever you need."

I turn away, gathering my papers, my bag, anything to avoid those eyes that once felt like home. All I can think is how far we've fallen, and how impossible it feels to climb back.

Chapter Six

I stare up at the two-story brick building where my husband works, debating what in the actual fuck I am doing here.

Am I really about to walk in and confront Constance?

A breath I did not know I was holding finally leaves me when I catch my reflection in the rearview mirror. Pulling out my phone, I text Samaya what I am about to do.

You got this. Ask and watch her reaction.

Not waiting for a reply, I shove the phone into my bag and get out of the car. Bailey Hall towers over me like a haunted house, its brick walls cold and unforgiving. My throat tightens.

Get it together, Halo. This is your life on the line.

Well, not your actual life, but the life you thought you had signed up for sits on the edge of a knife. I lift my chin and head for the stone steps.

"Good morning, Mrs. Roberts!" The intake desk guy chirps. It's Sean, a kid I had in first-year literature several semesters ago. He looks younger behind the counter, cheerful, the kind of campus kid who still believes the world is basically fair.

"Sean, hi. How's everything going? I didn't know you were working in Student Services now." I give him my teacher smile. The sound of it feels brittle in my own ears.

He shrugs, grinning. "Oh, I'm just covering today. I usually work in Counseling, but I'm doing my friend a solid since she covered for me when I had Covid last month."

"Oh no, I hope she's okay. Glad you're covering."

"Are you here to see Mr. Roberts? I think he's in a meeting with the president over in Garcia Hall." He rises, peering toward the inner door.

Of course he's in a meeting. That is precisely why I am here now.

"Uh, no. Well, sort of," I stammer. "I need to drop something off in his office." Better to say I dropped something off than admit I came to pick at a wound.

Sean waves me in with that bright, easy manner of his. "Be my guest. Good to see you, Mrs. R."

The VP's suite smells faintly of lemon cleaner and expensive coffee. My footsteps sound loud in the corridor. John's office sits like a glass box at the center of it all, and farther in, the row of small desks where the assistants sit, Constance's among them.

She is on the phone when I walk in. As soon as she looks up, color drains from her face. That reaction makes something in me solidify, like a key sliding into place. I smile, all civility and ice, and take the navy blue chair by the window that looks out over the east side of campus. The glass is cold against my cheek when I lean forward, watching her under my breath.

"Hi, Halo," she says from behind me. "John won't be back until noon."

I turn and walk toward her slowly. The click of her mouse sounds too loud. "That's fine. I'm actually here to see you."

Her fingers go to the tiny pendant at the base of her throat, twisting the thin gold chain like an anchor. "Oh. Ok. Were you trying to get something scheduled?" Her voice stumbles, then flattens. Her mascara looks fresh, the contour of her cheekbones precise, the skin under her eyes pale like porcelain.

I sit directly in front of her and look into her eyes. "No, thank you. I came to ask what happened between you and my husband the night you all had drinks last month." My words are measured, sharp. I do not let my gaze drop.

Heat blooms in her face and she opens her mouth, then shuts it again. Her hand flies to her throat and she looks away. Nervous, guilty, or both. Why would she be that unsteady if nothing happened?

"We all went out for drinks," she offers cautiously. "There was a whole group of us." Her tone is too careful, like she's walking a ridge.

"John told me you two stayed later after everyone else left," I say. "I saw texts on his phone the next day about how good he felt. So I'm asking you again, what happened between the two of you that night?"

A new, deeper red crawls up her neck. Her voice gets smaller. "I don't know what you're talking about. We only talked. I was telling him about my recent breakup and he was there for me." She chews the inside of her cheek.

I feel something hot and furious under my skin. "Why the hell are you talking to a married man, no less your boss, about your relationship issues? Don't you see how inappropriate that is?" The words spill out, sharp and cold.

Her eyes narrow. "I can talk to whoever I want about my relationship issues. It's not my fault your husband is more attentive to me than you'd like." A smirk flickers over her mouth and my vision goes red at the corners.

Standing up suddenly makes me tower over her. Her small frame does nothing to intimidate me. "You better stay away from my husband, you little bitch. I can have you fired with a single phone call. You do not want to fuck with me, Constance." The venom in my voice tastes metallic.

She stands too, hands landing on the desk like she means to steady herself. "Are you *threatening* me?" Her voice is higher than before, fragile and angry.

"This is not a threat. This is a warning. Whatever you think you've got going with John, it's over." My words land like stones on a river. I can hear my pulse in my ears.

She shakes her head, disgust curling her lip. "No wonder he never wants to go home."

My blood drums loud enough to feel in my teeth. Every word she says is a match lit to dry tinder. My hands clench at my sides. For a breath, I imagine leaning over that desk and wrapping my fingers around her pale throat. The thought is animal and unwanted, so I swallow it and let the rage compress into cold resolve.

"You heard me," I say, my voice low now. I collect my purse from the navy chair and walk to the door. Footsteps are hollow in the corridor. I almost nod to Sean at the front, but the motion feels ridiculous, so I leave without much more than the stiffest of goodbyes.

Once in the parking lot, I slide into the car and call Sam. My thumb taps the phone before I even say hello. "She definitely is seeing him." No preamble, just the fact like a splinter I can't stop touching.

There's a sharp intake of breath on the other end. "Holy shit. What did she say? Tell me everything."

I tell her the short version, how the color drained from Constance's face, the way she twisted her pendant, the smirk when she suggested John was more attentive to her. There's a long silence while she takes it in.

"Wow, girl. I am so sorry. Even though she didn't own up to it, it's obvious there's something there."

"Exactly," I say, exhausted and furious. "Ugh. At least I'm not teaching tonight."

"My last class ends at 4:30. Tacos and drinks later? We'll talk."

"You're speaking my language. Text me when you're ready." I end the call and sink back against the seat, staring at the dashboard. The car smells faintly of pine and the coffee I grabbed on the way in.

I decide to go home, because he won't be there until after I leave for dinner with Sam, and the last thing I want is to see him right now. If I saw him, I'm not sure what I'd do.

I would probably kill him.

Chapter Seven

I check my phone again and see a text from Sam apologizing because she's running late. I decide to order a drink now, mostly because I'm dying for one. We can order food when she gets here. My appetite has been nonexistent since my intense conversation with Constance earlier today.

I order a double martini and smile sweetly at the bartender when she raises an eyebrow. If she knew the day I've had, she'd make it a triple.

Picking up my phone to text Sam, I hear her voice and glance up expectantly.

"Oh my God," she says, completely out of breath as she approaches me at the bar. "Traffic was crazy and I had to stay a little after class to speak with a student about her test results."

I pat the stool next to me for her to sit down. "All good. I'm glad you're here now."

She cranes her neck and looks around the half-full restaurant. "Should we get a table so we can have some privacy? I want to hear what the fuck happened with you-know-who."

Good idea.

I turn to the bartender. "Can we grab a free table?"

Her eyes scan the room, then she shrugs and pops her gum. "Sure. I'll let Tony know you're moving, and he'll set you up with some dinner menus."

We thank her and walk over to a small circular table in the back corner of the restaurant. Sliding into the booth against the wall, I let out a sigh, reach for my half-drunk martini, and take a long sip. The alcohol is strong, but it's what I need to take the edge off.

The waiter, who I assume is Tony, saunters over and gives us both a once-over. His eyes linger just a second too long on my tits, and I roll my eyes. Guys in their twenties seem to have a thing for women in their thirties. Mommy issues, maybe. Either way, I'm not in the mood.

"What can I get you lovely ladies?" Tony wiggles his eyebrows first at Sam, then at me. I shoot a look at Sam, who shifts uncomfortably in her seat.

"I'll take another double martini. Can you also bring out some of the mini chicken tacos and some chips with guac?"

He scribbles quickly in his little black notepad, then looks to Sam. "And for you, miss?"

Her face is still buried in the menu. "Umm... I'll have a strawberry margarita and the queso dip to start." She looks up and smiles politely.

"Ooh," I say, touching the waiter's sleeve lightly. "Can I change mine to a strawberry margarita instead of the martini?"

He nods, jotting it down.

Sam gives me a look. "You sure you wanna mix alcohols?"

I shrug. "I'll be fine."

Once Tony leaves, Sam leans in. "Ok, so tell me everything."

Twenty minutes, a plate of chips and guac, and a margarita later, I've told her the entire story. She leans back, shaking her head in disbelief.

"Constance has a lot of nerve. Even if she hasn't already been involved with him physically, she's obviously down and willing for it to go there."

I finish chewing the chip in my hand. "Do you think there's a chance he hasn't actually cheated? Yet, at least."

Samaya looks thoughtful. "I think there's a chance, yes. But it's still completely out of line for her or him to be talking about her breakup over drinks. Why's he playing Mr. Friendly with some twenty-something when he's got a wife at home? Also, the whole text situation is pretty damning."

Tony reappears with our entrees balanced on a tray, setting the plates in front of us. The smell of chicken tacos hits my nose immediately, meat and spices sizzling beneath the steam. Beside me, Samaya's enchiladas make her eyes widen like a kid on Christmas morning.

He asks if we want another round, and I answer yes before Sam can stop me. She smirks but doesn't protest.

"This looks so fuckin good," I say, shaking out the red cloth napkin and laying it in my lap. We're quiet for a while, taking our first bites. The chicken is tender, the peppers perfectly charred, and I close my eyes to savor it. When I open them, Sam is gazing down at her plate in awe. She catches me staring, then laughs, and I join in.

After several minutes, another server drops off fresh drinks. I smile sweetly at her before taking a long sip. The liquor burns its way down, warm and sharp.

"You're drunk," Sam says, laughing and shaking her head.

I giggle too, unable to hide it. "I'm definitely buzzed," I admit. Then I lift the glass again and take another swallow.

"Mine's strong too," Sam says, making a face.

One hour and two more drinks later, Sam insists we leave. She signals for the waitress, who tells us Tony's already clocked out.

"Why," I whine. "I want to stay."

"You're slurring, Lo, because you're drunk," she teases, standing. She wobbles slightly. "I'm gonna pee, then our Uber should be here."

I nod, eyes closed, swaying to the beat of a rap song I recognize but can't name. I may be drunk, but I feel lighter.

"Mrs. Roberts?"

My eyes shoot open. A man is standing before me, vaguely familiar. I tilt my head, trying to get a better look, but my vision is foggy from too many margaritas.

He laughs and slides into the booth across from me. And what a handsome face it is. His jaw is square, his black hair in perfect waves, his brown eyes smooth and deep. Something in me stirs as I stare at this almost-stranger.

I prop my chin in my hands and smile flirtatiously. Then I hiccup. He laughs, and I bury my face in my palms.

"You're drunk. And you have no idea who I am, do you?" His voice is warm, amused.

Peeking through my fingers, I grin. "I know your face, but I can't place it."

"I was in your Creative Writing class. Six years ago."

I sit straight up. "Oh my God. Damien?! You look so different."

He chuckles. "I'm all grown up now, Mrs. Roberts."

"Please. Call me Halo," I say, my stomach warming under his gaze. "Gosh, how old are you now?"

"Twenty-seven," he says, smiling.

I can't stop looking at him. Maybe it's the alcohol, maybe not, but I'm drawn to him.

"Wow," I breathe. "You really are all grown up."

We stare at each other longer than feels appropriate. Still, I don't look away.

"Well, hello," Sam says suddenly. I glance up as she hovers at the edge of the table, looking between us.

Damien rises quickly, offering his hand. "Nice to meet you," he says sincerely.

"Samaya," she replies, shaking it, then shoots me a look. "You ready? Our Uber's almost here."

I stand, the room tilting slightly. Grabbing the table for balance, I hear Sam laugh.

"*Shut up*," I groan, giggling too.

Damien steadies me with one hand, smiling. "I got you, Halo. I'll walk you outside."

I let him guide me, grateful. Outside, the night air cools my flushed skin. Sam takes a call a few feet away, leaving me with him. I sway, and his arm slips around me, holding me steady.

Even drunk, I register how good it feels. He smells like peppermint and woodsy cologne, and I sigh.

"You ok down there?" he asks softly, his voice close.

Looking up at him, our eyes lock again. "You smell good," I slur. Then hiccup. We both laugh.

"Thank you. You look beautiful." His eyes dart away. "Sorry. I shouldn't say that."

"No, I appreciate it," I say quickly, wanting his gaze back. He looks down at me again, and his hand lifts a curl from my cheek. The warmth of his touch sends a jolt through me. I lean into it without meaning to.

"Halo Roberts," he says, his tone thick with something I can't name. My knees feel weak. A car pulls up at the curb.

"That's us!" Samaya calls, waving to the driver.

I step back from Damien and give him a small smile, unsure of what just passed between us.

"Good seeing you, Mrs. Roberts," he says politely.

"You too, Damien," I reply before hurrying into the car.

Chapter Eight

The first thing I notice when I wake is the sharp pain shooting through my neck. Groaning, I attempt to sit up and am instantly punished with a splitting ache in my skull.

I ease my head back down and squeeze my eyes shut, trying to breathe through it. The smell of coffee drifts through the air, and I catch the faint rustle of someone moving in the next room. With effort, I pry open one eye, squinting hard against the light, and force myself to take in the scene.

Where am I?

After a few steadying breaths, I brace for another attempt at sitting up. A moan slips out as I slowly manage to push myself upright. My hand runs along the smooth beige fabric beneath me, and I realize I'm on a couch. Scanning the room, I take in a large painting of an African woman hanging above a wooden table. The table holds a vase of fresh flowers and several candles, their wicks blackened but unlit. To my right, there's a narrow entryway leading into what looks like a hallway. To my left, a flat screen TV hangs neatly on the wall.

Nice place, I think hazily.

Footsteps approach behind me. I turn, groggy and still adjusting, to find Sam holding two steaming mugs. She wears a grin that's equal parts smug and sympathetic.

"Well, good morning, sunshine," she teases, setting the mugs down on the glass coffee table before us. "How are you feeling? Besides, I assume, incredibly hungover."

"Water," I croak, my eyes barely managing to focus on her.

She laughs, pats my shoulder, and disappears into the kitchen. When she returns, she's holding a tall glass of water and a bottle of Tylenol. Relief washes over me. I toss two pills into my mouth and drink like I've been crawling through the desert. By the time I come up for air, water is running down my cheek.

"Bitch," Sam cackles, shaking her head. "You drank that like you never had water before."

"It feels like that," I mutter, pressing the cool glass to my forehead. "My head is splitting."

"I mean, you were sucking down margaritas like the world was ending."

"Right now, I wish it had ended. I feel like death, Sam. And I have a class at two."

She glances at the clock on the wall. "Lucky for you, it's only nine-thirty. You've got some time to pull it together."

I sink into the couch's plush cushions and close my eyes, praying for the Tylenol to kick in.

"What a night," I mumble. "I don't even remember paying for all that food."

The words hang there, followed by a flicker of unease. I'm not someone who loses track like that. I like control. I like knowing where I am, what I've spent, how I got home. Lately, though, the edges keep blurring. One drink turns into several without me noticing, like I'm using the haze to dull something I don't want to name yet. The thought settles uncomfortably in my chest. This isn't me. Or at least, it never used to be.

Sam takes a slow sip of her coffee and chuckles. "That's because I paid. You were gone, sis. I didn't know you drank like that."

"Girl, I didn't either. Normally one glass of wine is enough. I don't know what got into me last night."

Her eyes sparkle mischievously. "Speaking of what got into you last night, who was that dude you were all over?"

My stomach drops. Then the fog in my brain clears enough to hit me with the memory.

"Oh shit," I groan, covering my face with both hands. Damien.

I search through the blurry snapshots in my mind, trying to stitch them together. His face flickers. I remember thinking he looked good, too good, and then it all goes fuzzy again. Just fragments.

"You were hugged up with him when we left La Rosa," Sam reminds me, her tone both playful and sharp.

"Fuck," I mutter, pressing my palms into my eyes. "Damien was my student five years ago. And here I am, a married woman, flirting with a man twelve years younger than me, a man who used to be in my class. I'm no better than John."

Sam's smile vanishes. "Stop. That man hasn't been your student for years, and he looked like a grown ass man last night. Do not compare yourself to John. You hugged him, yeah, maybe a little too close, but that's all it was."

Her words are meant to soothe, but guilt still gnaws at me. I've spent weeks resenting John for being too close to another woman, and yet here I am, replaying the warmth of another man's arms around me.

"I don't know what to do, Sam. Part of me thinks I should leave John. Another part keeps whispering about all we've invested, all the years we've spent. I feel like maybe we should fight for it. What would you do?"

She sets her mug down, her expression shifting from playful to serious. "Do you want my personal opinion or my therapist's opinion?"

"Both," I say, trying for a smile but failing.

"As your friend, I'd say the writing is on the wall. He is, or he will be, unfaithful. The question is whether you need to catch him in the act before you walk away. As a therapist, I'd tell you it sounds like you still want to honor your marriage. In that case, counseling might help. At least then you'll know if there's anything left to salvage."

I lean back, her words heavy on my chest. I never once pictured a life without John. In the beginning, he felt so certain, so sure of us. He used to show up early, waiting on the curb outside my apartment like he couldn't stand another minute apart. He'd take my hand like it was instinct, like choosing me was the easiest decision he ever made. I remember thinking, *this is what safety feels like.*

Even when his schedule filled up, he made time for us. Late dinners. Stolen afternoons. Slow walks along the shore in the summer, his arm slung loosely around my shoulders, the future unfolding effortlessly between us. Back then, I believed love was supposed to feel steady like that, unquestioned.

Those memories ache now, sharp and disorienting, because I don't know when certainty turned into distance, or when the man who once chose me without hesitation became someone I have to convince to stay.

"What are you thinking?" Sam asks softly.

I pick up my mug and blow gently across the coffee's surface before taking a sip. The familiar taste grounds me for a moment.

"I'm thinking that right now, I need to finish this coffee and find the strength to resemble a responsible adult."

She chuckles, squeezing my shoulder. "That's a start. Today is not the day to figure out your marriage. Let's get you hydrated, fed, and ready for your students."

***

Teaching my afternoon class went better than I expected, considering that only two hours earlier I was nursing the worst hangover I've had in years. If any of my students noticed the grocery bags under my eyes, they were gracious enough not to say a word.

I'm gathering my things when a light knock sounds at the door. I frown, assuming a student has forgotten something. But when I open the door, my whole body stiffens.

"Halo, hi. I'm glad I caught you before you left for the day."

It's Carlos Mendoza, Vice President of Academic Affairs at Shady Oaks. This man barely steps out of his office for anything short of a graduation ceremony. To see him in my classroom feels wrong, like a storm cloud hanging in the doorway.

"Hi, Carlos. What a nice surprise." My words feel like paper on my tongue. I try to sound pleasant, but even to my own ears, caution bleeds through.

He gestures at the rows of chairs. "Can we sit down? There's something I need to discuss with you."

"Of course."

We sit. His posture is cool, distant, stripped of the approachable facade he normally wears. My stomach twists. Something is coming, and I already know it won't be good.

"It's been brought to my attention that you had a verbal altercation with a fellow employee earlier this week," he says, clearing his throat.

"Ms. Keller contacted me, very upset. She said you yelled profanities and threatened to have her fired. She claims she had no idea why you were angry."

My jaw tightens. *What a bitch.*

Cunt-stance has the audacity to run crying to Carlos like she's some innocent victim. I can picture her crocodile tears, her wide eyes, her trembling voice as she spins the story to make herself look helpless. Meanwhile, I'm painted as the aggressor. I want to laugh at the absurdity of it, but the truth is I'm cornered.

I force my voice to stay calm. "Yes. Constance and I had a conversation that got heated. It won't happen again."

"It can't happen again," Carlos replies, his tone cold and clipped. "I don't know what the argument was about, and unless it involved the university directly, I don't care. What I do care about is that staff and students feel safe here. You've worked at Shady Oaks for years, which is the only reason I'm giving you a verbal warning instead of putting this in writing. But if something like this happens again, I will take action. That is policy."

Inside, I'm seething. My fists curl in my lap as I imagine Constance smiling to herself somewhere, pleased with the mess she's created. I want to tell Carlos that she's manipulative, that she's the one who crossed a line, but I know it doesn't matter. His mind is already made up. My reputation got bruised, maybe permanently, and I'm expected to sit here and nod.

So I do. I nod vigorously, my head bobbing like I'm eager to please. "I understand, sir. It won't happen again."

He stands, avoiding my eyes, and makes his way toward the door. Before leaving, he turns back.

"One more thing. Ms. Keller said she feels uncomfortable around you. I'll need you to stay away from her building for now. Just until things cool down."

Shock punches me in the chest. "What? But my husband works over there. I need to be able to see him when I want."

His expression hardens. "Then he can come here, or meet you somewhere else while you're on campus."

The humiliation is sharp and hot, like being slapped in public. Constance has not only managed to make me look unprofessional, she's dictated the terms of where I can and cannot go at my own workplace. I want to scream, to throw something, to demand fairness. But Carlos is already giving me more grace than he should. One wrong word and this could become official, a stain I'll never shake.

So I swallow the rage clawing up my throat. I nod, thank him, and watch him walk out the door.

The moment it closes, I snap. I lunge for my phone, hands trembling, vision blurred with tears I refuse to let fall. I dial Sam with shaky fingers, clutching the phone to my ear like a lifeline.

"Can you meet me?" My voice cracks, and I hate the desperation in it.

Chapter Nine

Sam and I meet at a little coffee shop near the college. I settle at a small table by the window, texting Jenna the latest updates while Sam orders her drink. My mind is still reeling from what Carlos said. The anger I felt toward Constance has multiplied, swelling into a seething rage that burns low in my stomach.

"Uh-oh," Samaya says as she slips into the chair across from me, setting her frosty iced coffee on the table. She drops her purse on the back of her chair, then fixes me with a look that tells me I have her full attention. "So, what happened?"

"Carlos came into my classroom after I finished my class."

Her eyes widen and she nearly chokes on her drink. "Carlos, Carlos? As in VP Mendoza?"

"Exactly." I sigh, exasperated. I lift my drink and take a long sip, letting the cool liquid soothe my throat. "So he comes in, all business, and tells me Constance went to him trying to file a complaint against me."

"For what? Confronting her about John?"

"Yes. She told Carlos I threatened her."

Sam's jaw drops. "Are you fucking serious? All you did was call her out for sleeping with your husband. It's not like you threatened her life."

I swallow hard and tuck a stray curl behind my ear. Her disbelief softens into concern when she sees my face.

"Wait," she says slowly. "You didn't actually threaten her, right?"

"Well... I sort of told her I could have her fired."

Sam gasps, loud enough that I don't even need to look up to feel the weight of her reaction.

"I know, I know," I say quickly. "I took it too far, didn't I?"

"Shit." Her voice drops into a murmur, her expression twisted with worry. "That's not good. What did he say? Is there going to be backlash?"

I bury my face in my hands. "For now it's only a verbal warning. But he also banned me from going to John's office, at least for now. Basically told me to talk to my husband on my own time."

Sam nods slowly. "I know this isn't what you want to hear, but that could've been way worse. Colleges don't play about that kind of thing."

I know she's right. I've worked in education long enough to understand how bad this looks. What I said was unprofessional, reckless, and I know damn well the fact that I'm a Black woman while the one who went running to Carlos is white makes it even worse. New York may be diverse, but Long Island isn't, and Shady Oaks still feels like it's stuck in another decade. John and I used to talk about this when he was applying for the VP job he now holds. Back when we talked about things. Back when we were still on the same page. Now it feels like we aren't even reading the same book.

The thought of him sharpens into dread. "Do you think he told Carlos what happened?"

"Girl, *Cunt*-stance probably told him already. I'm more surprised you haven't heard from him yet."

Smiling at the name play, I fumble for my bag, realizing I haven't checked my phone. My stomach sinks when I see the screen. Four missed calls from John. A string of unread messages.

What were you thinking?

We need to talk.

Why can't you let go of this fantasy that I'm cheating?

You're being paranoid.

Where are you?

I sigh, place the phone face down, and take a long sip of my iced tea. Condensation drips down the cup and pools on the table, the slow spreading ring of water perfectly matching the feeling of everything closing in around me.

I know I need to answer him. I know I need to face this marriage head-on. But if he won't admit the truth to me, will he admit it in front of someone else? Would therapy even matter? How did a decade of marriage unravel into this?

"What's happening, babe?" Sam asks gently, pulling me out of my spiral.

I meet her gaze and feel tears sting my eyes. "I don't know what to do or what to believe," I whisper. A tear slips free, betraying the mask I've tried to hold together. I'm not someone who breaks down in public. I'm practical, confident. Feeling lost like this is foreign, and it terrifies me.

"Lo, it's going to be ok," she says softly. "Right now it feels heavy and terrifying, but you will look back and realize this moment was necessary. For your growth. For your evolution."

Wiping my eyes with the scratchy napkin in my hand, I offer a weak smile. Deep down I know she's right, but her words feel distant, like light I can't quite reach.

"Yeah, I know. I just wish I could skip to that part," I say.

She nods, squeezing my hand across the table, rubbing her thumb over my trembling skin. "I'm here for you, sis. All that you need."

I nod again, afraid that speaking will unleash another wave of tears. I drain the last of my drink and let the silence settle between us. For once, silence feels like comfort.

But in the back of my mind, the question keeps circling, sharp and unrelenting.

What am I going to do about my marriage?

Am I staying with John and trying to fight for what's left, or am I finally leaving him behind?

Chapter Ten

When I open the front door, the house is quiet and dim. I step inside, closing it softly behind me, and walk through the entryway into the kitchen. Only the stove light is on, casting a soft glow that makes the room feel smaller, more intimate.

I relax my shoulders a little and set my purse on the table before heading to the cabinets for a glass. The bottle of whiskey is still sitting on the counter, and I know John must have been drinking earlier too. I pour myself a quarter glass and, without bothering to close the bottle, take a long swallow. The liquid burns its way down my throat and settles hot in my belly. I close my eyes, letting the warmth spread through me.

"You're home," a husky voice says behind me.

I jump, slamming my glass down on the counter so hard that whiskey splashes over the rim. My hand flies to my chest as I whirl around.

John stands there, shirtless, broad shoulders gleaming in the low light. His only clothing is a pair of loose basketball shorts. His eyes look tired and wet, like he's been drinking while waiting for me.

"Hey... yeah," I say, breathless. "I'm sorry I didn't call you back, I—"

I don't finish. He crosses the room in a blur, and his mouth crashes against mine. His lips silence me, his hands gripping my waist with such force I know I couldn't move even if I wanted to. But I don't want to.

The heat of his erection pressing against my stomach makes my resistance vanish.

I kiss him back, arms locking around his neck. His hands fumble with the button of my skirt. I try to pull away, but he kisses me deeper, harder, until I surrender with a moan.

My skirt slips to the floor. In one swift motion, he lifts me, setting me on the cool surface of the kitchen counter. His lips find mine again, urgent and hungry, then trail to my neck.

"John, I—"

"*Shhh,*" he whispers, unbuttoning my blouse. His mouth lingers over the tops of my breasts, his fingers already unhooking my bra. When both fall away, he inhales sharply, eyes dark with lust. For a second, I almost cry at the familiarity of that look.

He bows his head, taking my nipple into his mouth, tongue circling until I throw my head back in pleasure. When he switches to the other, my entire body arches toward him, desperate and alive.

He drops to his knees, pushing my thighs apart with his hands, his eyes locked on mine. His lips brush the inside of my thigh, teasing me.

"I love you, Halo," he murmurs.

Then his tongue is on me, sweeping over my clit before sucking gently, swirling until I cry out. My head falls back, and the world spins with the rhythm of his mouth. Ten years together and he still knows exactly how to unravel me.

Minutes later, my legs shake uncontrollably, nearly closing around his head. I feel him smile against me, smug in his control. He rises, freeing himself from his shorts, and positions me at the edge of the counter. His mouth claims my nipple again as his cock slides against me, thick and pulsing.

"Lo," he groans, eyes closing as he pushes inside.

I moan as my body stretches to take him. He moves deeper, each thrust opening me more, until I am clinging to him, nails digging into his shoulders. The intensity is unbearable, and before he's even fully inside me, I feel release crash through me.

"Shit," I cry, clenching around him as I come.

"Yes, that's right, baby—come for daddy."

My body melts, but he isn't finished. He lifts me off the counter, turns me, and bends me over the edge. His hands grip me—one on my hip, the other cupping my breast—as he thrusts into me from behind. My cries echo in the quiet house, the sound of skin against skin filling the space.

Moments later, his breath quickens. He mutters something low, unintelligible, before his body jerks against mine. His grip tightens, then loosens as he comes, collapsing into me.

We stay like that, panting, both trembling in the aftermath.

And then reality settles like a cold fog. My body stiffens. Slowly, I pull away, covering myself as I head toward the bathroom.

I need space. I need to think.

What am I doing?

Chapter Eleven

When I wake the next morning, John is already gone. The empty side of the bed feels cold, and for a moment I let myself relax. At least I have time to think, to figure out what the hell I'm doing.

The shame hits me as soon as I roll over. Instead of having the conversation we needed, I for sure fucked him last night. I gave in to his body when what I should have demanded was his honesty.

Constance must have told him about our conversation in his office. If she told Carlos, there's no doubt she ran straight to John. The little whore probably couldn't wait, certain she was getting me in trouble. But then why was he all over me last night? Maybe it was the alcohol, but my gut tells me it's something else.

Maybe he feels guilty. Maybe he knows he's caught. Either way, I hate that I let my guard down and gave him the impression that things are fine. They are far from fine.

The thought of him at work today, sitting mere feet from her desk, makes my stomach twist in knots of anger and anxiety.

I roll over and grab my phone from the nightstand. Scrolling past the unread messages from Jenna and Sam, I open John's text.

Good morning love. Let's talk tonight. I love you.

I read it twice, then type back, *Sounds good.*

Jenna and Sam are checking on me, asking about getting together. I tell them I'll see them this weekend. They haven't met yet, but I know they'll click. Not only because they both love me, but because they're both my kind of women. I've never been one for big circles of friends. I've always been a quality over quantity type, and from what I know about their lives, they'll get along just fine. I make a mental note to bring us all together soon.

I stretch my arms overhead, twist my back, and wince at the kink from being bent over the kitchen counter last night. Still naked, I drag myself into the shower.

The hot water soaks into my skin as I stand there, lost in thought. I squeeze conditioner into my palm, far more than a dime-sized amount, and work it into my curls. Coconut and argan oil fill the air, calming me for a moment. But then the guilt presses back in.

Last night should not have happened. I can't keep blurring the line between passion and destruction.

A loud crash snaps me out of my thoughts.

The sound is so sharp I squeal. My heart races.

What the fuck was that?

I turn off the water, straining to listen. The silence feels too heavy, too still. I push open the glass shower door, grab my black robe, and wrap it tight around my damp body. My pulse hammers as I creep toward the bathroom door. I had left it slightly ajar, and I peer through the crack, every nerve on edge.

Carefully, I push it open all the way. No creak, thank God. I pad to the top of the stairs and peer down. Everything looks normal. I release a shaky breath, relief flooding me.

Back in the bedroom, I grab my phone.

Were you just home? I text John.

I toss the phone onto the bed, but the unease won't let me leave it behind. I pick it back up and force myself downstairs, each step deliberate, bracing for what I might find.

And then I see it.

Glass covers the floor, glittering under the weak morning light. The bay window is shattered, and at the center of the wreckage lies a massive rock.

My hand flies to my mouth to stifle a scream.

My phone rings in my hand. I don't move my eyes from the scene as I answer.

"Hey, Lo, what's up? I just got your text." John's voice is breathless.

Too horrified to process that detail, I choke out, "John, the window is smashed. There's a huge rock. Someone threw it through our front window. I was in the—"

"What?" His voice is sharp and urgent. "What do you mean someone threw a rock through the window?"

"I mean I'm standing in our living room, the glass is everywhere, and there's a big rock on the floor. John, who would do this?" My own voice sounds shrill, shaky.

He sucks in a breath. "What the fuck. Holy shit. I'm coming home right now."

I nod, even though he can't see me.

"Halo? Are you safe? Call the police and make sure everything is locked. My gun is in the third drawer of our dresser, under my T-shirts, in the wooden box."

I stare at the screen.

Of course I know about the gun. I've known where it's kept for years. Still, seeing it spelled out like this makes my stomach drop. The way he says it. The urgency. The assumption that I might need it.

Panic seizes me. What if whoever did this is still out there? What if they're still here?

"John," I whisper, my voice breaking.

"I'm coming, baby. Get the gun and call the cops. I'll be there in twenty minutes, tops."

"Hurry," I whisper, but the line is already dead.

I swallow hard, dial 9-1-1, and double-check that the front door is locked and deadbolted.

"9-1-1, what's your emergency?" a woman's voice answers.

"Someone threw a huge rock through my window," I blurt, too loud, my voice trembling. "I don't know if they left or if they're still here. I need an officer to come."

She asks questions while I pace, telling me to calm down, assuring me help is on the way. I try, but my voice keeps breaking, words spilling too fast. This doesn't make sense. Ours isn't the kind of neighborhood where this happens. The bay window sits too far back from the street. Whoever did this had to walk up the driveway and onto our porch.

This wasn't random.

This was *intentional*.

When the dispatcher confirms an officer is en route, I hang up and sink onto the couch. My eyes lock on the glass, jagged and sharp, covering the carpet like a hundred tiny knives. Who would do this? And why?

A sharp knock jolts me upright.

That was fast.

I glance in the mirror above the couch, reaching up instinctively to fluff my loose curls. The absurdity almost makes me laugh. Who cares about my hair right now? Old habits die hard.

I open the door and come face to face with two officers. The man is tall and wiry but looks strong. His short blond hair is cropped close, and his dark blue eyes are piercing. The woman is shorter but solid, with tan skin, hazel eyes that flash against her dark features, and a hooked scar etched into her left cheek. I force my eyes away from it and back to her partner.

"Halo Roberts?" the man asks, glancing at the notebook in his hand.

"Yes. Thank you for getting here so quickly," I say, stepping back. "Careful, there's glass."

They walk past me into the living room. The woman slips on gloves and crouches near the wreckage, studying the debris. The man turns toward me.

"Do you have any idea who might have done this?"

I shake my head slowly. "I don't. Our neighbors are friendly. This is so unexpected. Do you think we were targeted?"

Even as I ask, I already know.

The woman rises, holding the object in her gloved hands. "This isn't a rock. It's a piece of broken cement." She turns it over and hands it to her partner.

My phone buzzes in my pocket. I excuse myself and step into the kitchen.

"What's happening?" John asks, still breathless. I can hear his car on the road.

"The cops are here now. They said it's cement."

"What the fuck. I'm almost there. Five minutes."

As I slip my phone back into my robe pocket, the male officer clears his throat. I turn, startled. He's got his notebook open again.

"I need your official statement, ma'am, before we go."

I nod, my throat tight, and follow him back into the glass-filled room.

I'm halfway through giving my statement when I hear tires screeching in the driveway. The crunch of gravel makes my whole body tense. Seconds later, John bursts through the door.

His chest is heaving, sweat darkening his shirt, his eyes wild as they dart from me to the shattered window. "Jesus Christ," he mutters, raking both hands through his hair. He stares at the cement block, then at the glass scattered across the floor.

"Are you okay?" he asks, rushing over, gripping my shoulders so tightly it almost hurts.

"I'm fine," I whisper, though my voice doesn't sound convincing.

The female officer shifts, watching him closely. "Sir, we'll need to ask you a few questions once we finish with your wife."

John nods distractedly, but his hand never leaves me. His thumb strokes my arm, absent, almost mechanical. His face is pale, eyes flicking between the officers and me.

For a moment I almost ask the question sitting heavy in my chest. Do you know who would do this? But the words choke off in my throat.

Because part of me doesn't want the answer.

Chapter Twelve

John and I sit at the kitchen island, both of us slouched on stools like two people who have been wrung out and hung up to dry. He looks as haggard as I feel. The house is too quiet, even after hours of officers moving through it, asking questions, writing things down that didn't add up to anything.

We hired a special cleaning crew to take care of the glass, the jagged carpet of shards that had swallowed our living room floor. Now the bay window is patched with a temporary board, but the smell of sawdust and industrial cleaner still lingers. The police didn't have solid answers, only promises to canvass the neighbors and follow up if anyone saw anything suspicious.

But the silence left behind feels worse than the chaos.

I've been turning it over in my head for hours. Who would want to do this? If it was some random act of vandalism, why our house? There are plenty of other nice homes on our block. It doesn't make sense.

I glance at John. His jaw is tight, his eyes fixed somewhere far away. He looks deep in thought, and the sight of him unsettles me. I've spent ten years memorizing that face, loving it, trusting it. Yet sitting here now, with this eerie quiet pressing down on us, I feel a rush of something cold and sharp, like I don't really know him at all.

The thought comes fast, strong, and then it's gone. But the trace of it lingers like a bad aftertaste.

When his gaze meets mine, unsmiling, I force myself to look away. My teacup trembles faintly in my hand. I take a sip to cover my nerves, but when I glance up again, he's still staring. The moment our eyes meet, he looks away too quickly, as if caught.

Who are you? The question flashes through my mind before I can stop it. An involuntary shiver runs down my arms.

"Cold?" His voice is soft, but steady.

I shake my head too quickly, gulp another mouthful of tea, and stand abruptly. "I think I'm going to take a bath. That'll help me calm down. Today has been... crazy."

He studies me for a moment, his eyes unreadable. Then he nods. "Good idea. I'll be down here a little longer. I have some work to finish. I'll come up soon."

I nod, avoiding his eyes as I turn toward the stairs. At the top, I glance back. He's still watching me, expression blank, but it makes my skin prickle. I give him a weak smile before hurrying upstairs.

The sound of the tub filling is soothing. I peel my clothes off and let them drop onto the floor, testing the water with my hand. Too hot. I adjust the faucet, let cool water mix in, and pull my curls up into a messy bun. My reflection in the mirror looks flat, drained. I stare blankly until I can't stand the sight of my own tired face.

Sliding into the water feels like a reprieve. I sink deeper, closing my eyes as the lavender oil I'd added drifts around me. The warmth loosens the knots in my back and shoulders. I let myself breathe.

But my mind won't let me rest. It circles back to the one question that's been chasing me all day: who threw that rock, or that slab of cement, through our window? And *why?*

Constance's face surfaces in my mind like a ghost. I know her scrawny frame couldn't have lifted something that heavy, but she's the only one I can think of with a motive. Maybe tattling to Carlos wasn't enough for her. Maybe she wanted to push me further, punish me harder. As if sleeping with my husband wasn't enough.

The water suddenly feels too hot, suffocating. I sit up, lean forward against the porcelain, and rest my chin on my forearm. My reflection stares back at me from the mirror across the room. My hazel eyes look tired, my face hollow. I make a mental note to try the new eye cream I bought at Ulta, as if that could fix anything right now.

A soft knock at the door makes me jolt, water sloshing around me.

Jesus, Lo, get a grip.

"It's just me," John says, pushing the door open slightly. His tall frame fills the doorway, his head resting against the frame. "You okay in here?"

"You scared the shit out of me," I mutter, trying to slow my breathing. "But yeah. The bath helped."

"I didn't mean to scare you, love. I'm glad it calms your nerves. It's been a hell of a day."

I nod, motioning for the towel on the hook beside him. He steps into the room, takes it down, and hands it to me before lowering himself onto the closed lid of the toilet. His eyes follow me as I rise from the tub, water streaming down my body. Wrapping the towel around myself, I move past him, but I can feel his gaze burning into me.

When I turn, my suspicion is confirmed. He's still staring.

"Lo," he says quietly. "I know we aren't in the best place right now, but I want you to know I love you. And I would never do anything to hurt you."

His eyes search mine. The weight of them is almost unbearable. I look away before he sees the disappointment that burns in me. My vision blurs with sudden tears, the black-and-white check of the tiles smearing under my gaze.

"Thanks," I murmur, my voice barely audible. Without looking up, I pull the door closed behind me and leave him sitting there.

The hallway feels colder than the bathroom, the silence heavier than the water I just left.

And the question that haunts me rises again, sharper than before.

Who are you, John?

I close the door gently behind me and walk down the hall toward the bedroom. My bare feet make no sound on the hardwood, but the silence feels heavy, almost suffocating. I dry my hair with the towel as I climb into bed, my body exhausted, but my mind refuses to quiet.

The sheets feel cool against my skin, and for a moment I let myself sink into them, pulling the blanket up to my chin. My eyelids flutter, but each time they close, the image of shattered glass on the living room floor returns. The cement slab, the sharp edges of danger glinting across the carpet, the fact that someone walked onto our porch to do that.

Sleep doesn't come.

Instead, I hear John's footsteps downstairs. Slow. Heavy. Pacing the kitchen.

At first I think he's cleaning something up or making himself another drink, but then the sound stops. A pause. Then his voice, low and clipped.

I freeze, my breath caught. The hum of his voice is muffled but unmistakable. He's on the phone.

I strain to hear, pressing my ear toward the crack in our bedroom door. His words float up in pieces, broken by the distance, but the tone makes my stomach twist.

"...I told you I'd handle it..."

Silence.

"...No, she doesn't know..."

Another pause, longer this time.

"...just don't do anything stupid."

My blood runs cold.

I pull the blanket tighter around me, my pulse hammering so loud I swear he'll hear it from downstairs. My mouth is dry, my hands clammy.

He doesn't know I can hear him. He doesn't know I'm awake.

When I finally hear his footsteps again, this time moving toward the stairs, I roll onto my side and squeeze my eyes shut. I force my breathing to slow, pretending sleep, though every nerve in my body is on fire.

The mattress dips as he slides in beside me. The scent of whiskey and soap clings to him. His hand brushes against my hip, lingering for a moment before pulling away.

I keep my eyes closed. I keep still.

But the words echo in my skull.

She doesn't know.

Chapter Thirteen

Standing in line at The Bean, the coffee shop next door to the college, I glance around for Samaya. She promised to meet me before work so I could spill everything. She isn't here yet.

The smell of roasted beans and sugar clings to the air, but even that comfort doesn't quiet my nerves. I didn't sleep last night. I tossed and turned, the sheets twisted around me like a trap. John's words replayed in my head on a loop: *I'd never do anything to hurt you.*

I thought they were supposed to soothe me. Instead, they made me question every second of the last ten years. If he could look me dead in the eye and lie, then what else has he hidden? There's something cruel about that kind of lie—when it comes from someone whose body you know as well as your own. It rips safety away, leaving a black hole of mistrust.

I shake myself from the spiral when I notice the girl in front of me. Her hair is a swirl of teal, pink, and blue, like spun sugar. It makes me think of Rainbow Brite, a flash of childhood from another life. She turns, catching me staring, and offers a nervous smile.

"I was admiring your hair," I say quickly. "Very cool."

Her smile softens into a grin, her braces flashing. "Thanks! My mom hates it, but what does she know?"

I laugh and shrug. "Well, I think it's dope."

She beams and turns back to place her order.

When it's my turn, I order the biggest coffee I can. My head pounds from lack of sleep, but it isn't exhaustion alone. It's dread. The image of John whispering into the phone downstairs while he thought I was asleep still lingers. *She doesn't know.* My stomach knots just thinking about it.

I carry my cup to a small round table near the front window and sink into the chair. The glass rattles faintly when I set it down, my hands still unsteady. Outside, the street is alive with the shuffle of backpacks, bikes, and the occasional car horn. The campus crowds blur together, diverse faces mixing in a way you rarely see outside of the university bubble.

When I spot Samaya's beautiful, curl-framed face cutting through the crowd, my chest loosens. She lights up when she sees me, her wide smile enough to make me believe, for a second, that everything will be okay.

"Babe!" she squeals, wrapping me in her long brown arms. "Oh my God, are you okay?"

"Sort of. Go order first, then I'll tell you everything." I glance down at her flip-flop-clad feet. "Girl, it's supposed to rain later. Aren't your feet cold?"

She laughs, her dimples flashing. "You can take the girl outta Cali, but you can't take Cali out of the girl."

We both giggle, the sound a little too light against the weight pressing on my chest.

When she returns with her coffee, she drops into the chair beside me. "Okay," she says gently. "Tell me everything."

I tell her about the slab of cement. About the shattered window. About the police questions that went nowhere. I even tell her about John's comment, the one that lodged itself in my chest like a splinter. *I'd never hurt you.*

What I don't tell her is the other thing. The moment I overheard him on the phone, his voice low and certain when he said, *She doesn't know.* The words come back to me with unsettling clarity, sharp enough to draw blood.

That part stays locked inside. Saying it out loud would force a conclusion I'm not ready to reach. Naming it would mean asking what she doesn't know, and whether I've already missed something critical. Without proof, without something solid to anchor the fear, it feels safer to carry it alone than to watch it take shape in someone else's eyes.

"Does she know where you live?" Samaya asks.

"She?" I blink at her, confused.

"Constance. Does she know where y'all live?"

The question chills me. "Oh my God, no," I say too quickly, too loud. But when I reach for my iced white mocha, my hand is shaking. I take a long sip to steady myself, eyes fixed on the ring of condensation the cup leaves behind. "Actually... I have no idea." The words fall from my lips quiet, alien, like they don't belong to me.

Samaya studies me, her sharp gaze softening as she lays her manicured hand over mine. "I'm not saying she does. And I'm definitely not saying she's behind what happened. But she's the only person who has it out for you right now. I doubt her scrawny ass could even lift a rock that big."

I let out a short laugh, my shoulders easing a fraction. "It crossed my mind, trust me. I didn't want to sound paranoid."

She nods, sympathetic. "What about cameras? Do you have anything on your house?"

I snort. "We don't live in the kind of neighborhood that requires cameras. Now I wish we did. The cops basically said without proof or witnesses, it's going to be hard to know who did it."

Her expression hardens. "Sounds about right. You damn near gotta be dead for the cops to take you seriously. Unless, of course, it's us they're being called on."

Her voice drops at that last word, *us*, and she gestures between the two of us.

I know her story. I know how the cops ignored her warnings about her ex-husband until it was nearly too late. The way she had to disappear, hide, survive. The way someone else—someone obsessed with her—killed him instead.

Her survival has always inspired me. But sitting here now, hearing her talk about how the system failed her, I can't help but wonder: is it failing me too?

Samaya breaks the silence by pulling out her phone. "What about this one?"

On the screen, a picture of a porch light.

I frown. "What about it?"

She laughs. "It's a camera."

I snatch her phone and squint. "What? It looks like a regular light."

"Girl, welcome to the twenty-first century. They even have ones that look like iPhone chargers. Spy stuff, new and improved."

"No shit," I mutter, scrolling through the photos.

"The porch light is the best for you. Hidden in plain sight. If someone comes back, you'll catch them."

I shiver at that thought, but I order it anyway. And because it's cheap, I add the charger block version too, even though I don't know what I'll use it for.

Samaya grins. "Good. People are crazy, and now at least you'll be ready."

But the word *ready* sits wrong in my gut. Because readiness means expecting something. It means believing someone might come back.

And the more I think about it, the more I realize I do.

***

I stir the pot absently, the wooden spoon scraping the bottom in slow circles. The smell of simmering tomatoes barely registers. My head is too full.

John texted earlier that we needed to talk when he got home. I can't tell if this is about the shattered window or the conversation with Constance in his office. That scene feels like a lifetime ago, though it was only days ago.

I set the burner on low and cover the pot, then turn to the sink to fill another pot with water for the pasta. The sudden click of the deadbolt sends my heart into my throat. I drop the pot back into the sink with a clang, clutching at my chest.

Get a grip.

It's only John. Still, my nerves have been strung tight since the break-in. I wipe my damp hands on the dish towel, fluff my curls, and force a deep breath. When I turn, he's right there behind me, closer than I realized. How did he move so quietly?

"Hey, Lo," he says in that husky voice that once melted me. "Something smells delicious."

He loosens his tie, unbuttons the collar of his crisp blue shirt, then leans down and brushes my lips with his. His mouth tastes faintly of whiskey.

"How was your day?" he asks.

"What did you want to talk about?" The words spill out before I can stop them.

He smiles faintly, releasing me. "We can talk later. Don't you want to eat first?"

I shake my head.

He sighs, his chest rising and falling. "Carlos called me into his office. He told me what happened with Constance. He said you won't be allowed in my office for a while."

Heat rises through me, fast and sharp. "And?"

"I told him I didn't agree. I asked for her to be transferred immediately."

My mouth falls open. "Transferred? On what basis? You can't just reshuffle people like that."

He inhales slowly and lets it out through his teeth. "Constance has been acting inappropriately for months. Coming on to me. Making comments. Touching my arm in ways that crossed the line. I finally told him everything. He supports the decision."

For a second, I only stare. Did he really say that?

"John, all the times I accused you, why didn't you tell me she was the one coming on to you?"

His eyes hold steady on mine. "Because you never would have believed me. You already thought I was sleeping with her. The last thing I wanted to do was admit she was getting worse."

I search his face, desperate for a crack in the mask. He doesn't flinch. His gaze never wavers. Could he really have gone to his boss and filed a complaint? Or is this another layer of lies? Shady Oaks doesn't take accusations like that lightly.

"I'm just in shock," I manage.

He studies me like he's waiting to see if I'll break. I know what he wants. Blind trust. Loyalty. My silence as proof of belief.

I force a small smile. "Well, it's a relief knowing you weren't the one behaving inappropriately. I'm glad the college is being supportive."

His jaw tightens almost imperceptibly. "Yes. I'm happy you're taking this well. With any luck, she'll be gone soon. Besides, I'll be out of town for a week anyway. Perfect timing."

The words pull me back sharp. "Out of town?"

"The new Student Success conference in Pennsylvania. I told you. It was in the campus-wide email." His tone is gentle, but his eyes are scanning my face again, gauging every reaction.

I nod, though the memory isn't there. "Oh. Right. I must have forgotten."

"They're trying to look more inclusive," he says, smirking and making air quotes. "You know how that goes."

"Yeah," I say weakly. The lack of diversity is no joke. It makes his smile feel like a weapon.

"When do you leave?"

"Sunday. I should be back the following Saturday." He stretches and turns toward the stairs.

Should be back.

The phrase lodges deep. My stomach twists.

I watch him walk away, his back straight, his stride steady. He looks like a man with nothing to hide, but the memory of his voice on the phone last night slams into me again.

She doesn't know.

Was that about me? About Constance? About someone else entirely?

I grip the edge of the counter, my nails biting into the wood. A chill runs down my arms despite the steam curling from the pot behind me.

He disappears up the stairs, and the house feels too quiet again.

I stand in the kitchen alone, trying to decide which terrifies me more: the possibility that John is telling me the truth, or the possibility that he isn't.

Chapter Fourteen

I release my Creative Writing Theory students ten minutes before the usual time for dismissal. As they gather their backpacks and purses in a rush of chatter and squeaky sneakers, I smile. I love my students, and after so many years teaching, I know the rhythm of their week. It's Thursday, which means for most of them, the weekend begins now.

The sigh that leaves me when the last student slips out is heavy. I gather the stack of lesson notes from the desk, shove them into my black leather bag, and reach for my phone. A new text from Jenna lights up the screen.

Yoga?? I'm going to the 5 pm class at Evolution.

Evolution is the little studio we sometimes manage to meet at. My first instinct is to decline, retreat home to stew in my thoughts. But instead, I find myself typing back a quick yes. A class and some friend time might pull me out of this fog. Besides, Jenna deserves an update.

Outside, the campus lawn is perfectly manicured, every blade of grass in line as if the grounds crew were waiting for me to notice. It's three in the afternoon and unusually quiet. I toss my bag into the trunk of my car, then hesitate, turning back toward Shady Oaks. I have time to spare, and my body could use the movement. A loop around campus feels better than sitting in traffic.

The oaks stretch high overhead, their branches like open arms. Squirrels dart across the path, bold in the absence of students. Birds call in a way that feels staged, almost too pretty. For the first time in weeks, my chest loosens, the steady pace of my steps pressing out the tension.

John and I used to walk this path together. In another life, it was our small ritual. A SUNY campus means perfect landscaping, no loose branches unless a storm tears through. I breathe it in, my curls safe in the low humidity, and think about how much I've always welcomed moody weather. Rain never chased me inside. As a girl, I would run into storms and dance, soaked through, wild and unbothered. Even now, walking through drizzle or snow feels cleansing. The elements give me something John can't.

By the time I reach the center of campus, I loop around the massive oak that seems older than everything else here and begin the slow trek back toward my car. My body feels lighter, but my mind—stubborn and cruel—starts to crawl back to him.

John insists nothing happened. He says he was guilty only of being too supportive, too involved in Constance's problems. He says she came on to him. He says he shut it down.

But my gut doesn't buy it.

His words replay in my head, each one rehearsed, each one polished, but hollow. His smile too careful. His eyes too guarded. It's like listening to a stranger wear his voice.

I stop walking for a moment, standing in the dappled sunlight, and let the weight of that realization sink in.

If he is lying, what else has he lied about?

A breeze cuts through, rattling the branches overhead. The sound is sharp, brittle, and for a second I feel exposed, as if someone is watching me from the shadow of the trees.

I shake it off, force myself back onto the path, but the shiver lingers.

***

As soon as Jenna sees me, she wraps me in a bear hug so tight I nearly lose my balance. The strength of it cracks something open inside me, and for a terrifying second I almost let the tears spill. I squeeze my eyes shut, biting down on my bottom lip, willing myself not to fall apart in the middle of the lobby. Her hands grip my shoulders when she pulls back, her gaze scanning my face like she's reading every unspoken word.

"Lo... babe, are you ok?"

I swallow the knot in my throat and force the air back into my lungs. "I'm ok. There's so much going on right now."

Her blue eyes harden, narrowing like shards of ice. "With John?"

The weight of her stare makes me want to crumple. The last real conversation we'd had was about John's affair. That truth, spoken aloud, feels like a bruise that hasn't healed. Now I have to drag her into everything that's happened since.

We walk in silence toward the yoga room, the soft squeak of our flip-flops echoing in the empty hall. The studio is quiet, still. We're early—no mats rolled out, no instructor yet, only the faint hum of the heater and the scent of lavender lingering from the last class.

I unroll my mat slowly, the sound of it snapping flat against the wood floor jarring in the silence. My legs fold beneath me as I sink down cross-legged, my palms resting heavy on my knees. Only when I finally meet Jenna's eyes do I find the courage to speak.

"Things have been... crazy. I thought John was having an affair. Then my dumb ass marched into his office and threatened her—told her I'd get her fired if she 'kept fucking my husband.'"

Jenna's eyes widen before she bursts out laughing, the sound bouncing around the quiet studio. "Lo, stop. You didn't!"

I can't help but laugh too, even as shame burns the back of my throat. "I really did, girl. What the fuck, right?" I shake my head. "Well, John says she was coming onto him all along, so now he's putting in some kind of complaint against her. Long story short, she might actually get fired for sexual harassment."

I lean back on my hands, waiting for her high-five, waiting for her to laugh with me at the absurdity of it all.

But she doesn't.

Her face goes still. Cold. She looks at me like I've spoken in a language she doesn't understand. My heart dips, and before I can backpedal, she shakes her head.

"Lo… that sounds like some sketchy shit. So all this time he was being harassed, but somehow he was still hanging out with her at bars? Still taking her calls? Still giving her all that extra attention? It doesn't add up. Why didn't he say anything before? Why didn't he tell you or report her sooner? Sounds like last-minute scrambling to put it all on her, to save his own ass. And now what, she loses her job while he comes out clean?"

Her words slice through me. I shift uncomfortably on my mat, eyes darting down to my trembling hands. "I don't think he would do all of this to cover an affair," I whisper, though I don't believe it. Not really.

"Babe." Jenna's voice softens, but it lands like stone. "I know you want to believe he wouldn't, but you know deep down there's more to the story."

Her hand brushes my shoulder gently, grounding me, and I almost lean into it. But the truth of what she's saying burns too hot. I shrug her off and paste on a tight smile.

"Well, either way, she won't be working with him anymore. So I don't have to worry."

Her mouth twists. "And what if that's a lie too? What if she's not some manipulative temptress but just a woman who slept with a man who outranked her, and now he's flipping it back on her to keep you in line? I'm not saying she's right. I'm saying they're probably both guilty."

My lips part, ready to argue, ready to deny, but the creak of the door opening cuts me off. Two young women giggle their way inside, their heads bent close, their whispers sharp and private.

Jenna's eyes search mine one more time. I can't hold her gaze.

Instead, I collapse forward onto my mat, folding into child's pose, pressing my forehead hard against the floor as if I can push the noise out of my brain. The mat smells faintly of rubber and lavender spray. My heart hammers against my thighs, my breath catching on each exhale.

I tell myself I came here for release, for stillness. But all I find is the thrum of my own mind, whispering over and over.

What if she's right?

The instructor breezes in just as the room fills with more students. Her voice is calm, lilting, the kind of tone that normally washes over me like a balm. Tonight it barely registers.

"Let's start in a comfortable seated position. Close your eyes. Let the day go."

I obey, crossing my legs tighter, pressing my palms into my knees. My eyes close, but instead of peace, I see shards of glass scattered across my living room floor. I hear John's voice on the phone, muffled, clipped. *She doesn't know.*

The instructor's voice floats through the room. "Notice your breath."

I try. *Inhale. Exhale.* But it's uneven, ragged. My chest feels too small for my lungs.

We move into cat-cow and my spine arches, but the stretch doesn't bring relief. I feel Jenna's eyes flick toward me, watching. She knows I'm not here. Not really.

When we rise into downward dog, my arms tremble more than they should. My hamstrings scream in protest, but it's not the pose. It's the adrenaline buzzing in my veins, the dread that coils in my stomach like a stone.

"Flow with your breath," the instructor says softly.

My breath snags. My body moves, but my mind won't. Every time I close my eyes, I see John's face, hear Jenna's words. *It doesn't add up.*

By the time we fold into pigeon pose, I'm shaking. My forehead presses to the mat, and suddenly I'm not in a studio filled with lavender and quiet bodies. I'm back in my house. The rock through the window. The gun in the drawer. The silence when I asked John a question he didn't want to answer.

Tears sting the corners of my eyes. I choke them back. Nobody here needs to see me unravel.

The teacher cues savasana, and bodies stretch out around me, still and surrendered. I lie flat, palms up, eyes staring at the ceiling.

This is supposed to be peace.

But all I feel is the echo of Jenna's voice inside my skull.

What if he's lying? What if you're the only one still pretending this is normal?

Chapter Fifteen

Class ends, the room buzzing with that familiar hum of post-flow chatter. Mats squeak against the hardwood, water bottles click open, and somewhere someone laughs too loudly. I roll mine up in silence, my body loose but my mind still tight as a wire.

Jenna moves slower, watching me like a hawk pretending not to be a hawk. Her blue eyes catch mine, unreadable.

"Lo," she says softly, "do you want to grab tea? Or come by the house? I'm worried about you."

The words are gentle, but they land like a weight pressing down on my chest. I know she means well, but I can already hear the unspoken follow-up: *Are you sure John isn't lying? Are you sure you're not ignoring the truth?*

I force a smile that doesn't quite touch my eyes. "I appreciate it, babe. Really. But I'm wiped. I think I just need to crash tonight."

She hesitates, her brows pinching. I can feel her trying to read me, trying to pry open the lock I've slammed shut. "Okay," she says finally, stretching the word like she doesn't believe it. "But call me if you need me. Please."

I nod too fast, clutching my mat like a shield. By the time I reach the door, guilt claws up my throat. But I shove it back down. I don't want another interrogation disguised as love. I don't want to be told I'm blind when all I'm trying to do is survive.

Outside, the air is thick with humidity, the kind that makes your skin sticky in seconds. My phone buzzes in my bag. A text lights up the screen.

Samaya: *You free? I've got wine and Thai food with your name on it.*

Relief crashes through me. No probing questions. No icy blue eyes searching for cracks. Just comfort. Just escape.

Half an hour later, I'm barefoot on Samaya's couch, curled under one of her oversized knit throws, a glass of red wine sweating in my hand. The smell of spicy basil chicken fills the room, warm and grounding. Sam listens the way only she can—quietly, with her whole body. No interruptions. No judgment.

"She thinks I'm naive," I confess, staring into the rim of my glass. "That I'm missing something obvious."

Sam tilts her head, curls brushing her cheek, her voice steady, almost professional. "Or maybe she doesn't understand what it's like to be in your position. People love to think they'd know what to do. But they don't."

I let out a shaky exhale. "Exactly."

Her smile is soft, knowing. She reaches out, resting her hand over mine for just a beat too long. "Lo, you're not crazy. You're protecting yourself the best way you know how. And sometimes?" Her eyes lock with mine, unwavering. "Protecting yourself means letting go of people who can't see you clearly."

Her words sink into me like honey and venom. Sweet. Dangerous. I nod slowly, letting them settle, letting them take root in the places I've been too afraid to touch.

***

John is already home when I walk in from Samaya's. His briefcase is tossed on the table, his tie draped carelessly over the back of a chair. A half-empty glass of bourbon sweats in his hand, the ice nearly gone. He doesn't even look at me.

"I heard from HR today," he says flatly, eyes locked on the amber liquid like it might give him answers. "The complaint's filed. Constance won't be a problem much longer."

A wave of relief loosens my chest. Proof he's on my side. Proof he's the victim, not me. Proof I'm not losing my mind.

But then my gaze drifts. His phone lies face down on the counter, silent and still, like a snake waiting for movement.

I shouldn't. God knows I shouldn't. But my fingers move before my brain catches up. I flip it over. The screen lights, and her name burns back at me. Constance.

The notification is short, almost casual, but it slices through me.

You still alone? I was at my mom's birthday thing.

My stomach flips. My mouth goes dry.

"Lo." His voice cuts sharp, snapping me out of it. "What the hell are you doing with my phone?"

I freeze, heat flooding my cheeks, my hand still hovering like I've been caught stealing. "Nothing. I just—" I shove the phone at him, desperate to cover my tracks. "Why is she texting you if she's harassing you? That doesn't look like a woman you've shut out, John. That looks like a woman you're stringing along."

He snatches it from me, his jaw tight, eyes dark. "She... she won't leave me alone. That's exactly why I filed the complaint."

My laugh is bitter, ugly. "Or maybe it's because you needed to cover your ass before I figured it out. Tell me the truth for once. Did you sleep with her?"

His glass slams against the counter so hard bourbon splashes, droplets scattering like shrapnel. "I'm not doing this again. I told you I didn't. You either believe me or you don't."

"I don't know what to believe." The words shake out of me, raw and broken.

His mouth curves—not quite a smile, not quite a snarl. "Then maybe you don't deserve the truth."

The words slice through me before I can even process them. He storms upstairs, each step pounding like a drumbeat, leaving me shaking in the kitchen.

The screen of his phone is seared into my mind. That text. Her name glowing like a warning flare. If she's blocked out, why is she still reaching? And more importantly, why does it feel like he wanted her to?

I'm too tired and too buzzed to cry. My body feels hollow as I sink into the couch, staring blankly at the dark TV screen. My mind turns to the work trip. That so-called conference. If that's even what it is.

I grab my phone instead, searching her name, my pulse hammering. Constance's Instagram lights up immediately. A new post. She's at some fancy restaurant, a tight black dress clinging to her like a second skin, a champagne glass sparkling in her hand. She has her arm around a bigger blonde woman I assume is her mother. The caption reads: *Happy birthday, Mom! The big 55—woohoo!*

My chest tightens as I zoom in on her smiling face. She looks stunning. She looks untouchable. She looks like a woman who has no reason to be afraid of consequences.

I roll my eyes and toss my phone aside, but the image sticks. Perfect smile. Perfect body. Perfect lie.

I consider texting Sam, but stop myself. Sam would tell me not to blame myself. Sam would tell me John was gaslighting me. She always knows the words I need. But I've already unloaded too much on her today.

As much as I hate the thought of John going away, I find myself craving it. A week without him under this roof. A week where I can breathe without his eyes on me. Sunday cannot come soon enough.

Because if I don't get space soon, I'll lose what little grip I have left. And I need to figure out if I'm sharing a bed with a liar.

Or with something worse.

Chapter Sixteen

By Sunday morning, my relief outweighs my suspicion. I grip the steering wheel as I pull into the departures lane at JFK, John silent beside me. The air between us feels heavy, like even the car knows I want him gone more than I should.

I glance sideways. He's hunched over his phone, thumbs flying across the screen. I roll my eyes and look back at the road, biting my tongue to keep from making some catty remark. The whole drive he's been buried in that phone. No music. No conversation—only tapping and scrolling. He wanted to get here abnormally early, muttering about heightened security procedures. The excuse felt flimsy. Everything about him feels flimsy.

When we stop, I climb out, determined to at least put on the mask of a picture-perfect wife. My heels click against the pavement as I round the car to help him with his bags. Only, there's one small carry-on in the back seat. That's it.

"Don't you need more than this dinky little bag?" I ask, eyebrows raised.

He rolls his eyes like a teenager. "I'll be fine, Lo. This is more of a retreat. I don't need suits besides the one I'm wearing now for the formal event on Thursday. Do you have to question everything I do?"

The sting is instant. My confusion flips to anger. I drop the bag in front of him like it's on fire. "I am so over this," I mutter, circling back to the driver's side.

I'm reaching for the door handle when his hand clamps around my arm. I spin around, ready to rip free. "I've got to move—they're wav—"

"No kiss?" His voice is suddenly soft, playful, his eyes warm in a way that makes my stomach twist. He leans down and brushes his lips against mine, tender. Too tender.

I stiffen, caught between revulsion and longing. His switch from anger to affection is whiplash. He releases me slowly, studying my face with an intensity that makes my skin crawl. When did he become so unpredictable?

"I know things are all fucked up right now, but I promise once I get back next weekend, I'll put more energy into us," he says. "I'll call you when I land."

I nod quietly, choking back the surge of anger that wants to claw out of my throat. He disappears into the crowd of travelers, swallowed by rolling suitcases and endless lines. I watch until I can't see him anymore, then let out a long sigh and slide back into the car.

As I buckle my seatbelt, my mind returns to that small bag. A week-long trip. One carry-on. My gut twists. Is this really a conference, or a cover for something else?

I ease the car into traffic, signs guiding me toward Long Island. Instead of fumbling with music, I let the silence hum around me, giving space to the thoughts circling like vultures. Maybe I should trust him. He did file the harassment complaint. He swore Constance would be out of the picture by the time he returned. Carlos was handling it. On paper, it all makes sense.

But my gut says otherwise. My gut says he's still tangled up with her.

I sigh audibly, fingers drumming the wheel. Maybe I should call Jenna. Except I can already hear her voice, sharp and scolding, telling me I'm pathetic for letting him go through with the complaint and having Constance punished. I don't need judgment. Not today.

"Hey Siri," I say. "Call Samaya."

The car's speakers click alive. "Calling Samaya."

Her voice comes after two rings, warm and easy. "Hey babe!"

A smile creeps onto my face despite myself. "Girl, I just dropped John off at the airport for his business trip." The sarcastic edge on *business trip* makes her laugh.

"How'd that go?" she asks, amusement threaded through her tone.

"Weird," I admit. "He was glued to his phone the whole way there, then got pissed when I pointed out how little he packed. One tiny bag for a week."

"That *is* weird," she says slowly. "What kind of event is this again?"

"He said it's a casual retreat for community college administrators, so he only needs one suit. Which he's already wearing."

Silence. I glance at the screen to make sure the call hasn't dropped. Finally, Samaya exhales. "I mean… I guess that could be true."

Her hesitation gnaws at me, but she shifts before I can respond. "Why don't you come over for dinner later? We'll order Thai or pizza. Take your mind off John. The last thing I want is you spiraling over whether he's cheating. Again."

Her words land like an anchor, grounding me. I check my mirrors, slide into the next lane, annoyed by a lumbering Pepsi truck slowing me down. "You know what? Let's do it. I was going to go home and rot, but screw that. I refuse to waste another minute feeling sorry for myself."

I can hear the grin in her voice. "That's the spirit. And since we're ordering in, you can still rot a little—with food and wine. Text me when you're home and I'll pick a place."

I laugh, tension easing from my shoulders. "Deal."

For the first time in days, I feel like I can breathe.

***

As soon as I walk in the door, I breathe out a long sigh of relief. I close it behind me and lean against the wood, letting my head fall back as I take in the empty foyer. The silence of the house feels heavier than usual, but I welcome it. My eyes flick instinctively to the bay window in the living room, the same one that had been shattered days ago. The new pane is clean and unblemished, but I can still picture the glass glittering across the carpet, the jagged edges framing the night air. Even with it fixed, the memory lingers, a bruise under the skin of the house.

Heading upstairs, exhaustion presses down on me like a weight. I sit on the edge of the bed and stare up at the ceiling, my mind as restless as ever. My phone pings. John.

Boarding now and taking off soon. Love you.

My thumbs move before my brain does. *Have a safe flight.* The words feel like muscle memory, as automatic as breathing. How many times have I typed those exact words to him before? Dozens, maybe hundreds, when we used to travel separately for conferences or family visits. Back then, it was genuine. Back then, my heart would ache when he left. Now it's just reflex.

It amazes me, the way the mind holds on to old patterns. If I had a dollar for every time I wondered how we ended up in this estranged place, I could have the house paid off twice over. Our cars too. The truth is, the shift didn't happen overnight. Ten months ago, things had already started to sour, though I tried to pretend otherwise. If I'm honest, the cracks showed long before that.

A memory flickers, sharp and unwelcome. Eight years ago, sitting at the dining table with wedding magazines scattered everywhere, John scribbling in a notebook. His vows.

"Babe, I want to get this perfect," he said, running a frustrated hand through his hair. "What's a better way to say this?"

I laughed, covering my eyes with my hands. "You're not supposed to show me, babe! That's cheating."

"I won't tell anyone," he teased, shoving the page toward me. "Just look at this one sentence, pleeeease."

I peeked through my fingers, gave him a few grammatical tips, and watched him light up as he scratched out lines and rewrote them, his tongue sticking out in concentration. When he finally finished, he leaned back with a smug little grin.

"I love you so much, baby. It's hard to put into words what you mean to me."

He pulled me into his arms then, and I sank into him without hesitation—certain, safe, sure.

I never could have imagined the shift. I never could have guessed that someday I'd be here, sitting alone on the edge of our bed, wondering if the man who once wrote vows in earnest is the same man lying to me now.

I pull my arm away from my eyes and sit up, shaking the memory off like a wet coat. I refuse to spend this whole week drowning in pity. I grab my phone and type a quick text to Samaya.

How early can I come over? I don't want to be alone another second.

My thumb hovers before I hit send. It's too easy to lean on her, too tempting to let her words smooth over the rough edges of my doubt. But the truth is, I need the company. I need someone to keep me from spiraling in this house that feels less and less like home.

Right now, I need it to be Sam.

Chapter Seventeen

When I arrive at Sam's, the vibe hits me right away. Candles glow in every corner, lavender drifts through the air, and my shoulders soften before I even close the front door. Sam smiles wide, but there's a flicker of caution in her eyes, like she's checking to see if I'll crack in her hands.

She takes my purse and sets it on the kitchen island. By the time I've hung up my sweater, she's already standing there with a glass of white wine outstretched.

"Girl, you are the best," I sigh, accepting it gratefully. The first sip slides down warm and steady, like my nerves might finally unclench. I flop into a white, high-backed chair at her kitchen table, watching her drag the chair beside me so we're face to face.

"How are you? Have you eaten? Are you hungry?" Her eyes search mine, sharp and gentle all at once. I want to look away. How do I look right now? Like someone unraveling? Like a wife who can't control her own damn life?

"I'm starving. Haven't eaten much today," I admit.

She immediately pulls up DoorDash. "What are you in the mood for?"

I set my wine down, smoothing my curls with one hand, like tidying the outside could cover the wreck inside. "How fucked up do I look right now?" My voice is barely above a whisper. "I can't even think. You pick something. The last thing I can do is make a decision."

"Totally fair." She scrolls through the options. "Chico's?"

Relief flickers through me at the mention of one of my favorite Tex-Mex spots. This girl knows me. "Yes. Three chicken street tacos, please."

I watch her order, draining my glass faster than I mean to. My eyes wander her spotless kitchen, candlelight painting the walls in soft gold. Everything feels safe here. Contained. Like I can finally breathe again.

Then my phone pings.

Just landed. Getting settled.

My stomach clenches. Of course. The second I let my guard down, John yanks me back into the pit. I tip my glass up and drain what's left.

"Food will be here in thirty-five," Sam says, glancing up. "Uh-oh. What's wrong?"

I slam the phone face down. "I don't even know where to begin." My hands cover my face. "Part of me is sick thinking he's lying about the trip, but another part of me..." I drop my hands and meet her eyes. "Another part of me feels free. And I like that part."

Sam nods knowingly, her voice smooth. "I get that. Trust me. Where do you think he really went?"

"No clue. But he barely packed anything. One light-ass bag. And Friday night I saw a text from Constance. She was basically apologizing for missing his call. I checked her Instagram and she was out at her mom's birthday dinner. That means he was calling her while I was in the same house with him."

Sam's eyes widen, then narrow. "Wow, Lo. How could he treat you like that? And you're not crazy. Men like John always lie."

My throat burns. "I blame them both. He's married. It's on him. But she knew he was married. What a fucking skank." My voice rises, sharp with wine and rage. "For all I know, they're together right now."

Sam leans in closer, a glint in her eye I can't quite read. "You said you were on her Insta?"

"Yeah." I grab my phone, but my glass is empty again. She notices, stands, and refills it before I can even protest.

"Check again. Maybe she posted today. Could give you a clue if they're together."

I fumble, unlocking my phone and switching to my burner account before typing her name. The newest post loads. A mirror selfie from last night—bathroom lighting, skimpy black dress, smug grin plastered across her face.

"Nothing new today," I mutter, tossing the phone aside like it burned me.

The doorbell rings, startling us both. Our food. Thank God.

I hate this. Hate that I'm playing detective, piecing clues together from Instagram posts when the only thing I should need is my husband's word. But his word doesn't mean anything anymore.

Sam sets down our plates, and the smell of grilled chicken and lime jolts my senses. My stomach growls. I bite into a taco and almost moan as citrus and cilantro explode against the salt. For a few seconds, I let myself disappear into the food, into something simple and good.

When I look up, Sam is watching me with approval, smiling. I grin sheepishly, wiping my mouth with a napkin.

She laughs, stabbing her fork into a plate of enchiladas. For a few minutes, there's nothing but food, wine, and quiet. No John. No Constance. No lies. Just us.

"This is what I needed to start my John-free week," I say after finishing my second taco, washing it down with a slow sip of wine. "I'm not spending this week worrying about him. And I'm *not* stalking that bitch's Instagram. This week, I'm clearing my head. I deserve that."

Sam nods, her voice suddenly low. "Good. The truth will come out. But let me tell you something about Constance. Women like her don't stop until someone makes them."

The words slice through the room. The candlelight flickers, like a shadow passed over it.

Then, just as quickly, she brightens again. "I don't want you to get hurt, babe; I care about you a lot. I'd do anything for you."

I chew slowly, her words ringing louder in my head than I want to admit. When I meet her gaze, she's smiling again, warm and calm, the Samaya I know.

The tightness in my chest loosens.

"Thanks for tonight, Sam. I needed this," I say, meaning it.

She squeezes my hand across the table. "You'll get through this, Lo. You're not alone."

For the first time all day, I believe her. I register the way her eyes linger on me a fraction too long and choose not to examine it, letting the comfort stand without asking more of it.

Chapter Eighteen

I walk out of my classroom Monday afternoon feeling more refreshed than I have in weeks. Teaching has always been my salvation. No matter what chaos is clawing at me outside those walls, the moment I'm standing in front of my students—listening to their voices, watching them light up when they share what they've written—I feel anchored again. They make me remember why I chose this life, why words matter.

I turn the key in the lock and hear the satisfying click, then nearly drop my bag when I notice someone standing to the right of my door.

Damien.

My spine straightens on instinct. My heart gives a strange flutter. I'm suddenly grateful I decided to dress up today instead of throwing on one of my usual sweaters. My jeans hug my hips nicely, and the white tank beneath my hot pink blazer shows just enough cleavage to blur the line between professional and something else.

"Damien!" I say, praying my curls aren't doing something wild. I reach a hand up to smooth them anyway—too obvious, too exposed.

He shifts his weight, looking nervous but steady. "Hey, Mrs. Roberts. I hope this isn't weird—me showing up here like this. But I realized I don't have your number, and I didn't want to use staff email just to ask if you'd grab coffee with me sometime."

The corners of my mouth lift before I can stop them. "First of all, please call me Halo. Or Lo is fine."

His shoulders relax. "Ok. Cool. So how about it? Coffee?" His eyes are hopeful, a flicker of something boyish but also bold.

"Yes. I mean, I'd love that. I'm free now," I blurt, then flush. "Unless you've got somewhere else to be."

"Let's do it, Halo." He says my name like he's tasting it, like he's making sure it sits on his tongue the way it should. The sound of it makes my stomach tighten.

"I need to drop my stuff in my car."

"Sounds perfect. I'm parked in the M lot too," he says easily.

We fall into step together, the silence charged but not uncomfortable. I pop open the hatch of my SUV and toss my bag inside, pulling out my wallet. He whistles softly.

"Nice ride, Mrs. Rob—Halo."

Heat creeps up my neck. The Mercedes wasn't even my choice, not really. John has always made sure our cars scream success. A symbol for the life we built. Or pretended to. I shut the hatch hard and mumble, "It's just a car," before walking away from it faster than I need to.

A few steps later, we stop at his car. A black Mazda CX-5. Clean, neat, practical. He hurries around me to the passenger side and opens the door before I can. My heart hammers a little harder at the simple gesture.

Sliding into the seat, I notice the leather is spotless. It smells like Black Ice from the tree dangling on the rearview mirror. There's a sleek black leather bag in the back, probably his work stuff. He slips into the driver's seat, and I realize I've been holding my breath.

"You're clean for a boy," I tease, letting a grin slip out.

He chuckles, mock-offended. "Now, Halo, did you think just because I'm younger I was out here living messy?"

His hand lingers on the ignition button, then he glances at me. His gaze drifts from my curls down the neckline of my blazer, tracing every line before snapping back up. I swear I hear his breath catch.

"I can't believe I'm sitting in this car with you right now. I won't even lie," he says, voice low. His eyes shine like melted cognac.

My chest tightens. "What makes you say that?" My voice doesn't even sound like mine—too soft, too small.

"I had the biggest crush on you when I was in your class. Shit, every guy in that class did," he admits with a laugh.

The laugh escapes me before I can stop it. "Boy, bye. You're lying."

But the memory stings with truth. Damien in the back row, tall and broad, always with that easy grin. Back then, I barely noticed. I was a married woman, a dedicated professor. My whole life was wrapped around John and the dream I thought we were building.

Now I sit in his car, a man in place of that boy.

Damien pulls out smoothly, his hand resting casually on the wheel. I sneak a glance at him, tracing the line of his jaw, the low-trimmed beard, the fullness of his lips. My stomach flips when he catches me looking.

"Like what you see?" he asks without looking away from the road.

I flush, stammering, "I can't believe how different you look. Well, not different. Just more... grown."

He barks out a laugh. "It's been a few years. But that didn't answer my question. Do you like what you see?"

I swallow. "I do."

His smile spreads slow and confident. He backs into a spot at a small coffee shop near campus, parking with ease. His arm stretches along the back of my seat, close enough for me to feel the warmth radiating from him. His eyes lock onto mine, pulling me in deeper.

"I do too," he murmurs, brushing a curl from my forehead with the barest touch. "I'm not sure how you've done it, but you're even more beautiful now."

The fluttering in my belly ignites, rushing heat downward, spreading until I can barely breathe. His eyes don't move from mine, dark pools pulling me under.

Jesus.

"Thank you," I whisper. My voice trembles, betraying the storm inside me. Desperate to break the spell, I push the door open. "Shall we go inside?"

***

When I get back home, I'm practically floating. Damien and I sat in that coffee shop for nearly three hours, talking, laughing, trading memories of the classroom days. Hearing him tell stories from his side of the desk was hilarious and humbling, like opening a window into a world I'd never seen before. For the first time in weeks—maybe months—I felt light. I felt like myself again.

But the second I close my front door, the weight slams back into my chest. The silence of the house presses in, suffocating. I glance at my phone and see John's name on my missed calls list. He tried reaching me while I was with Damien. My jaw tightens.

I scroll through my notifications.

Jenna: *Hey babe, checking in! Let me know if you want company while John is away.*

I hesitate, thumb hovering. I haven't spoken to her since yoga, since she called me out for not being a girl's girl. I tell myself I'll text her later, but the truth is I don't want another lecture.

Next message.

John: *Busy day. Love you.*

My lip curls. *Love you.* The words feel empty. A script he's memorized, nothing more.

I'm about to toss the phone onto the couch when another text buzzes through. A number I don't recognize.

Hey it's Damien. Thanks for today. I really enjoyed your company.

A smile breaks across my face before I can stop it. I type back quickly: *Hey you. Yes, me too. Thanks for the good company.*

Almost instantly, my phone lights up with a red heart reaction. The smile lingers even as I toss the phone aside and head into the kitchen.

The clock above the oven reads almost four. Too early for dinner. Maybe a snack. I pull lettuce from the fridge, chop a cucumber, toss in some cherry tomatoes. The motions are mechanical, but my mind is somewhere else entirely.

Damien's laugh. The way his eyes softened when he said my name. How he didn't push when I brushed off John with a vague *out of town for work.* He just nodded, like he understood without needing every detail. That kind of attention, that ease, was more intoxicating than the strongest wine.

I open the fridge again, grab the balsamic, and drizzle it over the bowl. The dark liquid pools across the greens, and suddenly my chest tightens.

John.

Constance.

The anger returns like a switch flipped. I grab the salad and my phone, carrying both back to the couch. I scroll straight to Instagram and type her name, fingers shaking with fury.

Her latest post nearly knocks the breath from me.

All packed and ready for my mini vacay! The caption is paired with a selfie in the mirror. Constance's lips are pursed in a kiss, a duffel bag slung over her shoulder. Her hashtags hit me like a punch: *#vacationmode #baecation.*

It was posted at 9 p.m. last night.

My fork clatters onto the table.

Are you fucking kidding me? What are the chances she's leaving on a trip the exact same week John is gone? The bile rises in my throat. My hands tremble as I scroll back up to stare at her smug, painted face, the word *baecation* screaming at me from the screen.

"Unbelievable," I hiss to the empty room.

My thumb hovers over Sam's name, and I hit call. Straight to voicemail.

Ugh.

I slump back against the couch cushions, the salad untouched on the table. My stomach is in knots anyway. My mind is a spinning reel of images: John in his crisp suit, his single carry-on; Constance in her tight black dress, boarding a plane with him, laughing, clinking glasses of champagne while I sit here alone.

His text flashes in my memory. *Busy day. Love you.*

Busy. Right.

He isn't busy. He's balls deep in that bitch.

My hands tighten around the phone, and before I even realize what I'm doing, I'm texting Damien.

Are you free later?

The response comes so fast it feels like he was already waiting for it.

Absolutely.

My pulse kicks in my throat. For the first time all day, the weight inside my chest loosens.

Not relief exactly. Something sharper. Something that feels danger-ously close to freedom.

CHAPTER NINETEEN

Streetlights throw long shadows as I turn into Damien's apartment complex, my grip on the wheel too tight. My pulse hammers in my ears, louder than the hum of the Mercedes. I tell myself I'm only here for company, for distraction, but my body betrays me. Every nerve knows I'm lying.

I slide into a visitor spot and cut the engine. He's already waiting outside, leaning against the hood of his car like he knew I'd come. That easy smile curves his lips, but it's the steady way he looks at me that makes something in my chest ache.

For a second, I can't move. I sit staring through the windshield, fighting the voice in my head telling me to turn around, to go home, to crawl back into the safety of my marriage—no matter how broken it is. Instead, I push the door open and step out, the night air cool against my flushed skin.

"Lo." His voice is low and certain, and the sound of my name on his tongue feels like a key sliding into a lock I didn't know was waiting.

He opens the door for me, letting me step into his space first. His apartment is simple but spotless, the faint smell of coffee and cologne curling through the air. Clean counters. A sofa that looks untouched. Blinds drawn tight against the night.

"Cozy," I say, my voice higher than I intend.

He shrugs out of his jacket, tossing it onto a hook. "It does the job. You want water? Coffee?"

"Water's fine."

I sink onto the couch, smoothing my blazer over my thighs, my heart thudding in my ears. He returns with two glasses, handing me one before lowering himself beside me. Not too close, but close enough.

The silence stretches. It isn't empty. It hums.

"You okay?" he asks finally, his gaze sliding to mine. "You seemed different today."

"Different how?" I ask, stalling. My thumb traces a bead of condensation on the glass.

"Lighter. But like something was still weighing on you."

A brittle laugh escapes me. "You're observant for someone who barely knows me anymore."

"Or maybe I pay attention."

The words sink deeper than they should. I shift, crossing my legs tight, caught between spilling everything and staying locked up.

"It's nothing dramatic," I lie. "Work. Marriage. Just heavier lately."

He doesn't push. He only watches me, his patience more dangerous than pressure. My chest tightens. I glance away before the heat in his eyes burns me alive.

"Do you have anything stronger than water?" I ask, my smile weak but daring.

His mouth curves, and he disappears into the kitchen. When he returns, there's a bottle of Crown Royal in his hand and two short glasses. He pours, raises his glass.

"To whatever this is," he says.

I clink his glass, take a swallow, and feel the fire spread through my chest.

The words tumble out before I can stop them. "John is cheating on me with his assistant."

The confession hangs heavy in the air. My hand flies to my mouth.

"Shit," Damien whispers, draining his own glass fast.

"Yup," I say, smiling like it's a joke. My stomach twists. "That's the headline of my life. Everything else is side stories."

His brows pull together, his voice sharp with disbelief. "I don't get it. You two were the power couple. Everybody looked up to you. How could he cheat on you? You're beautiful, intelligent, you're—" He trails off, shaking his head.

The compliment lands harder than I expect, loosening something in me. I smile, real this time, even as it aches. "I thought we had the perfect marriage too," I say. "Until I didn't."

I set my glass on the table. The second it leaves my hand, he sets his down too and shifts closer. The air thickens. His knee brushes mine. His cologne—wood and spice—wraps around me, and I feel my body tighten, my pulse quicken.

His thumb brushes my cheekbone, soft but deliberate. My eyes flutter shut, a tremor rolling through me. When I open them, his gaze is still locked on mine.

"What are you gonna do about it?" he asks softly.

"About John?" My voice cracks on his name.

He nods, his hand steady against my face.

I exhale, throat tight. "I don't know. Some days I want to burn it all down. Other days I'm terrified of what comes next."

His knee presses firmer against mine. "You don't deserve to live like that. Always doubting. Always wondering. You deserve more."

The words cut deep and soothe all at once. My eyes sting.

"I haven't told many people," I admit. "It feels different telling you."

"Why me?"

I swallow, my heart in my throat. "Because you don't look at me like I'm pathetic. You seem to... see me."

The silence that follows is molten. His hand slides into the curls at the back of my neck, his forehead lowering to mine.

"Lo," he whispers, his breath warm against my lips.

Every part of me aches to close the distance, to give in, to forget John even exists. My body screams yes, but my mind still whispers no.

I close my eyes, trembling. "I can't."

He pauses, then presses his forehead more firmly to mine before pulling back just enough. "Okay," he murmurs. "I'm sorry, and I understand."

The restraint burns hotter than a kiss. His hand lingers at my neck, his thumb brushing the edge of my jaw. My body hums like a live wire.

I pull in a shaky breath, dizzy.

What the hell am I doing?

Chapter Twenty

The silence of my house presses in on me the second I step through the door. It should feel like relief, but it doesn't. The air feels too heavy, the rooms too empty, and all I can think about is Damien leaning closer, his warmth still clinging to my skin.

I tell myself I should be proud for stopping things before they crossed the line. Instead, my body hums with restless energy, every nerve still alive with the memory of his nearness. My cheek tingles where his hand had lingered, phantom sparks firing every time I let myself replay the way he leaned in, the way his voice dropped when he said my name.

I kick off my heels and wander into the kitchen, pretending the ritual of ordinary life can save me. A glass from the cupboard. The refrigerator light spilling cold brightness into the dark. Water filling the glass. I go through the motions, but they mean nothing. Every clink, every hollow sound makes me think of the loud thud of my heartbeat in his apartment. Every shadow along the wall holds his outline, watching me.

By the time I collapse onto the couch and pull a throw blanket over my lap, my body is on fire with memory. No comfort in the fabric, no relief in the cushions. Just Damien's eyes, steady and unflinching, carved into me. Just my own breathless whisper of *not yet* when everything inside me screamed *yes*.

The glow of my phone breaks the dark. One text.

Did you make it home safe?

Damien.

My thumb hovers. Whatever I type next will be a step closer to the edge I swore I wouldn't cross. I start anyway.

I keep thinking about you.

I delete it.

Another try.

I shouldn't have let it feel like that.

Delete.

My chest tightens as I stare at the empty text field, my pulse loud in my ears. The truth presses forward anyway, insistent and reckless. That I wanted him closer. That a part of me wanted to forget every rule I've ever made for myself and let the moment take over completely.

I close my eyes and clear the screen, leaving nothing behind but the echo of what I almost said.

Jesus, Lo.

I settle on the safe answer, fingers tapping out a thank you for listening, a confirmation that I made it home. The three bubbles appear. My breath catches. They vanish.

And then my phone rings.

His name on the screen. My pulse leaps into my throat. I freeze, thumb hovering over *decline*, the rational choice. I shouldn't answer. God, I shouldn't.

But I do.

"Hey," I say, praying my voice doesn't betray me.

"I wanted to check you got home okay," he says, his tone warm, easy, unrushed. The sound of it slips under my skin, loosening something clenched tight inside me. John never calls to make sure I'm safe. John assumes.

"Yeah," I breathe, sinking deeper into the couch. "I'm here. Exhausted."

He laughs softly, and the sound runs a line of heat through me. "You don't sound exhausted. You sound... restless."

I bite my lip, smiling even though no one can see me. "Maybe both."

The silence that follows is charged, the kind that vibrates even through a phone line. Then his voice again, gentle and steady. "Lo, if you ever need anything, I'm here. I know we're just reconnecting, but I mean it. I got you."

My heart thuds. Words jam in my throat. "Wow. Thank you. I really appreciate you. Tonight was... good for me."

We talk for a few more minutes about nothing. Plans for tomorrow. Little things. Normal things. The sound of him is enough to make me forget, for a breath, that my world is collapsing.

When the call ends, I let the phone slip from my hand onto the couch. The silence crashes back, heavier than before.

This pull toward Damien was *not* on my bingo card for this year. Not on any card. Ever. But it is undeniable. And it is not just his body or mine that wants this. Something deeper in me is reaching—clawing—craving.

Chapter Twenty-One

By Tuesday afternoon, I've nearly convinced myself that last night was nothing more than a blip. A weak moment I can fold into the bigger mess of my emotions. I've repeated it so many times in my head that I almost believe it. Almost.

But when I step out of the English building and see Damien leaning against the iron railing, the story I built to protect myself shatters on the spot.

He is waiting. I can see it in the way his shoulders are relaxed, in the way his hands are shoved casually into his pockets like he has all the time in the world, in the way his head tilts slightly—as if he knows the exact moment I will appear.

My stomach flips violently. Heat crawls up the back of my neck, prickling across my scalp. I should keep walking, turn toward the faculty lot, pretend I don't see him. But his eyes find mine the second I step into view, and that small, steady smile spreads across his face like he knew without question I would pass this way.

"Lo."

Just my name, but it slices clean through the chatter of students around us. Everything else drops away. His voice finds me like a thread, tugging straight to the center of my chest.

"Hey," I manage, my voice thin and unsteady. I clutch the strap of my bag so tight my knuckles ache. "Shouldn't you be grading papers or something?"

He shrugs. Easy. Careless. But his eyes never move off me. "Maybe I was waiting."

The words land with a weight I can feel in my bones. *Waiting.* My pulse pounds in my throat so hard I can barely breathe. I glance away, desperate for a distraction, pretending to study a group of students weaving across the quad. Their laughter is too bright, sharp as glass. It belongs to another world entirely.

"About last night—" I start, but the words shrivel up on my tongue. My mouth goes dry.

Damien tilts his head, waiting me out, patient in a way that makes me feel naked.

"I was… tired," I finish, hating the sound of it immediately. Weak. Lame. A lie so thin he could tear through it without trying.

He doesn't call me out. He doesn't press. He lets the silence expand between us, thick and unbearable, until I want to crawl out of my skin. Then his voice comes, quiet and sure. "You don't have to fake it with me. Not after what you told me."

The air shifts. My stomach tightens. I try to swallow, but my throat feels raw. My instinct screams to run, to end this before it becomes too dangerous. But I stay rooted where I am, my body tilted toward him like gravity has chosen sides.

A breeze cuts across the lawn, carrying the faint tang of cigarette smoke from somewhere nearby. The scent snaps me to the moment, to the awareness of my pulse hammering in my ears. John never waits for me like this. John never sees me like this.

Damien leans slightly closer, his voice pitched low so only I can hear. "Coffee. Off-campus. Tomorrow."

Coffee. One harmless word, wrapped around something much sharper. Every nerve in my body lights up.

"I can't," I blurt, adjusting the strap of my bag again, desperate to anchor my hands. "I shouldn't."

He studies me, eyes steady on mine. Then he says my name like it's something fragile. "Lo. It's just coffee."

But we both know it isn't just coffee.

I shift my weight, my body screaming to move, to create space before I do something reckless. I turn as if to leave, but his voice follows, quiet and certain. "Tomorrow?"

I freeze. My heart slams so hard I think I might be visibly shaking. It would be easier if he broke eye contact, if he looked away, if he gave me a way out. But he doesn't. His eyes are locked on mine, patient and unflinching, like he's already decided.

The world keeps moving around us. Students laugh, sneakers scuff across the pavement, someone calls out to a friend. But none of it touches me. I feel like I'm underwater, suspended in this moment where everything tilts on one reckless choice.

"Okay," I whisper. The word falls out of me before I can stop it.

His smile spreads, slow and sharp, like he knew I would break eventually. My chest constricts with both dread and something dangerously close to desire.

I walk away on legs that don't feel steady, the sounds of campus swallowing me whole. But all I can hear is my own voice, that single word echoing like a promise I can't take back.

Okay.

***

My chest is still tight from the drive home when the phone buzzes in my hand. For a second, I hope for Damien, his name lighting up the screen like a spark I shouldn't want. Instead, it's John. My stomach drops. *Shit.* I never texted him back last night.

Made it through another long day. Crazy meetings here. You good?

That's it. No *I miss you*. No *wish you were here*. Only sterile words, the kind you'd fire off to a coworker when you're stuck in a meeting. I stare at them until my chest aches before forcing my thumbs to type back.

Yeah. I'm good.

A minute later, the phone rings.

"Hey, babe," John says, clipped and distracted. "Just checking in. We've got this dinner thing, so I don't have long."

There's noise in the background, muffled but sharp enough to twist my gut. Laughter. High and feminine. The clink of glasses. Business trip, he said. Business dinners. Always vague, never clear.

"Dinner thing," I echo, bitterness thick in my mouth. "Sounds fun."

He chuckles, distracted. "Fun isn't the word. Half these people don't even know what they're talking about." A pause. "Anyway, I'll call when I can. Don't wait up."

The line clicks dead.

I stare at the black screen, the weight of it heavy in my palm. He didn't ask about my classes. Didn't ask if I'd eaten. Didn't even pause long enough for me to say goodbye.

The silence around me swells until it feels like it has teeth. It presses in, loud and suffocating. Two truths rise up whether I want them to or not. John is lying. Damien sees me in five minutes more clearly than John has in years.

The guilt comes quick and sharp, stinging in my chest. Comparing them feels wrong, but the echo of that woman's laugh in the background makes it impossible not to. My fingers twitch with the urge to check Constance's Instagram, to scan her posts for hints. But I don't let myself.

I am thirty-nine years old. I will not become the pathetic wife squinting at another woman's selfies for proof.

Fuck that.

I scroll right past John's name and land on Sam's. If I need grounding, it won't come from him.

She answers on the second ring, her voice warm and steady, the kind of tone that usually reels me back in. I spill everything. John's half-assed check-in, the laughter in the background, the gnawing suspicion that keeps me awake at night. The words tumble out until I can't catch them.

Finally, I stop pacing, breath ragged. "Tell me I'm not losing my mind," I plead, raw.

"You're not crazy, Lo," she says gently. "I hate that you're stuck in this. Constance needs to chill out..." She trails off, and for a moment I think that's it.

But then her voice sharpens, quieter now, almost dangerous. "She won't stop, Lo. Women like her push until they get what they want. She feeds on attention. She wants John, and she'll tear through you to get him."

A cold shock shoots through me. The words hang like smoke. I laugh, brittle and thin. "Jesus, Sam, you sound like you're plotting my legal defense. Full mob-boss energy."

Her laugh breaks the heaviness, quick and real. "God, listen to me. I was married to a psycho, remember? Sometimes I go dark. Don't mind me."

I breathe out, some of the tension leaving my shoulders. I forget sometimes how much she's endured. The abuse. The hiding. The way his murder shattered her world. And still she sits with me, listens to me unravel, steadies me. It feels like a kind of miracle.

Then guilt crashes in. I am piling my chaos on top of hers, weighing her down when she has carried more than most people could ever survive. But she doesn't flinch. She just keeps showing up.

When we hang up, I'm left alone in the dark. The hum of the fridge is the only sound. Sam's laugh lingers in my ear, and for a moment it almost makes me lighter. Almost.

But then Constance's name burns through my thoughts again, glowing like neon behind my eyes. The memory of her texts. Her voice curling around John's. Maybe Sam is right. Maybe women like her don't stop until they take what they want. And maybe John is already letting her.

I curl deeper into the couch, pulling the throw blanket tight around me. Part of me wants to believe him. To cling to his story about the complaint, about being harassed. God, I want to believe it. But every time I see his face in my mind, hers is right there beside it.

The other part whispers louder. The part that says I could walk away. That I don't have to fight for a marriage that feels like it's rotting from the inside. That I could finally be free.

The thought splits me open, relief tangled with terror. Who am I without him? What does my life look like when the perfect-couple mask is ripped away? Could I even keep teaching at Shady Oaks?

I sigh and sink into the cushions. Tonight, I have no answers. Tonight, I am simply a woman caught between the life I built and the one I am afraid to want.

I grab the remote and flick on the TV, letting the noise fill the silence. Anything is better than the truth pressing in with it.

Chapter Twenty-Two

The morning hits too fast.

I wake tangled in the sheets, my head foggy, chest heavy, like I barely slept. I can't even remember crawling into bed. Sam's words from last night still echo—sharp one second, soft the next. One thing feels certain now. John is lying. Constance is a threat. I'm not crazy.

Dragging myself to the bathroom, I stand in front of the mirror. The woman staring back is worn down. Skin pale. Dark circles bruised under her eyes. Curls piled into a bun that looks less chic and more desperate. I splash cold water on my face, hoping it will shock me awake, hoping it will peel away the confusion sticking to me like a second skin.

John's voice worms back in from our last call. Flat. Distracted. No tenderness, no curiosity about my day. Only sterile updates and the sound of glasses clinking, women's laughter breaking through like a cruel reminder. Every time I try to believe he's innocent, that text from Constance glows again in my memory like neon.

You still alone?

I shove the thought aside and spray my curls into some kind of order. Black slacks. A blouse that looks more put together than I feel. My students don't need to see the cracks spidering underneath my surface. They don't need to know their professor is unraveling, held together with caffeine and denial.

By the time I grab my bag and keys, the pit in my stomach has turned restless. It isn't just John. It's Damien. The way his voice dropped low the other night. The heat of his hand against my skin. The way I almost didn't say no. That memory trails me like a ghost as I lock the front door.

In the car, I flatten my palm against the steering wheel, eyes closed, forcing one deep breath.

Just get through class. One foot in front of the other.

But as soon as I pull out of the driveway, the thought hits, uninvited. Coffee later. Damien.

It lands inside me like both a promise and a threat, and for the first time all morning, exhaustion gives way to something else.

Anticipation.

***

The cafe hums with restless energy. Espresso machines hiss, chairs scrape against tile, voices layer over one another until it becomes one constant buzz. Normally that kind of noise would grate on me. Today it feels like protection. Like maybe if the world stays loud enough, no one will notice how close Damien and I are leaning across this too-small table.

He lifts his cup, smirking over the rim. "Still with the oat milk, huh? What's next, ordering one of those pumpkin spice things just to make my teeth ache?"

I stir the foam in lazy circles, refusing to break eye contact. "Please. This is a vanilla latte. A classic. Not everything has to scream basic fall starter pack."

"Mhm," he says, tilting his head. "Says the woman who made me stand in line for fifteen minutes because she couldn't decide between a muffin or a croissant."

I laugh, shaking my head. "Indecision is a sign of intelligence, thank you very much. My brain was weighing serious options."

"Serious," he repeats, his lips twitching like he's fighting back a grin. "Chocolate chip or blueberry. Very high stakes."

"You're just bitter I didn't offer to split it with you." I lean forward on my elbow, the space between us shrinking without me even realizing.

His smile lingers longer this time. A second too long. "Maybe."

Something in the air shifts. Quiet but sharp. The playful back-and-forth dissolves, leaving a silence that stretches across the table like a live wire. I glance down at my cup, pretending to study the foam pattern, but the truth pulses hot in my chest. The heat has nothing to do with the coffee.

He's watching me. I can feel it without even looking.

"You headed back to campus after this?" Damien asks finally, his voice lighter than his expression.

I shake my head too quickly. "No. My afternoon's wide open." My pulse thuds against my throat. "You?"

He leans back, stretching enough to remind me how much space he takes up. "Free as a bird."

The words hang there. Heavy. Waiting.

I should laugh it off. Make a joke about errands or papers or anything else to break the spell. But I don't. Instead, I trace a fingertip along the rim of my cup, my eyes locked on the swirl of milk and coffee.

"So..." The word catches in my throat. I force it out softer, almost a whisper. "What now?"

His chair scrapes against the floor, slow and deliberate. The sound cuts through the cafe noise like a blade. When I finally look up, the glint of humor in his eyes is gone. What's left makes my breath stutter.

"Now," he says, voice low, steady, certain, "I think we get out of here."

The noise of the cafe blurs into nothing. It's just me, him, and the weight of a decision I already know I'm about to make.

Chapter Twenty-Three

The silence between us stretches from the cafe to Damien's car. It isn't awkward. It thrums, heavy, like static before a storm. Every step, every glance, every flicker of air between us feels charged with something we have been circling for too long.

"Your car or mine?" he asks at the curb, his voice low, meant only for me.

"Yours," I whisper, already betraying myself.

The drive is short but stretched thin with anticipation. Afternoon sunlight cuts across his profile in golden slashes, highlighting the sharp line of his jaw, the curve of his mouth. My hands knot in my lap, restless. Every time I glimpse my reflection in the window, my face looks flushed, my eyes fever-bright, like I am already guilty.

We climb the stairs, my pulse a drumbeat in my ears. His keys jingle, the lock clicks, and when the door swings open, the light spilling in feels like permission. I hover at the threshold, heart pounding, and then I step inside.

The door shuts, and the world shrinks to this room, this man, this choice.

"You want a drink?" Damien asks, his voice steady, almost casual.

"I'm fine," I murmur. My throat is too dry for anything.

His gaze holds mine. He doesn't move at first, just studies me like he is memorizing every flicker of doubt. Then, slow and deliberate, he closes the space between us.

"You don't have to be here," he says softly. "You could walk away."

"I know." My voice catches on the truth. "But I don't want to."

Something breaks in him at that. His hand comes up, fingers grazing my jaw, light as a question. I lean into it before I can stop myself. The kiss begins soft, hesitant. Then it's like a dam bursting. His mouth devours mine, hungry, urgent, and I answer with equal force.

His hands grip my waist, and I clutch his shirt in fistfuls, pulling him closer, desperate for more contact. He backs me against the counter, his lips trailing fire along my jaw, down the side of my throat. My head falls back, a gasp slipping out unguarded.

He lifts me onto the counter easily, spreading my knees with his hips. The cool surface beneath me only sharpens the heat inside my body. His hands slide under my blouse, rough palms against my bare skin. I shiver, arching into his touch. My blouse is gone in a blur, forgotten on the floor.

His mouth finds my collarbone, then lower, lips tracing the lace of my bra, teeth grazing until I moan. He pulls the fabric down and takes me into his mouth, sucking until my back bows off the counter. My fingers dig into his shoulders, urging him closer, needing more.

I tug at his shirt, yanking it up, desperate to feel his skin. When it's gone, I run my hands over his chest, down the ridges of his stomach, feeling the muscle shift beneath my palms. He groans low in his throat, the sound vibrating against me as he kisses harder, faster, his hands everywhere.

His fingers slip under my waistband, tugging my slacks down, and soon they're pooled on the floor with everything else. His touch slides higher, stroking, teasing, until I'm writhing against him, my breath breaking into sharp, uneven sounds.

"Lo," he murmurs against my ear, his voice hoarse. "Say stop and I will."

"Don't stop," I whisper, desperate, almost begging.

That's all he needs. He lifts me from the counter, carrying me down the narrow hallway. I cling to him, legs locked around his waist, our mouths crashing together over and over, tongues tangling. We stumble into the bedroom, sunlight spilling across the bed in pale gold stripes.

He lays me down like I'm something precious and tears the rest of the distance away. Clothes vanish in frantic motions, piece by piece, until there's nothing between us but heat and hunger. His weight presses me into the mattress, grounding and electrifying all at once.

His hands roam, mapping every inch of me. His mouth follows, kissing lower and lower until I am gasping, trembling, calling his name. The pleasure builds sharp and hot, crashing over me in waves until I am shuddering beneath him, undone.

When he finally enters me, it's slow at first, a stretch that steals my breath. His forehead rests against mine, his eyes locked on me, searching, waiting. Then we move together, the rhythm urgent, unrelenting. The sunlight paints him gold as he thrusts, his body strong and certain, and every sound I make feels like release, like confession.

I hold onto him like I might drown if I let go. His lips find mine again, swallowing my moans, his pace quickening, deeper, harder, until I am spiraling all over again, breaking apart under him.

And when he finally follows me over the edge, his name on my lips and mine on his, it feels like the world outside no longer exists.

For the first time in years, I am not thinking of John, or Constance, or the wreckage of my marriage.

I am only here.
With Damien.

Chapter Twenty-Four

I drag myself into the bathroom, heavy-limbed and foggy from a night of tossing. The mirror is brutal. My auburn hair looks extra red in its tangled knot; mascara faintly smudged beneath my eyes, skin pale under the harsh light. I stare at my reflection until my throat tightens.

The woman looking back at me feels distant. She doesn't look like the professor who stood in front of her students yesterday, or the wife who once laughed so easily in John's arms. She looks like someone trapped between two lives, one splintering apart, the other catching fire too fast to control.

I splash cold water on my face, willing the sting to strip away the guilt clinging to me like a second skin.

In the kitchen, I go through the motions: grind the beans, fill the kettle, wait for the hiss and sputter. The smell of coffee blooms warm and bitter in the air, wrapping around me like memory. Every morning of my marriage started this way. Only now, the silence that fills the house doesn't soothe. It suffocates.

I pour into my favorite chipped mug and lean against the counter, both hands wrapped tight around the warmth. The first sip burns, sharp and punishing, but I take it anyway. Maybe I deserve the sting.

My phone buzzes. John.

Be home tomorrow night. Flight gets in late.

That's it. No *I miss you.* No *how are you.* Only logistics and increasing distance.

My chest tightens. For a second, I let myself remember the John I married, the man who kissed the back of my neck while I poured coffee, who texted me dumb jokes just to hear me laugh. I wonder if that version of him ever existed, or if I was too blinded by love to see the cracks spreading underneath.

The silence grows louder. The clock ticks too hard. My own breath sounds uneven. Guilt slams into me, hot and relentless. *You cheated. You crossed the line.* It doesn't matter if you felt invisible. It doesn't matter if your heart has been dying inch by inch. The vows were yours too. And you broke them.

But then, like a shadow rising through the guilt, comes the darker thought I can't shake. What about his vows? What about Constance's perfume on his jacket, the text glowing on his phone in the middle of the night, the hollow way he has looked through me for months? If he's been breaking us apart piece by piece, why should my guilt weigh more than his?

Why am I the one bleeding over promises he shredded first?

I set the mug down too hard. The ring it leaves on the counter looks like a stain that won't ever wash out. Maybe our marriage is only that now, damage baked into the surface no matter how hard I scrub.

I squeeze my eyes shut and breathe through the ache. I don't know what hurts worse, that I betrayed him last night, or that part of me doesn't regret it.

Another buzz.

I need to see you.
Damien.

My stomach lurches. I slam the mug down again, coffee sloshing over the rim. Two men, two choices, two versions of myself colliding in the same breath.

I should be grading papers, preparing lesson plans, getting my head on straight before class. Instead, all I hear is Damien's voice from last night, warm and steady, the way his hands anchored me like I was something precious instead of something broken.

I swipe the message away, shove the phone into my bag, and grab my keys. My students don't care about my marriage. My colleagues don't care that I'm unraveling. Today, I'll smile. I'll teach. I'll nod through the meetings.

But beneath it all, I know the truth.

I'll see him again before John comes home.

***

The rest of the day crawls by without incident, but when it's finally over I feel like my nerves are frayed wires buzzing under my skin. Instead of numbing myself with a drink before meeting Damien, I decide to hit the 4 p.m. happy hour yoga class at Evolution. My body aches for release. I haven't been back since that awkward class with Jenna, and the memory sits heavy in my chest.

We haven't spoken since then either. One half-hearted text a few days ago and nothing more. I'm not angry with her, not really. I don't have the strength to be scolded again. And the last thing I want is to drag her through my gnawing suspicion that John and Constance are together on his so-called business trip. Still, the truth presses in as I grab my mat. I miss my friend.

I sigh and drive to the studio, blasting R&B loud enough to rattle the windows, trying to drown the static in my head. It only half works. Between the unresolved attack on my house, the endless churn of questions about John and Constance, and the confusing pull of Damien, my mind feels like a storm that won't settle.

The parking lot is packed, but right as I circle, a spot opens in front of the door. I slip in quickly, thinking maybe my luck is finally shifting.

Inside, I step to the desk, giving my name to the girl typing cheerfully behind the counter. I'm pulling out my wallet when a familiar voice drifts across the room.

"I know, right? I'm fucking sweating."

I turn before I can stop myself. Jenna. She's stepping out of the studio, laughing with another woman at her side. She looks radiant, her lavender sports bra and leggings clinging to her glowing, post-flow skin. The sight lands like a punch. A sharp sting of jealousy hits me, unexpected and mean.

"Lo!" she exclaims, her eyes lighting up. She rushes over, arms already wide. "Oh my god, what a surprise."

I force a smile that doesn't reach my eyes. "I was literally just thinking about you." The words fall flat, and I see it register on her face before she smooths it away with practiced ease.

Her friend lingers politely behind her, pretending not to notice the shift. Jenna hugs me tight, her body still warm from practice. "Please call me, okay? I want to catch up." Her voice is bright, but her eyes are serious. Almost pleading.

My throat tightens. I nod quickly. "Yeah. Definitely."

She squeezes my hand once before letting go, then turns back toward her waiting friend. I watch them walk out together, their laughter spilling into the hallway, and something aches deep in my chest.

I collect myself, shove my mat under my arm, and head toward the studio doors. It's time to breathe. To fold myself into shapes that will quiet the chaos in my head. At least for an hour.

Chapter Twenty-Five

Being on Damien's couch again feels forbidden and foreign, like I've stepped outside my own life and into someone else's story. The cushions are worn, the fabric soft against my legs, but all I can think about is how close he is. How tomorrow John will be home, and this will all feel like a dream I won't be allowed to remember.

"He's back tomorrow night," I blurt, the words tumbling out before I can stop them. "John. His flight lands late."

Damien leans forward, elbows braced on his knees, eyes locked on mine like he's trying to see past the words. "And how do you feel about that?"

A brittle laugh slips out. "Like I'm supposed to. Guilty. Like the wife who made a mistake and needs to go back to pretending." My palms press together, gaze fixed on the floor. "But part of me dreads it. Going back to silence and lies."

His expression shifts, softens, though there's tension in the set of his jaw. His voice drops lower, more deliberate. "Lo... you need to know something."

I glance up, wary.

"This isn't casual for me. It never was." He exhales sharply, like he's been holding this back too long. "Even back when you were my professor, I admired you. The way you taught, the way you carried yourself, how you seemed untouchable but still human. You made me want to be better than I was. You made me believe I could be. I know it sounds crazy, but I've had feelings for you since I was twenty-one. They never really went away."

The air leaves my chest in a rush. Shock and something warmer pool in my stomach, stealing my breath.

"Damien..." My voice is thin, almost lost.

"I'm not asking you for promises," he says quickly, shaking his head. "I know you're married. I know this is messy. But I can't sit here and let you think this is nothing. You're not some accident or distraction to me. You're the woman who walked into a lecture hall years ago and made me see the world differently. You're someone I respect. Someone I've wanted for a long time."

Respect. The word makes my throat close. When was the last time John looked at me with anything close to that?

I force a weak laugh, trying to cut the intensity. "So you're telling me I was your professor crush?"

The corner of his mouth twitches, softening the moment. "You were. But it's not that anymore. It's not just that. I don't want the fantasy version I built in my head; I want you—the real you, even when you're unraveling, especially then."

Something inside me trembles—fear, desire, maybe both. "You make it sound so simple."

"It is simple," he murmurs, leaning in just enough that I can feel the warmth radiating off him. "I care about you, Lo. That doesn't change just because your husband gets home tomorrow."

I swallow hard, pulse pounding. It should scare me, how certain he is. Instead, it pulls me closer, like I've been waiting for someone to say those words for years.

Silence stretches thick between us, the kind that thrums with unspoken choices. His hand brushes mine on the cushion, feather-light but searing. I don't move away.

His eyes search mine, waiting. Always waiting. And when I finally tip forward, closing the space, it doesn't feel like a mistake.

It feels inevitable.

The kiss catches fire instantly—no hesitation, no testing. His mouth crushes mine with a hunger that mirrors my own, and I match it, pulling, grasping, desperate. His tongue teases past my lips, and I taste the whiskey he must have had earlier, warm and sharp. My body arches into him before my brain can keep up.

He grips my waist, lifting me into his lap like I weigh nothing. My thighs tighten around him, my hands fisting his shirt to pull him closer. His mouth leaves mine to blaze down my throat, hot, open-mouthed kisses that leave me gasping.

We barely make it to the hallway. My back hits the wall with a dull thud, his hands pinning me there, mouth trailing fire along my collarbone. A sharp gasp tears out of me, shameless, and I don't care if the neighbors hear.

It's reckless. Messy. Nothing like the first time. That was nerves and restraint. This is raw need.

We stumble toward his bedroom, colliding into the doorframe, laughing breathlessly against each other's mouths. Clothes peel away in frantic pieces—my blouse tugged over my head, his shirt yanked down his arms. His skin is hot, smooth, muscles taut under my palms. I trace the lines of his chest and he groans low, the sound vibrating through me.

By the time he lays me back on his bed, my pulse is thundering so hard I swear it shakes the room. His hands roam everywhere, sure and hungry, like he's memorizing me. His mouth finds mine again, then lower, trailing across my breasts, sucking gently until I cry out and arch beneath him.

"Lo," he rasps, his voice rough against my skin. "You don't know what you do to me."

My fingers trace the sharp edges of his close-cropped fade, skimming the heat of his scalp before sliding down to the strong line of his neck. I tug him closer, breath catching in sharp gasps as his weight settles over me—solid, unyielding, impossible to mistake for anything but power. He grounds me, anchors me, makes me forget there's a world outside this room at all.

And then he's inside me—slow at first, deliberate, stretching me open until all I can do is gasp his name. The rhythm builds fast, deeper, harder, like we're both too far gone to stop. I clutch at his back, nails digging into skin, and he groans into my ear, the sound raw and unguarded.

The air thickens with the slap of skin, the rustle of sheets, the sound of our ragged breathing. Every thrust pushes the guilt further from my mind, replacing it with pure sensation. My body answers him with abandon, chasing release like it's the only thing left that matters.

When it breaks, it shatters me. Heat crashes through my veins, sharp and consuming, and I cry out against his shoulder, my body clenching hard around him. He follows a moment later, his hips jerking, his voice low and guttural in my ear as he comes undone.

After, we collapse into the sweat-damp sheets, tangled together. His chest rises and falls under my cheek, and I listen to the slowing rhythm of his breath as his fingers trace lazy circles on my arm.

That's when the weight hits. Tomorrow John will be home. Tomorrow I'll have to smile across the dinner table and pretend this never happened.

But tonight, wrapped in Damien's arms, I let myself stay. Just a little longer.

Chapter Twenty-Six

The last straggle of students drifts out of the seminar room, voices trailing down the hall, their laughter fading into the echo of footsteps on tile. I linger at my desk, stacking papers I don't actually plan to grade today, buying myself a few more minutes before I have to face the quiet. My phone buzzes against the wood.

John.

Flight lands at 7. See you tonight.

Two lines. No softness, no warmth. A cold timestamp and a command. My chest tightens, but right behind the ache comes the darker thought I can't shake. If he's been sneaking around with Constance all this time, why should my guilt weigh heavier than his?

I flip the phone facedown and press both palms to the desk. The grain of the wood blurs as my eyes lock on it, refusing to move. Less than twelve hours and he'll be home. Less than twelve hours until I have to look him in the eye and pretend I don't see her name glowing behind my eyelids. Less than twelve hours until the fragile cocoon I've spun around myself—the stolen days with Damien, the laughter that reminded me of who I used to be, the warmth of someone looking at me like I still mattered—will be ripped away.

My stomach twists. Part of me wants to scrub the house clean, reset the stage, slip back into the version of myself John won't question. Another part of me wants to burn it all down. How do you welcome someone home when you don't even know if they're still yours?

I press my lips together, scoop my bag off the desk, and walk out before the silence swallows me whole. By the time I reach my car, I barely remember crossing the lot.

The drive home is a blur, my thoughts circling the past week like vultures. I don't feel like the same woman John left behind. For starters, I've had an affair. A whole-ass affair. The guilt pricks at me, sharp and relentless, but mostly there's anger. Not anger at Damien—not really—but at John. His lies, his distance, his carelessness carved the hollow space where Damien fit so easily.

At home, the urge to clean hits hard. Maybe it's distraction, maybe it's penance, but I can't stop myself. I move from room to room, straightening stacks of books, wiping counters that don't need wiping, throwing in a load of laundry just to hear something other than my own thoughts. Damien hasn't even been in these rooms, but the space still feels tainted, heavy with secrets.

And beneath it all is the urge to tell someone. To say it out loud before John walks back through the door. Jenna would judge me—I know that much. Even at the studio the other day, her eyes said more than her words. She could barely believe I was "okay" with John's transfer request for Constance. No—Jenna's not the one.

My thumb hovers over Sam's name instead. She's been quiet lately, but when I called earlier this week, she did pick up. She's always been steady. Safe. The kind of friend who reels me back in when I'm about to spin off the edge.

John's coming home... drinks later??? I type and hit send before I can stop myself.

Her reply comes almost immediately, fast as always.

Oh shit! YES. I'll call you after my next meeting.

Relief loosens my shoulders, the knot in my chest easing slightly. For the first time all day, I let myself breathe.

***

I scan the room and spot Samaya tucked into a booth in the far corner of Luigi's. The place is alive with Friday night noise—forks scraping against plates, bursts of laughter spilling from the bar, the warm scent of garlic and tomatoes hanging heavy in the air. My stomach growls even though I wasn't hungry five minutes ago.

Sam stands when she sees me, arms open, and I nearly collapse into her hug. It hits me how much I've missed her. This week has been nothing but Damien and my students, and suddenly the comfort of a familiar face feels like water in the desert. Her perfume smells faintly of coconut and sun, a small reminder that there is life outside my own chaos.

We slide into the booth, the vinyl squeaking beneath us, and Sam pushes a menu across the table.

"Let's get you a drink."

The waitress appears almost immediately—a young woman with glossy braids piled into a bun. She's balancing a tray of empty glasses and grins like she's been running on caffeine since sunrise.

"Give me two minutes to clear this table and I'll be right back to start you ladies off," she says, her voice light and practiced.

I smile, already grateful, and flip through the cocktail list. When she returns, I order a lemon drop martini. Sam asks for a Jack and Coke. The waitress repeats the order quickly, then disappears again, weaving through the crowd with the kind of grace that only comes from years of practice.

Sam leans forward, eyes sharp, elbows braced on the table.

"So. How are you feeling about John coming home?"

I trace the rim of my sweating water glass with one finger. Condensation slicks my skin, my pulse damp and frantic beneath it. Where do I even start? She has no idea what I've been up to. Suddenly, I wonder if she'll judge me.

I glance at her properly for the first time since sitting down. She looks tired—faint shadows under her eyes. When my gaze drifts to her hand wrapped around her water glass, I notice scrapes along her knuckles.

"What happened?" I nod toward her hand.

Sam reddens slightly and tucks it into her lap.

"I was doing some home improvement stuff," she says quickly.

I tilt my head, teasing.

"Since when are you a handyman?"

She laughs—a quick burst—just as the waitress returns with our drinks. The lemon drop is bright yellow, sugar dusting the rim, and I grab it before the words are out of her mouth, resisting the urge to gulp it down in one swallow.

We clink glasses. I take a long sip and let the sharp tartness coat my tongue, steadying me enough to blurt the thing I promised myself I'd keep buried.

"So I may or may not have slept with a guy who was in my class a few years ago."

Sam must have been mid-sip because she sputters, coughing, nearly sending Coke across the table. Her eyes widen.

"Jesus, Lo," she gasps, grabbing a napkin. "Give me a little warning next time."

I can't help but laugh, sliding another napkin her way.

Her lips curve into a smile as she shakes her head.
"Okay. Explain."

I exhale hard, leaning back against the booth. The hum of the restaurant swells around us. A couple at the next table argues softly in Italian. A waiter sets down a steaming plate of lasagna nearby, the aroma thick in the air. It all feels oddly distant, like I'm in a bubble with Sam.

"I'm sorry—it just came out. But I haven't really seen or talked to anyone but him all week. I tried reaching out earlier, but you didn't text back."

"Sorry, babe. I've been swamped with work."

"I get it." I take another gulp of my drink. "But yeah. I don't even know how I let it happen. It was... familiar. And with everything happening with John, I guess I needed to feel wanted."

Sam tilts her head, studying me.
"Validated?"

"Exactly." I stare into the lemony swirl of my martini. "Like someone actually saw me. With John, I feel like I've been invisible for years. The only time he notices me is when he's annoyed."

Sam's face softens, though her voice sharpens with honesty.
"That's not nothing, Lo. You're allowed to need more."

Her words sting in their truth. I let out a brittle laugh.
"It's also not nothing that I slept with him while my husband's off God knows where. What kind of woman does that?"

"The kind who's been neglected," Sam says evenly. "The kind who's human. Don't act like this makes you a monster."

Her words should soothe me, but they leave me hollow. My voice drops, raw.
"I don't know how I'm supposed to face John tonight. Do I confront him about Constance? Do I just smile and pretend? I don't even know

if I want this marriage anymore. But I also don't know who I am without it."

Sam leans across the table, her gaze holding mine like a lifeline. "You don't have to decide that tonight. See how he comes home. See what he shows you. Let him do the work for once."

I nod, though it does nothing to ease the weight pressing on my chest. The thought of John breezing in, suitcase by the door, like nothing has changed makes me want to scream.

Sam lifts her glass, tapping it against mine with a small smile. "To whatever happens. And to you not falling apart before you even know the truth."

I sip, but the martini burns hotter than it should. "I swear, sometimes it feels like I'm already unraveling."

Her grip finds mine again, firm and steady. "It's not about holding the pieces. It's about deciding which ones are worth keeping. You'll get there."

Her words are solid, grounding, but they don't dissolve the dread building inside me. As the restaurant buzzes around us, all I can think about is that in a few short hours John will walk through the front door—and everything I've been doing this week will be sitting there in the room with us.

***

The sound of the key in the lock makes my stomach seize before the door even swings open. The metallic scrape rattles through me like a warning bell. When the door finally gives, John steps inside like he never left, dragging the air with him. His single suitcase drops with a dull thud, echoing through the entryway. His cologne—sharp, heavy, and suffocating—fills the space before I can even see his face.

"Hey," he says flatly, almost bored, like this is just another Friday. His eyes skim over me, quick and detached, then flick to his phone. He sets it face down on the counter with practiced ease, the motion so familiar it feels rehearsed.

My hand tightens around the glass of water I'm holding. My voice comes out too even.
"Hey. Long trip?"

"Exhausting." He shrugs, loosening his tie, fussing with his coat as if hanging it neatly is the hardest thing he's done all week. "Meetings all day, dinners all night. Barely slept."

I study him, cataloguing every detail. The faint tan deepening the cut of his jaw. The loosened collar of his shirt, undone like it's been tugged open too many times in laughter. He doesn't look tired. He looks alive. And that burns. Because Damien is still on my skin, guilt has been gnawing at me all day, and yet right now rage tastes sharper.

"You didn't call much," I say, setting the glass down with a crack against the counter. "A few texts. One rushed phone call. That's it. I didn't even know what city you were in."

His jaw ticks, a twitch he can't quite hide. Finally, his eyes lock onto mine, steady and hard.
"I told you it was packed. I didn't exactly have time for play-by-plays."

I laugh, short and cutting, like a blade slipping free.
"Too busy to text your wife, but not too busy to—"
The word sticks in my throat, thick as bile, but I force it out. "Constance."

The change is immediate. His expression hardens, eyes narrowing, mouth curling into a cruel half-smile.

"Jesus Christ, Lo. Again with this? You sound insane."

"Do I?" My voice rises, shaking but fierce. "Because she texted you before you left. Because she's all over your phone. Because when I close my eyes, her name is burned into the backs of my lids and you don't even try to make me believe otherwise. Tell me the truth. Are you still seeing her?"

His hands curl into fists at his sides, knuckles white. For a breath, I think he might strike me. Instead, he snatches his phone off the counter, jabbing at the screen with violent precision. His voice is cold steel.

"You want proof? Fine. Fuck it. I'll call her right now. You can ask her yourself."

My stomach knots as the line rings. Once. Twice. Each chime is a blade slicing through the air. Then voicemail.

The silence that follows is deafening.

John slams the phone down on the counter so hard the sound ricochets through the room. I jump, the glass rattling in the sink. His voice is a snarl.

"Happy now? She's probably ignoring me because she knows you've gone completely off the rails. You've embarrassed yourself. You've embarrassed me. Do you even hear how paranoid you sound?"

I open my mouth, but nothing comes. He is pacing now, his body wound tight, shoulders rolling like a storm about to break. Then he spins, sudden and violent, and drives his fist into the cabinet door. The wood shudders, dishes clattering inside.

My breath lodges in my throat. Instinct takes over, pulling me back a step, every muscle locked, my body screaming danger. He has never laid a hand on me. But standing here, the cabinet still trembling, his fist red and shaking, I know how close that line really is.

"Unbelievable." His voice is ragged. He grabs his suitcase, movements jerky. "I'm not doing this anymore. You clearly need time to… I don't know, get your head straight. I'll be at the apartment in the city until you can calm down."

"You're running away," I manage, my voice splintering.

He stops at the door, turning just enough for me to see the rage carved into his face.

"No, Lo. I'm done babysitting your insecurities. Call me when you're ready to be a wife again."

The door slams, shaking the frame.

For a long moment, I can't move. My heart is pounding so hard it drowns out the silence. Finally, my knees give and I drop into the nearest chair, staring at the cabinet like it's evidence in a crime scene. Slowly, I rise and trace the dent where his fist connected with the wood, my hand trembling.

A hollow ache opens in my chest. It isn't just an argument anymore. It's proof—a mark burned into the house itself. Proof that I am not safe here.

My throat closes until breathing feels impossible. I thought the worst thing John could do was lie to me.

But now I'm not so sure.

Chapter Twenty-Seven

The silence after John leaves is almost worse than the shouting. The door slams, rattling the frame, and then there's nothing—only the echo of his voice still vibrating in my chest.

I stand frozen in the kitchen, staring at the dent in the cabinet. My pulse is still hammering, my skin damp with sweat, the sting of adrenaline buzzing under my skin. The mark is shallow, just splintered wood—but it might as well be carved into me. Proof that the man I married can break more than furniture if he ever decides to.

I can't stay in this quiet. Not tonight.

My hand fumbles for the phone on the counter. I don't even think before pressing Sam's name.

She answers on the second ring. "Lo? What happened?" Her voice is alert, tight, like she already knows I'm on the verge.

My words tumble out, shaky. "He—he lost it. Slammed his fist into the cabinet like he was going to rip it off the wall. And then he stormed out, said he's staying in the city."

There's a pause, just her breathing. Then her tone drops lower, steady and sure. "Lo, that's not normal. That's violence, whether he touched you or not. You need to take this seriously."

Her certainty presses into me, heavy, and for a moment I feel like a child being scolded. "I don't know what to do," I whisper. "I don't even know who I am with him anymore. I'm—" My voice breaks. "I'm scared."

"You should be," she says quietly. "But you're not weak. Don't let him make you believe you are. Eat something. Rest. And whatever you do, don't let him see you break when he comes crawling back."

Her words are meant to be solid ground, but they only make me feel more unsteady. "Thanks," I murmur, and we hang up.

The silence rushes in again, heavier than before. I stand there staring at the cabinet, phone still in my hand, my chest tightening like the walls are pressing in.

I can't sit here alone.

My thumb scrolls without thinking, landing on Damien's name. Before I can stop myself, I press it.

The phone barely rings once. "Lo?" His voice is warm, steady, like he's been waiting for me to call.

I swallow hard, the words catching in my throat. "Hi."

There's a pause, then his voice softens. "Wait—wasn't John supposed to be home tonight?"

That question splits me open. My chest caves, the pressure I've been holding in all night breaking loose. "He... he came home," I whisper, my voice already shaking. "And he lost it, Damien. He slammed his fist into the cabinet like he was trying to break the whole kitchen apart. He looked at me like... like I was the enemy."

Silence on his end—heavy, but not judgmental. Only listening. And that's enough to push the tears free. My breath hitches, hot tracks running down my cheeks. "I'm sorry. I shouldn't be dumping this on you. I just—I don't know where else to go."

His voice is quiet but certain. "Don't apologize. You're not dumping anything. You're scared, and you don't deserve to feel this way." Another pause, firmer this time. "Come over. Please. Don't sit in that house alone tonight."

The words land in me like a lifeline. I nod even though he can't see me. "Okay."

"It's going to be okay, Lo," he says gently. "Please drive safe."

When the call ends, the silence of the house rushes back in—but it's not crushing this time. Because I have somewhere to go. I grab my keys with trembling hands, glancing one last time at the cabinet door. Then I leave it behind.

***

I don't remember the drive to Damien's. My hands stay clenched around the wheel the entire time, white-knuckled, like I'm holding on to something stronger than myself. When I finally pull into his lot, the tremor in my body hasn't left. It feels like I'm buzzing under my skin, a live wire that won't stop sparking.

Damien is already outside waiting, arms crossed over his chest, his expression unreadable in the glow of the streetlamp. The moment he sees me, though, his face softens. He strides toward the car before I can even cut the engine.

I open the door, and he's there—steady hands closing around mine as if to anchor me. "Lo," he murmurs, his voice low, certain. "You're safe now."

The words almost undo me. My throat tightens, my eyes burn, and for a second I can't move. Then I'm stepping out of the car, into him, letting his arms wrap around me like a shield. He smells like cedar and soap, clean and grounding, and I bury my face against his chest as if I can press the night out of existence.

He doesn't rush me. He holds me, his palm smoothing slow circles over my back until my breathing steadies. When I finally pull away, my cheeks are wet. I swipe at them quickly, embarrassed, but Damien catches my wrist gently.

"Don't hide," he says. "Not from me."

Inside his apartment, the familiar warmth hits me. The faint scent of laundry detergent, the scattered books, the neatness that feels lived-in but not sterile. I sink onto the couch, suddenly so tired I could collapse, and he disappears into the kitchen. A minute later he's back, pressing a glass of water into my hands.

"Drink," he says softly. "You've been through enough tonight."

I take a sip, the coolness grounding me, and set it on the table. "He looked at me like—like I was the enemy," I whisper. "I've never seen his face like that. He hit the cabinet, Damien. Hard. I thought for a second he might..." The words choke off.

Damien crouches in front of me, his hands warm on my knees. "But he didn't," he says carefully. "And you're here now. That was not your fault. Do you hear me?"

My laugh comes out brittle. "I feel crazy. Like maybe I'm imagining how bad it was."

"You're not crazy." His voice is sharp, certain. "Lo, that's what abusers do. They make you question yourself. But I heard your voice on the phone. I see you right now. You're scared, and you have every right to be."

I blink down at him, the weight of his words hitting harder than I expected. No one has said it out loud like that. Not even me.

"I don't know who I am anymore," I admit, my voice breaking. "I don't know how to go back to pretending everything's fine."

He shifts closer, resting his forehead against my knee. It's such a simple gesture, so human, that my chest aches. "Maybe you're not supposed to go back," he says quietly.

The silence that follows is heavy but not suffocating. His words linger—warm and dangerous, a seed I can't ignore.

When I reach down to touch his cheek, he looks up at me, eyes dark and steady. "Thank you," I whisper. "For not making me feel insane."

He presses a kiss against my palm, lingering, reverent. The intimacy of it makes my stomach flutter. This isn't the wild, reckless heat of the other night. This is slower. Deeper.

He shifts onto the couch beside me, pulling me against him. His arm wraps firm around my shoulders, and I let my head fall against his chest. The steady thud of his heart is a balm, easing the tremor still running through me. I close my eyes, inhaling the warmth of him, letting the world blur out.

My phone buzzes on the table, jolting me. Sam.

You okay?

I hesitate, then type back with fingers that still shake. *Safe. I'm with Damien.*

Three dots appear, then vanish. A moment later: *Good. Stay safe. Call me tomorrow.*

Relief washes through me. I set the phone down again and curl closer to Damien. "Sam knows I'm here," I murmur, almost to myself.

He nods, tightening his arm around me. "Good. I'm glad she does."

For a long while, we don't speak. The hum of the fridge in the kitchen, the muffled sound of a car passing outside, the rhythm of his breathing—all of it steadies me in a way I didn't realize I needed.

When he finally tilts my chin up, his eyes search mine. "You don't have to decide anything tonight," he says softly. "Not about him. Not about me. Just... be here. Let me hold you."

I nod, tears pricking again, and lean into the kiss when it comes. It's slow, careful, nothing like the desperate hunger of before. His lips move against mine like he's memorizing me, like he's giving me space to breathe even in the closeness.

When he pulls back, his forehead rests against mine. His breath is steady, grounding, and his voice is barely more than a whisper. "You're stronger than you think, Lo. Stronger and smarter than he ever gave you credit for."

The words slip under my skin, deeper than comfort, closer to truth. For the first time all day, I let myself believe it.

The hours blur after that. We stay curled together on the couch, voices low and unhurried, sharing pieces of ourselves that feel stolen from time. His hand traces idle patterns on my arm, not asking for more, not taking—only giving me the steady weight of his presence. The chaos in my chest loosens with every breath, every heartbeat pressed against my ear.

When sleep finally drags me under, it's not John's anger I carry into the dark, not Constance's name burning neon in my mind. It's Damien—the heat of his skin, the strength of his arms, the quiet promise in the rhythm of his chest.

For the first time in months, maybe years, I don't fall asleep bracing for impact.

I fall asleep feeling safe.

CHAPTER TWENTY-EIGHT

Saturday morning drifts in slow, honey-colored light. I wake to the faint hum of traffic beyond the window and the warmth of Damien's arm heavy across my waist. For a few disoriented seconds, I forget where I am. The sheets aren't mine. The scent—cedar, detergent, something faintly sweet—isn't mine either.

Then I remember. Last night. The slam of John's fist against the cabinet, the sound of my own breath catching in fear, the way Damien's voice steadied me when I thought I was unraveling for good.

I exhale into the pillow, feeling the knot in my chest loosen enough to let me breathe.

Damien shifts beside me, murmuring something low and incoherent, half-asleep. His hand tightens slightly at my hip, like even in dreams he's making sure I don't slip away. The thought makes something deep inside me ache. When was the last time John even noticed if I rolled to the far side of the bed?

I lie still, listening to Damien's breathing until it steadies again, and only then do I slide out carefully, tugging the blanket back over him. My feet find the floor, cool against my skin, and I pad toward the kitchen.

The apartment is quiet, sunlight cutting stripes across the hardwood. There are dishes in the drying rack, a single mug with yesterday's coffee stain inside. It feels lived-in. Unpretentious. Not the curated, spotless house John insisted we keep—every surface wiped down, every pillow fluffed to prove some image of control.

Here, the imperfection feels like oxygen.

I find coffee in the cabinet and start the pot. The hiss and drip fill the silence, and I lean against the counter, palms pressed flat. My hands still tremble faintly from last night, and I wonder how long before my body stops reacting like danger is waiting in every corner.

When the smell thickens in the air, Damien appears in the doorway, shirtless, hair mussed from sleep. His eyes find me instantly, soft but alert. "You okay?" His voice is rough—that morning rasp that hits me low in my stomach.

I nod, swallowing the lump in my throat. "Yeah. Just... needed to move."

He crosses the kitchen in three easy strides and wraps an arm around me, pressing a kiss into my temple. The contact unravels me more than it should. My shoulders drop, my body leaning into his without thought.

We drink coffee together in mismatched mugs, sitting at his small kitchen table like it's the most natural thing in the world. He tells me a story about his brother crashing their mom's car when they were teenagers, his hands animated, his laugh filling the room. I laugh too—really laugh—head back, throat open. It feels foreign and familiar all at once.

The weekend stretches out in moments like that.

We cook dinner together, chopping vegetables side by side, hip bumping against hip in his narrow kitchen. He teases me about the way I grip the knife too delicately, calls me "Professor" every time I correct his grammar with mock seriousness. When the pasta sauce splatters across my shirt, he laughs until tears roll down his face, then kisses me until I don't care about the stain anymore.

Later, sprawled on his couch with an old record spinning low in the background, I let him pull me into his lap. My cheek rests against his chest as he traces slow circles on my arm. The steady thrum of his heartbeat becomes the metronome of the evening, drowning out the noise in my own head.

At night, it deepens. Our touches shift from playful to reverent—slower than before, but no less hungry. This time there is no frantic edge, no need to outrun guilt. This time, it feels like discovery. Like we are memorizing each other. He whispers things against my skin that make my throat tighten—not dirty promises, but confessions. That I make him feel alive. That he can't stop thinking about me. That he doesn't want this to end.

Each time I tell myself not to believe it. But my body betrays me, melting under his words, craving them almost as much as his hands.

By Sunday afternoon, I almost forget there is a world outside. We order takeout and eat straight from the containers, his knee brushing mine under the table, his grin boyish when I steal the last dumpling. My phone buzzes twice—once with a message from Jenna, once from John—and I leave it face down, unread.

But the illusion fractures when Sam checks in.

Just after sunset, my phone lights up again, her name glowing across the screen. Damien watches me hesitate, then hands me the device. "Answer. She'll worry."

I step into the bedroom, voice low. "Hey."

"Where are you?" Sam's tone is sharp but not unkind. "I've been thinking about you all day."

The truth slips out before I can second-guess it. "I'm with Damien. I didn't want to be alone."

There is silence. Then a long exhale. "Okay," she says finally. "As long as you're safe." She doesn't ask for details. Doesn't push. Just lets me know she's there if I need her.

When I hang up, Damien is leaning in the doorway, arms crossed. His expression is unreadable. For a second, panic grips me. What if this is too much, too soon? But then he steps forward, takes my face in his hands, and presses a soft kiss to my forehead.

"I'm glad you didn't sit in that house alone," he murmurs.

The words lodge in my chest. Simple. Solid. Everything John hasn't been in years.

That night, curled against him under the thin sheets, I wonder if this is what it feels like to start over. Not clean. Not without mess. But with choice.

Because when Tuesday comes, I will have to face the campus, face John, face whatever this week has cracked open. But for now, for this one suspended weekend, I let myself believe it's possible. That I can breathe again. That maybe—just maybe, I am not as broken as I thought.

Chapter Twenty-Nine

By the time I pull into the lot at campus, the bubble of the weekend has burst. The memory of Damien's steady breath against my skin feels like it belongs to someone else. I spent two days wrapped in warmth, laughter, the fragile illusion that I could pause my life—but the moment I cut the engine in the parking lot, reality claws back in.

My phone buzzes. An email notification flashes across the screen.

Carlos, VP of Student Services.

Halo, please stop by my office when you get to campus.

Short. Serious. My chest tightens.

Had something else happened? Was this about the Constance situation or John's transfer request? If I hadn't confronted her in that hallway, if John hadn't gone behind my back to HR, maybe I wouldn't be spiraling now. But Carlos's clipped tone from our last conversation is enough to set me on edge.

I don't even head toward my own building. I steer over to staff parking near Student Services, palms slick on the wheel. By the time I walk through the glass doors, my pulse is hammering in my ears.

The student at the front desk nods me toward Carlos's office. Through the half-glass panels, I see him pacing with the phone pressed tight to his ear. His face is grave. My stomach flips.

I push the door open. His eyes flick up and, without missing a beat, he ends the call, gesturing me in with a sharp wave. His office manager offers me a polite smile that falters when she catches his expression. She ducks her head and disappears.

"Good morning, Lo. Sorry to pull you in before class," Carlos says, unbuttoning his suit jacket as he lowers into the leather chair behind his desk. His voice is even, but tension rides under every word. "There's been—" He cuts himself off. "Have you spoken with John?"

The shift catches me off guard. I tense. "Uh, not this morning."

Carlos nods, like he's debating what to reveal. "I need to reach him. He wasn't in the office yesterday."

My throat is dry. He's not the only one who can't keep track of John. I force a thin smile.

He leans forward, forearms braced on the desk. "I need to be direct. Constance's mother filed a missing persons report this weekend. She said her daughter never showed up for their family dinner on Saturday night. Didn't call, didn't text. That's not like her."

The words thud inside me. Missing.

Carlos exhales, watching my face. "Her mom said she was worried immediately, but when Constance didn't show for work this week either, she went to the police. A detective reached out to campus yesterday morning asking about her schedule and who she had been in contact with."

My chest tightens, a cold prickle racing down my arms. "Why would the police—" I stop, realizing I don't want to finish the thought.

Carlos straightens, his expression grave. "And, as you probably guessed, your name came up. Not only because of John's transfer request—because of what happened in my office."

My throat goes dry. "What do you mean?"

His brow arches. "Lo, Constance filed a complaint after that meeting. She said you cornered her, raised your voice, and told her to stay away from John. She framed it as a threat. That's not just gossip. It's documented."

Heat floods my face. I want to argue, to twist it, but the memory is too sharp. Constance smirking. My own voice rising. The words I hurled at her like knives. I never thought anyone would take it seriously.

"I was upset," I manage, the words brittle. "It wasn't a threat. It was just me being angry. That's all."

Carlos doesn't blink. "Be that as it may, the detective is going to want to hear your side. I thought you should be prepared before they call."

The thought of being contacted by a detective feels like I've suddenly stepped into someone else's life. I'm still trying to process the news, let alone consider that I may be brought in for questioning.

The office feels too small, the hum of the fluorescent lights drilling into my skull.

Missing. Constance is missing. And somehow, I've been pulled into the center of it.

***

The gust of wind that smacks me in the face as soon as I push open the heavy oak doors of the Student Services building blasts me out of my polite trance. The air is sharp and biting, and it wakes me up enough to fully register what I've just been told. My heels clatter against the stone steps as I make my way down to the lot where my car waits, every click echoing louder than it should.

By the time I sink into the familiar leather of the driver's seat, my chest is tight and my brain is racing. Constance is missing. My husband's boss thinks I—or John—might have something to do with it. The words replay like a scratched record.

I tap John's contact on the dash. The phone connects through the Bluetooth, his smiling face flashing on the screen. As it rings, I back out of the parking space, gripping the wheel with white-knuckled hands. I have a class in forty-five minutes, but the idea of standing in front of my students feels absurd. I don't even know where to go.

The call clicks to voicemail. His voice fills the car, and I stab at the screen to hang up before the beep. Rage boils up in me so fast I curse out loud, the sound tearing through the silence.

I pull into the staff lot closer to my building, letting the car idle as I stare at the dashboard. My thumb hovers over Damien's name. He's been my soft place lately, the person I want to reach for when everything feels like it's caving in. The thought of hearing his voice is tempting in a way that makes my chest ache.

Then reality cuts in.

Dragging him into this would be selfish. Reckless. I picture the mess of my life spilling into his—the questions it would raise, the scrutiny it would invite. He doesn't deserve that. He doesn't deserve to be collateral damage in a marriage that's already imploding. If the police ever found out about us, it wouldn't just ruin me—it would pull him under too.

My stomach twists as I lower my phone. Wanting him is one thing. Risking him is another.

Instead, I scroll to Jenna. A lawyer. My *friend*. My last line of defense. A sharp pang of regret slices through me. She's been trying to reach me for weeks. I brushed her off, dodged her texts, convinced myself I didn't need her advice. And now, the second I feel the ground crumbling, she's the only person I want. The guilt stings almost as much as the fear, but I push the thought down and hit call.

She picks up on the second ring, her voice clipped but warm. "Lo? What's wrong?"

The sound of her steadiness cracks me open. "Jenna," I whisper, my throat catching. "I think I'm in trouble. Carlos called me into his office. He said Constance is missing. And he told the detective about me confronting her last week. He made it sound like I'm already under suspicion."

There's a beat of silence, but I can feel her mind moving fast. Then her voice shifts into something steadier, sharper—the tone she uses when she means business. "Okay. Here's what you need to do. If the police reach out, stay calm. Answer their questions honestly, but keep it simple. Don't guess, don't speculate, and don't volunteer more than what they ask. If you're not sure about something, it's okay to say you don't remember. And if at any point you feel overwhelmed, tell them you'd like me present before you continue. That's your right."

I press the phone harder against my ear, nodding even though she can't see me. "Okay. I can do that."

Her tone softens a fraction. "Good. But I don't want to do this over the phone. Can you come into the city this afternoon? Meet me at my office and we'll go through everything together. I want to know exactly what happened between you and Constance, and I want you to have a clear plan moving forward."

Relief loosens my chest just enough for me to breathe. "Yes. I'll be there right after my class. It's only seventy-five minutes."

"All right," she says firmly. "We'll sort this out. One step at a time."

My tears spill hot down my cheeks. "I didn't do anything, Jenna. I just—"

"I know," she cuts in gently. "And that's why you need to protect yourself. Right now, you are vulnerable. You are married to the man everyone knows she was sleeping with, and you already had a confrontation with her. That's enough to make you look bad even if you are completely innocent."

My chest heaves. I grip the steering wheel so tightly my fingers ache. "This is going to ruin me."

"It's not going to ruin you," she says firmly. "Not if we're smart. I need you to stay calm. If anyone approaches you, you tell them you're represented. You give them my name and number. Nothing else."

Her tone softens completely then, the lawyer melting into the friend I've leaned on for years. "Lo, I've got you. You are not alone in this. We will get through it together. Breathe. Go teach your class, then come see me. Keep your head down. And call me the second you're on your way here."

I close my eyes, pressing the phone tight against my ear like I can climb inside her steadiness. "Thank you," I choke out.

"Always," she says. "Now wipe your face, pull yourself together, and remember who you are. You are stronger than this storm. Don't let them see you crack."

The call ends, but her words linger, wrapping around me like armor. And under the relief, guilt churns hot and sour. I shut her out when she tried to be there for me, and still she answered on the first ring. Still, she steadied me when I could barely breathe.

For the first time since stepping out of Carlos's office, I let myself inhale fully—but it tastes of shame as much as salvation.

Chapter Thirty

Jenna closes the thick file folder on her desk with a soft thud, the sound final. Her office smells faintly of paper and peppermint tea, the kind of scent that should be calming but only makes my chest tighter. City traffic hums faintly through the glass behind her, and I sit perched on the edge of a sleek chair that feels too hard for how wrung out I am.

We've gone through everything. The confrontation with Constance. The way Carlos looked at me this morning. The questions the police might ask if they call me in. Jenna has taken notes, her pen flying across the legal pad with a precision that makes me feel both terrified and protected.

She pushes her glasses up the bridge of her nose, looking at me in that way she does when she wants her words to stick.
"Lo, you keep your answers simple. Don't speculate, don't fill in blanks they haven't asked about. The truth is enough. If you feel like you're cornered or you don't know how to respond, you pause. That's it. Do not let their silence pressure you. Silence is not your enemy here."

I nod, though the idea of ever sitting in that room without her makes me want to crawl out of my own skin.

"Good," she says. "If they reach out again, I'll be there. You're not doing any of this alone." Her voice softens then, that friend side slipping through. "You look exhausted. Promise me you'll get some rest."

I try to smile, but it doesn't reach my eyes. "Rest feels impossible right now."

She walks me to the door, resting her hand lightly on my arm. "One step at a time. Let me carry some of this weight with you."

I thank her, mean it, and step out into the afternoon noise of Manhattan. The honking taxis and endless stream of pedestrians feel surreal, like I've walked into a movie set. For a moment, I stand on the sidewalk, the sun bouncing hard off the glass towers, my body heavy and my mind refusing to settle.

John still hasn't returned my calls. The thought of him sitting in our apartment, stonewalling me—maybe laughing at me—makes my blood simmer. The apartment isn't far from here. Five blocks. I can Uber it, leaving my car safely in Jenna's private parking area for staff.

Before I can talk myself out of it, I turn uptown, weaving into the current of people. My heels strike the pavement in rhythm with the pounding of my heart.

If John won't answer the phone, then he can answer me face to face.

***

The elevator groans its way up, each floor lighting like a countdown I can't escape. By the time it dings on ours, my chest is tight, my stomach sour. The hallway feels endless. I fish my keys from my bag, fingers trembling, and unlock the apartment door like I'm bracing for a fight I already know is waiting.

The moment I step inside, I know. The air is heavy, thick with the stale bite of whiskey. The TV glows in the corner, muted, flashing images across the walls like ghosts. John is sprawled on the couch, a glass in his hand, his shirt rumpled, his jaw dark with stubble. His eyes find me, flat and unreadable, and a bitter smile curls his mouth.

"Well, look who's here," he says. His voice is low, but sharp enough to cut skin.

I shut the door behind me harder than I mean to. "I've been calling you all day. Do you even care what's happening right now? Constance is missing, John. Missing. And people already think we had something to do with it."

His jaw tightens. He drops the glass onto the coffee table with a crack that makes me flinch. "Don't say her name."

The heat in my chest boils over. "Don't you dare tell me what I can or can't say. I confronted her because you were sleeping with your assistant. And now she's gone, and guess who looks guilty? Us. You. Me. And you're sitting here, drunk, ignoring my calls."

He's on his feet in an instant, towering over me, his face twisted with fury. The sudden movement makes my body jolt back a step, but I hold my ground.

"You think this is on me?" His voice explodes, filling the room, rattling through my ribs. "You think I made her disappear? Do you have any idea what you've done? You couldn't keep your mouth shut, and now the detective wants me in tomorrow morning for an official statement. Do you hear that? They're looking at me because of you."

My blood runs hot. "Because of me?" My voice cracks but keeps climbing. "You cheated on me with her. You dragged us into this mess. Don't you dare put this on me, John."

His chest heaves, his fists tight at his sides. For a terrifying second, I think he's going to punch the wall, the table—maybe even me. His whole body hums with violence he's choking down, and the air between us feels charged, unsafe.

He steps closer, close enough for me to smell the whiskey on his breath. His voice drops, ragged, almost a growl. "You want the truth so badly? Fine. I fucked her. Are you happy now?"

The words hit like a slap. My throat closes, my stomach twists. I knew. God, I knew. But hearing him spit it at me now—not because he's sorry, not because he loves me, but because he's cornered—guts me.

"You admit it now," I whisper, my voice shaking. "Only because you have no choice. Because she's gone and the cops are circling. Not because you ever intended to tell me the truth."

Something flickers in his eyes—guilt, rage, maybe both—but it's gone before I can pin it down. He steps back, dragging a hand over his mouth. His voice stays venomous. "Everything happening right now is because you couldn't leave it alone. Remember that. This is on you."

The words hang in the air like smoke. My body feels pinned in place, my skin prickling with heat. I want to scream back, to claw at him for all the ways he's broken us, but the way he's looking at me makes my throat close. His stare is sharp, unblinking, and for a second I don't see my husband at all. I see a man I don't recognize—someone capable of things I don't want to believe.

He paces a few steps, running both hands over his hair before slamming his fist against the edge of the counter. The sound cracks like a gunshot, and I flinch hard, my stomach lurching. He doesn't even notice. His chest rises and falls like he's fighting something back, something feral.

"You had to confront her," he spits, not even looking at me now. "You had to stir everything up. Do you ever think about what you do to me? To us? You ruined this. You ruined everything."

Tears burn hot down my cheeks, but I can't stop staring at him—at the way his hands clench and unclench, at the way his voice breaks like he's splintering from the inside out. For a terrifying moment, I think he's going to turn that fury on me, and all I can hear is the frantic pounding of my own heart.

The room tilts. My heart slams against my ribs so hard it hurts. I stumble toward the door, vision blurred with hot tears. My hands shake so badly it takes two tries to twist the lock.

When the door finally clicks shut behind me, I stagger into the hallway like I've been spit out of a nightmare. My chest heaves, my legs barely working, and I don't know if I'm shaking from rage or terror.

I press my back to the wall, sliding down until I'm crouched low, my hands over my mouth to keep the sob from spilling out. My husband admitted to the affair—but only because Constance is missing. Only because he had no choice. And as much as I want to believe he's not capable of more, I can't stop asking myself the question that keeps splitting me open:

What if he is?

***

I don't remember the drive home. My hands must have steered the wheel, my foot must have pressed the pedals, but it's all a blur. The next thing I know, I'm inside my house, lights off, sitting on the edge of my bed with my phone pressed to my ear, sobbing so hard I can barely breathe.

Sam's voice is steady when she answers, no hesitation at all. "Stay put. I'm coming over."

Now, she's here. She slips through my front door with her arms full—takeout bags dangling from one hand, her purse and phone clutched in the other. She doesn't ask permission, doesn't wait to be invited. She just comes in, kicks her shoes off, and wraps me in her arms.

"I'm so glad you called. You shouldn't be alone right now," she murmurs into my hair, holding me while I shake. "Breathe, babe."

The house is dark except for the dim lamp she switches on. My living room feels foreign, like I've wandered into someone else's life. I can still smell John's cologne in the air, faint and bitter.

Sam guides me to the couch, sets the food on the table, and nudges a container toward me. "Eat something. Take a few bites."

I pick up the fork, but my hands tremble too much to manage more than a mouthful. The taste barely registers.

She doesn't push. She sits close, her body angled toward mine, patient and steady. When I finally find my voice, I spill everything. The meeting with Carlos. The silence from John. The fight in the apartment that left me raw and shaking. My words come out ragged and broken by tears, and when I reach the part where John finally admitted the affair, Sam takes my hand and squeezes.

Her eyes never flinch. She does not interrupt. She simply holds the space and lets me pour the rest out.

When I'm finished, I collapse back against the cushions, hollow and spent. Sam tucks the blanket around my shoulders and says quietly, "No wonder your body is wrecked. You've been holding all of this alone."

My chest caves. "He scared me tonight, Sam. The way he looked at me. The way he hit the counter. I don't even know if he—" My throat closes. "I don't know what he's capable of anymore."

Her hand finds mine again, grounding me. "Your body knows when you're not safe. Listen to that. And remember, you don't have to figure it all out tonight. You've got me. You've got Jenna. You're not carrying this alone."

Tears roll fresh down my face, but the release feels different this time—less frantic, more like my body is finally unclenching.

Sam moves through my house like she's lived here forever. She clears the food, starts a load of laundry, fills a glass of water, and sets it in front of me. The ordinary rhythm of it steadies me in a way I didn't realize I needed.

By the time she coaxes me toward my bedroom, I feel like I'm moving underwater. She smooths the blanket over me and crouches so we're eye level. Her voice is soft but certain. "Rest now. Tomorrow, we'll figure out the next step."

When she clicks the light off, the house falls quiet. I curl into the pillow, my body still trembling, but for the first time since John's eyes burned through me in that apartment, I let myself close mine.

Chapter Thirty-One

I wake before the alarm, the thin gray light of morning slipping through the blinds. My body feels wrung out, heavy with exhaustion, but I push myself up anyway. Today has to be different. Today has to be calmer. I shower, pull on clothes, and fix my hair, like routine alone might glue me back together.

The silence of the house presses in too close, so I flick on the TV for company. The morning news fills the room, the polished anchor's voice steady and detached.

"...still no word on the whereabouts of Constance Keller, the twenty-six-year-old who serves as the Executive Assistant to the Vice President of Student Affairs at Shady Oaks University in Shady Oaks, New York. Keller was last seen late Friday night leaving a restaurant downtown near the Shady Oaks campus. She is five foot three, with shoulder-length blonde hair and green eyes. She was reported missing when she failed to show up for a family event on Saturday."

A photograph fills the screen. Constance smiling, bright and alive, her green eyes catching the light. My stomach drops so fast it makes me dizzy.

The anchor continues, the words slicing clean through the room. "Local police are asking anyone with information to come forward."

The co-anchor leans in, her voice softer but no less cutting. "It has been nearly four days since her last confirmed sighting. Her loved ones are desperate for answers."

Desperate for answers. The phrase echoes inside me like a bell. My chest burns as I remember her face in the office, the way her eyes flashed when I confronted her. And now that same face is everywhere, reduced to a missing person report, a set of details scrolling across the bottom of the screen.

The broadcast cuts to grainy footage of the restaurant's exterior, then a blurred shot of a parking lot. My body goes cold. I snatch the remote and click the TV off, my hands trembling so hard I nearly drop it.

The silence that follows is unbearable. I press my hand against my chest, trying to calm the frantic thud of my heart. It is not only that Constance is gone. It is that her disappearance is no longer mine to wrestle with in private. It belongs to the public now. To the world. And that means the eyes of the world will eventually turn to me.

I sink into the kitchen chair, my legs weak, my whole body trembling. I told myself this morning would be the start of something steadier, that I could walk into my classroom and act normal. But normal is impossible now. Not when Constance Keller's ghost is on every screen, asking questions I cannot answer.

My phone buzzes against the counter. A text from a colleague, just one word: *Did you hear about Constance???* I don't even open it. My chest seizes at the thought of what they're saying about me, about John.

I shove the phone into my bag and stand, forcing myself into motion. Coat, keys, lesson plan. It all feels mechanical, like I'm moving my body through steps I've rehearsed a thousand times.

My reflection in the hallway mirror stops me cold. I look like someone else—pale, eyes ringed, jaw tight with something between fear and rage.

"You're fine," I whisper to myself, though the words sound empty. "Just teach your class."

Outside, the air is cold and biting, the kind of morning where breath hangs like smoke. I grip the steering wheel too tightly on the drive to campus, my mind replaying the news anchor's voice, Constance's smiling face filling the screen.

By the time I park and gather my things, my stomach is a knot. I tell myself all I have to do is get through fifty minutes. Fifty minutes of standing in front of a room of freshmen who don't know any better, pretending everything is fine.

But as I walk across campus, students streaming past me with their coffees and earbuds, I feel the glances. Quick, darting. Too long to be nothing, too short to be polite. My pulse stutters. I know that look. Have they seen the news too, or am I tripping?

By the time I reach the door to my classroom, my heart is pounding. My hand lingers on the knob, slick with sweat. I draw in one deep breath and push it open, willing myself into my role.

Professor. Not wife. Not suspect.

The room is already half-full when I walk in. Normally that would mean chatter, phones buzzing, the low hum of first-years who still don't know how to act in a college classroom. But today the noise drops the second I set my bag on the desk. It doesn't disappear, though—it shifts, thins out, turns sharp around the edges. Whispered fragments. Quick glances that flick away when I look up.

I force myself into routine. Bag down. Syllabus stack straightened. Marker in hand. If I just move through the steps, maybe I'll feel in control again. I uncap the marker and scrawl across the board: *Character arcs. Conflict. Resolution.* The words look sterile, like they belong to a different life.

The door creaks and more students shuffle in. Two girls take the front row, their heads tilted together, whispering behind cupped hands. One looks up at me, wide-eyed, then snaps her gaze back down, her cheeks going pink. A boy in the back elbows his friend, showing something on his phone screen, and both of them turn their heads toward me at the same time. My stomach twists hard.

I grip the marker tighter and keep writing. But the whispers don't stop. They rise and fall like waves, laughter bubbling up too loud, then cutting short when I turn. The air buzzes with it. I can feel it in my skin, in my pulse.

By the time the clock says it's time to start, the tension is a live wire. I turn to face them, and that's when a girl in the front blurts out, her voice hesitant but clear. "Professor Roberts... is it true? About your husband's assistant?"

The silence that follows is brutal. My heart spikes, my face burning hot.

From the middle row, another voice chimes in, louder, too casual. "I saw them together all the time. The blonde lady, right? Keller? She was always hanging around his office."

A murmur ripples through the room. Someone whispers, "Yeah, I thought she was, like, his shadow or something."

Then a boy by the window smirks, not even trying to lower his voice. "Bet she wasn't just taking notes." His friend snorts, choking back a laugh.

The marker slips out of my hand and clatters to the floor. The sound is too sharp, too final. The class startles, but no one says a word.

My whole body trembles as I bend down, retrieve the marker, and set it back on the ledge. My hand won't stop shaking. I turn, forcing my voice into something steady. "I saw the news this morning, just like you did.

Yes, Constance Keller is missing. That's all I know. I don't have details, and if I did, I wouldn't be sharing them here."

For a beat, no one moves. Their eyes dart from me to each other, wide and restless. The silence is worse than the whispers.

A girl near the back finally mumbles, "Sorry, I didn't mean anything... I just..." Her words trail off, flimsy and unfinished.

But another boy mutters under his breath, "Still shady though," and I swear my ears ring from the heat of it.

I grip the edge of the desk so tightly my knuckles ache. "This is a creative writing class, not a gossip column. Open your books."

Chairs scrape against the floor as they shuffle papers and fumble with notebooks. The noise is normal, ordinary, but it doesn't ease the weight pressing down on me. The tension hangs thick, and I can feel their eyes still flicking back to me, curious, skeptical, pitying.

I start talking about conflict and resolution, my voice tight, my throat raw. The words feel empty as they leave me. I know none of them are listening. Not really. They're all wondering the same thing: *What does she know? What is she hiding?*

Under these fluorescent lights, with their eyes locked on me, I feel the truth settle like ice in my chest. I am no longer solely their professor. I am a headline; a piece of the story they're passing back and forth like a rumor that keeps growing.

***

When the last students leave my classroom and the door swings shut, I sag against the desk, my breath leaving me in one long rush. Relief tastes bitter. I survived the class, but barely. My hands still tremble as I gather my papers, sliding them into my bag with too much force.

"Lo?"

I whip around at the sound of my name. Damien stands in the doorway, leaning against the frame, his dark eyes searching mine. The sight of him hits me like a wave. The relief scares me almost as much as the wanting. For a second, all I want to do is run to him, bury my face in his chest, let him hold me until the world disappears.

But the weight of the campus presses down on me, heavy and watchful. The walls here have ears. I keep my distance, clutching the strap of my bag like a lifeline.

He steps inside, closing the door halfway behind him. "I saw the news," he says softly. "And I saw your face when you walked across the quad this morning—are you okay?"

The question almost undoes me. I swallow hard, blinking back the heat that burns at the corners of my eyes. "No. Not really. Everyone's staring. They were whispering about me the whole class. Asking questions about her. About John." My voice cracks. "I can't keep pretending I'm fine."

Damien crosses the room slowly, careful, like he knows I'm strung tight as a wire. He stops close enough for me to feel the pull of him, but not close enough to be obvious. His voice is low, steady. "You don't have to pretend with me. Not ever."

I close my eyes for a moment, wishing I could lean into him, wishing I didn't care who saw. But I do. Every glance feels like a knife right now. "I can't... not here. Not on campus."

"I know." His hand hovers for a beat, then drops to his side, restrained. "Then let's not do this here. Meet me later tonight at my place. No eyes or whispers. Just us."

The words make my chest ache. The word *us* feels dangerous and intoxicating all at once. I nod before I can think better of it. "Yes. Please."

He gives me the smallest smile, then nods once. "Get through the rest of your day. I'll see you tonight."

I swallow hard, the knot in my throat tightening. I want that more than anything—to let my guard down, to let him be the safe place I run to. But the paranoia is eating at me. Every shadow outside the classroom window looks like someone watching. Every whisper feels like it's about me. The thought of another secret coming out, of anyone finding out about Damien and me, makes my skin crawl.

He must see it on my face—the hesitation, the fear—because he steps back a little, giving me space. "It's okay if you're not ready," he adds quietly. "We can wait. Whatever you need."

The gentleness in his voice almost breaks me. I nod, my heart hammering. "I just... I can't afford more eyes on me right now. I can't risk it."

"I understand," he says simply. "We'll keep it quiet. We'll be careful. But I'm here, Lo. Whenever you're ready."

His words ease something in my chest. Not gone, but lighter. I manage a shaky smile. "Thank you."

He hesitates, just a beat, then steps forward and pulls me into a quick hug. It's brief, careful, the kind that could almost pass for harmless if anyone were watching. Still, my body reacts instantly, my breath catching as his hand presses between my shoulder blades before he lets go.

He nods once more and turns for the door.

Then he's gone, leaving me alone in the echoing quiet of the classroom. I stand there for a long moment, the ghost of his warmth still clinging to me, wrestling with the fear and longing tangled together inside my chest. Wanting to trust him. Needing to protect myself. A balancing act on a razor's edge. I don't know which will cut deeper if I fall—trusting him, or never letting myself try.

Chapter Thirty-Two

The silence in the house greets me like a gift I don't deserve. I kick off my shoes by the door, drop my bag on the kitchen chair, and stand there for a long moment, listening. The refrigerator hums. Pipes creak somewhere in the walls. Outside, the night is heavy and quiet. No John. No reporters. No whispers following me down the hall. Just me.

I didn't realize how badly I needed to be alone until now. Every hour of today has pressed down on me, piled one thing on top of another until I could hardly breathe. At least here, with no one watching, I can start to think. Or maybe thinking is the last thing I should do.

John admitted it. Not because he wanted to come clean. Not because he owed me the truth. But because the walls were closing in. Because Constance Keller vanished, and her name was about to come out whether he said it or not. He confessed like a man being forced, dragged by the hair into the light. And all I can hear, looping over and over, is his voice, spitting it at me like a curse.

Everywhere I look, there she is. Constance. On the news, her face framed with the words Missing Person. Five foot three. Shoulder-length blond hair. Green eyes. Assistant to the Vice President of Student Affairs. Gone since Friday night, last seen leaving a restaurant near Shady Oaks.

She was my husband's mistress. Now she is missing.

I grip the edge of the counter, replaying the voices from my classroom today. Students whispering, trying and failing to be discreet. A couple of them bold enough to say it outright. They'd seen John and Constance together all the time. One boy even laughed about it, like it was some kind of joke. My students. Barely out of high school, yet they saw through my life more clearly than I did.

I'm supposed to be their professor. Their authority figure. Instead, I am a scandal. A punchline.

The silence presses harder. I pour a glass of water and sit at the table, wrapping my arms around myself. I know too much about cases like this. Too many hours spent listening to Crime Junkie, letting other people's nightmares become entertainment. The spouse is always the first suspect. If not the spouse, then the scorned wife. That would be me. Wife. Rival. The woman with every reason to hate her.

It doesn't matter if I never touched her. People don't care about the truth. They care about stories, and the one being written around me is ugly.

The vibration of my phone makes me jump.

Damien.

Hey. Just checking in. You okay?

The words almost undo me. My throat tightens. I type with shaky thumbs. Not really. Today was a nightmare.

His reply is instant. *I figured. I'm here if you need me. Call or come by. Doesn't matter the hour.*

I close my eyes. For a second, I let myself lean into that. Into him. Just knowing someone is steady when everything else is falling apart. I want to drive to him right now, crawl into his arms, and let him hold all of this. But I don't. I set the phone back down on the table, staring at the glow of the screen until it fades.

Another vibration.

Pax.

I blink at the name. My younger brother usually calls when something's on his mind. His texts are normally messy. Too many words, run-on thoughts, or stupid memes that make me roll my eyes. Not this. Not a single sentence.

You know that missing chick?

My stomach flips. The word chick makes my skin prickle.

Constance? Yeah why?

Dots appear. Vanish. Appear again. My pulse ticks with them. Finally:

Just curious. Since she worked with John it looks like.

The air feels thin. I type back, fingers stiff. *Yeah, she did.*

I expect more from him. Pax has never been one for subtlety. Normally he'd be blowing up my phone with questions, demanding the whole story. Instead, the silence stretches.

When he finally replies, it's short.

Is she the one you thought he was cheating with?

My chest aches as I type back. Yup. That's all I can manage. I don't want to bleed this wound any further tonight.

I brace myself for his anger. For him to curse John. For him to say he's on his way over. But there's another long pause. My phone sits heavy in my hand, screen dark. When it finally buzzes, his words make my stomach lurch.

Shit that's crazy.

I stare at the message, waiting for the rest, waiting for something that sounds like my brother. But nothing comes. The glass goes black again, leaving only my faint reflection, pale and blurred.

I tell myself not to read too much into it. Maybe he's in the middle of something. A date. Work. Maybe he's distracted and doesn't want to get pulled into my storm tonight. Still, it's strange. Off. He's never this clipped with me.

I set the phone face down on the table, as if that could quiet the unease crawling through me. But it doesn't. My chest stays tight. My thoughts spiral.

I walk to the sink, rinse my glass, rinse it again, only for the motion of doing something. The silence swells behind me. I flick on the TV for noise, and the news blasts back at me. Constance's face. Her name in bold across the screen. Reporters reciting every detail of her last known steps.

I switch it off.

The house feels smaller suddenly, the walls pressing closer. I grab my phone again, half-thinking I'll text Pax back and force him to give me more than a line. But I don't. I let it sit in my palm, screen dark and heavy.

Somewhere deep down, I know I won't sleep tonight.

***

The TV murmurs low in the background, just enough noise to fill the silence. I don't remember turning it back on, much less closing my eyes, but when the sharp buzz of my phone slices through the quiet, I jerk awake with a gasp. The room is dark, only the glow of the screen lighting the shadows. My heart is already hammering before I even look.

A local number I don't recognize. I already know who it will be before I answer.

Something about it coils in my stomach as I check the time. 8:48 p.m. At this hour, it can't be good. I swipe to answer, my voice still rough with sleep. "Hello?"

"Mrs. Roberts? Detective Ruiz." His tone is steady, matter-of-fact. "Sorry for the late call. I need to set up a time to meet with you about Constance Keller."

Her name slices through the haze of sleep. I sit up straighter. "Oh, yes. Of course."

"Would you be able to come down to the station tomorrow morning? Say ten o'clock?"

I swallow hard. "Yes. I can do that."

"Good. We'll go over a few things then." A pause, just long enough to make my skin crawl. "Appreciate your time."

Before I can ask a single question, the line clicks dead.

I sit there frozen, the phone still pressed to my ear long after the call ends. The silence that follows is louder than the TV ever was.

Ten o'clock. Tomorrow.

My mind skids to John. He was supposed to speak with them today. What did he say? What did he give them? The bile creeps up fast and bitter. I can almost see him, sitting across from Ruiz, spinning his story. Pointing the finger not at himself but at me. John has always been careful with his image, careful with his words. Why wouldn't he offer me up if it took the heat off him?

The thought is so sharp I nearly text him. My thumb hovers over his name in my contacts, aching to ask, *What did you tell them?* But I stop myself. The worst thing I can do right now is give him the satisfaction of seeing me panic.

I drop the phone face down on the couch cushion and press the heels of my hands into my eyes until I see stars. The truth is, I don't need to text him. I know. I know in my gut he threw me under the bus. The husband's affair. The wife's confrontation. The mistress now missing. It all lines up too perfectly.

I can already hear the story being built around me, brick by brick. Bitter wife. Humiliated professor. Maybe she snapped. Maybe she wanted revenge.

The clock on the wall ticks past nine. Each second feels like it's marking down to something I can't stop.

I pull the blanket tighter, but the chill that settles into me isn't one I can shake off.

Tomorrow I'll face Detective Ruiz, and I can't stop wondering if they'll see me as a witness or start to imagine me as something else. The waiting feels worse than anything that might come next.

Chapter Thirty-Three

The waiting area of the station is colder than it should be. The air smells faintly of bleach and burnt coffee, and the hard plastic chair digs into my spine. I keep my hands folded in my lap to keep them from shaking, nails pressed into the skin of my palms. Stay calm, I tell myself. You have done nothing wrong.

I repeat it over and over, a mantra, even as my pulse races loud enough to drown out the voices of the officers milling behind the counter. A man in uniform laughs at something on his phone. The sound is jarring, too casual for the gravity pressing down on me.

The glass door opens and a woman in plain clothes steps out. Mid-forties, dark blazer, hair pulled into a no-nonsense ponytail. Her eyes scan the room, then land on me.

"Mrs. Roberts?"

I rise on unsteady legs. "Yes."

"Detective Adams," she says with a brief nod. "Come with me."

I follow her down a narrow hallway that smells faintly of old paint and something sour I can't name. My heels click against the tile, too loud in the quiet. We stop at a small gray door. She pushes it open and gestures me inside.

Detective Ruiz is already there, seated at a rectangular table, a styrofoam cup in front of him. The room smells like coffee that's been sitting too long. And something else, something metallic, like pennies and damp wool.

"Have a seat," Adams says, sliding into the chair opposite me. Ruiz sits to her left, his eyes steady but unreadable.

I lower myself into the chair, my body stiff. The metal legs screech against the floor. A recorder sits at the center of the table, its red light blinking like an accusation.

Ruiz leans forward slightly. "Thank you for coming in, Mrs. Roberts. We won't take too much of your time. We need some clarification on a few points."

I nod, though my throat feels too tight to speak.

Adams takes out a notepad, flips to a clean page. "First, we understand you knew Constance Keller through her role at the college?"

"Yes," I manage. "She was John's assistant."

Ruiz's gaze sharpens. "We've spoken with your husband. He admitted they were having an affair."

The words land like a punch to the chest. My face stays still, but inside I burn. He told them. Of course he did. My husband confessed to strangers what he would not say to me until he had no choice.

Adams tilts her head. "And we understand you confronted Ms. Keller about the affair the week before she went missing?"

"Yes," I say, voice low. "I did."

"Tell us about that."

I swallow hard. "I... found out she was the one he was seeing. I went to confront her at her office. I asked her to leave him alone. I didn't threaten her. I didn't touch her. I just..." I pause, words catching. "I wanted her to stay away from my marriage."

Adams scribbles a note. Ruiz studies me, eyes narrow. "Would you say it was heated?"

"It was emotional," I admit. "I was upset. But I didn't hurt her. I walked away."

They let the silence stretch. The red light on the recorder blinks steadily. My heart is so loud I'm sure it's being captured too.

"Did you see her again after that?" Adams asks.

"No."

"Did you contact her in any way?"

"No."

Ruiz clears his throat. "Your husband said she stopped responding to him that week. That she seemed distant. Do you think your confrontation played a role?"

My jaw tightens. He would say that. He would frame me as the reason she pulled away. I shake my head slowly. "I don't know what she was thinking. All I know is, I told her what I needed to say, and that was the end of it."

Adams leans back, her expression softer than Ruiz's. "We need to ask about your husband. Do you believe he's capable of harming Ms. Keller?"

The question hits me sideways. My first instinct is to defend him, to say no, never. Eight years together rise in my mind. Birthdays, holidays, small private jokes. But then flashes of last night surface, the rage in his eyes, the venom in his voice.

"I..." My throat locks. I take a breath. "He's been angry lately. Quick to snap. Different. But I don't..." My voice falters. "I don't want to believe he would ever do something like this."

Ruiz presses. "Different how?"

"Short-tempered. More secretive. When I asked questions, he shut me out. He started staying at the city apartment more. When he was home, it felt like he wasn't really there. And when I finally confronted him about the affair, he…" I shake my head. "He didn't deny it. He was furious with me for saying it out loud."

Adams scribbles another note. Ruiz leans back, his gaze still pinned to me. "Would you say you're afraid of your husband?"

The air leaves my lungs as I think about John's recent outbursts. I force myself to stay still, to keep my face even. "Sometimes," I admit quietly. "Yes."

Saying it out loud feels like crossing a line I can't uncross. The silence afterward feels weighted, as though the room itself is leaning in.

Adams speaks gently. "Lo, you understand we have to ask these questions. We're trying to build a timeline, a sense of who Constance was with, who might have wanted to hurt her. We know this is difficult."

Difficult. The word feels too small for the avalanche of dread crushing my chest.

I nod. "I understand."

"Is there anything else we should know?" Ruiz asks. "Any details you haven't shared yet? Even something that seems small."

I shake my head quickly. "No. That's everything."

The recorder's red light blinks on, off, on. My hands tremble in my lap. I think of every true crime story I've ever devoured, every time the spouse sat in this exact chair and thought they were telling their truth, only to have it twisted.

I'm terrified of saying too much. Terrified of saying too little. Terrified, period.

Adams closes her notebook. "That will be all for today. Thank you for your time."

I nod again, my body stiff as I rise. My legs feel unsteady, but I force them to carry me to the door.

The hallway outside smells like coffee again, sharp and stale. I keep my eyes straight ahead, but inside my mind won't stop racing. John told them. He gave them everything. I can't shake the feeling that in doing so, he handed them me.

***

I sit in my car and grip the steering wheel until my palms ache. The station's brick facade fills the windshield like a wall I barely made it through. I can still smell the stale coffee from that room, still hear the tiny click of the recorder, still see Detective Adams's level eyes and Ruiz's steady stare. My chest is tight. The edges of my vision fuzz. I keep replaying my answers, hunting for a word I should not have used, a pause that sounded like guilt.

I am not a suspect, I tell myself. They did not say that. I am a wife who got cheated on, who confronted the other woman, who now sits in a parking lot trying not to pass out.

I unlock my phone and call Jenna.

She answers on the second ring. "Tell me everything."

"It's done," I say, and my voice scrapes. "They asked about the confrontation, about John. They told me he admitted the affair. They asked if I thought he could hurt her." I swallow hard. "I said I didn't want to believe that."

"Good," she says. Calm. Professional. "You told the truth. Did they press you on timeline specifics?"

"Friday night. Where I was. They wanted my movements again. I gave them everything. Work, home, texts. I heard myself say the same sentences three times, like I was reading off a cue card."

"Fine," she says. "Repetition is normal. Listen carefully now. No more meetings without me. Not phone calls, not quick pop-ins, not five-minute clarifications. If they reach out again, you tell them I represent you and we will schedule together. You did well today. Now we change the rules."

"I felt like a person of interest," I whisper.

"You are a person of interest to the story," Jenna says. "Not necessarily to the case. But the gap between those two things will eat you alive if you let it." A softer breath. "Go somewhere quiet. Eat something that is not coffee and panic. And call me if you remember anything you did not say."

"Jenna," I say, "do you think John threw me under the bus?"

A pause. Not long, but not nothing. "I think John is protecting John. Which means you need to protect yourself."

The words land like a small anchor in a storm. "Okay."

"Text me when you get home," she says. "Or when you get to wherever you are going instead of home."

We hang up. The silence in the car roars. I stare at my reflection in the rearview mirror and almost do not recognize her. The wife of the man. The professor whose students whisper. The woman who sat under fluorescent lights and tried to line up her life in straight pieces for strangers.

I scroll to John and hit call before I can talk myself out of it.

He answers on the fourth ring. His voice is raw and thick. "What."

"You talked to them yesterday," I say. "What did you say?"

"That is how you start a conversation," he snaps. "What did you say. What did you do."

The smell in that interview room slides back into my nose. "They already knew about the affair, John. You told them. I am asking what else you told them."

He snorts. "I told them my wife is vindictive. I told them you confronted Constance. I told them you have been drinking more than usual. I told them you are obsessed with your true crime garbage and now you think you are the star of one."

The world tilts. "You told them I have been drinking?"

"You want me to lie to the police now," he says. "Is that your legal advice? Because they asked about your little stunt in my office like it was a movie and guess who gave them the screenplay. *You.*"

My hands shake on the wheel. "You cheated on me with your assistant. I asked her to stay away from my husband. That's the full story!"

He exhales fast, a sound full of disgust. "The story is you do not know when to stop. You stirred things up. *You* made a scene. Now she is gone and everyone thinks I did it or you did it or both. Do you understand what this is going to do to my job??"

"Your job," I say, and the words come out shredded. "*Your job.*"

"You are ruining my life," he says. "If you had just left it alone."

A laugh slips out of me, ugly and small. "What happened to the man I married?"

"People change," he says. "Grow up."

The line goes dead. I pull the phone away and stare at the blank screen until my eyes burn. The urge to throw it across the car pulses through me, then drains away. All the fight leaves my body at once, like someone pulled a plug.

For a second I just sit there, suspended in the aftermath, waiting for my brain to catch up to what my ears heard. Vindictive. Drinking. Obsessed. Star of one. The words replay in his voice, each one landing with the precise cruelty of a man who knows exactly where to cut.

My throat tightens, but no sound comes. Not a sob. Not a scream. Just that hollow, stunned quiet that follows an impact. My hands are still on the wheel, but they do not feel like mine. They are cramped into place, knuckles white, as if my body is trying to keep itself anchored to something solid.

He told them.

Not just the affair. Not just Constance. He gave them my weaknesses like a list. He handed them the version of me he wants them to believe. The unstable wife. The angry woman. The one who drinks. The one who makes scenes. The one who is easy to blame.

And the worst part is how cleanly he did it. No hesitation. No guilt. Like he has been practicing.

A laugh tries to rise and dies halfway up my chest. This is what eight years bought me. Not loyalty. Not protection. A man who can turn my life into evidence the second it serves him.

I swallow hard and taste bitterness, sharp as metal. My pulse thuds behind my eyes. I try to slow my breathing, but my lungs keep snagging on the same thought, again and again, like a hook in fabric.

If he can say those things about me to the police, what else has he said. What else has he been building, quietly, behind my back.

I picture him in that interview room, sitting under fluorescent lights, looking composed. I can see him wearing the right expression, the concerned husband, the wronged man caught in a tragedy. I can hear him saying my name in that calm voice, making it sound like a warning.

Lo is emotional. Lo drinks. Lo is into true crime. Lo confronted her. Lo has been spiraling.

A sick heat crawls up my neck. I press my tongue to the roof of my mouth, fighting the urge to gag. I am suddenly aware of how alone I am in this car, in this moment, in this version of my life. No witness. No protection. Just me and the story he is already writing.

My eyes flick to the station in the windshield. Brick. Windows. A flag. A place where the truth is supposed to matter. My stomach twists because I know better. In rooms like that, truth is only as useful as the shape it can be forced into.

I blink hard, once, twice, as if I can clear him out of my head. It does not work. The blank screen keeps reflecting my face back at me, pale and tight, and I realize something that lands heavier than the call itself.

He is not afraid for Constance.

He is afraid for himself.

And if saving himself means sacrificing me, he has already started.

My fingers loosen on the wheel, finally, and the ache in my palms blooms as the blood comes back. I breathe in through my nose, slow, controlled, like I am teaching myself how to survive my own body.

Do not call him again, I tell myself. Do not beg. Do not explain. Do not chase the version of him you thought you married.

But the fear does not listen to logic. It sits in my ribs and watches the station and waits for the next phone call, the next question, the next person to look at me and decide what I am.

I text Damien because I need a voice that does not slice me open.

Me: *Just finished. I feel sick.*

Damien: *Where are you?*

Me: *Station lot.*

Damien: *Meet me two towns over. Sayville at The Shed. 30 minutes*

I do not trust my voice enough to call. I tap the steering wheel with my fingernails until the feeling comes back into my hands, then pull out of the space and onto the road like I am learning to drive for the first time. The radio stays off. The town rolls past in slow strips of gray and red brick. A woman in a puffer jacket drags a dog that refuses to move.

A kid in a hoodie crosses against the light and flips off a honking car. It all looks like a movie I cannot hear.

The bay air meets me as I turn onto Main Street in Sayville. It smells like salt and old wood and fried onions. The Shed sits tucked back from the street with strings of lights winking under the awning. Inside, the noise is warm. Not loud, but alive. The kind of hum that cushions you if you let it.

Damien is already there, corner table, back to the wall like he is protecting me from the door. When he sees me, he stands. He does not fold me into his arms. He does not touch me at all. He lets me see his face and the steady way he is looking at me.

"You okay to sit?" he asks.

"I think so."

We slide into the booth. A server appears with water and a paper menu that swims a little in my eyesight. Damien orders for both of us without asking, and somehow it feels like relief. Burgers. Fries. Two beers. He waits until the server leaves before he speaks again.

"Tell me what they asked."

"The confrontation," I say. "Where I was Friday night. Whether I thought he could hurt her." The words crumble as they come. "They told me he admitted it. Like it was a favor."

Damien's jaw tightens. He does not swear. He does not roll his eyes. He just listens in that way he has that makes people tell him the thing they did not plan to share.

"I felt like I was handing them pieces that would be used to build a cage," I say. "Even though I told the truth. Even though I did nothing wrong."

"You told the truth," he says. "That matters."

"Does it?" I ask. "In stories like this. Does it matter at all."

"It matters to me," he says. A beat. "And to Jenna. And to anyone who actually cares about facts. Eat something. Please."

The beers arrive cold enough to sweat. I take a long sip and feel it hit my empty stomach like a small iron weight. Food comes fast. Steam rises off the fries in curls. I pick one up and it burns my fingers in a way that reminds me I am still in a body. I eat because he asked me to. The salt drags me back toward the table inch by inch.

Damien keeps his voice low. "What did John say when you called him?"

"That I am ruining his life," I say. "That I should have kept my mouth shut. That I made this happen."

His nostrils flare. He looks at the table, then back at me. "That is what cowards say when the house is on fire and they smell their own smoke."

A sound leaves me that might be a laugh or a sob. "I hate him and I still want to defend him. I spent eight years doing that. I do not know how to stop."

"You do not have to stop tonight," he says. "You have to eat and breathe and keep your head above water."

"Jenna said no more meetings without her. She said protect myself because he will protect himself."

"Good," he says. "That is what we are doing."

We eat in small stretches of quiet. The lights along the window glow soft. A couple at the bar clinks their glasses and a group in hoodies argues about hockey. Normal sounds. I let them fill me up.

"Tell me something that is not about him," Damien says after a while. "Tell me what you are afraid of that has your name on it."

"My students," I say before I can pull it back. "They were looking at me like I am a sideshow. A girl asked if it was true. A boy made a joke.

I dropped a marker because my hand would not work. I could feel the room waiting for me to break."

"Kids love a story," he says. "You know that."

"I do," I say. "I also know how fast a story becomes a verdict."

He nods. "Then we give them nothing to hold onto. You keep your class boring. You keep your head down. You do not repeat scenes in parking lots. You do not drink alone. You do not text him when the nightmares wake you up."

"You say that like it's easy."

"I say that like I will help," he says. "You can lean. I am not going anywhere."

It is too much and exactly what I need. I take another drink to push down the feeling that rises in my throat. The fries are half gone. My burger sits in two bites and I do not remember eating most of it.

"Pax texted me last night," I say, because it has been humming in the back of my skull. "He asked if I knew the missing girl. He called her a chick. He was weird. Short. Not himself."

Damien's eyes sharpen. "Weird how?"

"He asked if she was the one I thought John was cheating with. I said yes. He replied that it was crazy. Then nothing. He usually floods me. He felt like someone I do not know."

"Call him tonight," Damien says. "Or tomorrow morning if tonight feels like a mountain. You do not need another question mark."

"Do you think I am being paranoid?"

"I think fear is a system. Your body is trying to keep you alive. Sometimes it fires too hard. That does not mean it is wrong."

I look at him and try to absorb the calm in his face. The room feels less sharp now. My hands are steadier. The food goes somewhere useful. I can feel it.

"Thank you," I say. "For being here."

He gives the smallest nod. "Always."

We pay. He walks me out. The air outside is colder than I expected, the sky the color of slate. Across the street a string of lights wraps a tree and makes it look like a constellation fell and forgot where it was going. The lot smells like damp leaves and oil. I breathe it in like medicine.

At my car he stops a step away, not touching, close enough that if I took one breath forward I could rest my head against his chest. I do not move.

"You are going to get through tomorrow," he says. "You will call Jenna before you do anything. You will text me if you feel yourself slipping. And you will remember you did not do this."

I nod. "What if they already decided who I am?"

"Then we change their minds," he says.

A small laugh escapes me. "You make that sound simple."

"It is not simple," he says. "It is work. Luckily we both know how to work."

He waits until I am in the driver's seat. He does not leave until my headlights cut across the lot and I pull away. I watch him in the rearview mirror until he becomes a tall shape under the tree and then a darker piece of night.

On the drive home the road feels both familiar and strange. The same old storefronts become landmarks in a city I do not trust. My phone is face down on the passenger seat, but I can feel it like a pulse. I imagine texts I cannot see. I imagine headlines that have not been written. I imagine Detective Ruiz's voice saying my name.

At a red light I pick up the phone and type a message to Jenna that I am home. I type another to Pax that says *hey, checking in*. I do not hit send on the second one. I stare at it until the light turns green and someone honks behind me.

Home is dark and still. I stand in the doorway and listen to the quiet like it might answer me. The kitchen smells like nothing. The living room looks staged for a life I do not live anymore. I set my keys in the bowl and my phone on the counter and press my palms to the cool stone until the buzzing in my head softens.

The rug has been pulled out from under my life. That is the truest thing I know.

My phone lights once on the counter. A number I do not recognize. It goes dark before I can grab it. I leave it there and let the dark hold me a little longer.

Chapter Thirty-Four

The hours after lunch crawl like years. I pace the house, sip wine I don't taste, stare at the TV without seeing. Every thought leads back to the station, to Ruiz's steady eyes, to John's slurred voice spitting blame at me. I try to read, I try to shower, I even try to pray. Nothing sticks. My mind keeps looping the same few images, like if I replay them enough they'll change.

What I really want is not food or sleep or silence. It is Damien. The way he looks at me like I'm not broken. The way his voice cuts through the noise. The way my breathing slows when I sit across a table from him.

The wanting tips into something sharper, lower. My body remembers the heat between us, the weight of his hand steady on my back, the way his mouth hovers a breath too close when he tells me to breathe. It feels less like desire and more like instinct, like my body has already decided what it needs.

I send the text before I can think myself out of it. *Can I come by later?*

The reply comes quickly. *You're always welcome.*

The words settle into me, warm and dangerous. Always. No questions. No caution. I tell myself I'll just sit, just breathe. I don't believe it.

By the time I pull into his driveway, night has settled thick and dark over the town. His porch light glows like a beacon. My chest tightens as I climb the steps, pulse quick and unsteady, but when he opens the door, the tension slips, just enough to let me step inside it.

"Lo," he says softly, and my name sounds different in his mouth, gentler than I've felt all day. I don't know when I started measuring myself by how carefully other people handle me.

The air between us shifts. No prying eyes here, no students watching, no colleagues whispering. Just me and him and the quiet permission of being unseen.

He takes my coat, his fingers brushing mine. It's a small touch, but my body reacts anyway, like it's been waiting for proof I'm still real. The living room smells like cedar and clean laundry. Familiar. Safe. My nerves hum beneath my skin.

"You okay?" he asks.

I shake my head. "No." The truth comes easier than I expect. "I don't want to think tonight. I want..."

He cups my face, steady, grounding. "Then don't think. Just be here."

Something in me loosens. Not the fear, exactly, but the grip it's had on my throat all day.

I kiss him hard, too hard, pouring everything I've been holding into that single contact. He tastes like beer and heat and the promise of quiet. His arms come around me and the panic dulls, not gone, just pushed far enough back that I can breathe.

I stop caring about careful. About tomorrow. About who this makes me. I push closer, needing the weight of him, the certainty of his hands. I know this will complicate things. I also know I don't care tonight.

"Lo," he murmurs, not stopping me.

"Yes," I say, already past restraint. "Please."

The kiss deepens. His hands slide down my back, anchoring me when my thoughts start to scatter. My body responds faster than my mind, choosing sensation over spirals, closeness over questions.

The world narrows. No missing person. No detectives. No husband who turned into someone I don't recognize. Just breath and warmth and the relief of wanting something that wants me back.

For the first time since Constance's face filled every screen, I feel something other than fear. I feel present. I feel alive in my body again.

Damien lifts me, sure and steady, and I cling to him, not thinking past this moment, not trying to justify it. I let myself have the night.

***

Morning drips in slow through Damien's blinds. For a moment I don't know where I am. The sheets smell different, cedar and detergent, not the faint lavender of my own. Then I feel the weight of his arm brushing my hip, hear his steady breathing, and it all comes back. Last night. The rush. The relief. The fire. It settles into me quietly, without panic.

I lie still, watching the light cut across the floorboards. He sleeps on his stomach, one arm bent, face turned toward me. His jaw is slack, his mouth parted slightly, and I can see the faint shadow of stubble along his cheeks. He looks peaceful in a way that feels impossible. Not untouched by the world, but resting anyway.

Peace is a stranger to me now. Still, it sits at the edge of the bed like it's considering staying.

I let myself watch him a moment longer, memorizing the shape of him in this light, then carefully slide out of bed. My body aches in ways that remind me of his hands, his mouth, his steadiness. The ache feels good, grounding, like proof I am still here and still capable of wanting.

Clothes scattered across the floor, I gather them quietly, pulling my blouse over my head and smoothing my skirt. The mirror catches me as I pass. My hair is a mess, my eyes softer than they were yesterday. I look like someone who slept. Like someone who was held.

I pause at the door and look back at him one last time. His breathing doesn't change. He shifts a little deeper into the pillow, one hand curling near where I was. There is no regret in me, only the awareness that this was a shelter, not an escape.

"Thank you," I whisper, though he can't hear me. Not for the night, exactly. For the way my body remembers how to be calm when it's with him.

The drive back feels dreamlike. The town is barely waking up. Bakery windows fogged with early bread. Joggers huddled against the chill. A dog straining at its leash, determined to get somewhere important. My car hums beneath me, steady and mundane, and for a few minutes I let the ordinary carry me.

My thoughts try to fracture anyway. The interview room. Ruiz's steady eyes. John's voice dripping venom through the phone. Pax's strange, clipped text. Each memory presses in, testing the calm. But every time panic starts to build, I picture Damien's hand on my face, the weight of his body grounding mine, and my breathing evens out again. I don't pretend it fixes anything. It just gives me enough space to keep going.

By the time I pull into the faculty lot, I'm repeating a mantra under my breath. *Normal. Normal. Normal.* Not because I believe it, but because I need something steady to hold onto as I step into the day.

***

In my office, I build my armor. Buttoned blouse, hair pinned back, notes stacked neatly. I line up my pens like soldiers, a small illusion of order. The ritual matters more than I want to admit. My reflection in the tiny mirror on the back of my office door looks pale but composed. I force a smile at myself. Too sharp. I try again, softer. Passable.

When I step into the classroom, the air is different. Brighter. Lighter. My students shuffle in, clutching notebooks, yawning. Some laugh about something in the hallway. For once, no one looks at me like I'm a headline. The absence of scrutiny feels almost suspicious, like the quiet before a sound returns.

"Morning," I say evenly. "Find your seats. Let's get started."

They do. Laptops open. Pens click. I start slowly, easing into the lecture. Narrative structure. Three-act arcs. Setups and payoffs. Safe material. Familiar. My voice holds steady, and I cling to that steadiness like proof.

I write *Exposition* on the board and hear a girl whisper to her neighbor, but when I glance back, they're only passing gum. My chest loosens. Not everything is about me. Not today.

I ask a question about foreshadowing. A boy in the front row answers, fumbling but earnest. I nod, build on it, move on. A couple of kids laugh at a joke I crack about clichés, and the sound lands clean, unforced. It almost feels like muscle memory, like slipping back into a version of myself I know how to be.

For forty-five minutes, I am not the wife of the man who cheated. Not the woman detectives are circling. Just Professor Roberts, talking about story, about choices and consequences that belong to fictional people.

When class ends, I gather my notes slowly, reluctant to let go of the calm. The students file out, chatting about lunch plans, exams, weekend trips. Anything but me. For the first time all week, I don't feel their eyes following me.

Relief trickles through me like warm water, tentative but real.

"Halo."

I jump, clutching my papers tighter than necessary. Carlos stands in the doorway, hands in his pockets. He looks the same as always. Tidy blazer, hair smoothed back. But his expression is careful, measured in a way that makes my stomach tighten.

"Carlos," I say, my smile clicking into place. "What brings you by?"

"I'm checking in." He steps into the room and closes the door. His eyes sweep over the empty desks before settling back on me. "I know this has been... difficult."

The word lands and slides right off. Too small. Too polite. I nod once, because that's what's expected.

He clears his throat. "I wanted you to hear it from me before it spreads. John requested some vacation time. Effective immediately."

The word hits harder than I expect. "Vacation."

"Yes," Carlos says. "Given the whispers on campus. The atmosphere. He thought it best. I agreed."

My face tightens before I can stop it, but I smooth it quickly. Inside, something twists. Vacation. As though this is a break he earned. As though he isn't stepping out of the frame before it collapses.

I press my hands flat on the lectern to ground myself, feel the solid wood beneath my palms. "I understand."

Carlos tilts his head, studying me. "You handled class well today. Professional. That's what people will remember."

The compliment tastes thin, but I swallow it anyway. Professional. The word feels like both shield and sentence. "Thank you."

He hesitates, then adds, "If you need anything, my door is open."

I nod again. "I appreciate it."

He leaves quietly, the door clicking shut behind him.

The room feels too bright now. The air too thin. I sit on the edge of the desk and let the silence swell around me. The relief I felt only minutes ago has curdled. John on "vacation." Carlos's careful tone. The way everything is being arranged to preserve John's image while mine fractures out of sight.

I gather my notes and slide them into my bag with deliberate calm, even though my hands are trembling. My marriage has become a cautionary tale. My name is being spoken in hallways I can't hear, shaped by mouths I don't see.

Still, for one hour this morning, I held the mask in place. I taught my class with no issue and I was not undone.

I press my palm flat against the cool wood of the lectern one last time, steadying myself. I will keep standing. I have to.

Chapter Thirty-Five

I stop counting the days. They slide past in a smear of headlines and whispers, each one heavier than the last. Sometimes I'm sure it's only been a few nights since Carlos called me into his office. Other times it feels like years have collapsed into the silence between me and John, his anger so thick I can taste it. The absence of him has weight now. It presses in different ways depending on the hour.

I measure time differently now. By the flowers left outside the student center, wilting, then replaced with new bouquets. By the candles that burn to puddles of wax before strangers relight them. By the way my phone keeps buzzing with numbers I don't recognize, reporters circling like vultures, patient and relentless.

The police keep coming back, circling me with the same questions over and over, as if repeating them will pull out an answer I don't have. Each visit leaves me feeling scraped raw, like something essential has been rubbed thin. On campus, conversations fall quiet when I walk by. Constance's face follows me everywhere. On posters. On the news. Glowing from the phone screens of students huddled together in the hallways. I learn to keep my eyes forward, to pretend I don't see her watching me from every surface.

It isn't until the vigil that I realize how much time has really passed. A week, someone whispers. Maybe more. Candles flicker in a hundred hands, wax dripping onto frozen ground, voices lifting into the cold night air. Her smile, too bright for the darkness, beams from every poster taped to every wall. I stand at the edge of the crowd, unsure where I belong in a space built for grief I'm not allowed to claim.

And then, one morning, the world tilts again.

The call comes just after dawn. My phone shatters the quiet, buzzing against the nightstand. For a second I think it's John, drunk again, needing someone to blame. The reflex is automatic. But the number is local, unfamiliar, and something in my chest drops before I even answer.

"Mrs. Roberts," Ruiz says when I pick up. His tone is clipped, official. No wasted words. "We need you to come in immediately. There's been a development. Bring your attorney."

That's all. No explanation. Only the weight of those words pressing down on me until the room feels smaller, until my breath turns shallow and tight. Development can mean anything. Everything.

I'm still clutching the phone when I dial Jenna. My hand shakes enough that I have to steady it against the mattress. She answers instantly, voice sharp with alertness.

"They called me," I manage. "Said it's urgent."

"I'll meet you there," Jenna replies. "Lo, don't say anything until I'm in the room. No matter what."

I hang up and sit there in the quiet, the early light creeping in around the edges of the room. Somewhere between the vigil candles and this call, something has shifted. I don't know yet whether it's hope or dread. All I know is that the waiting is over, and whatever comes next is going to ask something of me I'm not sure I can give.

***

The Suffolk County Police station waiting area hums with phones and printers, voices muffled through glass. I sit stiff-backed, knees pressed together, palms slick with sweat. I tell myself I have nothing to hide, but my body won't believe me. It braces anyway, like truth is something that has to be defended.

Detective Adams appears in the doorway, her expression unreadable. "Mrs. Roberts. Ms. Green." She nods once at Jenna. "This way."

We walk the same hallway as before, but today every step feels louder, heavier. The interrogation room seems smaller, colder, like it has been holding its breath. Ruiz is already seated, a manila folder resting on the table in front of him. The sight of it makes my stomach lurch. I can feel my pulse in my throat.

Adams closes the door and sits. "Thank you for coming in on such short notice."

I swallow. My throat feels raw, scraped thin.

Ruiz flips the folder open. He doesn't slide it toward me, not yet. He pulls out a stack of glossy photographs and spreads them facedown across the table.

My pulse spikes. My body reacts before my mind does, a cold rush flooding my limbs.

Adams's voice is calm, almost soothing. "Before we begin, Mrs. Roberts, we need to ask again about the last time you saw Constance Keller."

My hands knot in my lap. "At the college—a little over a week ago."

"And that was when you confronted her about the affair with your husband?"

"Yes." The word comes out barely more than breath.

Ruiz flips one photo over. The camera's flash bleaches out the edges, but the center is all too clear. A pale arm stiff against the mud, fingers curled grotesquely.

My chest seizes. The room tilts.

Jenna's voice slices in. "She's already answered this in detail."

Ruiz ignores her and turns another photo face-up.

I wish he hadn't.

Constance lies sprawled like a doll dropped wrong. Her limbs are twisted into angles no body was meant to hold. One arm bent beneath her, the wrist swollen and purpled, fingers frozen into a claw. Her knee juts outward, bone pressing at skin, the joint bent grotesquely, impossible for the living.

Bruises mar nearly every inch of her. Dark blotches ring her neck, a violent collar of purple that makes me look away too fast. My vision blurs at the edges. Her cheek is blackened and mottled, her skin stretched until her face looks less like a woman and more like a mask.

Another photo. Her torso. Her shirt is torn, mud ground into the fabric. Gashes line her arms, scratches from fighting, skin shredded raw. Her hair is caked into the dirt, strands glued together with blood and soil, pulled tight across her face.

I can't breathe.

My throat convulses. Bile rises. I press my nails deep into my palms until they sting, anchoring myself to pain I can control. The table feels too close. The air feels used up.

Ruiz doesn't take his eyes off me. He wants to see me crack. Wants me to give him something he can shape into guilt.

I force myself not to look again, but the images are already burned into me. Her bent knee. Her clawed hand. Her bruised throat. They loop behind my eyes, relentless.

Adams's voice cuts in, quiet but sharp. "These are difficult to look at. But someone left her like this. Someone who wanted her hidden, but not enough to care if she was found. Do you understand why we're asking if you were angry?"

I shake my head too quickly, vision swimming. "I didn't—" The words choke off, caught somewhere between my chest and my mouth.

Jenna taps her heel once under the table. *Hold steady.*

I bite my tongue, tasting blood, forcing my face blank. Inside, I'm unraveling. I can't stop seeing her body bent and broken like discarded trash. I can't stop wondering what kind of person could do this, and what kind of person they are hoping I'll look like.

Adams leans forward. "Did you and Ms. Keller have another confrontation after that day on campus?"

"No." My voice cracks despite my effort. "I never saw her again."

"Did you ever believe your husband was capable of violence?"

Images slam into me. John's slammed doors. His voice rising to a roar. The darkness in his eyes when I accused him. My lips part, but no sound comes. The room seems to wait.

"Speculative," Jenna cuts in flatly. "And irrelevant."

The detectives don't argue. They let the silence stretch. The photos sit between us like open wounds. Like proof of something I'm supposed to account for.

Finally, Ruiz leans back. "We know Constance was seeing someone else. Did you know about that?"

My body jolts. "No."

His gaze doesn't waver. He waits, measuring the tremor in my voice, the twist of my hands, the way my breath refuses to settle.

The fluorescent light hums louder, relentless, drilling into my skull. I can't unsee the images. Her hair. Her hand. The scarf twisted into something unrecognizable. My chest heaves, and I bite my tongue hard enough to keep myself present.

Adams tilts her head, eyes narrowing like she's trying to see through skin. "You seem upset."

My laugh is sharp, bitter. "Wouldn't anyone?"

Neither detective responds. They watch me. Every twitch of my mouth. Every tremor of my hands. Waiting to see what breaks first.

At last, Ruiz gathers the photos, sliding them back into the folder one by one. Each makes a faint scrape against the table, deliberate, almost ceremonial.

"That's all for now," he says, closing the folder. Then he looks up at me, expression unreadable. "I'd appreciate it if you stayed in town for the time being, just in case we have a few more questions."

My chest tightens, the room suddenly feeling smaller. I nod anyway. "Of course."

My chair screeches as I stand, knees wobbling. Jenna rises with me, her hand brushing mine under the table, steady and grounding.

"You did fine," she murmurs. "Nothing they can twist."

But her voice feels far away. My head is filled with Constance. Her twisted arm. Her swollen face. The way her body looked like something no one came back for.

Across the lot, a figure walks up the steps toward the station. Head down. Shoulders tight.

Pax.

My chest squeezes. For a second I tell myself it's not him. It can't be him. Confusion coils in my stomach, fast and sharp. Why would he be here?

But when he looks up just enough for me to see his face, the air leaves my lungs.

It's him. My brother.

What the hell is he doing here? How did he know I had an interview with the police? Maybe he saw the news that she was found. But Detective Ruiz said they hadn't released details yet.

"Lo." Jenna's voice cuts through, sharp and steady. "Drive."

I blink hard, forcing my grip to tighten on the wheel.

Of course Pax could be here. People come and go from a police station every hour of every day. Parking tickets. Witness statements. I'm spiraling, seeing shadows where there aren't any. I shake it off, tell myself it's nothing, and put the car in gear.

The drive to Jenna's condo is quiet, city lights streaking across the windshield. My fingers ache from gripping the wheel, and Jenna doesn't push me to talk. Not until we're parked outside her building.

She unclips her seatbelt and exhales. "You did good in there. They were circling, but you held your ground. Don't let them make you doubt that."

I nod, but my stomach won't unknot. "It felt like they wanted me to break. Like they were waiting for me to admit I hated her enough to…" I can't finish.

"They wanted you to feel that way," Jenna says firmly. "That's the tactic. Pressure, silence, repetition. But you didn't give them anything new. That's what matters." She squeezes my arm, softer now. "I meant what I said earlier. You're not walking into that station again without me. Ever."

I nod again, forcing a thin smile, but the image of Constance's body won't leave me. The broken branches. The mud. The way her body looked arranged by someone else's decision.

Jenna grabs her bag and pauses with the door open. "Get some rest, Lo. Seriously. You need to shut your brain off for a few hours."

When she disappears inside, the silence swells too big in the car. My reflection in the rearview looks like a stranger, eyes too bright, face pulled tight with something I don't know how to name.

I sit there, wondering about John, wondering if the cops have brought him in yet, wondering how much longer before everything snaps.

Realizing I'm almost out of gas, I head to BP, taking care to stick to the back roads, telling myself I just need to fill the tank. At the gas station, the fluorescent lights buzz overhead, casting everything in a sickly glow. I sit long after the pump clicks, staring at nothing, not ready to face my own driveway.

I scroll my phone instead, thumb hovering before I finally type: *You up?*

Sam responds almost instantly: *Yes. Come over.*

She has been my nonjudgmental anchor, the only person who doesn't look at me like a headline. I toss the phone onto the passenger seat, start the engine, and pull out slowly.

This time I don't aim for home.

I take the back roads, headlights carving through the dark, my mind drifting into all the places I don't want it to go.

Chapter Thirty-Six

I curl into the couch with a glass of wine, the stem slippery in my fingers. Sam sits across from me, legs folded under her, slipping into therapist mode the way she always does. It's subtle, almost unconscious, but I can feel the shift. I unload everything. The phone call about Constance. The way the detectives twisted my words. How Jenna kept shutting them down. How it felt like the walls pressed in with every question, closing ranks.

"I swear the chair was designed to make you confess," I mutter, rubbing the back of my neck. "Hard as stone. The light buzzing overhead, just bright enough to make you sweat. They didn't even have to say anything half the time. They looked at me like they were waiting for me to break." I take a long sip and let the warmth spread. "If Jenna hadn't been there, I think I would've."

Sam hums softly, absorbing it, then tilts her head. "Okay. But Lo. Why was Pax there?"

The question lands heavier than the wine. Heavier than the room.

I swirl what's left in my glass, staring at the dark liquid. "I don't know. Honestly, I told myself I was imagining it. There are a hundred reasons someone might be at a police station. Maybe he was giving a statement about something else. Maybe he had a ticket." My laugh comes out thin and brittle, the sound of a bridge trying not to crack. "He didn't see me."

Sam's eyes stay on me. She doesn't blink. "And you didn't ask him?"

I shake my head. "I didn't. I couldn't. Not there. Not then." I don't add that I was afraid of the answer. That naming it would make it real.

She leans forward, elbows on her knees. "Then ask him now."

The air catches in my throat. "Sam, I can't just call my brother and say, 'Hey, why were you walking into the police station after they found John's mistress dumped in the woods.'" My voice drops, quieter, truer. "I know how that sounds."

"You can," she says. "And you should. Because if you don't, it's going to eat you alive."

Her words dig under my skin, finding something already sore. I stare at my phone in my lap, thumb hovering over Pax's name. My hands are shaking. "He won't answer me. Or he'll blow me off the way he always does when he doesn't want to talk."

Sam doesn't move. "Then text him. Don't give him a chance to dodge your voice."

I sit there longer than I mean to, the silence broken only by the soft crackle of candle wicks. The room feels too quiet for what I'm about to do. Finally, with a breath that feels like it might split me open, I type: *I saw you at the station. Why were you there?*

I hit send before I can change my mind. My stomach flips as the screen goes quiet, like I've just thrown something fragile and don't know where it will land.

Minutes pass. My wineglass is empty before I realize I've drained it. Sam refills it without asking, her hand brushing mine in quiet reassurance. I don't thank her. I just nod.

Still nothing.

I check the phone again. And again. Every second stretches longer than the last. The room feels smaller, the shadows cast by the flickering candles taller, sharper.

Finally, the screen lights up. A single message.

Are you home?

Then,

We need to talk.

My heart slams once, hard, like it's trying to get my attention. Sam's eyes meet mine across the coffee table, steady but alert.

A hundred thoughts rush through me. Pax is my brother. The one who knows how to make me laugh when no one else can. The one who's always brushed things off with a joke, a shrug, a change of subject. But this. *We need to talk.* That isn't him deflecting. That's him bracing.

What could he possibly mean? Why didn't he say it on the phone?

The phone feels heavy in my hand. Not threatening. Just loaded, like I'm holding a weight whose purpose I don't understand yet. My chest tightens with the not knowing, with the sense that whatever comes next won't fit neatly back into the life I had before.

Sam watches me, her expression meant to be encouraging, though I can see the confusion under it. She doesn't ask what I'm going to say. She knows I've already decided.

I'm at Sam's. Come here if you want to talk.

I hit send and set the phone on the table, my fingers brushing the rim of my glass. My chest is tight, but not with fear. More like anticipation. I want something real from him. Anything that cuts through the guessing.

Minutes drag. Sam tops off my glass again and I sip, glancing at the phone every few seconds. Still nothing.

"He'll respond," she says. It sounds less like comfort and more like a directive.

I set the phone back down and stare at it, willing it to light up. The silence stretches, thick and uncomfortable. The room seems to close in with every minute that ticks by.

What could he possibly need to tell me that requires being face to face? My mind flips through possibilities, none of them settling. A fight. Trouble at work. Something about John. Something worse. The not knowing itches under my skin, and with every second the phone stays dark, my chest tightens a little more.

Finally, the phone buzzes. One new message.

Okay. Send me the address.

Relief flickers through me, quick and fragile. I type back immediately, fingers steadier now, and hit send. The dots appear, vanish, then reappear.

I'll come by in 30 min.

I lean back against the couch, pulling the blanket Sam tossed over me tighter around my shoulders. My body feels braced, like it knows something is coming. "Well," I mutter, lifting my glass, "at least this might finally be more eventful than the last time I tried to get him to talk."

Sam studies me, her expression unreadable in the candlelight. "Then let's see what he has to say."

***

The knock at the door is sharp enough to make me flinch. Sam opens it, her body angled like a guard, but then Pax steps inside. His eyes go straight to me, bloodshot and wild, his chest rising and falling too fast. He looks like someone who has been running from something and lost anyway.

Sam lingers by the door, studying him openly. "Wow," she murmurs after a beat. "You two really are cut from the same cloth. Same eyes, same nose even. No mistaking it."

Pax gives her a short nod, doesn't even try to smile. He's pacing already, back and forth across Sam's rug like a caged animal. His jacket is half-zipped, his hands buried deep in the pockets until suddenly they're out again, rubbing his face, dragging across his braids, pressing the crown of his head like he's afraid his skull might split open.

"Lo," he says, voice breaking on my name. "There's something I need to tell you. I should've told you before, but I couldn't. I didn't know how."

My throat tightens. My body goes very still. "Tell me now."

He stops pacing for a second. His eyes are wild, desperate, searching my face for something he hasn't earned yet. "I was seeing someone. You remember, I told you. I think I even told you her name."

My stomach flips, slow and sick, because I already know where this is going. "Yeah. Yes, you told me her name was—"

He cuts me off. "Grace. She told me her name was Grace," he says, his voice ragged. "Grace. That's all I knew her by. She said she was new to the area. She said she didn't have family here. She said she worked some boring job she hated. She made up a whole life. And I—I believed her." His laugh breaks loose, sharp and ugly. "I was falling for her, Lo. I thought she could be the one for me, you know?"

He stops again, laughter collapsing into something closer to a sob. "And then one morning, I wake up, and her face is everywhere. The news. The internet. My phone blowing up. Only it isn't Grace. It's Constance. Faculty member. Missing. Mistress to your husband." His voice fractures around the word husband, like it cuts him on the way out.

Sam inhales sharply behind him, but I can't take my eyes off Pax. Cold spreads through me, slow and absolute, like my body is trying to catch up to what he's saying. Grace. Constance. The names slide over each other in my head, refusing to stay separate. Two women collapse into one, and with them, two versions of the past. It's not fear that grips me. It's disorientation. The sickening realization that the whole time, we were all touching the same lie from different sides.

"The girl I loved wasn't real," he says, voice shaking. "Do you understand what that does to your head? Every memory. Every word. A lie." His hands rake over his hair again, pressing until his knuckles nearly go white, like he's fighting to stay in his own body.

I've never seen my brother like this. Hollowed out. Stripped down to nerve and bone. A shiver moves through me, thick with the sense that something irreversible has just been spoken aloud. My heart drops hard, then keeps dropping, like the truth has its own gravity.

I swallow. My mouth is dry. "When did you realize?"

"The second I saw the news," he says, voice hoarse. "Her photo. Her smile. I knew. My stomach dropped out. And then I saw where she worked. With you. With John." His face twists into raw panic. "That's when it all came together. The woman I was in love with was living a whole other life. She was with him too. My own sister's husband."

The words land heavy and wrong. My lungs forget how to work.

"She lied about everything," he says. "And now..." His chest heaves. He forces his eyes to mine, desperate. "Now the cops think I'm the liar. They pulled my texts with her. She was messaging me the night she disappeared. The last person she reached out to. They look at me like I put her in the ground."

He shakes his head, like he can't believe his own life anymore. His voice drops into something close to a plea. "I didn't, Lo. I swear to you. I loved her. I would've done anything for her. I didn't kill her. You have to believe me."

The silence that follows hums, thick with everything he's just laid bare.

I look at him. Really look. His hands trembling. His chest tight with grief he's holding back by force. The boy I grew up with still there beneath the wreckage. Whatever fear flickered earlier burns out completely. This is someone I know. Someone I trust without question.

He could never do this. Not him. Not the person standing in front of me, breaking open in Sam's living room.

My heart softens as certainty settles in, steady and unmovable.

"I believe you," I say, without hesitation.

Sam doesn't move or speak. Her hand slips over mine anyway, steady and sure, anchoring me to this couch, this room, this moment, while the storm of Pax's confession settles into something solid and real.

We sit there together in the glow of Sam's warm lamplight, the truth between us jagged and terrible, but clear. I don't question it. I don't second-guess what I've heard. Some truths arrive fully formed, leaving no room for doubt. Only the quiet understanding that nothing will ever be the same again.

CHAPTER THIRTY-SEVEN

The door clicks shut behind Pax, and the silence he leaves in his wake feels louder than his words. My whole body is buzzing, like someone plugged me into an outlet. The hum of Sam's refrigerator fills the kitchen, steady and strange. The soft tick of her wall clock is relentless. The smell of the sandalwood candle she lit earlier curls around me, warm and grounding, but I feel untethered, floating somewhere above myself, watching my own hands tremble in my lap.

Sam leans back on the couch beside me, her glass of wine balanced between her fingers. The amber glow of the lamp softens her face, but her eyes stay sharp. She waits a long moment before speaking, giving me space to breathe, though my chest still feels locked. Finally she says, "Lo... do you believe him?"

The answer leaps out before I can think. "Yes." My voice is too quick, too hard. The word tastes like iron on my tongue. I grip the stem of my glass too tightly, like if I let go I might shatter right there in front of her.

Sam tilts her head, watching me. Her tone is calm, even, but I hear the weight behind it. "Do you believe him because you really think it's true, or because he's your brother and you need it to be true?"

Heat flares under my skin, sharp and defensive. "Sam. He wouldn't lie about something like this. I know him. He's not violent, and he damn sure isn't capable of murder." The words come fast, instinctive, like muscle memory kicking in.

She doesn't argue. She studies me, steady and patient. "I'm not saying he's guilty. I'm saying it's complicated. Messy. And you can't afford to pretend it isn't."

The words land heavy. My throat tightens. I think of Pax when we were kids, before life got so tangled. He was the little brother trailing behind me, always asking questions, always wanting to tag along. I was the one who carried his backpack when it was too heavy, the one who walked him home when he was scared of the dark. I was supposed to be the anchor. The protector. Seeing him unravel now makes something ache in my chest, like I missed the moment when the ground started to give way beneath him.

But I do know him. I know the way his left eyebrow twitches when he's holding something back. The way he rubs the back of his neck when he's cornered. The way his laugh comes too quick when he's lying. I've always been able to read him like a book. And tonight, what I saw wasn't deceit. It was devastation. Raw and unguarded. A grief so wild it scared me, not because I thought he was lying, but because I'd never seen him so gutted.

The weight of that realization makes me dig in deeper. "He's not lying," I say again, quieter this time. The words feel less like an argument and more like a vow. If I keep saying it, maybe I can hold the truth in place.

Sam reaches for the bottle and pours us both another glass. Her hand brushes mine as she sets it down. "Lo, I just want you to be careful. Keep your eyes open. That's all I'm saying."

I finally take a sip, the wine burning its way down my throat, spreading warmth through the cold panic lodged in my chest. Sam's hand slides over mine where it rests on the cushion, her thumb moving in a slow, steady circle. "Whatever happens, you're not alone in this," she says. "You have support. No matter what."

I close my eyes and let her words wash over me. Gratitude swells, tangled with guilt. She didn't sign up for this storm. Didn't ask to be pulled into my mess. But she stays anyway, grounded and present, even after everything she's already carried in her own life.

I glance around her living room, letting the details steady me. The flicker of candlelight. The green leaves of her plants leaning toward it. The stacks of books on her coffee table, worn spines and open pages. Everything here feels alive, held. A small sanctuary against the chaos that keeps trying to swallow my life whole.

When I finally stand and slip into my coat, my body feels heavier than it should. I tell Sam I'm heading home, though the thought of walking into that house alone makes my stomach knot.

At the door, I look back at her one last time. She gives me a small nod, an unspoken promise that she'll hold the line for me, no matter what comes next.

Out in the cold night, the air shocks my lungs. I clutch my coat tighter, breath fogging in the glow of her porch light. And beneath the hum of everything else, one thought pulses steady in my chest.

I believe Pax.

***

The drive home is too quiet, too long. Sam's voice, Pax's revelation, the shadows of everything I've just heard—they rattle in my skull like coins in a jar. By the time I pull into my driveway, the street looks almost ordinary, which feels impossible. My world is unraveling, yet the neighbors' porches glow soft with twinkle lights, and someone's TV flickers behind closed blinds.

For one fleeting moment, I almost believe I'll make it inside unnoticed. The hope feels naive the second it forms, like tempting fate just to see if it's listening.

Then the door of a car creaks open across the street.

A man steps out, the kind of man who blends into crowds until he doesn't. Dark jacket. Camera bag on one hip. A microphone in his hand. The logo on his chest is sharp under the streetlight—News 12 Long Island.

My chest tightens like a rope pulled taut. It feels physical, involuntary, like my body knows this is the moment everything tips from private disaster into public spectacle.

"Mrs. Roberts?" His voice carries low but clear, polite in a way that's nothing like polite. "Do you have a comment on the discovery of Constance Keller's body?"

I stop dead halfway up the walkway. My keys dig into my palm until it hurts. How does he know already? Ruiz said the details weren't public. Was it leaked? Did John talk? Did someone in the department slip?

The thought coils tighter and tighter, like a rubber band stretched to snapping. I can feel the pressure building behind my eyes, the kind that comes right before tears or something worse.

The man takes a step closer, notebook flipped open like he already knows the story he's writing. "Were you aware she was last seen leaving a restaurant near campus? Did your husband ever mention her movements the night she disappeared?"

My throat won't work. All I can manage is the shake of my head as I force myself up the steps.

He calls again. "Mrs. Roberts, can you confirm whether you confronted Ms. Keller about her relationship with your husband?"

The words hit like blows. Everyone knows. The whispers on campus, the questions from students, and now this—broadcast, public, forever.

I jam the key into the lock, twisting so hard I'm afraid it'll snap. Inside, I slam the door, drop my bag, press my back flat against the wood. My heart is a drum. Loud enough that I'm sure he can hear it through the door.

How do they know already? How did it leak so fast?

The silence of the house presses down, not comfort but suffocation. Pax's words echo in my head. Constance's body twisted, broken. And now the reporters are circling like vultures, smelling blood.

I yank the curtains shut, check the lock twice, then sink onto the couch with my arms wrapped tight around myself. The air feels too thin, every breath shallow. I count them anyway, one, two, three, like I was taught, even though it doesn't help.

I thought tonight would end in quiet. Instead, the story has already slipped out of my hands. I understand now that silence is no longer mine to choose.

Tomorrow, there won't be one reporter. Tomorrow they'll multiply. They'll wait, watch, pry. I don't know how long I can hold before I break.

Chapter Thirty-Eight

The ache behind my eyes that means I slept but never rested. For one thin moment, I believe today will be quiet. Then the weight returns. The photos. Pax's voice. The reporter in the dark.

I sit up and make myself move. If I do the small things in the right order, maybe the big things will not swallow me whole.

Closet first. I slide open the door and stare at color-blocked rows like they belong to a steadier woman. I pick the pink pantsuit because it looks like competence. High-waisted trousers, sharp crease. Cropped blazer with clean lines. It reads bright instead of broken. It says I am still a person with a job and a spine. I lay it across the bed like armor.

Hair next. I pad to the bathroom and peel off my satin bonnet. My curls have formed a wild crown in my sleep, coiled and flattened in uneven places. I stand under the light and study myself the way other people will today, trying to find the version who can survive it.

Spray bottle, warm water. I mist until my hair sighs back to life, sections waking up under my fingers. A palmful of leave-in worked through from ends to roots, then the wide-tooth comb, gentle, patient. I part it into four, clip three, and rake a curl cream through the free section until it clumps into glossy ropes. Gel after that, scrunching upward until my hands make that sticky-soft sound I have known since middle school. I plop with a cotton T-shirt for a few minutes while I brush my teeth, then release and coax the curls with a diffuser, low heat, head tipped sideways. Edges last: a little control, a soft brush, nothing too severe. I shake once, and the shape settles. Big. Defined. Unruly in a way that is mine.

While I work, my mind paces. What will the day bring? Will Ruiz call again? Will students watch me like a headline? Will Pax answer if I text? Will John do something I cannot fix?

The coffee ritual is supposed to help. Grind, pour, bloom, wait. I pad to the kitchen, flip the switch on the kettle, and pull down the bag of beans. The first whir of the grinder cuts through the morning quiet. I measure the grounds into the dripper and reach for a mug. I do not look out the window. I do not.

I look.

Six of them. At least. Parked along the curb like scavengers, two leaning against cars with paper cups, one checking a tripod, another speaking to someone I cannot see. Jackets with station logos. Camera bags. The kind of smile that belongs to people who think they own the story.

My stomach drops hard enough that I have to grip the counter. It takes me a beat to realize the kettle is boiling and the steam is ghosting past my hand. I switch it off and back away from the window.

Phone. Jenna.

She answers on the second ring, voice awake and ready. "Talk to me."

"They multiplied," I say. "News vans. Six, maybe more. They are outside my house."

"Okay," she says, steady. "Here is what you are going to do. You are not answering questions. You are not opening your door. Text Carlos and ask if campus security can meet you at the faculty lot so you do not have to cross campus alone. Do you have a garage or side exit?"

"Side door through the laundry room."

"Good. Use it. Bring your keys, your bag, sunglasses, and a mask if you have one. People are less brave when they cannot read your face. Put your phone on video before you step out and keep it pointed down. If anyone blocks your path, you repeat one line: 'I have nothing to share.' Not 'no comment.' Say 'I have nothing to share.' Then keep walking."

I pull open the drawer and grab the big sunglasses I wear to the beach. "What about my car? They are parked right by the driveway."

"You can call a rideshare to the side street and walk to it through your neighbor's yard if that neighbor is friendly. If not, get in your car and go slow. If someone follows, do not go straight to school. Drive to the police station or a public lot and call me. And, Lo, vary your route. Do not be predictable this week."

I press the phone to my cheek and breathe in her certainty, like oxygen. "Thank you."

"One more thing. Keep your hands visible when you walk out. No rummaging in your purse. It keeps the footage boring. Reporters do not air boring footage."

A laugh slips out of me that sounds like a crack. "Copy."

"Text me when you are in the car. I will call Carlos. Do not engage with anyone. Not even a 'good morning.' Nothing."

We hang up. I slide the sunglasses into my bag and fish out a simple black mask. When I turn around, the room looks wrong. My pink suit on the bed, my careful hair, my tidy mug waiting under the dripper. A life I built, now under glass.

My phone buzzes again. Damien.

I answer before I can think. "Hi."

"I saw the morning updates," he says. His voice is tentative. "How are you holding up?"

My breath is shallow. "Well, for starters, there are reporters outside my house. Six, maybe more."

"Are you okay?"

"I am pretending to be."

A quiet breath. "I am worried about you."

The words loosen something in my chest that nearly tips into tears. I hold the edge of the counter and stare at the coffee I am not pouring. "Jenna is walking me through getting out. She told me not to engage. Wear sunglasses or a mask."

"Good. Do that. I can drive over and run interference."

"No," I say, too fast. "It will make it worse. They will film you. I cannot have that."

"I do not care if they film me."

"I do." My voice softens. "The last thing I need is news breaking about... us. Please."

He lets the moment settle. "Then I will meet you for lunch. Not on campus. Two towns over again. Name the spot and time when you can breathe."

I shake my head, even though he cannot see me. "Let's see how the morning goes."

"Lo," he says, lower now. "One more thing. Be careful with John. If he calls, if he shows up. Do not be alone with him right now."

The caution lands like a weight I recognize. "I know."

"I mean it."

"I know," I say again. "Thank you."

"I am here," he says. "Text me when you are moving."

We end the call. The silence that follows is thick. I pour the water over the grounds, watch the bloom rise and collapse, and feel my hands start to steady. I take two sips standing at the sink because sitting feels like an invitation to fall apart. Then I set the mug down and get dressed.

The pink pantsuit slides on like a decision. White shell tucked in. Simple gold hoops. Low block heels for walking fast. I add the mask and sunglasses to the bag and stand in the hallway staring at the laundry-room door as if it might bite.

I text Carlos. *Reporters outside my house. Can campus security meet me at the faculty lot so I can go straight to my office?*

Three dots. Then: *Yes. 8:20 at the back entrance. I will alert them. Do you need a dean's lot pass for the week?*

Please, I type. *Thank you.*

I slip my phone into my bag, start the video, and angle the camera toward the floor. The little red light at the corner of the screen feels like a talisman. I put on the mask and the sunglasses and crack the side door.

The cold air hits first. Then the voices. Distant at the front of the house, bright and hungry.

I lock the door behind me and move along the side yard, close to the hedges. The grass is damp against my shoes. My breath sounds too loud inside the mask. I cut through the gate and step into the driveway.

They see me.

"Mrs. Roberts," a woman calls, already walking toward the lawn, heels sinking into damp earth. "Do you have a comment on the discovery of Constance Keller's body?"

Another voice. "Did you confront her about the affair, Mrs. Roberts?"

"Was your husband abusive?"

"Did you ever threaten Ms. Keller?"

The questions fling themselves at me like gravel. I keep moving. I do not look at faces. I do not break stride. I hold my bag close enough to feel the phone hum against my palm.

"I have nothing to share," I say, even and low.

"Did you know Ms. Keller was seeing someone else?" a man shouts.

"I have nothing to share."

"Did your husband tell you where he was that night?" someone else asks.

"I have nothing to share."

The key fob beeps. My car unlocks. I open the door, slide in, and shut out the noise in one blessed click. My hands shake, but the mask hides the worst of it. I keep the camera rolling on the passenger seat as I start the engine and back out slow. No one blocks me. They know the line. They have their footage. They will use it anyway.

At the stop sign, I check the mirror. A sedan eases off the curb behind me. Another pulls away from farther down the block. I turn right instead of left. Then left instead of right. I vary my route the way Jenna said. Two turns later, only one car remains. At the next light, I change lanes and let a delivery truck slide between us.

When I hit the main road, my phone buzzes in the bag. Jenna: *Security confirmed. They will be at the back lot at 8:20. Do not go to your office first. Text me if anyone follows you.*

Another buzz. Damien: *Breathing with you. Let me know about lunch.*

I glance at the mirror again. The sky is pale. The road wet. Curls settling against my cheeks, a curtain of ordinary hiding the chaos. I grip the wheel and keep going.

Today I will teach in a pink suit and pretend I do not hear the whispers. I will answer only to my name and to my lawyer. I will not break on camera.

I will survive the next hour, then the one after that. Then I will see what the day brings.

Chapter Thirty-Nine

Campus looks almost normal from a distance: brick and glass catching the weak morning light, maple leaves beginning to flare red. But as I roll past the main gate, it's obvious nothing is normal. Clusters of students stand in tight circles, phones up, eyes darting toward my car like I'm part of an exhibit. Two men with badges I don't recognize linger by the student union, a camera bag at their feet. A woman in a fitted blazer walks backward, lips moving in practiced concern as her cameraman tracks her every step.

I park in the back lot, bay three, exactly where Jenna told me. Campus security waits inside the service entrance—two officers who look more like kindly uncles than muscle. One holds the door open as I slip through, sunglasses and mask in place, phone camera already recording like a talisman.

"Professor Roberts?" the taller one asks, voice pitched low.

"Yes," I answer. It feels safer than *that's me*.

"Dean's office asked us to walk you to your building," he says. "Lot's a circus up front."

"Thanks," I manage.

The halls smell of floor cleaner and old paper. Silence inside is a different kind of loud—the echo of my heels, the drum of my pulse.

When we turn into my department, Carlos is waiting outside my office, hands clasped. His tie is straight; his face is not.

"Lo," he says, relief and dread braided together. "Can we talk?"

The officers fall back, pretending not to listen. I slip the sunglasses into my bag. "I have class in fifteen."

"I know. Just a minute."

We step inside my office. It's the same cramped square of calm I left last week: books stacked two deep, a cardigan draped on my chair, a plant still fighting for life. Carlos shuts the door carefully, as if the air itself might break.

"I'm sorry to do this now," he says. "But we need to address the situation." He gestures vaguely—outside, the reporters, the whispers, the shadow of Constance's face across campus. "Our students are anxious. Faculty are fielding questions. Public Safety has concerns."

"And optics," I say before I can stop myself.

His eyes flicker. "We need to protect you," he corrects, careful. "And the school. It's a very visible moment."

My throat tightens. "I'm here to teach. That's the one thing I can still do."

"You will," he says. "Today. But after that..." He exhales like every word has weight. "We're asking you to take the rest of the week off. Paid. A wellness pause. We'll cover your sections."

A wellness pause. The phrase bruises.

"This isn't about guilt," he adds quickly. "You're not under any institutional investigation. It's temporary. Until after this initial announcement or the memorial next week."

"It won't calm by then," I say flatly.

"I know. But it's also about safety. There are reporters at every gate. We can't guarantee you won't be ambushed. Or filmed. And one wrong clip could spiral."

I don't need him to finish. I've already seen the thumbnails: *Professor at Center of Scandal Snaps at Student.*

"Halo," he says, softer, the voice I remember from retreats and the day he hired me. "Teach this morning. Then go home. Let us handle the rest."

There's no answer that won't split me open. "Fine," I whisper.

Relief loosens his shoulders. "Thank you." He glances at the clock. "Security can stay close to your room. Do you want me to make the announcement?"

"No," I say. "I'll do it."

He hesitates at the door. "If you need anything—"

"I'll call," I lie.

The officers reappear, quiet bookends, as students start to gather outside my classroom. Their voices are pitched higher, their laughter too quick, the effort of pretending normal. One boy leans against the frame scrolling his phone, but I can feel his eyes flick up at me. A girl whispers behind her hand until both fall silent when I approach.

The noise swells—the scrape of chairs, the thud of books, the rustle of papers. But the moment I step into the doorway, the volume fractures. Phones lift, sly angles catching me without asking.

"Good morning," I say evenly, setting my bag on the desk. "Let's get started."

I keep it dry on purpose. Structure. Stakes. A paragraph on tension that feels like autobiography. My voice doesn't falter even as their eyes press against me like heat. Two whisper in the back and pretend they aren't. A girl in front nods too eagerly. A boy asks how you decide what to reveal to keep readers hooked. I meet his eyes and answer like a professional: you reveal what serves the story, hold what the story cannot hold yet, never forget your reader is watching.

For forty minutes, I make it boring. I call on quiet kids. I let silence stretch until it chafes. I refuse to be a headline.

When the clock strikes, I close my notebook. "Before you go," I say, throat tight, "I need to let you know I'll be out the rest of the week. Professor Ames will cover your sections. Check your email for details."

A ripple moves through them. Whispers crest. A hand shoots up—the same boy, greedy for the headline. "Is it because of—"

"We're done," I cut him off. "Send assignment questions to the course email."

They file out. Some bolt. Some drag it out. A girl lingers by my desk. "Professor Roberts?" Her voice barely above the scrape of chairs. "I hope you're okay."

"Thank you," I manage. When she's gone, my legs go soft. I sink into the chair, pulse racing.

My phone buzzes. **Jenna:** I'm here. Side entrance by Facilities. Two minutes.

I text back: *On my way.*

Packing slowly so my hands won't shake, I slip the sunglasses on and mask up. The officers flank me again as we weave through crowded halls—faculty with clipped smiles, students whispering in our wake. The service stairwell smells of damp concrete. Somewhere above, a reporter's voice bleeds in through a cracked window.

We reach the Facilities door. The taller officer peeks out before holding it halfway. October air spills in with the distant clatter of voices.

Jenna waits at the curb, navy coat buttoned, sunglasses like a shield. She waves me forward without breaking stride, already moving toward the gray sedan.

"Professor," the officer says quietly. "We'll be around all week."

"Thank you," I say, meaning it.

I step out. The campus noise swells like weather gathering—questions, cameras, the low thrum of a crowd smelling blood. Jenna has the car door open before I reach it.

"Don't look left," she murmurs. "Get in."

The door shuts. The world muffles.

She drives with the confidence of someone who never second-guesses exits. Past dumpsters, loading bays, the back of a theater where a set is being painted blue. No one notices. The circus is at the front gates.

"You did what you needed," Jenna says, eyes on the road. "Well handled."

I peel off the sunglasses and press my fingers to my nose. My head feels packed with wool. "They asked me to take the week."

"I assumed they would." She doesn't soften. "They'll frame it as wellness and safety. It's optics."

"It feels like being peeled out of my life," I say, startling myself with the words. "Like they're making room for the story to swallow me."

"They're covering their flank," Jenna replies. "That's what institutions do. It doesn't mean you're guilty. It means they're scared."

"I'm scared," I whisper. "I don't want to go home."

"You're not. You're coming with me. You'll sleep, shower, not look out a window."

The knot in my chest loosens. "Thank you."

"Always. Two things: don't respond to press emails. Forward them to me. And if John calls, let it go to voicemail. If he shows up, call 911, then me."

"Okay."

She nods, satisfied. The rest of the drive is quiet but not empty. When we pull into her building's underground garage, I feel something I haven't in days: the edge of safety. It doesn't last—fear never lets it—but it's enough to carry me to the elevator.

As the doors shut, the image of the girl by my desk flickers up: *I hope you're okay.* Carlos's words echo, careful and padded, but still cutting.

The elevator dings. Jenna unlocks the hallway with her fob. "We'll regroup in an hour," she says. "I'll call Carlos about coverage. Draft a statement for your out-of-office."

I nod, throat tight.

She turns, finally meeting my eyes. "Lo. What they're doing is for them. What we're doing is for you. Don't confuse the two."

The doors open.

Her condo is clean and simple, not cozy but lived in. A stack of books by the armchair, framed prints on the wall, plants thriving despite her sixty-hour weeks. It doesn't embrace you, but it doesn't reject you either.

Jenna drops her bag on the counter, kicks off her heels with a sigh. "Tea, wine, or something stronger?"

I hover in the doorway, arms wrapped around myself. "Whatever knocks me out."

She raises a brow. "So, wine."

It tugs a brief smile out of me. But it dies quickly. "They looked at me like I'd already done it. Like I was just there to slip up."

"That's the job," she says, tugging glasses down from the cabinet. "They circle until you bleed. You didn't."

I sink onto the couch, still in my suit, body rigid. "It doesn't feel like enough."

"It never does," she says softly, pouring.

I hold the glass like it might break. The wine is dark, nearly black. One swallow does nothing to quiet the knot in my chest.

"They'll twist everything," I mutter. "Every word I say will get re-arranged until I sound guilty."

"Then I'll untwist it," she says. "That's my job."

The television clicks on. Constance's headshot fills the screen—too-bright smile, eyes startled by the flash. Beneath it, the banner scrolls: *Tragic Discovery: Local Professor Found Dead.*

The wine curdles in my stomach. I set the glass down too hard.

The anchors talk, voices pitched with false gravity: tragic, gruesome, investigation ongoing. They don't say how. They don't say where. But Ruiz's photos are burned into me, edges slicing through memory.

"She's not a headline," I whisper. My throat burns. "I mean, I know we had issues, but Jesus Christ... She's not a soundbite for them to wedge between car commercials."

Jenna mutes the volume. Silence is worse.

"She's gone, Lo," she says carefully, "and sadly, the press will make her a spectacle. It's what vultures do."

I press my palms into my eyes until sparks bloom. "John's probably loving this. Playing the accused cheating husband, the betrayed man, whatever makes him look softer. Meanwhile I'm shoved out of my class-room like I'm the danger."

"Don't give him that power," Jenna snaps back. "The college is cov-ering its ass. That's all this is. But it's not about him unless you let it be."

I drop my hands, stare at the screen again—Constance's smile frozen too alive. My chest feels like a rubber band stretched to breaking.

"Everybody's watching," I murmur. "The cops, the college, the reporters. Waiting for me to trip."

"Then don't," Jenna says simply, settling beside me. "You hold. I'll do the rest."

The TV flickers: yellow tape, trees, anchors mouthing speculation.

"She deserved better than this circus," I say.

"She did," Jenna agrees. "All victims do."

I drain the glass, but it doesn't soothe. "I can't stand that John's out there spinning this while I'm shoved aside."

"Optics," Jenna reminds me. "Not truth. Optics fade."

"Tell that to the cameras outside my house."

She exhales, turns the TV off. "Then we make a plan. Tomorrow, you don't step outside without telling me. You don't speak to the press. If they push, you call."

It should sound protective. Instead, it makes me feel smaller.

"How did my life turn into this?" I whisper.

Jenna leans back, blue eyes steady, equal parts steel and tenderness. "Because other people made choices they couldn't live with. That's not yours to carry."

Her words sting, but they steady me too. Because I am carrying it—every grotesque image, every whisper, every flashbulb. And one wrong move still feels like it will snap everything.

Chapter Forty

Jenna is still at work, and I can hear the hum of her refrigerator from the couch where I've been camped with my laptop for hours, pretending I'm answering emails but really only refreshing news tabs, like maybe one headline will finally make sense of my life.

I try John's number again, more out of habit than hope. It rings once, then skips to voicemail, that robotic voice telling me the subscriber is not available before the beep I never let myself get to. I hang up, stomach sour. He hasn't answered since the night we tore each other apart in the apartment. He hasn't explained. He hasn't even lied well enough to sound like he cared.

A push alert flashes across my screen, and my body reacts before my brain does, thumb pressing it open like maybe this time it's about someone else. It isn't.

College Dean Confirms VP John Roberts on Leave of Absence. Cooperating with Police in Keller Case.

The headline stares back at me in bold font, unreal, as if someone printed my private nightmare in block letters and pushed it across the world. Another alert pings before I can even process the first. VP steps back amid scandal. Then another: Roberts cooperating with police after mistress's disappearance. They are all running it, each outlet with its own flavor of sensationalism. The words blur together until the meaning is simple and sharp: John is no longer just my problem. He's public property now.

I slam the laptop shut too hard, the sound cracking through Jenna's living room like a shot. I press my palms into my eyes until stars burst against the darkness. My chest is heavy with something I can't name—shame, rage, grief—but underneath it all is the sick knowledge that I can't hide anymore. The story has legs. It's sprinting without me.

I flick on the TV even though I know better, the remote shaking in my hand.

And there he is.

John.

The footage is jerky, someone's phone camera catching him outside the apartment in the city. Reporters swarm the front steps, microphones jutting like weapons, their voices climbing over each other until it's just noise. He stumbles through them, shielding his face with one hand, muttering something I can't hear. His shirt is wrinkled, collar pulled half sideways, jacket falling off one shoulder like he put it on in a hurry. He looks drunk. I know that stagger, that loose jaw, the way his eyes don't quite land where they should.

Unshaven. Hair unkempt. The faint sheen of sweat on his forehead even though the caption on the corner of the screen says it's barely sixty degrees. His mouth moves, lips shaping words I can't hear, but the way his head jerks tells me he's cursing at them, telling them to get out of his way.

A woman's voice cuts clear in the din: "Mr. Roberts, did you kill Constance Keller?"

My stomach knots. The audacity of it, shouted like she's asking him about his schedule, not murder.

He doesn't answer. Doesn't even flinch. He fumbles with his keys, almost drops them, then shoves them into the lock wrong twice before the doorman steps in, gentle hand on his back, guiding him inside like a child too clumsy to make it on his own. The reporters keep shouting even after the glass doors close, their reflections warped across the surface like ghosts.

I can't look away.

It's grotesque. It's humiliating. And the worst part is the traitorous ache inside me, the one that makes me want to throw the remote at the screen and scream, but also the one that wants to pull him upstairs, shove a glass of water into his hand, cover him with a blanket before he combusts in front of the entire city. I hate myself for that ache. Hate myself for not knowing whether to scream at him or save him.

Because he was my husband. My partner. The man I built eight years with, brick by brick. And now he's unraveling in public like some tragic cliché, a man too obvious to be innocent and too pathetic to be guilty.

The anchors break in, their voices full of that false gravitas reserved for tragedy they don't actually care about. "We've learned that Vice President of Student Affairs John Roberts has taken a leave of absence from the university, citing personal reasons, though sources tell us he has been questioned by police multiple times regarding the disappearance of Constance Keller. Keller, twenty-six years old, was last seen leaving a restaurant near the Shady Oaks campus late Friday night. She failed to appear at a family event on Saturday, and her vehicle was found in a downtown parking lot. Colleagues describe her as dedicated, ambitious, and well liked."

The segment shifts, B-roll rolling across the screen. Constance's faculty photo, her smile too bright, dissolves into shots of the campus gates, the college seal gleaming in the morning sun, students walking past with their heads down as if they can feel the cameras in their spines. Then back to the anchors, who lean closer to the desk. "There is speculation about her relationship with Mr. Roberts. Some students report seeing them together on campus frequently, raising questions about the nature of their connection. Roberts has not been charged with any crime and continues to cooperate with investigators."

Speculation. Questions. The words slide under my skin like glass splinters.

I mute the volume, but the images stay burned in: John's wild eyes, Constance's too-bright smile, the reporters' microphones like bayonets.

My phone buzzes. A text from Sam: *You okay? Saw the news.*

I don't answer. Because I don't know.

The more I replay it, the more certain I am that people will believe John did it. Maybe he did. Maybe I've been making excuses for years, turning slammed doors and late nights into quirks instead of warnings. Maybe Constance pushed him one step too far.

I pace Jenna's condo, restless, barefoot on the hardwood. My reflection stares back from the glass balcony doors, pale and hollow, hair still wild from this morning's routine. I look like someone waiting for a knock on the door.

Why hasn't he called me?

If he's innocent, wouldn't he want me to know? Wouldn't he claw his way toward me, desperate for an ally? Unless he knows I can't save him. Unless he knows I wouldn't try.

The TV flashes again. A new clip, a student interviewed outside the library. She's clutching her phone like a lifeline, eyes darting nervously at the camera. "We all saw them together," she says. "Mr. Roberts and Ms. Keller. They were close. Like, too close. People joked about it."

The screen cuts to a boy in a hoodie, his grin too wide for the topic. "Honestly, he looked whipped. Always walking her to her car, always talking in low voices. I mean, we all figured something was going on. Guess we were right."

The anchors nod solemnly, feeding the story. Feeding the public. Feeding the beast.

My phone rings again. Unknown number. For a second I imagine it's Ruiz, calling me back in for another round, another stack of glossy horrors spread across a table. I let it go to voicemail. A reporter this time, bold enough to leave a message: *We'd love your perspective on Mr. Roberts, Mrs. Roberts. A simple comment, anything to set the record straight.*

Delete.

I collapse back onto the couch, knees to my chest, watching the muted loop again. Reporters shouting. John fumbling his keys. The doorman's hand on his back. Over and over, as if repetition will give me clarity, as if I'll find some hidden truth in the angle of his stumble or the tilt of his head. I want to scream at him through the screen: Say something. Defend yourself. Defend me. But he doesn't. He disappears inside, leaving the vultures to circle and me to drown in questions I cannot answer.

The man on that screen is not the John I married. He isn't the one who used to cook pasta at midnight, who kissed me with laughter still on his lips, who once drove three hours to surprise me with flowers because I said I missed home. That John is gone. This one is slipping away, and I don't know if I should chase him or let him fall.

By the time Jenna comes home, I'm still on the couch, still staring at the black screen long after I turned the TV off. She drops her keys and studies me for half a second, then clicks her tongue in disapproval. "Turn it off, Lo," she says, even though I already have.

"I can't," I whisper, voice ragged.

She sits beside me, posture sharp, presence steady. "He's circling the drain," she says. "And the press will be happy to push him under. But you don't go with him."

I want to argue. I want to say but he's my husband, as if that still means anything. But the words won't come. Because maybe it doesn't anymore. Maybe all that's left is pity tangled with rage, love warped into something unrecognizable.

I press my face into my hands and breathe through the darkness, but it doesn't clear. It only tightens.

Because John is slipping away, and the world is watching.

Chapter Forty-One

Jenna is still at her desk when I slip into the guest room with my phone. The blinds are shut tight, the muted TV in the living room murmurs about another "development," and my stomach twists. I scroll to Pax's number before I can talk myself out of it. He answers on the second ring.

"Lo," he says, voice rough like he hasn't slept. "You okay?"

I close my eyes. "I was going to ask you the same thing."

There is a pause, the sound of him dragging a hand down his face. "The cops pulled me in this morning. Questions, forms, the whole thing. They said I was the last person she texted."

My body reacts before my mind can argue, a brief drop like an elevator slipping a floor. The words hollow me out. "Were you?"

"Yeah." His laugh is sharp and without humor. "She wanted to come by. I told her not tonight. I thought she was just being dramatic, you know how she got when she felt cornered. I figured she would cool off." His voice breaks, then hardens. "And now she's gone."

I press my palm to my chest like I can steady my own heart. "They let you go?"

"They didn't have anything. They wanted to rattle me. I answered everything, swore on her grave, and they sent me home." His breath shudders. "John's the one they should be tearing apart, not me. He destroyed her. He paraded around with her like a trophy while still playing family man with you. He made her believe she was the one who would finally matter, and then he left her to bleed out."

The venom in his voice makes me flinch, but there is something else under it, a rawness that sounds like disbelief. "Pax," I say carefully, "we don't know what happened yet."

He exhales through his teeth. "I know enough. I saw her change before I understood why. At first she was lighter, like she finally believed she mattered to someone. But then it shifted. She got restless, frantic, like she was chasing something just out of reach. I didn't know it was him until after she disappeared."

The line lands like a stone in my stomach. He says it clean, without hesitation, but there's a bitterness that coats every word.

"I should have asked more questions," Pax mutters, voice low. "Should have dragged the truth out of her instead of pretending everything was fine. I should've—"

He cuts himself off, the silence between us jagged. I watch his jaw tighten, the effort it takes for him to keep whatever comes next locked down.

"You couldn't have known," I say, without hesitation. The words come easily, solid and sure. This isn't something I need to think through. He's my brother. I know who he is.

The tension eases just enough, settling into something heavy but bearable. There are things no one could have seen coming. This is one of them.

"I hate him," Pax says suddenly, low and certain. "I hate that he gets to stand there and act like he's the victim. I saw him on the news, looking drunk, all pathetic. People will eat it up. Poor John Roberts, his life in shambles. No one will say what he really is."

My throat feels dry. "And what is he, Pax?"

"He's a coward," he spits. "A liar. And if he had one ounce of decency, he'd admit it was his fault she's dead."

Something about the way he says it makes my skin prickle. Fault. Not guilt. Not killer. Fault.

"Listen," he says, softer now, the rage collapsing into exhaustion. "I know you've got enough on your plate. I... I can't stop thinking I should have gone to her that night—that maybe if I had said yes, she'd still be here."

"You can't do that to yourself," I whisper. "You didn't know."

"Doesn't matter," he says. "I'll never forgive him. And I'll never forgive myself."

The line goes quiet except for his breathing. My chest feels like it's caving in.

"Pax," I say finally, "I'm glad you're safe. I just... I needed to hear your voice."

"You always can," he says, gentle now. "But promise me something, Lo. Don't let him twist you up. That's what he does. That's what he did to her."

"I promise," I murmur, even as the words settle uneasily in my chest.

We hang up, the quiet rushing back in. His voice stays with me for a while afterward, steady and familiar, grounding in a way I didn't realize I needed.

***

Jenna's door clicks once and the condo exhales. I stand in the quiet for a count of ten, phone cooling in my palm, Pax's voice still vibrating in my ear. He sounded believable. He always sounds believable. Believability has always been his armor. Mine too, once. He also sounded like a live wire, hot enough to burn through whatever touches him.

I move to the kitchen and rinse a glass I don't need to wash. Running water helps. It's something I can control. My reflection in the window looks faint, grainy, like a woman I wouldn't trust in a lineup. I dry the glass, place it precisely on a coaster, and breathe until my pulse comes down.

Jenna emerges in stocking feet with two mugs and a tea tin tucked under her arm. She studies my face the way surgeons study scans. "How's your brother?"

"Stressed," I say. "They questioned him again and let him go." I keep the rest in my mouth: the last texts, his hatred for John, the guilt that leaked out and vanished like it had never been there.

"Good," she says. Not relief, just a note in the ledger. She sets the kettle on and flips the TV to the evening broadcast. The glow washes the room flat and cold.

Constance's photo fills the screen, her hair slightly off, her smile too careful. Beneath it, a new banner crawls: **Breaking Development.**

My stomach drops.

The anchor leans into her script. "We are learning more tonight about Vice President of Student Affairs John Roberts, who has taken a leave of absence as investigators continue examining the death of his colleague." Her voice softens. "Students tell us Roberts and Keller were often seen together. Sometimes late. Sometimes arguing. One student described Roberts as protective, another as quick to anger."

B-roll smears across her words. Campus gates. The quad. A flyer taped to a lamppost: **Candlelight Vigil for Constance.** A sticky note beneath it: **You mattered.**

They cut to a girl outside the library. She hugs a hoodie tight, eyes rimmed red. "He was always with her. Not inappropriate, just... always there. Watching. He didn't really talk to us. He looked past us."

Next, a boy on the student union steps, grinning too big. "I saw them arguing once. She yanked her arm back. He stepped closer. That's all I saw." He shrugs, satisfied. "Drama."

My tea rattles in its mug when the kettle clicks. I hate the boy for his shrug. I hate the camera for loving it.

Jenna pours without looking away. Steam ghosts up around my face. The anchor leans forward. "Detectives have also spoken to another close contact of Keller's. We are not naming that person because they have not been charged. Meanwhile, pressure mounts on Roberts to make a statement."

Close contact. Not named. Being unnamed feels worse than being accused. It means someone else gets to decide when you appear. The words scrape like a key across paint. I picture Pax in some gray room under brittle light, hands clenched, mouth drawn thin. *I told her. He ruined her.* His voice cracks in my memory. He almost said more. Almost.

My phone buzzes. Damien.

You okay?

Relief crashes into me like an open window on a heavy day. I type, erase, type again. *I'm fine.* Lie. Edit. *Hanging in.* Closer.

He replies instantly. *Saw the news. Want me to come by?*

A yes rises too fast. Wanting him feels less like desire and more like gravity. I swallow it. *Not home. At a friend's place.*

The typing bubble flares, stutters. *I wish you'd let me help. Even for an hour. I could drive. We could sit. No one has to know.*

Jenna slides her mug closer and catches my angled phone. She doesn't ask. "Work?" she says.

"Colleague," I lie. The word tastes metallic.

She lets it pass. Onscreen, cell footage plays: John stumbling through microphones, the doorman steering him inside. A reporter shouting, *Mr. Roberts, did you kill Constance Keller?*

I brace for pity. Instead I see my own hands tightening his jacket so he wouldn't shame himself. My own hand opening the door and letting him collapse through it. Both images flicker and vanish.

The anchor's voice cuts again. "Friends of Keller describe her as ambitious and under enormous pressure. One colleague, anonymous, said she had recently seemed afraid. She had been receiving messages."

Jenna swears softly. "Anonymous is doing a lot tonight."

"People love to hear themselves talk," I say. My voice shakes anyway.

The ticker scrolls: **Vigil set for Saturday. Family releases statement. Counseling offered.** My name isn't there, but I feel it ghosted underneath, waiting for the moment someone needs it.

Damien again: *I'm at the edge of town already. I can pick you up. Ten minutes of quiet. You don't even have to choose where.*

My chest aches with wanting. He's steady in ways no one else is. He's dangerous, but he's a raft. I type *Another night. Thank you.*

He answers with a single dot. A breath. Then nothing.

Jenna's phone lights. She frowns. "The college wants a statement. Something supportive, student-focused. You don't have to do it."

"Would it help?"

"It'll help them. It won't change anything for you." She nods at the screen. "Or out here."

On TV, a student shifts uneasily. "I saw Roberts yell at a groundskeeper once. He snapped. Maybe stress. I don't know."

I think of John's voice when it cut through walls. The slam of our door, the crack it left in the frame. The man who used to press his cold nose to my neck because he knew it made me laugh. He refuses to balance.

"Eat," Jenna orders gently. "Soup. Bread. You won't sleep, but you'll stay upright."

I tear bread without tasting it. The anchor recites the rosary of facts: last seen, car found, body discovered, phone and wallet nearby. Each word is a bead I can't stop touching.

Close contact. The phrase gnaws. Pax's voice in my ear again: *I told her not tonight. She would cool off.* The words are stones I keep picking up, setting down, trying to weigh.

I open my messages to him, write nothing. Anything I send looks like surveillance. My phone buzzes before I can decide.

Pax: *You still at your friend's?*

Yes.

Pax: *Need anything?*

I read it three times. Love and protection can wear the same face. A kindness or a cover. I can't tell which.

I'm okay. You?

Pause. Dots vanish, return. *I will be.*

I lock the phone and press it to my chest.

Jenna catches the motion. "Want me to call Ruiz in the morning? Ask him to stop feeding kids quotes?"

"They'll find someone else to talk to," I say. "There's always someone."

She tilts her mug against mine. The hollow clink sounds like nothing. "Then we make it boring. Bored reporters leave."

The screen shifts to a live shot outside the NYC building. A reporter stands where I once carried groceries while John fumbled the keys and laughed. Now she says neighbors heard shouting. That he's been asked to return to the precinct. I try to picture him walking through the doorway steady, shaved, sober. I can't.

Damien again. *I'm here if you change your mind.*

I type *Thank you.* Delete it. Type *Take care of yourself.* Delete again. I pocket the phone.

Jenna places a hand on my forearm. Firm. "Most of what you do won't be seen. Be careful anyway."

"I keep thinking about his keys," I say, startling both of us. "He used to miss the lock before speeches. He'd laugh, call his hands stupid. He didn't laugh this time."

"Because he knows how it looks," Jenna says. "And maybe because he is what it looks like."

I flinch. "Do you think he did it?"

"I think it doesn't matter what I think. What matters is you don't let it ruin you."

Her hand squeezes once, then pulls away.

Later, I stand at her window with the city washing blue below. A woman in a red coat smokes across the way, framed like a painting. Everything feels framed tonight. Cropped. Chosen.

My phone hums again. Pax.

Night sis. Love you.

I stare at the words until they stop being words. I think of him as a boy with scabbed knees and pockets full of pennies. I think of his voice an hour ago, how he said *fault* like it cut him to speak it.

Love you too. Sleep.

Onscreen, the reporter reminds viewers of Saturday's vigil. Anyone with information should contact the police.

Everyone wants something. The cops want answers. The press wants headlines. The college wants quiet. Pax wants absolution. Damien wants ten minutes.

I want the version of my life where Constance is alive, John is steady, and my reflection doesn't look like evidence.

The night presses against the glass. I let it. Holding is its own kind of endurance. I don't break. Not yet.

Chapter Forty-Two

After two nights at Jenna's, I tell her I need to go home.

She doesn't argue, not exactly. She studies me over the rim of her coffee mug and says, "Call if you change your mind," like she already knows I won't.

Her condo was safe. Clean lines, plants that refused to die, silence broken only by the news. But it wasn't mine. My things weren't there. My ghosts weren't there either, and part of me needed them—needed to be back inside the walls where everything had cracked, so I could touch the edges and decide if they were real.

The drive feels longer than it should. By the time I turn onto my block, I know why. Vans choke the curb. News 12. NBC. A channel I don't even recognize. Reporters lean against their cars with coffee cups, chatting like this is just another day at work. One looks up, notices me, and the group straightens like a flock of birds alerted to prey.

My stomach drops.

I inch past, pulse loud in my ears. A camera hoists onto a shoulder. Another car brakes too hard as the driver fumbles with their phone to record. By the time I pull into my driveway, the swarm is in motion. Microphones appear. Voices call my name.

"Mrs. Roberts, have you spoken to the police again?"

"Did you know about the affair?"

"Are you attending the vigil?"

"Do you think your husband is guilty?"

Each question slams against my windshield like hail. My hands lock around the wheel. For a second, I think about throwing the car in reverse and peeling out, but there's nowhere to go without making it worse, without becoming footage.

I slam the gear into park, grab my bag, and make a break for the front door.

Flashes pop, white-hot in my eyes. Questions overlap, tangled in static. Someone shoves too close, the smell of their coffee sour on their breath. My keys slip once, twice, before I jam the right one in.

The door opens and I stumble through, slam it shut hard enough to rattle the frame.

Silence.

Except not silence—my heartbeat hammering, my breath scraping. The muffled thrum of voices still outside, dulled now, like bees against glass.

I press my back to the door. I don't cry. I don't breathe for too long either. My body feels locked, as if still being watched.

This is home. My space. My safety. And yet it feels invaded, the air too thin, the walls too porous.

I peel myself off the door and wander room to room, checking locks, blinds, windows. The living room smells faintly stale, like no one has lived here in weeks. Mail piles on the counter. A plant droops in the corner, yellowing leaves curled inward like fists.

Upstairs, our bedroom looks the same but not. John's side of the bed is untouched, the pillow too neat. I want to rip it apart, shake it, scream into it. Instead, I sit on my side and let the mattress dip under me, the familiar weight pressing back like a memory that refuses to fade.

The TV remote is still on the nightstand. I grab it on instinct. The screen flares alive.

Constance's face fills it immediately. Not the headshot this time. A candid one—her laughing at some campus event, eyes bright, hair pulled into a careless ponytail.

The banner beneath her reads: **CANDLELIGHT VIGIL: COMMUNITY INVITED TO HONOR LIFE OF CONSTANCE KELLER**

Her name sprawls in capital letters, larger than life, larger than death. The anchor's voice drips solemnity. "The service will be held Saturday evening at the Riverbend Event Center. Friends, colleagues, and students are encouraged to attend. Organizers tell us it will be a chance to honor her legacy, to celebrate her contributions, and to offer support to her grieving family."

Footage cuts to students taping posters, arranging flowers, hugging each other in the drizzle outside the student union. Someone strums a guitar in the background, soft chords that sound rehearsed for the cameras.

My throat tightens.

I hated her. That's the truth. I hated the way she looked at John, the way she smiled like they shared something I didn't. I hated the fact that she did share something I didn't, and that she smiled about it anyway.

But she didn't deserve this.

No one deserves this.

The screen flashes to a close-up of a flyer taped crooked to a wall. **You mattered.**

I shut the TV off before my stomach flips inside out. The black screen stares back, my reflection pale, curls unruly, eyes too big. I look like someone waiting for a verdict.

I pace. Kitchen to living room. Living room to hall. Up the stairs, down the stairs. The house feels both too empty and too crowded. Reporters murmur outside like a pulse. Every time I pass a window, I'm sure one of them will be standing there, camera ready, waiting for the moment I crack.

By late afternoon, exhaustion settles heavy. I sink into the couch with my knees pulled up, phone clutched in my hands.

News notifications light the screen every twenty minutes. **No official statement from John Roberts. Unnamed person of interest questioned again. Memorial expected to draw large crowd.**

I scroll until my thumb aches. Every story circles the same points. They all land on John. His absence, his silence, his face caught mid-blink in a grainy photo outside the NYC apartment.

Pity and rage war inside me. Part of me wants to scream at him. Part of me wants to shield him, to shove him inside and lock the world out before he implodes on live TV. Loving him feels like a reflex my body hasn't learned how to shut off yet.

I close my eyes and imagine standing at the memorial. The candles. The faces turned toward Constance's family. The whispers when they notice me. The microphones lurking at the edges, waiting for me to break.

I don't know if I can do it.

I don't know if I can live with myself if I don't.

My phone buzzes in my hand, jolting me. A text from Sam.

You home?

Yes, I type back.

How bad?

I glance toward the blinds. A shadow moves outside. A camera clicks faintly. *Bad.*

Call?

I press the button before I can think. Her voice fills the line, warm, steady. "Lo?"

"Yeah." My own voice sounds scraped raw.

"You okay?"

"No," I admit. "They're everywhere. The house feels like a cage."

She hums softly, thinking it through. "Tomorrow. Lunch. My treat. Somewhere far enough away you can breathe. We'll talk. We'll plan."

Relief bleeds through me, fragile but real. "Thank you."

"Always," she says. Then, "And Lo?"

"Yeah?"

"Please try to eat something and remember to drink water. Get some protein in you."

My throat burns. I bite down hard, press my hand to my face until the sting passes. "Okay."

When the call ends, I curl into the couch. Outside, voices rise and fade. Inside, the house settles around me like a question I can't answer.

Tomorrow, I tell myself. Tomorrow I'll leave these walls, even if only for lunch.

Chapter Forty-Three

The restaurant smells like onions and fryer oil, the kind of smell that settles into sweaters and refuses to leave. Forks scrape against chipped plates. A baby fusses in the booth behind me, soothed by a tired-looking mom. Somewhere near the bar, a man argues with the Mets game on the mounted TV like the outcome will change if he yells loud enough.

Life is happening here. Ordinary, mundane, messy life. And I am sitting in the middle of it with a stomach that feels lined in glass, waiting for someone to drop a stone. My shoulders stay lifted, braced for impact that doesn't come.

Nassau County is only an hour from Shady Oaks, but it feels like another country. No reporters in the parking lot. No students whispering as I pass. An array of strip malls and neon signs, the rumble of the Long Island Expressway outside. Distance buys me air. Not much, but enough to swallow without choking.

Sam slides a glass of water across the table to me. "Drink," she says. It isn't a suggestion.

I take a sip, then another. The water tastes faintly of metal, but it settles my throat. My hands stop trembling enough that I notice. "Thank you."

She studies me with the same look she uses on patients who pretend they're fine while bleeding under the skin. Her curls are pulled back in a knot, a pair of readers perched on top of her head though she isn't using them. Always ready. Always steady.

I pick at the napkin until it frays at the edge, the tiny tearing sound oddly satisfying. "I want to go tomorrow."

Her eyes don't flicker. "To the memorial."

"Yes." The word comes out harder than I meant. I feel it hit the table between us. I soften it. "I should go. I need to."

Sam leans back, arms crossed loosely over her chest. She doesn't argue right away, which makes my stomach tighten. Silence with her always means she's turning the thought over, testing for cracks. I hold my breath without meaning to.

Finally, she says, "Are you sure?"

I expected it. I still flinch. "I knew her. Not well, not enough, but enough. It would be worse not to go." Worse to stay invisible. Worse to let fear decide.

"You don't owe anyone that," she says.

"That's not what this is." My fingers knot in the frayed napkin, twisting until it threatens to tear clean through. "This isn't for them. It's for me. And for her."

Sam nods slowly, like she's measuring how much of that I believe myself. "Then I'll come with you."

I exhale, shaky, the tension spilling out of me in one long breath. "You don't have to."

"Of course I do. You think I'd let you stand in that crowd alone while every eye cuts into you like you're next on the chopping block?"

Her voice is gentle but fierce enough to make something hot sting behind my eyes. I blink hard, steadying. "Thank you."

"Always," she says.

A waitress drops two menus in front of us with a distracted smile. "Specials are on the board. I'll give you a few minutes." She's gone before we answer.

Sam doesn't touch her menu. She keeps her gaze steady on me, like she's waiting for the next thing to crack open.

I pretend to read mine. Words blur. Burgers. Pasta. Soup of the day. None of it matters. My appetite is a ghost I can't resurrect.

"What about John?" she asks quietly.

The menu lowers before I even think. "What about him?"

"Do you think he'll be there?"

The question slices sharper than I expect. For a moment, I picture him walking into that chapel, shoulders hunched, tie askew, eyes bloodshot and pleading. Reporters swarming like gnats. Microphones shoved in his face. The grieving man. The betrayed man. The accused man. All masks he could wear with equal ease.

But then I shake my head. "No. He won't. Not after the footage. Not after the cops. He'll hide."

Sam arches a brow. "You sound certain."

"I'm not," I admit, voice thin. "That's the problem. With John, I never know anymore. He could disappear or he could throw himself in front of the cameras. Either way, it'll be about him."

"And you?"

I don't answer right away. My reflection stares back from the restaurant window, fractured by streaks where the cleaner missed. My curls are still damp from this morning, springing in wild coils no amount of cream can tame. I look like a woman pretending to hold it together because there is no other option.

Finally, I say, "I just want to stand there without flinching. I want to prove to myself, maybe, that I can."

Sam reaches across the table and rests her hand over mine. Warm. Solid. "Then that's what we'll do. We'll stand."

The words are simple, but they steady me more than anything has in days.

The waitress returns, pen poised. Sam orders soup and salad. I mumble something about a sandwich I won't eat. The waitress scribbles, whisks the menus away.

We sit in the lull of clinking silverware and low conversation. My nerves buzz louder than all of it, my body half-expecting someone to say my name too loudly.

Reporters are probably camped outside my house right now. Maybe more than before. The story has shifted from whispers to headlines. John's leave of absence. The footage of him stumbling into our building in the city, drunk, eyes glassy. Students calling him intense. Protective. Quick to anger.

The news has a way of sharpening suspicion until it gleams like truth.

Sam sips her water, watching me over the rim. "You look like you're somewhere else."

"I'm always somewhere else now," I say.

She doesn't smile. She doesn't tell me I'm being dramatic. She nods.

The baby behind us quiets. A song from the nineties hums through the speakers. Someone laughs too loud near the bar. Normal life insists on itself, relentless and indifferent.

I grip the edge of the table. "Do you ever feel like the world keeps moving, and you're stuck in place, watching it pass like a parade?"

"All the time," she says.

Her honesty cracks something in me, and I almost laugh. It doesn't come out right. It wobbles, half-broken.

The waitress drops our plates with the hollow clatter of ceramic. My sandwich is too big, piled high, meat sweating under the light. The smell turns my stomach.

I pick at the bread, tear it into pieces. "If I don't go, people will say I'm hiding. If I do go, they'll say I'm guilty. There's no version where I win."

Sam spears a crouton. "So stop trying to win. Show up because you want to. Leave because you're ready to. The rest is noise."

Her certainty is maddening and comforting in the same breath.

I chew a bite I can't swallow and finally set the sandwich down. "Reporters will be everywhere. They'll push microphones in my face. They'll ask if I killed her."

Sam's fork pauses midair. "And you'll walk past them. Because you don't owe them a thing. I'll be right beside you."

I close my eyes. Try to imagine it. Try to believe it without shaking.

Her hand finds mine again, squeezing tight. "Lo, listen to me. The memorial isn't about them. It isn't about John. It isn't about the cops .It's about Constance. If you want to honor her, then do it. Everything else is background noise."

My throat burns. I nod, because I can't speak without breaking. The word *honor* scrapes. This woman slept with my husband, smiled in my face, took what wasn't hers. Still, my body knows this ended wrong—no betrayal earns a grave.

The rest of the meal passes in fits and starts. I push food around my plate. Sam actually eats. She tells me about a patient who brought her cookies as thanks, about her neighbor's dog that keeps digging under the fence. Small things. Life things. I cling to them like driftwood.

When the check comes, she grabs it before I can reach. "You can get the next one," she says, already tucking her card into the sleeve.

We step out into night air colder than I expect. The street hums with traffic, headlights streaking past. A couple walks by laughing, their breath fogging white. Somewhere down the block, a siren wails and fades.

I hug my coat tighter. The sky is wide and dark, pressing down. "Tomorrow," I say quietly.

"Tomorrow," Sam echoes.

We stand there a moment, letting the night settle. My pulse is a taut wire, stretched too thin, but her presence anchors me.

I think of Pax, of his texts, of the word fault in his mouth. I think of John, maybe drinking in some dim apartment, maybe rehearsing his performance. I think of Constance's face frozen on every screen, smiling a smile she didn't mean.

Tomorrow, I will stand in the room where they say her name and pretend I belong.

Chapter Forty-Four

I sit at Sam's vanity in borrowed slippers, hair pulled into sections, twisting curls one by one until they lie the way I want them. My dress hangs on the back of the door: black, simple, chosen to blend into a crowd, not stand out from it. Not invite interpretation.

The guest room smells faintly of lavender and some kind of fruity plug-in, Sam's careful touches everywhere. I stayed here because my house had become a stage set, reporters staking out the front lawn, waiting to catch me leaving. Waiting to catch my face doing the wrong thing. Here, no one knows. Here, for a few more hours, I can pretend I am just another woman getting dressed for another obligation.

By the time we drive into town, the late afternoon sky has shifted to a dark, bruised gray. The Riverbend Event Center rises ahead of us, glass and stone catching what little light there is. It looks less like a funeral hall and more like the kind of place you'd hold a gala or a wedding. Intentional, I realize. Designed to be photographed. A beautiful backdrop to soften a brutal truth.

The building is two stories, modern but softened by details meant to comfort: wide glass doors framed in black steel, ivy climbing the stone façade, lantern-style lights glowing even in daylight. The entrance opens onto a courtyard landscaped with care, hedges trimmed into clean lines, flowerbeds spilling with late-season mums in shades of burgundy and gold. A fountain trickles at the center, its sound delicate against the hum of arriving voices. It is all very calm. Very controlled. Grief arranged so no one has to look at it too closely.

Inside, the reception area spreads wide, marble floors polished to a mirror sheen, a chandelier catching and scattering light across the room. To the left, a restaurant opens its doors, tables draped in white cloth, silver set in neat lines, a bar gleaming behind bottles of amber and clear. Waitstaff in black move silently, setting trays of hors d'oeuvres, arranging candles. It smells expensive. Like lilies and polish and something floral meant to soothe.

Straight ahead, double staircases curve upward to the balcony that runs the length of the second floor. From above, you can see down into the courtyard, a vantage point that feels both powerful and exposed. The railings are wrought iron, intricate scrolls softened by flickering candlelight placed at intervals. Already, people lean against it, looking down at the space where the memorial will begin. Watching. Always watching.

Everywhere, people are dressed in dark hues, but the effect is less somber and more curated. Grief, but styled. Mourning that knows it may be captured from the right angle.

At the far end of the hall, an easel holds a blown-up portrait of Constance. Her smile is wide, captured mid-laugh, hair gleaming under natural light. Beneath it, vases overflow with flowers, handwritten notes tucked between stems. A guestbook lies open on a podium, names scrawled across its pages, the ink still wet.

I feel the familiar, unwelcome contradiction settle in my chest. This woman slept with my husband. She lied to my face. She smiled while doing it. And still, looking at her photo, something in me resists the easy story. Whatever she did to my marriage, she did not earn this ending. Two things can be true, and neither cancels the other.

It is beautiful. It is classy. It is exactly the kind of stage you could grieve on and be photographed at in equal measure.

Sam squeezes my hand as we step inside. "Breathe," she whispers. "You're not alone."

But already, I feel the eyes on me. Not cruel. Not kind. Curious. Assessing. As if I am another exhibit they didn't expect but are determined to interpret correctly.

The hum of the room thickens as Sam and I move deeper into the hall. People cluster in twos and threes, leaning close as though grief is best shared in whispers. But I know better. Those glances, those pauses when I pass are not mourning. They are measuring. Taking notes. Deciding where I fit.

I catch the eyes of colleagues I recognize from faculty meetings: a history professor who once asked if I would co-lead a seminar, the librarian who always remembers my coffee order. Their faces soften when they see me, then harden again, like they do not know which version of me is safe to acknowledge. The widow. The wife. The woman who didn't know. Or the woman who did.

Carlos stands near the back with a knot of administrators. His tie is somber gray, his eyes restless, scanning the room like a man waiting for a crisis to break. He nods once when our eyes meet. Nothing more. No comfort. No distance. Just neutrality, which somehow feels heavier than either.

I look again, searching the clusters and corners. Every nerve in me expects to land on John. Expects the shape of his shoulders, the cut of his suit, his eyes darkened by whiskey and anger. I brace for the split second where the room will tilt around him.

But he isn't here.

The space where he should be is empty, and relief runs through me so sharp it almost hurts. Relief, followed immediately by the unease of knowing that wherever he is, he is being watched just as closely. Absence, too, is a statement.

The memorial begins slowly, the crowd shifting as ushers guide people to seats lined in rows facing the stage. The lights dim a fraction, a hush rolling across the room. On the stage, a college official speaks first, his words polished, rehearsed: devoted colleague, bright future, community in mourning. They sound like press release sentences. Safe. Hollow. Designed not to offend.

Then Constance's family takes the microphone. Her younger cousin stumbles through a poem she wrote in high school. An uncle reads a passage from scripture, his voice flat, eyes fixed on the words. My hands rest in my lap, fingers locked together so tightly my knuckles ache.

And then her mother steps forward.

She is a large woman with brassy blonde hair teased high, her black dress cut sharp at the shoulders. The mic nearly trembles in her grip, not from nerves but from fury. Even from the fourth row, I can smell the sour-sweet trace of gin on her breath.

"My daughter," she begins, voice ragged and too loud. "My girl was everything. She worked harder than anyone in this room. She deserved better than this." Her accent rides every syllable, pure Long Island, vowels dragged, consonants clipped. "She was taken from me, from all of us, and don't you think for a second we won't find out who did it."

The room stiffens. My jaw tightens until it aches. Heat blooms behind my eyes, sharp and sudden, and I have to blink hard to keep my vision steady. Her words crackle like static in the air.

"She told me she was scared," the mother goes on, eyes blazing now. "She told me someone was watching her. And now she's gone. So whoever you are, whoever you think you are, you will not get away with this. Not with my girl."

A ringing fills my ears. I press my palms flat against my thighs, grounding myself in the pressure, the fabric, the fact that I am still here. Somewhere behind the rage and grief, cameras adjust their angles.

Her voice breaks, but her rage does not. She slams the mic back into its stand, shoulders heaving as family rushes to steady her, to usher her back into the front row. A murmur runs through the audience. Discomfort. Fascination. Hunger. The anchors in the back corner lower their cameras for only a second before raising them again.

Sam leans toward me, her whisper a tether. "Hey... isn't that your brother?"

I follow her gaze.

In the shadow of the far corner, half-hidden by the iron staircase, Pax sways. His hair is braided down neat, but his shirt clings damp to his chest, as though he's been sweating. His eyes are glassy, unfocused, his body rocking on unsteady legs. My first instinct is not suspicion. It is panic. A sharp, physical fear that he will fall. That someone will notice. That cameras will pivot.

For a moment, I think he will tip forward into the crowd.

The world tilts. The mother's vow still hangs in the air, sharp as broken glass, and across the room, my brother looks like he is already falling.

***

Thankfully, after about forty-five minutes and a few glasses of water, Pax looks less unhinged. We've moved to the upper balcony and are standing near the railing, taking in the sun's slow setting. Orange and dark, purply grays fill our vision, and my mind betrays me, leaping to the gray, mottled skin from Constance's death photos. The image lands without warning, sharp and invasive. I bristle, wondering if I will forever be ambushed by those horrific flashes, my brain filing them under memory instead of mercy.

Pax assures us he's fine, his voice steadier now, and Sam and I make our way back downstairs, Sam stopping to use the restroom while I linger in a corner of the stairwell. The murmur of voices from the reception hall swells and ebbs like a tide carrying the weight of too many conversations. I press my back to the wall, trying to breathe through the press of images in my head—Constance's face, Pax swaying, the mother's vow—when a sharp voice cuts through the noise.

"*Her.*"

The word hangs in the stairwell, louder than it should be, jagged with accusation.

I freeze. My body locks before my mind can catch up, like a prey animal sensing teeth.

At the bottom of the stairs stands Constance's mother. Stocky, broad-shouldered, face flushed from drink or grief or both. She's gripping the railing, knuckles white, eyes locked on me with a focus that feels almost physical, like a hand around my throat.

"Her," she says again, pointing a finger up the steps. "That's the one."

Conversations outside the stairwell falter, thinning into silence as a few heads turn our way. The sound of clinking glasses and murmurs dulls under the weight of her voice. I can feel the room tilting toward us, attention sharpening.

My chest tightens. "Mrs. Keller," I start, but the words are brittle, already breaking apart in my mouth. I am suddenly, acutely aware of how alone I look standing here.

She climbs one step, then another, each one landing like a blow. "You think I don't know? You think I didn't hear what you did to my daughter? You threatened her. You screamed at her. She told me." Her voice quivers and rises all at once, grief spilling over into rage so fast it steals the air from the stairwell. "Now she's gone. And you're here. Walking around like nothing happened."

A hot, hollow shock spreads through my chest. This is what it looks like when grief needs a body to aim at.

I take a step back, instinct driving me down the stairs, trying to draw her away from the small crowd that's begun to gather. But she follows, relentless, her fury snapping off her like sparks. My pulse pounds so hard it feels visible.

"She didn't deserve this. She didn't deserve you or your husband!" she shouts, her voice thick with Long Island bite. "Everyone knew he was the problem. Everyone knew he was dragging her down. And you—" She jabs the air with her finger. "Did you want to solve your little problem by getting rid of mine?"

The words slam into me with such force my vision blurs. My brain scrambles, trying to separate accusation from reality, blame from possibility.

Gasps ripple through the cluster of people in the hall. Someone fumbles their phone out, the glow of the camera catching the edges of our faces. I register it distantly, like watching myself through glass.

My throat burns. "That's not true," I manage, but my voice is swallowed by the swell of her accusations. I can hear how weak it sounds, how insufficient denial is against a mother's grief.

"She *hated* you!" Mrs. Keller roars. "You wanted her gone. You couldn't stand that she had him. Now she's in the ground, and you're standing here like butter wouldn't melt in your mouth."

The crowd thickens, closing in, silence heavy with judgment. My pulse races so fast it feels like my body might lift right out of itself. Somewhere inside me, a quieter truth keeps repeating: I hated her. And she still didn't deserve this.

Then Sam's voice slices through the noise. "Enough!"

She pushes forward, eyes blazing, body angled between me and Constance's mother. Her hand clamps around my arm, steadying me, anchoring me to something solid before I can float completely away.

But the damage is done.

Phones are out. Eyes are on me. And the words—*did you want to solve your little problem by getting rid of mine?*—hang in the air, sticky and poisonous, already looking for somewhere to land.

***

Sam's car is parked at the far end of the lot, shadowed under a row of trees. The lights from the memorial hall glow faintly behind us, muted by the glass. The second the door shuts, I fall apart.

It's not quiet crying. It's violent, gasping, body-wracking, something that feels like it's tearing out of me from some bone-deep place. My chest heaves like it's trying to split open. I clutch at my stomach, at my face, anything to hold myself together, but the sound keeps coming, raw and humiliating.

Sam doesn't start the engine. She doesn't talk at first either. She lets me break. Then she leans across the console and grips my wrist.

"Lo. Breathe. Right here. With me."

I shake my head hard, throat seizing. "I can't. I can't, Sam. Did you hear her? She said I wanted Constance gone. She said—"

My voice shatters. The words collapse into another sob. I slam the heel of my hand against my thigh, furious with myself, furious with everything. "I shouldn't have come. I shouldn't have walked into that room. God, I shouldn't—"

"Stop." Her tone is sharp enough to slice through the spiral. Her eyes pin me in the dim light, steady where mine are wild. "You don't let her words take you down. She's grieving, she's drunk, and she's cruel because she's in pain. That doesn't make her right."

I press both palms into my eyes until I see stars, my body still trembling. "But I did threaten her. I said things to her on those stairs I can't take back. I—"

My breath snags, memory spooling out like barbed wire. Constance's sharp face. Her smirk. The way rage had boiled over and spilled from me like poison. "What if she was right? What if everyone thinks—"

Sam cuts me off again, quieter this time but no less fierce. "You're not a murderer, Lo. Don't let them write that story for you."

Her words scrape against the knot in my chest. I want to believe her. I want to climb into the safety she's trying to offer, but my body won't stop vibrating, every nerve still screaming that I've been exposed, stripped raw in front of too many eyes.

I slump back against the seat, fingers digging into the upholstery. My heart won't slow down. My throat feels like it's closing, a rubber band tightening around it. Even here, away from the crowd, I feel like I'm still standing under their stares, their whispers crawling across my skin.

Outside, headlights sweep across the windshield. For one horrible second, it feels like cameras have followed us out here too, like there's nowhere I can hide. I duck my head until the beams slide past, my body locked rigid, lungs stuttering.

The silence that follows is heavy, sticky, suffocating. The hum of the building, the faint tick of cooling metal in the car—it's all too loud.

And then it isn't silent at all.

It starts like a ripple, muffled through walls and glass, just enough to prick my ears. Then sharper. A voice raised. A collective intake of breath. Then a scream—high and jagged, slicing through the night.

The sound stretches, warps. For a split second it doesn't register as a scream at all, just a high ringing note that swells and swells until it drowns out everything else. The world feels half a beat behind itself, like I'm watching through thick glass. Sam's mouth moves, but I can't hear her. My hands don't feel like mine. Then the noise crashes back into place all at once, too loud, too real, snapping me hard into my body.

I jolt upright, stomach dropping like an elevator cut loose. "What was that?"

Sam's head snaps toward the building, eyes narrowing. Another scream tears loose, louder this time, tangled with shouts. The sound swells into chaos, the unmistakable surge of a crowd reacting to something awful.

A chill runs up my arms. My fingers curl into fists against my knees.

Whatever is happening in there, it isn't just grief anymore.

It's something worse.

Chapter Forty-Five

The first scream rips through the night, sharp enough to slice through the closed windows. Sam and I are frozen from it. A second scream follows, louder, shriller, echoing like it ricocheted off the building's stone walls.

We look at each other. Her knuckles are white on the steering wheel.

"Lo," she says. Just my name, but the weight of it carries a hundred unspoken things.

Then the third scream comes, and the sound is raw enough to peel the air.

For a split second, it doesn't register as a scream at all. It stretches, warps into a high ringing note that swells and swells until it drowns out everything else. The world feels half a beat behind itself, like I'm watching through thick glass. Sam's mouth moves, but I can't hear her. My hands don't feel like mine. Then the noise slams back into place all at once—too loud, too real—snapping me hard into my body.

Sam fumbles the window down. Cold night air slams inside, thick with chaos. Voices, footsteps, the unmistakable crash of chairs shoved aside. People pour out of the double doors of the hall, not in lines or clusters anymore but in a flood. Dresses snag on heels, suits hang askew, someone shoves past another, and the noise swells—panic, disbelief, hysteria.

The crowd pours into the courtyard below the balcony like water breaking a dam.

"What the hell," Sam breathes.

But I already know. Not the details, not yet, but I know the pitch of fear in those screams. I've heard it enough times in earbuds, through true-crime podcasts that narrate the unraveling of someone's life. This isn't grief. It's horror.

I push my door open.

"Lo!" Sam's voice is sharp, but I'm already out, my legs moving without me. Asphalt under my shoes. Cold air flooding my lungs. My chest is tight like a rubber band stretched too thin, but I can't stop.

The night smells of exhaust, perfume, something metallic I can't place yet.

More people spill from the doors. Voices overlap, jagged, frantic.

"Oh my god, is he dead?"

"Did he fall—did he jump?"

"Who is it?"

"Somebody call 911, for Christ's sake!"

Sam catches up beside me, matching my steps. Neither of us says anything. We don't need to. The noise is drawing us forward, toward the courtyard railing.

The crowd there has formed a circle, messy but magnetic. People are half-shielding each other, half-craning to see. A few phones are raised, camera lights cutting through the dusk like interrogation beams. I hear someone retching. Another sobbing. A woman says over and over, "Oh god, oh god, oh god."

Sam grabs my arm. "Lo, maybe we shouldn't—"

But I can't stop. I push forward until the bodies part enough for me to see.

The sight hits me like a blunt instrument.

A man lies face down on the pavement. Too tall to be anyone small, too broad to be frail. His limbs are bent at grotesque angles, twisted like a puppet whose strings have been cut and yanked at the same time. One arm juts wrong from the shoulder, his legs splayed in a way no living person could arrange. His jacket is bunched, collar nearly over his head, spine making a broken line under the fabric.

And then there's the blood.

It pools from beneath his body, thick and spreading in a fan across the concrete, a stain blooming wider with every second. Dark. Shiny. Wrong. The smell catches then—iron, raw and unmistakable.

For a heartbeat, I don't recognize him. It's a body, a crumpled ruin. Then my brain catches a detail: the shoes. Expensive leather, scuffed at the toes, but I know them. I bought polish for those shoes once. I remember him bragging about the brand, about how they lasted forever.

Recognition slams in like a car crash. The slope of his shoulders. The long line of his legs, even broken. The expensive jacket. The hairline at the back of his neck.

It's John.

For a second, the name doesn't land. It skids, refuses to stick. My brain slides right past it like it's protecting me from the impact.

Then my stomach drops. Hard. Cold floods my veins, sharp and immediate, like I've been submerged. My vision narrows. Sound dulls, as if someone has stuffed cotton into my ears. Every muscle in me screams no, but my eyes won't let go.

I hadn't seen him arrive. I hadn't thought he would. My mind keeps insisting there must be a mistake, that this is a body shaped like him, dressed like him. But he's here, and he's—

"Oh god," I whisper, though it barely sounds like language. My throat feels flayed raw.

Sam digs her nails into my arm. "Lo. Don't. Don't go closer."

I don't answer. I can't. My body won't obey me in either direction. I'm not moving forward or back. I'm locked in place, every joint seized, like my feet have fused to the ground.

My chest is hollow, a vacuum where breath should be, echoing with the questions ricocheting around us.

"Is he dead?"

"Did you see what happened?"

"Did he jump?"

"Who pushed him?"

The words don't mean anything yet. They're just noise, stacking on top of each other, piling up without shape. Phones flash. Someone shouts for an ambulance. Somewhere, a siren starts—distant, unreal, rising and falling like it belongs to another night.

And then something cracks.

Air punches back into my lungs too fast. My hands start to shake, violently, like they're trying to fling something off. Heat surges up my spine, sharp and nauseating. My vision blurs, then swims back into focus, cruelly clear.

I can't tear my eyes from the ruin on the ground. From John.

The man I married. The man I hated. The man I once would have thrown myself across fire for.

My chest caves in. A sound tears out of me before I can stop it—too loud, too broken, not a word at all. My knees buckle, and if Sam doesn't catch me, I'm not sure I stay upright.

Nothing is left but this shattered shape, bent in ways no body should bend, and the unbearable truth slamming into me all at once.

The world isn't collapsing anymore. It already has.

Chapter Forty-Six

The sirens slice through the night before I even register that I'm screaming. My throat burns, raw, but I can't stop the sound from tearing out of me. My knees hit the concrete beside John's body, hard enough to jar my bones. My hands hover, useless, trembling inches above him.

He's broken. Bent. Blood pools thick and black beneath him.

Someone grabs my shoulder. "Ma'am, please—"

I twist away. "That's my husband!" My voice fractures. "That's my—"

The word won't finish. My chest collapses inward, breath punched clean out of me. My vision tunnels, narrowing to the jagged angles of his limbs, the way his head tilts wrong against the pavement.

The crowd surges. People press closer, craning, phones already raised. Flashes rip through the dark, white and merciless. I want to knock every screen from their hands, smash them into the ground. How dare they. How dare they turn him into this—into footage, into proof, into a body for consumption.

"Back up! Back up!" a uniformed officer shouts, arms spread wide. More cops flood the courtyard, barking orders, forcing the onlookers back.

Red and blue lights strobe across everything, warping faces, turning the night sickly. Paramedics drop beside John, voices clipped and urgent, hands moving with brutal efficiency. One checks his neck. Another fits an oxygen mask over his face even though his mouth hangs slack, blood streaking his jaw.

I rock forward on my knees. "Please," I beg. "Please help him."

One paramedic glances at me. His eyes don't soften. They don't need to. I see the answer there, already decided, already sealed.

"Lo." Sam is suddenly beside me, arms wrapping tight, trying to pull me back. I can't move. I'm locked in place, my body refusing every instruction except stay.

Then one of the paramedics straightens.

His voice is loud. Final. "Time of death, 20:47."

The words don't land all at once. They echo, hollow, like they're bouncing around inside an empty room.

Dead.

Declared. Official.

The officers move faster now, efficiency snapping into place. Two of them grip my arms and haul me upright.

"*No!*" I thrash, the sound tearing out of me. "Let me stay—let me—"

"Ma'am, you can't be here," one says, voice firm, practiced. "We need space. You need to step back."

They pull me away. My heels scrape uselessly against the concrete. My hands reach for him, grasping air as the distance widens. I lose sight of his face. All I see is the stretcher, the straps, the way his legs hang too loose as they lift him.

My scream collapses inward. My ribs ache with the force of it, but no sound comes out.

The courtyard boils with voices.

"Did he jump?"

"No, someone pushed him—I swear I saw—"

"Oh my god, that's Roberts—"

"They're not letting anyone leave—"

A megaphone crackles. "Everyone stay calm. Nobody leaves until we've spoken with you."

The noise slams into me from every angle. I press my hands over my face, but it doesn't block anything. John on the stretcher. Blood smeared across the pavement. The straps cinched tight over his chest like he might still move.

My stomach heaves. I fold forward and retch, bitter acid burning my throat as it hits the ground. Sam's hand rubs my back, murmuring something I can't hear. My ears ring. The world feels thin, unstable.

Cameras still flash.

"Mrs. Roberts, did you see what happened?"

"Were you with your husband when he fell?"

"Do you believe he jumped?"

The words make me nauseous. Vultures. Parasites.

I wipe my mouth with the back of my hand and stare at the dark stain spreading across the concrete.

Nothing fits. John unraveling. John stumbling past reporters. John fumbling his keys. John falling—or being pushed.

My brain scrambles for order. There is none.

Police begin pulling people aside, taking statements beneath the pulsing lights. The air smells like gasoline and something metallic—blood, sweat, fear.

An officer approaches. "Mrs. Roberts, we need you to come with us."

I nod. The movement feels delayed, like my head is lagging behind the command. My mouth tastes like iron. My legs barely register the ground.

They guide me into the back of a squad car. Sam stays close until the door shuts, her face the last thing I see.

At the station, the fluorescent lights hum, invasive and relentless. Ruiz sits across from me with another officer I don't recognize. His gaze is steady, assessing.

"Mrs. Roberts," Ruiz says gently. "Tell us what you saw tonight."

I give them fragments. The balcony. The screams. The body. My voice dies when I reach John. The pen keeps moving anyway.

When they finish, Ruiz leans back. "We'll need to search your home. For any notes. Anything that might explain this."

"Explain?" A broken laugh slips out. "You think he jumped?"

The other officer doesn't blink. "Given the circumstances, it's a possibility."

The room tilts. John—cornered, humiliated, swallowed by scrutiny—throwing himself into the night. Or someone else finishing what the pressure started.

I can't hold the thought. I can't breathe.

I excuse myself and call Jenna. My hands shake so badly I almost drop the phone.

"I'm on my way," she says immediately.

She arrives within the hour, solid and unflinching. Sam stays close, pale but grounded. Together, they hold me upright through the rest.

When it's over, when the questions finally stop, we step into the cold night. Sirens wail somewhere distant, unreal.

An officer pauses. "Mrs. Roberts—where has your husband been staying recently?"

"No," I say before he finishes. "Not home. The city. Our apartment on East 62nd. Midtown." My voice sounds mechanical. "We were having issues. He'd been there about two weeks."

The pen scratches fast. "We'll notify NYPD."

A note? The idea feels absurd. John never explained himself.

When the cruiser pulls away, Jenna already has her keys out. "Come on," she says, decisive. "We're not doing this on the curb."

I let them guide me forward, my body moving on borrowed strength, the night closing in around what's left of my life.

***

The three of us drift into my house like we're trespassing, even though my name is still on the deed. Nothing feels familiar anymore. Not the pictures on the walls, not the furniture we chose together, not the quilt draped over the couch. Everything hums with absence, the air thick with it.

Jenna moves first, purposeful, checking locks, windows, lights. Sam lingers in the living room, her gaze sweeping the stack of unopened mail, the coats slumped on their hooks, the blanket bunched at the end of the couch.

I remain just inside the doorway, numb. The last time John stood here, we barely spoke. He'd kept his jacket on, eyes glassy from too much bourbon, muttering something about being late. He never unpacked. He left again that night for Manhattan.

The memory slices clean and deep.

The house feels more like mine without him, and also impossibly emptier. His absence presses harder now that it's permanent, a weight that doesn't shift no matter how I breathe.

The police said they'd coordinate with the NYPD. That they'd sweep the city apartment. Look for a note. For something that might explain his state of mind. I picture strangers in gloves opening drawers, sifting through our life. His socks still rolled into pairs. His cufflinks resting in their dish by the bed. They'll look for handwriting. For intention.

"What if they find something?" I whisper.

Sam meets my eyes, gentle but steady. "Then you'll know."

"And if they don't?"

"Then you'll still know," Jenna says. Her voice is calm, edged with steel. "That man was not simple. Don't expect a neat ending."

I sink onto the couch, palms pressing into my eyes. My skull throbs, crowded with the day's images. John on the pavement. His name shouted by reporters. The word suicide hovering unspoken but everywhere.

Sam crouches in front of me, resting a hand on my knee. "We'll wait for the call from NYPD," she says. "You don't have to do this alone."

I nod, but it feels performative. Because no matter who sits beside me, when that phone rings, the truth will be mine to carry.

The night stretches, taut and breathless. Every sound in the house sharpens. The tick of the clock. The hum of the refrigerator. The low thud of my own pulse.

Waiting for news from Manhattan feels like waiting for a verdict.

We don't talk much after that. There's nothing left to say. John is gone. Dead. Maybe jumped. Maybe pushed. No one knows yet, and the police aren't offering answers.

Sam settles beside me, her hand warm on my arm. Her eyes hold something I can't quite name—fear, pity, maybe both. "You're not alone," she says quietly.

The words are meant to comfort. Instead, they echo. Because in the places that matter most, I am.

I pick up my phone, my hands still unsteady. One name glows on the screen.

Pax.

My thumb hovers, then presses. The line rings. Once. Twice. Three times.

His voicemail answers—rough, casual, unchanged for years. I listen all the way through, waiting for the beep, but nothing comes out of me.

I end the call.

The silence afterward is so complete it feels like another body in the room.

Sam squeezes my arm. Jenna sets the untouched tea on the table. None of us speak. None of us know how.

I pull the blanket around my shoulders, the phone heavy in my hand, and breathe around the truth pressing in from all sides:

My husband is dead. Constance is dead.

Every single part of me is bracing for whatever comes next.

Chapter Forty-Seven

The morning doesn't fit.

It comes in soft and golden, a perfectly ordinary fall dawn, the kind where the air feels sharp enough to clear your head if you let it. Birds scatter across the yard. The neighbor's sprinkler hisses, rotating in its lazy arc. Somewhere down the block, a dog barks—sharp, repetitive.

Sam is still asleep upstairs. Jenna left before dawn, heels clicking against the tile, already shifting into lawyer mode. I nodded when she whispered that she'd call later, but I don't remember the words. Only the emptiness after the door closed.

I sit on the patio with my knees pulled to my chest, a mug of coffee cooling between my palms, and none of it feels like mine. Not the birds. Not the sprinkler. Not the dog. Not even this house, though I've lived here long enough to know every creak in its floorboards.

Because inside, John's toothbrush is still in the cup. His jacket still hangs on the hook by the door. His shoes are still lined up by the mat. Evidence of a man who will never come home again.

And outside, the world is already deciding who he was, what he did, why he died.

I scroll through headlines until my vision goes fuzzy.

John Roberts, College VP, Found Dead After Weeks of Scandal. Did Pressure Push Him Over the Edge? Memorial Marred by Tragedy.

The words blur, rearrange themselves. They've already labeled it a jump. A choice. A headline packaged neatly for the morning broadcast.

But I was there. I saw the chaos, the screams, the way people covered their mouths as if sound itself were poisonous. I saw his body twisted below the balcony—but I didn't see him fall. No one did. Not really.

My stomach tightens. What if someone pushed him? What if I missed it by seconds? What if Constance's furious mother followed through on her promise?

I press the mug to my lips, but the coffee is cold now, bitter sludge that scrapes my tongue. I set it down, grip the arms of the chair, and tell myself to breathe.

Two nights at Jenna's condo were all I could manage before the walls started to close in. I needed my own bed, my own bathroom, my own silence. Now, in the thin morning light, I wonder if that was a mistake. The reporters haven't swarmed yet—not since the memorial—but I can feel them out there, idling in cars, waiting for the next angle.

I pick up my phone before I can talk myself out of it and dial Ruiz.

He answers on the second ring, voice clipped, already in motion. "Mrs. Roberts."

"Why are they saying he jumped?" My voice cracks on the last word. "The news. Every station. They're all saying it was suicide."

A pause. Then, "We haven't confirmed that."

"But they're running it everywhere."

"I know." His tone softens, just a fraction. "The autopsy is scheduled for ten this morning. Until then, the cause of death is undetermined."

"Then how—" I stop, digging my nails into my thigh. "How can they just... decide?"

"Speculation sells," he says flatly. "Don't read into it. We'll release an official statement once the medical examiner reports back."

My throat is dry. "Do you think... do you think he—"

"I can't share theories," Ruiz cuts in. "We have one lead we're pursuing, but that's all I can say. For now, hang in there. Stay close to your people. Let us do our job."

A lead. The word punches me in the gut. "What kind of lead?"

"Mrs. Roberts." His voice sharpens. "That's all I can share."

I close my eyes. "Okay."

"We'll be in touch after the autopsy." He hangs up before I can ask anything else.

I set the phone facedown on the table. My hands won't stop trembling. A lead. Does that mean a witness? A camera? Or did they find something at the scene no one told me about?

My mind loops back to Constance's mother in the stairwell, her face red and furious, her voice lodging in my bones. *Did you just want to get rid of your problem?* The way her finger jabbed the air, spit flying with every word. She could have gone up there. She could have shoved him over the railing and called it justice.

Or maybe John couldn't take the weight anymore. Maybe he leaned forward and let gravity finish what the whispers started.

I don't know which thought makes me sicker.

The patio door slides open behind me. I flinch, but it's only Sam—hair a messy halo, one of my old sweatshirts slipping off her shoulder. She squints against the light, barefoot on the deck.

"You're up early," she murmurs, voice still thick with sleep.

"Couldn't... not." My throat feels scraped raw.

She pulls out the chair beside me and sinks into it with a quiet sigh. For a long moment, she just sits there, eyes on the street, the hush of morning stretching between us. Then she reaches for my mug, takes a sip, and grimaces. "Cold."

I laugh, but it's hollow.

Sam sets the mug down and looks at me fully. "You've been staring holes in the air since I came out here."

"The news," I whisper. "They're all saying he jumped."

Her expression tightens. "And you're believing them?"

"I don't know what to believe." The words spill out before I can stop them. "I keep seeing him lying there. I keep hearing people scream. But I didn't see him go over. None of us did. What if it wasn't him? What if someone—"

"Lo." Sam's voice cuts steady, her hand closing around mine. "Breathe."

I inhale, shaky. The exhale feels like it might split me open.

"You don't know yet," she says. "Nobody does. The cops will figure it out. You can't fill in every blank before they do."

Her hand is warm, anchoring me, and I want to believe her. But the images keep cycling: Constance's body bent in the mud. John crumpled on the courtyard stones. My brother swaying in the corner, eyes glassy, unmoored. Every piece feels connected, even if I can't see how yet.

"I don't know how to do this," I admit. "I don't know how to sit here drinking coffee while everyone else is out there deciding who I am, what I did, what he did."

Sam squeezes my hand tighter.

The sun climbs higher, spilling light across the yard, but it doesn't warm me. My skin feels thin, my insides raw. I rest my head against her shoulder and let the quiet hold us for a minute, just long enough to remember I'm still here.

***

By late afternoon, the house feels heavy, like it's swallowed all the voices that used to move through it. Sam is still here, padding around in socks, pretending to tidy things up. She moves glasses from one counter to another, straightens throw pillows I never noticed were crooked. It's her way of trying to hold the walls steady while my insides tilt.

When the knock comes—sharp, deliberate—both of us freeze.

"Reporters don't knock that politely," Sam says after a beat. She's already moving toward the door.

But when I pull the curtain back, it's Detective Ruiz. His suit looks like it's been slept in, his tie loose, his face carved deeper than I remember. Behind him, a squad car idles at the curb, lights off. He doesn't look like a man here to break news for cameras. He looks like a man here to bury it in me.

"Mrs. Roberts." His voice is flat, practiced. "Can I come in?"

Sam hovers close as I open the door. "Yeah. Of course."

He steps inside, scans the entryway like it might reveal secrets, then follows me into the living room. Sam sits across from him, arms folded, a shield in human form. I lower myself into the armchair, knees pressed tight together. My hands twist in my lap.

Ruiz opens his folder, glances at his notes, then looks at me. "The autopsy results are in."

My chest tightens. "And?"

"Your husband had a high blood alcohol content," he says. "Over twice the legal driving limit. He also had cocaine in his system."

Sam exhales a low curse.

My stomach drops, but part of me isn't surprised. I've seen John drunk—sloppy, mean. I've heard rumors, whispers that he dabbled when he traveled for conferences. I never wanted to believe them. Now it's ink on paper, cataloged in a lab report.

Ruiz keeps going, steady and clinical. "Toxicology doesn't tell us the cause of death, but it does tell us his state beforehand. Combined intoxication like that impairs judgment, balance, motor control. If he leaned too far over the balcony railing, the substances could explain why he didn't correct himself."

I taste bile. "So you're saying he jumped."

"I'm saying it's consistent with either a fall or a jump," Ruiz corrects. "But not all falls are the same. The medical examiner looked closely at the injuries. Certain patterns can indicate whether a body was pushed."

Sam leans forward. "Like what?"

"Defensive wounds," Ruiz says. "Bruising on the arms consistent with being grabbed. Skin under the fingernails if there was a struggle. Angle of impact—someone shoved from behind often lands differently than someone who leaned or climbed."

I close my eyes, force myself to breathe. Constance's photos flicker behind my eyelids. Now John's body joins them—twisted, bent—an image I won't be able to scrub away.

"What did they find?" My voice barely carries.

"No defensive wounds," Ruiz says. "But..." He pauses, his gaze narrowing. "There was a bruise across his upper arm. It could have come from being grabbed. It could have come from hitting the railing on the way down. We can't say with certainty."

Sam mutters, "Convenient."

Ruiz ignores her, eyes locked on me. "Mrs. Roberts, is there anyone you can think of who might have wanted your husband dead?"

The question splits something open.

I want to scream his name. I want to list them all—the reporters, Constance's mother, half the campus. Maybe even myself, on the darkest nights. But my mouth stays closed.

"People were angry," I say finally. "Constance's family. Her friends. Students. He... he wasn't kind when he was drinking. And if he was using—" My voice breaks. "I don't know."

Ruiz doesn't blink. "We received a statement from a witness. They said they saw Mr. Roberts arguing with a man six or seven minutes before he fell. They didn't get a clear look at his face. Possible hooded sweatshirt, male voice. That's all we got right now."

My blood goes cold.

Images collide: Pax in the corner of the hall, swaying, glassy-eyed. Pax muttering that he hated John—for what he did to me, for what he did to Constance. Pax sounding like he had things lodged in his throat that wouldn't stay buried.

Sam straightens, arms folding tighter. "So it could have been anyone."

"Anyone," Ruiz echoes. But his eyes linger on me, heavy with something he doesn't name.

I swallow hard. My throat feels scraped raw. "

Sam cuts in, sharp. "So what, you're going to line up every man in Long Island who owns a hoodie?"

Ruiz reddens as he snaps his folder shut. "We'll follow the lead. That's all I can say."

The room goes dense. My pulse roars in my ears. I can feel Sam's eyes flicking toward me, reading every twitch, every shadow. She knows I'm thinking it. She just doesn't know how close I am to breaking.

Ruiz rises. "We'll be in touch."

I stand too fast, knees weak, and walk him to the door. His hand lingers on the knob. "One more thing. If you remember anything—anything at all—about your husband's state of mind or who he might have spoken to that night, call me."

I nod. "I will."

He leaves, the squad car pulling away slow and silent. The moment the door shuts, Sam turns on me. "Lo. What was that look on your face?"

I press my back to the door, the wood cool against my spine. "I don't know."

"Bullshit." Her voice cracks with urgency. "You thought of someone."

I cover my face with both hands. My palms smell like soap, coffee, fear. My words come muffled. "Pax."

Sam stills. "Your brother?"

"He hated John. He said—he said things. He was there, Sam. At the memorial. Swearing he was fine, barely holding it together." My voice shakes. "What if it was him? What if he—"

"No." Sam cuts in too fast, too fierce. "Don't do that. Don't make that leap. You don't know what you saw. You don't know what Ruiz knows. Your brain is stitching monsters into every shadow because that's what trauma does."

But her eyes flick away—quick, unsettled—because she knows it isn't impossible.

I push off the door, knees threatening to buckle. "If it was him... if he pushed John..."

Sam grabs my arms, grounding me. "Then we'll deal with it. But not by destroying yourself before you have facts."

I collapse onto the couch, the air knocked out of me. Pax's voice echoes in my head—not dark, not damning. Just tired. *She would cool off. I told her not tonight.* Ordinary words, spoken without ceremony, now lodged in my chest like splinters. I don't know what they mean. I don't know if they mean anything at all.

That's what scares me most.

Everything sounds different once it's replayed through shock. Every memory bends. Every sentence shifts its weight. I can't tell what's real anymore and what my mind is rearranging to survive the pressure of it all.

I feel threadbare. Like if someone asks me one more question—one more *what if*—I'll come apart entirely.

Sam sits beside me, close enough that her warmth steadies the shaking in my bones. I lean into it because I don't trust myself to sit upright on my own. We don't speak. The silence isn't peaceful—it's strained, humming, stretched thin.

I stay very still, afraid that if I move, something else inside me will finally snap.

Chapter Forty-Eight

My phone lies face-down on the counter, a black slab I can't seem to touch. It's been almost two days since Pax's voice filled my ear, and the silence since has thickened into something heavy, suffocating. It presses on my chest when I wake up. It follows me room to room. Every hour stretches longer, denser—especially since the update from Detective Ruiz. Especially since everything stopped being hypothetical.

Finally, I flip the phone over. The screen lights my face too bright. My thumb hovers, useless, suspended above my brother's name like it's a fault line. My chest tightens, breath shallow and sharp, as if even this choice—whether to call him—might tip something I can't put back.

One ring.

Two.

My throat locks, bracing for voicemail, for the relief and disappointment all at once.

"Lo."

The sound nearly takes me down. His voice is raw, hoarse, stretched thin in a way that makes my stomach clench. It's still *him*, but frayed, like a wire stripped of insulation.

"Pax." My mouth tastes like metal. "Where are you?"

He exhales a sharp laugh, humorless. "Where do you think? Watching the circus. They're eating John alive on TV, and he's not even around to defend himself. Not that he deserves defending."

The bitterness scrapes like glass. I feel it catch under my ribs. My grip tightens on the phone, knuckles aching. "He's dead, Pax," I say. "He fell."

"Fell." He spits the word out. "That's what they're calling it? A man like him doesn't just fall."

A chill slides through me, slow and invasive, settling deep in my gut. My mind scrambles, trying to reframe, to soften. "What are you saying?" I ask, though part of me already wishes I hadn't.

"Nothing." Too fast. Too sharp. Then quieter, heavier: "Just that the world's better off with one less bastard pretending to be noble."

Something inside me twists. His voice carries an edge I've never heard before—not grief, not anger exactly, but something sharpened by both. Against my will, an image flashes: the balcony railing, John swaying, the empty air beyond it. My stomach revolts.

No.

Not Pax.

Not my brother.

I tell myself it's shock. That grief warps tone. That rage sounds different when it's been caged too long. But the thought doesn't release me. It hooks, digs in, refuses to stay hypothetical.

"Pax," I whisper, my voice smaller than I expect. "Were you there?"

The silence that follows is unbearable. It hums, high-pitched and electric, loud enough that I can hear my own heartbeat thudding in my ears. My skin prickles. I hold perfectly still, like movement might make whatever this is real.

When he finally speaks, it's with a hollow laugh. "You sound like them. Like Ruiz. Like the rest." A beat. "I thought you knew me better than that."

The shame hits hard and fast. I try to speak, to explain, but my words collapse before they reach my mouth.

"I gotta go," he mutters, clipped. And before I can catch him, the line goes dead.

I stand rooted in the kitchen, phone pressed to my ear like it's fused there, like if I move I'll shatter. My pulse races, loud and uneven, a warning bell I can't silence. The sick weight in my stomach won't ease.

I don't know if I imagined the danger in his voice. I don't know if it was always there and I just never needed to hear it before.
I don't know which version of him I'm supposed to believe—the brother I grew up with or the man who just sounded like he might light the match and watch it burn.

Jenna. I need Jenna.

She picks up on the second ring, her tone brisk but gentle. "Tell me you're okay."

"I spoke to Pax." My voice wavers despite my effort to keep it steady. "He sounded... different. Bitter. Like he knew something about John. About the fall."

A long silence stretches between us. I imagine her jaw tightening, her mind already mapping outcomes. When she exhales, it's controlled. Measured. "Lo, listen. If you keep this to yourself, it'll look like you're protecting him. And if anyone ties you to both John and Constance, you'll be right in the center of that storm. You don't want that."

The words land heavy. I press a hand over my eyes, shaking my head, the room tilting slightly. "But he's my brother. If I say something—" My voice cracks. "If I'm wrong—"

"You're not condemning him," she cuts in. "You're protecting your-self. You're telling the truth about what you heard. Ruiz decides what it means. That's his job, not yours."

Her logic is clean. almost surgical. It doesn't account for loyalty, or childhood, or the way loving someone rewires what you're willing to see. My throat tightens anyway. "So you think I should tell him."

"I think you have to," Jenna says firmly. Then, softer: "Don't spiral, Lo. You don't know what any of this means yet. All you know is your brother sounds like a man drowning. Ruiz will decide if anyone else was pulled under."

We hang up.

I sit there staring at my phone, drafting the text three separate times. Each version feels like a betrayal. Each version feels like a lie. My thumb finally commits before I can change my mind.

Detective Ruiz—this may mean nothing, but I spoke to my brother Pax tonight. He sounded bitter about John's death. It unsettled me. I thought you should know.

The second it sends, the phone feels heavier in my hand. Not relief. Not guilt exactly. Something closer to vertigo—like I've stepped off something solid and won't know the damage until I land.

I sink into the kitchen chair, staring at my reflection in the dark window. The glass warps me, stretches my face into something thinner, older, less certain. I barely recognize her.

I've told myself a dozen times that I didn't kill anyone. That I'm doing what I can to survive this. That telling the truth doesn't make me disloyal.

But right now, sitting alone in this quiet house, I don't feel innocent.

***

The phone rattling against the wood table jolts me out of whatever shallow half-sleep I'd slipped into. My hand jerks, nearly knocking the mug beside it onto the floor.

Ruiz.

My heart is already racing as I answer, throat dry before I even speak. "Detective?"

His voice is clipped, official, but not unkind. "Mrs. Roberts. I'm sorry to have woken you. I got your message about your brother. Thank you for letting me know."

The *thank you* lands wrong. Heavy. Final. Like a door locking somewhere behind me. For a split second, I want to take it back—to shove the words back into my mouth, pretend I never sent that text. "I don't know if it meant anything," I say too quickly. "He just... sounded bitter. Strange. It unsettled me, that's all."

"I understand." Papers shift on his end. The sound makes my shoulders tense. "Do you know where Pax is right now?"

Something tightens low in my body, instinctive and sharp, like an animal bracing. "No. Why?"

"Because he hasn't been home." Ruiz's voice firms, professional steel slipping through. "We had a unit sitting on his place. No sign of him since yesterday afternoon. His phone's pinging all over the county. He's moving."

The word *moving* hits me wrong. My stomach drops, hollowing out. My brain scrambles for explanations—work, avoidance, panic, anything that isn't what Ruiz is implying. "Maybe he doesn't want to be harassed," I say, breathless. "You've been questioning him. He probably just—"

"With all due respect, Halo," Ruiz cuts in, calm but sharp as glass, "your brother has a lot more to worry about than whether he did or didn't push John."

For a beat, the world stutters.

Sound dulls, like someone shoved cotton in my ears. The room tilts, just slightly, enough that I grip the edge of the table without realizing I've moved. My brain snags on the word *push*, refuses to process it. Push implies hands. Intent. A moment where choice exists.

I squeeze the phone until my fingers ache. "What... what does that mean?"

"I can't share details yet," Ruiz says. "But we're following a lead, and it's strong. Right now, I need to know if you've spoken with him again since the call you mentioned."

My head shakes before my mind catches up. "No. Only that one call." I hear how thin my voice sounds and hate it. Like a child trying to sound certain.

Silence stretches on his end. It presses against my chest, heavy and deliberate, as if he's letting the weight settle on me on purpose.

"If he reaches out again, Mrs. Roberts," Ruiz says finally, "I need you to contact me immediately. No hesitation. Do you understand?"

My mouth says yes before my body agrees. "Yes." The word feels borrowed, detached. Like I've just signed something without reading it.

"Good." His tone softens, barely. "I know this is difficult. But the sooner we find him, the sooner we can put the pieces together."

The line clicks dead.

I lower the phone to the table, hands trembling so badly I have to set it down twice before it stays. The screen goes dark, reflecting my face back at me—washed out, eyes too bright, like I've been crying even though I haven't.

More to worry about than pushing John.

The phrase loops, ugly and relentless. My chest tightens until breathing feels optional. I don't know if I'm terrified *for* my brother or terrified of what they're circling him for. I don't know which truth would hurt less. I don't know if loyalty means silence or survival anymore.

Images collide in my head—Pax's voice on the phone, bitter and frayed; John's body broken on the pavement; Constance's mother pointing at me like she could burn me alive with accusation alone. Everything feels connected, but I can't see the pattern yet. Just the knots.

My hands curl into fists in my lap. I feel implicated without knowing how. Like proximity itself has become a crime. Like loving the wrong people long enough eventually makes you guilty by association.

The room feels smaller now. Claustrophobic. As if the walls have leaned in while I wasn't paying attention.

I press my palms flat on the table and focus on the grain of the wood, the solidness of it, grounding myself in something that doesn't ask questions. My pulse still won't slow.

Chapter Forty-Nine

S leep never really comes. My body lies down, but my mind stays wired, replaying Pax's voice until it's no longer his—just a rasp of guilt and accusation echoing in my head. By the time the gray edge of dawn slides through the blinds, I'm not waking up, I'm giving up.

My chest feels tight, like someone cinched a belt beneath my ribs. Every inhale is shallow, every exhale unfinished. I keep thinking about Ruiz's voice from last night, low and measured, the weight of it hanging long after I hung up.

Pax has more to worry about than John's fall.

The words throb like an ache.

And what about me?

I can't decide which is worse—the silence from Pax, the headlines tearing John apart, or the possibility that everything I thought I knew about my family is slipping, piece by piece, into a pit I can't crawl out of.

I move through the rooms like they belong to someone else. The photos on the walls feel staged. The couch looks too neat. The stack of bills on the counter could be props in a set I've been dropped into against my will.

The floorboards creak as I wander, the sound loud enough to press against my skull. I catch my reflection in the hallway mirror and stop. My face looks pale, waxy under the early light. The bruised hollows beneath my eyes make me look older. Worn down. I try to look away, but my reflection keeps dragging me back like an accusation.

I grab the coffee pot and set it to brew, watching the slow drip, drip, drip like it's the only thing I can still control. I wrap my hands around the empty mug, waiting for it to fill, needing the weight of something warm in my palms. When it's ready, I take it out back.

The patio boards are slick with dew, the air sharp with chill. The yard is the same patch of grass and wet leaves it's always been, but it feels smaller now. Boxed in. I sit hard in one of the chairs and clutch the mug until the ceramic scalds my hands.

For a while, I just breathe. Or try to. Each inhale scratches, like I'm pulling air through broken glass. The coffee tastes bitter, harsher than usual. Or maybe that's just me.

My phone buzzes on the table beside me. Messages stack one over another, the screen lighting up with names I haven't thought about in months—people from graduate school, colleagues from conferences, old neighbors, even a distant cousin. Condolences. Prayers. Promises of meals dropped off or ears held open.

I'm so sorry. I can't imagine what you're going through. Let me know if you need anything.

They don't know what to do with me. I don't know what to do with them.

I turn the phone face down.

A few minutes later, it buzzes again.

Damien.

His name freezes me. My throat tightens before I even answer.

"Lo," he says, voice low, cautious. "I saw the news."

I don't respond right away. *The news* is everywhere now—John's name plastered across screens, headlines written like verdicts.

College VP Dead in Apparent Fall.
Investigation Shadowed by Scandal.

They don't even bother with the word *tragedy.*

"Are you okay?" Damien asks.

The question pulls a laugh out of me—sharp, ugly. "Do I sound okay?"

Silence. Then, softer: "I'm worried about you."

"I don't need you to be worried about me." The words come out harsher than I mean. "I need people to stop circling like vultures, waiting to see what pieces of me fall off next."

"Lo—"

"Don't. Please." I close my eyes. "I can't carry your pity too."

He exhales, the sound dragging across the line. "Fine. No pity. Just—if you need anything, you can call me. You don't have to go through this alone."

The words are gentle. They still sting. Because the truth is, I am alone. Jenna tries. Sam stays close. But at the end of every day, I'm the one inside this house, sitting with silence and ghosts.

"I have to go," I say, before my voice can break. I hang up before he can answer.

The mug is empty, and my hands tremble as I set it down.

Time moves strangely after that. One moment stretches into the next until I can't tell whether hours have passed or only minutes. The air warms. Sunlight creeps across the patio. Inside, I hear Sam moving—footsteps, the fridge opening. She's making herself small, giving me space. I'm grateful and resentful at the same time.

A knock comes mid-morning. My body locks. Every nerve strains. For a second, I'm sure it's reporters—that they've found me again, that they'll never stop.

But it's only a neighbor holding a foil-covered dish. "I made a casserole," she says awkwardly, eyes flicking past me into the house like she's looking for signs of death on the walls.

I thank her, take it, shut the door before she can ask questions. The smell of cheese and onions seeps through the foil, heavy and sour. I can't imagine eating any of it.

I leave the casserole untouched on the counter. The smell fills the room like a dare. My stomach knots and refuses.

The house goes quiet again.

I drift back to the hallway mirror and catch myself once more. I look like someone I wouldn't trust—hollow eyes, hair tangled from sleep, a mouth pinched tight against words I'll never say. I tilt my head, and for one sick moment I half expect Constance's ruined face to stare back at me instead of my own.

I tear my gaze away and return to the patio, mug clutched in both hands as if heat alone might anchor me.

My phone lights up again—more messages, more condolences. I don't pick it up this time. The silence is heavy, but it feels safer than letting another voice in.

The yard blurs at the edges. Leaves, fence, sky—everything tilts slightly, like I'm looking through warped glass.

Inside, Sam stirs. The clink of dishes. The scrape of a chair. She's awake now, moving carefully, waiting for the moment she thinks I can handle her.

I don't feel ready.

The house doesn't feel like mine anymore. Not after everything. Worse—it feels like it's waiting.

Waiting for the next call. The next knock. The next collapse.

I sip what's left of the coffee, bitter grounds thick on my tongue, and set the mug down hard enough that the ceramic cracks against the table. The sound rings through the morning stillness like a warning bell.

For the first time all morning, I'm certain of something:

This is only the eye of the storm.

Chapter Fifty

The phone rings around ten in the morning, splitting the quiet like a blade against bone. I flinch so hard the spoon in my hand rattles against the rim of the mug. The sound feels enormous, accusatory. Across the table, Sam lowers the newspaper she hasn't been reading—the same page turned over three times, her eyes tracking lines without absorbing a single word.

"It's him," I whisper. My throat tightens before I even swipe to answer, like my body already knows what's coming and is trying, uselessly, to brace.

Detective Ruiz doesn't waste breath. His voice is clipped, precise, built for delivering damage efficiently.

"Mrs. Roberts. I wanted to update you directly before the news cycle gets ahead of us."

My pulse kicks once, hard, then scatters. My heart doesn't race so much as stutter, like it's forgotten the pattern. "Okay."

"The state lab confirmed DNA collected from under one of Ms. Keller's fingernails. The profile is a direct match to your brother, Paxton Carter. Based on that, a warrant was issued this morning for his arrest."

The words don't arrive all at once. They come piece by piece, each one landing and staying.

Direct match.

Your brother.

Warrant.

Arrest.

They stack in my chest until breathing feels optional.

Beside me, Sam's hand flies to her mouth, trapping a sound that's half gasp, half grief. I don't look at her. If I do, I might fall apart in a way I can't come back from.

"DNA?" I hear myself say, my voice distant, thin, like it belongs to someone calling from another room.

"Yes, ma'am. It's conclusive. And it narrows our timeline. This isn't public yet, but it will be soon. I wanted you to hear it from me."

Something inside me gives way—not a clean break, but a slow collapse. My tongue feels thick, useless. My mouth won't shape the thoughts fast enough to keep up with the fear.

"So..." My voice cracks. I clear my throat, try again. "So he killed her."

The words taste poisonous.

Ruiz clears his throat, steady as a metronome. "We don't speculate. What I can tell you is that DNA establishes physical contact at or near the time of death. Mr. Carter will be brought in for questioning today."

The kitchen tilts. Not spins—tilts, like gravity has shifted just enough to throw me off balance. My knees fold without warning and I drop into the chair, the impact jarring, humiliating. For a second, I can't tell if I'm sitting or collapsing.

"But... Pax said—" My voice breaks apart mid-sentence. I press my palm flat to the table, as if I can anchor myself there. "He told me they only talked. He said she was different, but he never—"

The words scatter, frantic, trying to outrun the truth forming behind them.

Sam scrapes her chair closer and crouches beside me, one hand gripping my knee, the other braced against the table. Her eyes lock onto mine, fierce, grounding, like she's trying to keep me from floating out of my own body.

Ruiz doesn't soften. "I need you to think carefully. Does your brother have somewhere he'd run? A cabin, a friend out of state, anywhere he'd go if he felt the pressure closing in?"

The phrase pressure closing in hits something raw. My stomach heaves. Heat floods my throat and I swallow hard, fighting it back. "No." I shake my head, too fast. "He wouldn't run. He's not—"

Innocent.

The word rises automatically, reflexively, like muscle memory. But it fractures before it leaves my mouth, splintering under the weight of everything I've just heard.

Silence stretches. I can hear the scratch of Ruiz's pen, the faint hum of an office line, the sound of a world continuing while mine stalls out.

"We'll keep you updated," Ruiz says finally. "Please stay put today. And if you hear from him, do not engage. Call us immediately."

It takes effort—actual effort—to force sound out of my throat. "Okay."

The line clicks dead.

I stare at the phone for a beat too long before dropping it onto the counter like it burned me. My hands shake violently now, the tremor no longer subtle enough to hide.

"Lo?" Sam whispers.

I shake my head hard, like I can dislodge the words if I do it enough times. "DNA," I croak. Saying it makes it real. "They found his DNA on her."

Sam lowers herself into the chair beside me, slow, careful, like sudden movement might shatter me. "What does that mean, exactly?"

"It doesn't mean anything," I say immediately—too fast, too sharp. Panic disguising itself as logic. "Not like that." I flatten my palms against the counter, grounding myself in the cool surface. "They were seeing each other. Of course his DNA was on her. That's not evidence—it's proximity."

The words come easier now, lining themselves up into something that almost sounds convincing.

"People leave DNA everywhere," I continue, clinging to the thought like a lifeline. "A hug. A hand on an arm. He could've been in her apartment days earlier."

Sam doesn't interrupt. That scares me more than if she had.

"It could've transferred," I add quickly. "From her clothes. From his car. From anything." I swallow. "They make it sound definitive, but it's not. It can't be."

My chest tightens anyway, the argument already slipping through my fingers.

"It could mean they argued," I say more quietly, conceding ground inch by inch. "That things got heated. That she scratched him and stormed out."

My stomach twists violently. I press my fist to my mouth, breathing through the nausea, through the image my mind insists on assembling.

"That still doesn't make him a killer," I whisper, as much to myself as to Sam.

I shake my head again, slower now, deliberate. As if repetition can reinforce reality. "He wouldn't do that. He couldn't."

The words feel thin, fragile. But I hold them anyway, because without them, there's nothing beneath my feet.

"There has to be another explanation," I say. "There just has to be."

Sam's eyes shine. Her lips tremble. "Dear God, Lo."

I press both palms to my temples, trying to keep my skull from splitting under the pressure. "What if telling Ruiz made me the nail in Pax's coffin?" The thought detonates fully now. "What if I just handed them the last piece they needed?"

Sam's voice sharpens, cutting through my spiral. "You did what you had to do. Don't twist this into your fault. Pax made his own choices."

Her words don't settle. They burn.

Guilt spreads hot and relentless, crawling through every vein until I want to claw it out of my skin.

***

By late afternoon, my body feels hollowed out, like something essential has been scooped from me and left behind a shell that still moves out of habit. I've been awake for too long, grieving in fragments—John's body on the courtyard stones, the weight of his name turning into a headline, the way the house now feels like a place he once occupied rather than a life we shared. Every room carries a faint echo of him: his jacket on the hook, his shoes by the door, the toothbrush still angled toward the sink like he might come back and need it.

Sam insists I try to eat something, but the casserole a neighbor dropped off sits untouched on the counter, the smell of cheese and onions souring the room. It feels obscene to consume anything when everything else has stopped. Hunger never arrives; it just circles and leaves. I sip cold coffee because holding the mug gives my hands something to do, something solid to anchor them when my thoughts start sliding sideways.

Time doesn't move correctly anymore. Minutes stretch, then vanish. My body keeps bracing for the next impact—the next siren, the next headline, the next phone call that will explain everything or ruin what little is left. I tell myself I've already absorbed the worst of it. My husband is dead. My marriage is over in every way that matters. The world knows things about us that were never meant to be public.

I'm wrong.

The knock on the door detonates through the silence. My mug tips, coffee spilling across the table and dripping onto the floor.

Sam's already moving, cautious, peeling the blinds back with two fingers. She exhales like she's been holding her lungs hostage. "It's Detective Adams."

My legs don't want to work, but somehow I open the door.

"Mrs. Roberts." Adams's voice is quieter than Ruiz's, but it carries a weight that makes my stomach clench. She steps inside, takes in the room—the untouched casserole, the sour smell, the exhaustion hanging like a fog. Her gaze flicks to Sam, then pins me. "May I?"

I nod, numb.

We move into the living room, sitting arranged like chess pieces waiting for a hand to strike.

Adams opens her notebook but doesn't look at it yet. Her eyes lock on mine. "I want you to hear this directly, so you're not blindsided when the rest of the world hears it."

Sam crosses her arms tight, like armor.

Adams breathes once, then says, "Paxton was located this morning and brought into custody. He has spoken to us at length."

My heart jerks sideways. "And?"

Her mouth tightens. "He admits to being with Constance Keller the day she died. He claims it was not premeditated. He says they were hiking. They argued. He confronted her about lies—about seeing someone else. According to him, she slipped after he shoved her. She struck her head against rocks. He insists it was an accident."

The word rattles in my skull like a loose bullet. Accident.

I squeeze my hands until my nails bite half-moons into my palms. "An accident," I echo, hollow.

Adams doesn't flinch. "He also admitted to confronting John Roberts at the memorial hall. He says John knew what had happened to Keller—though he did not explain how—and that he was furious about John's involvement with her. He claims the argument escalated. He says he pushed John from the balcony."

Sam sucks in a sharp breath like it burned her throat.

My ears roar. The room sways. I taste bile.

"He said it like that?" I manage, the words shredded.

Adams nods once. "He did. He frames both incidents as heat-of-the-moment reactions. Rage. Betrayal. But his admissions align with the evidence—the DNA, the witness who saw a man in a hood, the trajectory of the fall."

My body shakes so hard my teeth chatter. "No," I whisper, then louder. "No. He's my brother. He wouldn't—" The sentence collapses into sobs.

Sam reaches for me, but I stumble back, hands clamped over my face. The sound that rips out of me doesn't feel human—it's keening, raw, torn from a place deeper than lungs. "He's all I have left," I choke. "And now—"

Adams leans forward, her voice firm but not cruel. "Mrs. Roberts, I know this is unbearable. But your brother's actions belong to him. Not to you."

Tears flood hot and relentless. I drop my hands, my face a ruin. "You don't understand. We already lost so much. And now..."

Adams softens, but her words don't bend. "Now it's about accountability. He will have his chance in court. But you needed to hear it from me, not the six o'clock news."

The silence after her words is crushing.

Sam clears her throat, steady despite the shake in her hands. "What happens now?"

Adams closes the notebook with finality. "Now he's charged. Murder in the second degree for Keller. Manslaughter for Roberts. The DA will announce soon. I suggest you brace yourself. The press will come hard."

She rises, pausing at the door. "I'm sorry for what this means for you."

The door shuts behind Adams, and the silence is immediate, cavernous, like the house itself has swallowed its own breath.

Sam turns toward me, face pale, eyes wide with the same horror I feel vibrating in my bones. She reaches for me, but I stumble backward, crashing into the wall hard enough to rattle the picture frames. My hands grope at the wallpaper as if I could tear my way out of my own body.

"No," I gasp, the word tearing my throat raw. "No, no, no."

The air feels heavy, poisoned. My lungs refuse to cooperate. I claw at the collar of my shirt, yanking the fabric until it stretches, until I can feel the cold sting of air against my damp skin.

Sam takes a cautious step. "Lo—"

Her voice shatters me. I bend at the waist, gagging. Bitter acid rushes up, and I barely make it to the sink before I'm heaving, retching until my stomach is nothing but spasms and spit. The sound is animal, guttural. I grip the edges of the counter, knuckles white, legs trembling so hard I can hardly hold myself upright.

Sam's behind me, gathering my hair in her hands, murmuring something low and steady, but her words dissolve in the roar inside my head.

DNA.

Murder.

Pushed him.

My brother's name stapled to crimes that will never unstitch themselves from him.

I rinse my mouth, but the taste of bile won't leave. The faucet runs too loud, too clear. I slap it off and stagger back, pressing both palms against my face.

Images batter me. Pax as a boy, running barefoot through summer grass, chasing fireflies, laughter spilling out of him like sunlight. Then Pax now—hands cuffed, head bowed, police shoving him into the back of a squad car.

I choke on a sob so violent it bends me in half. I collapse onto the kitchen floor, cheek pressed against tile that feels like ice. My body shakes, shudders, betrays me.

Sam drops to her knees beside me, trying to gather me into her arms, but I shove her away, my palms hitting her shoulder. "Don't—" I can't breathe. "Don't say it wasn't me. I opened my mouth—I gave them what they needed."

Tears streak her face. "Lo, listen to me. This is not your doing."

But her words are knives. I slam my fists against the tile, again and again, until my skin splits and stings. "I should have protected him!" My scream cracks into sobs. "I should have shut up. I should have—God, Sam—"

She catches my wrists, firm but gentle, her voice breaking. "Stop. Stop. You can't bleed for his sins. You can't."

Her face blurs. My whole body is slick with sweat, trembling uncontrollably. My stomach knots, cramps, but nothing's left to throw up.

I curl into myself, fetal on the floor, rocking against the cold tile like the movement could trick my body into safety. Sam lowers herself beside me, wrapping her arms around my shuddering frame. Her chin rests against the crown of my head, her heartbeat pounding against my ear.

I sob until my throat is sandpaper, until my chest burns, until my body has no sound left to give.

And still, the images won't stop.

Her fingernails clawing him.

John's body falling.

Pax's hands, red, guilty.

Worse than any of it—the thought that my voice, my words, were the final nail sealing his coffin shut.

Sam whispers over and over, "It wasn't you. It wasn't you."

But I can't believe her. Not when guilt has already stitched itself into my skin, my blood, my breath.

I squeeze my eyes shut, wishing for darkness, for silence, for anything but this truth:

My brother is *a killer*. What. The. Fuck.

The walls press inward. The room bends. My breath tears in jagged bursts.

Chapter Fifty-One

I don't remember lying down. One moment I was curled on the kitchen floor, Sam's arms around me, my body wracked with sobs that felt endless. The next, I was staring at the ceiling in my bedroom, the room warped and humming, the little white pill I'd swallowed finally dragging me under.

Valium. I hadn't touched them in years. Last night I didn't ask, didn't think. I opened the bottle Sam held out like communion and let it dissolve against my tongue.

Sleep came, but not the kind that heals. A heavy, drugged collapse. Dreams blurred with memories until I couldn't separate Pax's laugh as a boy from Pax in handcuffs, head bowed as they shoved him into the back of a squad car. My mind replayed the detective's words on a loop, her voice and my own screams tangled together in some grotesque duet.

He admits. He pushed. He murdered.

When I wake, the world is too bright. The light through the blinds is merciless, cutting into my skull. My mouth is dry, my tongue thick, and every muscle aches as though grief itself has bruised me.

For a moment—one blessed, stupid moment—I don't remember. I lie there staring at the ceiling fan, watching the blades whirl shadows across the plaster, thinking maybe I overslept, maybe I'll have to rush to class, maybe the casserole smell still lingers in the kitchen.

Then it hits.

The weight. The truth. My brother confessed. Constance. John. Both gone. Both his.

My chest caves like something dropped from a height onto it. A hollow implosion. I press my hand against my sternum as if I could keep my heart from seizing.

Sam is somewhere in the apartment; I hear the soft clink of a spoon against a mug, the shuffle of slippers on tile. I try to move, but my body feels foreign—skin too tight, bones too heavy. When I finally swing my legs out of bed, the floor tilts and I catch myself on the nightstand. My phone buzzes where it lies facedown.

I almost don't look. Almost.

But the sound is insistent. Calls. Texts. More texts. The screen lights up with a relentless stream of notifications, the world clawing its way into my life before I've even found my balance.

I swipe, and the flood pours in.

Screenshots from colleagues. Links from numbers I don't recognize. Social media posts forwarded like they're passing around gossip at a barbecue.

Newsday: *"Long Island Love Triangle Ends in Tragedy, Brother Behind Bars."*

News 12 Long Island: *"Professor at Local College Entangled in Family Murder Mystery."*

The Shady Oaks Gazette: *"Halo Roberts: From Faculty Darling to Tabloid Tragedy."*

Each headline slices deeper. Each ding of my phone is another blade.

And then the locals. The ones who cut the deepest.

On Facebook, a woman I vaguely remember from PTA writes in a community group: *"Never trusted her. Always thought she looked smug at Stop & Shop. Guess she had secrets of her own."*

Another post: *"Can you imagine being her student? Yikes."*

Someone else: *"Whole family's toxic. Should've seen it coming."*

I drop the phone onto the bed like it burned me. My stomach lurches, bile rising at the back of my throat. They don't know me. They don't know Pax. They don't know anything.

But they'll devour it anyway.

I stagger toward the bathroom, splash water on my face, and stare at my reflection in the mirror. My eyes are swollen slits, rimmed raw. My skin is grayish, stretched over bones that look too sharp. I look less like a woman than a ruin. A cautionary tale.

The phone buzzes again from the bedroom. Again. Again. I slam the faucet off and grip the sink until my knuckles blanch, but it doesn't stop the sound—the endless pull of the outside world demanding I let it in.

By the time I shuffle into the kitchen, Sam has already made coffee. She's perched on the edge of a chair, her phone glowing in her lap. She looks up, her face a careful mask.

"Don't look," she says, even though we both know it's too late.

"I already did." My voice is barely there. A rasp.

Something in her expression crumbles, but she doesn't reach for me. She pushes a mug across the counter. "Drink."

I wrap my hands around it, though my stomach revolts at the thought of swallowing anything. The warmth against my palms is the only thing keeping me tethered.

My phone rings again. This time it's a name I know.

Jenna.

I let it ring once. Twice. Sam gives me a look that says *answer.* So I do.

"Lo," Jenna says, her voice clipped, already in lawyer mode. "You holding up?"

The laugh that bursts out of me is jagged, humorless. "Define holding up."

"I've seen the coverage." She doesn't waste time. "And I'll be blunt. The rumors are already swimming. Affair, cover-up, you name it. If you don't say something soon, they'll write your story for you."

I sink onto the chair, the mug trembling in my hands. "What am I supposed to say? That my brother killed two people but I didn't know? That I was too busy drowning in my own marriage to notice?"

Jenna's silence on the other end is heavy. Then, "You tell the truth. That you didn't know Pax was involved with her, because he knew her under another name. That you're devastated by what's happened, but you had no part in it. You control what you can control. That's the only way forward."

I press my fist against my forehead, eyes squeezed shut. Her words clang around inside my skull, but none of them make sense. Control? There's nothing left to control. Everything I built—my marriage, my reputation, the idea that family meant safety—has already turned to ash.

"I can't—" My voice cracks. "I can't even breathe, Jenna. How do you expect me to stand in front of cameras when I can't even stand up?"

Her tone softens slightly. "You don't have to do it today. But soon. The press is ruthless, especially here. Long Island loves a scandal. They'll camp outside your house if they smell blood. You need to be ready."

Sam's watching me, her eyes steady, pleading.

I want to tell them both to go to hell. I want to throw the phone across the room, crawl back into bed, let the Valium drag me under until none of this is real.

Instead, I nod, though Jenna can't see me, and whisper, "I'll think about it."

When I hang up, the silence is instant, crushing. Only the tick of the kitchen clock, the low hum of the refrigerator. My phone lights up again—more calls, more texts. My name is bleeding across a thousand screens.

I press the heels of my hands into my eyes, hard enough to spark stars. For one reckless second, I wish I could peel off my skin, step out of this body, leave the mess of it all behind.

But when I open my eyes, I'm still here. Still Halo Roberts. Still the sister of a killer.

No one, not even Jenna, can tell me how to live with that.

***

By noon, I can't hide inside anymore. The phone keeps buzzing, Sam keeps watching me like she's afraid I'll shatter all over again, and Jenna's words echo like a gavel: *You need to be ready.*

But before press statements, before lawyers, there is this: a body that used to be my husband.

The funeral home is tucked off Montauk Highway, wedged between a shuttered deli and a vape shop. The parking lot is nearly empty. The November wind slices straight through my sweater as I climb the steps, and for a moment I can't force myself to push the door open.

Inside, everything smells faintly of lilies and disinfectant. Too clean. Too polite. The receptionist looks up, eyes soft in a way that tells me she already knows who I am. Long Island has a way of making sure bad news moves faster than the tide.

"Mrs. Roberts?" Her voice is hushed, rehearsed sympathy. "This way."

My legs carry me, though I feel detached from them, as if I'm floating a few inches behind my own body. We move down a hall lined with framed pictures of beaches at sunset, like they're trying to sell serenity.

The director meets me in a small office. He is a man in his sixties, suit pressed too tightly, voice grave but efficient. He gestures to a chair. "I'm so sorry for your loss."

Loss. The word feels ridiculous. As if I misplaced John like a set of keys.

He begins with questions, all in that same practiced tone: burial or cremation, visitation or private family service, casket or urn. I stare at him, unblinking, until he clears his throat and rephrases. "Would you like him embalmed, or—"

"Cremation," I say. The word scrapes up my throat. It feels like betrayal, but the alternative is worse.

He nods, jotting notes. "We can arrange that. I should let you know... the injuries to your husband's face are extensive. A viewing may not be advisable."

The room tilts, but I grip the arm of the chair, nails digging into the upholstery. "I want to see him now."

He hesitates. "Mrs. Roberts—"

"I need to see him." My voice is flat. Steel wrapped in exhaustion.

A pause, then a nod. "Of course. Just a moment."

The hallway to the preparation room is too bright, the hum of fluorescent lights buzzing like hornets. When he pushes the door open, cold air spills out.

I see him... John.

My husband.

Laid out on a metal table beneath a sheet.

The director folds the sheet back from his shoulders with delicate precision, but the face—Christ, the face. Swollen, bruised, split. The human shape is still there, but blurred. Broken.

My knees threaten to give out. I grip the edge of the table to keep myself upright.

It's him. But it's somehow also not.

For a heartbeat I expect his chest to rise, his eyes to open—some cinematic moment where he takes my hand and tells me it's all been a mistake. But the air is cold, the body still, and the truth is undeniable.

John is dead.

My husband. My partner and my betrayer.

The man who held me through anniversaries, who whispered promises in the dark. The man who lied, who kept secrets, who shattered me long before the fall that finished the job.

A sob claws its way out of me, raw and violent. I press my fist to my mouth to stop the sound, but it breaks anyway, echoing off the sterile walls.

"I loved you," I choke. "Even when I hated you. God, John..."

The director stands quietly at the doorway, gaze respectfully averted.

I lean closer, near enough that my tears splash onto the sheet. His skin is waxy, alien. I want to kiss his forehead, but the thought terrifies me. I hover instead, whispering into the cold space between us.

"I don't know how to do this without you. Even after everything... I thought we had more time. I thought..." My voice collapses. There are no words left.

The director clears his throat softly. "We can proceed with the cremation arrangements whenever you're ready."

Ready. As if anyone ever is.

I straighten, shaking, and nod. My body moves on autopilot—signing forms, agreeing to choices, letting the machinery of death grind forward while inside I am still screaming.

When it's done, I step back into daylight. The air tastes metallic, sharp. Cars rush past on Montauk Highway—people going to work, grabbing lunch, living lives untouched by mine.

I press both hands against my stomach as if to hold myself together.

This is real. This is permanent.

John is gone. Pax is behind bars. And I—I'm the one left standing in the wreckage, the one they'll all look to, the one the cameras are already circling.

For the first time, the thought flickers through me like a match struck in the dark: *Maybe Jenna is right. Maybe I need to speak.*

I don't go straight home.

The thought of those walls closing in, the phones buzzing, Sam's eyes tracking my every move—I can't. Instead, I take the long way, following Montauk Highway until it forks near the water. My hands move on instinct, turning toward the bay.

The lot by the marina is half-empty. A couple of gulls pick at scraps near a Dumpster, their cries sharp against the steady crash of waves. I park at the far end and sit for a moment, engine ticking as it cools, staring out at the gray expanse.

The water is rough today, whipped by a wind that cuts through my coat the moment I step outside. The air tastes of salt and iron. Clouds hang low, heavy, threatening rain. It's the kind of day that makes the bay look endless. Unforgiving. But alive. Always alive.

I walk to the railing and grip it with both hands, knuckles burning in the cold. The tide churns below, restless, insistent. For the first time since yesterday, my chest loosens just enough to let in air that doesn't scrape.

The memory comes without warning.

It's summer, and we're at Robert Moses Beach, the sky stretched wide and painted pink and gold as the sun slips toward the horizon. The sand is still warm beneath my feet, heat lingering from the day. I kick off my shoes and laugh when a wave sneaks up too close, soaking the hem of my dress.

John steps behind me, arms sliding easily around my waist, like they belong there. His chin rests on my shoulder. He smells like salt and sunscreen—familiar, comforting. I lean back into him without thinking, letting myself be held, letting the moment exist without question.

"You and me, Lo," he says, his voice steady, certain in that way it used to be. Like nothing could touch us. "No matter what."

I believe him completely. There's no doubt, no hesitation. Just the ocean stretching endlessly ahead of us and the quiet certainty that this—us—is forever.

The sound of the waves fades, and the memory dissolves.

I close my eyes as the words crash back into me, sharp and merciless. *No matter what.* A promise broken in a hundred small ways long before his body ever hit the ground.

The wind stings my face, and before I realize it, tears are slipping free—hot against the cold air—falling faster than I can stop them. My chest heaves, but it's different than last night's keening. This isn't disbelief. It's quieter. Lower. The grief of someone who knows there is no undoing.

I let it come.

I let the sobs shake me, my breath tearing ragged against the wind. I cry for John, for Pax, for the girl I was before all this. For the family dinners that will never happen again, the anniversaries already stolen, the faith in love I'll never get back.

The bay roars back at me, endless, indifferent. And somehow that indifference is a comfort. The water doesn't care about headlines or press releases or gossip in Stop & Shop aisles. It just moves. Crashes. Recedes. Returns.

I press my wet face into the crook of my sleeve, the fabric damp with salt and snot, and whisper to no one, "I'm still here."

The words feel fragile, but they're true. Against all odds, against the shattering of everything I thought I knew, I'm still alive.

The wind lashes harder, carrying spray that stings my skin. I let it. For a few minutes, I let the cold bite me, let the water rage without needing to control it.

When the sobs finally taper, I feel emptied—scraped hollow—but steadier somehow. Like the tide has taken just enough weight to let me stand upright again.

I turn back toward the car, my face raw, my body trembling, but my feet move. Each step is proof: I haven't collapsed. Not yet.

Maybe Jenna's right. The world is going to demand something from me. The press. The college. The town.

But first, the water demanded my tears.

And I gave them.

Chapter Fifty-Two

Sam leans close, steady hands guiding the brush across my cheekbone. I've never felt more like a corpse being painted to look alive. The foundation is cool against my skin, powder rising in faint clouds between us.

"Keep still," she murmurs, though her own voice trembles.

Across the room, Jenna paces like a general before battle—papers in one hand, phone in the other, eyes darting between me and the clock on the wall. "We've got less than an hour. They'll be setting up cameras now. Lo, remember: short, clear sentences. No speculation. You're not here to defend your brother. You're here to speak your truth."

My truth. The words feel foreign. My truth is a tangle of grief and rage and guilt I can't untie.

Sam dabs at the corner of my eye, where tears keep threatening to break the makeup she's worked so hard to apply. "Almost done," she says softly, as though this is any ordinary morning—as though I'm not about to stand in front of Suffolk County with my entire life ripped open.

Jenna stops pacing and fixes me with a stare. "They'll try to twist your words. Don't give them anything extra. Stick to the statement. Keep your voice steady. Look directly at the cameras."

I nod, though my throat is closing.

Sam's hand rests briefly on my shoulder. "Breathe," she whispers.

For a moment, the three of us are suspended in this strange tableau—grief, care, strategy. In one hour, it will all unravel under the blinding lights.

"Let's run it again," Jenna says. She reads aloud the draft she's written, her lawyer's cadence sharp and precise.

"I want to address the recent events that have devastated my family and our community. I had no knowledge of my brother's involvement with Constance Keller. During their relationship, he only ever referred to her as Grace, the name she gave him. I had no idea that Grace and Constance were the same person until after Constance went missing. I am heartbroken over her death, and over the loss of my husband, John Roberts. I cannot undo what's been done. What I can do is speak the truth: I did not know. I grieve with you. I ask that you allow the courts to do their work without dragging innocent lives into the fire."

The words hang in the room.

"Say it," Jenna orders.

My mouth feels dry, but I force the words out, my voice rasping them into existence. Each syllable tastes like blood.

Sam squeezes my hand when I falter. Jenna doesn't let up. "Again. Louder."

By the third run, I sound almost steady. Almost.

When the black sedan pulls up outside, Jenna gathers her things and snaps into motion. "Let's go."

The ride to the municipal building is silent except for the tick of the blinker and the occasional cough from the driver. Sam sits close beside me, her hand folded over mine. Jenna scrolls on her phone, fielding texts from reporters and the DA's office, her face an unreadable mask.

As we approach, the crowd comes into view—dozens of cameras clustered at the steps, microphones already hoisted, reporters in heavy coats with their hair lacquered against the wind. Behind them, locals hold up cell phones, hoping to catch their slice of the scandal. Suffolk County on full display.

The car door opens. Noise slams into me—voices calling my name, questions thrown like stones.

"Mrs. Roberts! Did you know about your brother's affair?"

"Lo, did your husband know what Pax did?"

"Are you protecting him?"

"Do you feel guilty?"

Flashbulbs burst, blinding. I grip Sam's arm, but Jenna is already in front of me, slicing a path with her voice sharp as a whip. "One at a time! She will make a statement, and that is all."

We reach the podium. The microphones cluster like a nest of vipers.

I grip the podium, the paper trembling in my hands. My voice sounds too loud through the speakers, but I force the words out line by line.

"I want to address the recent events that have devastated my family and our community. I had no knowledge of my brother's involvement with Constance Keller. During their relationship, he only ever referred to her as Grace—the name she gave him. I did not know that Grace and Constance were the same person until after Constance went missing."

A murmur ripples through the crowd. I steady myself against the microphones jutting toward me and continue.

"I am heartbroken over her death and over the loss of my husband, John Roberts. I cannot undo what's been done. What I can do is speak the truth: I did not know. I grieve with you. I ask that you allow the courts to do their work without dragging innocent lives into the fire."

The final words break slightly, but I keep my chin lifted.

For one thin, fragile second, silence holds. Then the questions explode again—shouted accusations and speculation—but my voice has already been recorded, captured, broadcast. My truth, however small, is now in the air.

That silence lasts only a breath. Shouting surges back, sharp and overlapping, questions hurled like stones.

"Mrs. Roberts, are you saying you never suspected Grace was Constance? How could you not know?"

"Why did your brother hide her real name from you? Were you covering for him?"

"Did your husband John know that Constance and Grace were the same woman?"

"Neighbors say Constance was seen leaving your house once—is that true?"

"Were you jealous of Constance, knowing she was with both your husband and your brother?"

The words batter me from every direction. They echo off the marble facade, cut through the November wind, pile on top of each other until they're no longer questions but a roar.

My vision narrows. Cameras flash white-hot, blinding, disorienting. I grip the podium harder, fingertips numb, as if the wood could keep me from being dragged under. My chest tightens, every breath jagged and shallow.

I hear *jealous* and *covering* and *blame yourself*, each word a nail driven into my skull. Everything else dissolves into static.

Sam's hand presses firmly against my back—a grounding weight. I can't look at her or anyone else, but I feel the heat of her palm through my coat, the silent reminder: breathe.

Jenna steps forward, her voice slicing through the noise like steel. "That's all. No questions. Mrs. Roberts has made her statement."

The crowd ignores her, surging forward, microphones reaching, voices rising.

I step back from the podium, knees threatening to buckle. My throat burns with words I'll never say. My body shakes, but I keep my chin lifted—just enough to hide the cracks.

The driver pulls the car door open. Sam guides me toward it, shielding me with her own body. Questions follow us down the steps, ricocheting against the building—accusations, insinuations, demands.

When the door slams shut behind me, the sound is almost violent. Noise cuts off, replaced by the suffocating quiet of the car. My ears still ring with echoes—*jealous, blame, blind eye*—words that will replay later, in the dark, when there's no one left to stop them.

Sam whispers, "It's over."

It isn't. Not really. The cameras got what they wanted. The town got its drama. I am still the woman they will strip bare in headlines, hashtags, and whispers at the bagel shop.

I press both palms against my thighs to stop the shaking, but it doesn't work. The tremor lives inside me now, stitched into my blood.

The car jerks forward, merging into traffic. For a few blissful seconds, the tinted windows shield me from flashes and voices, from vultures clutching microphones. The ringing in my ears doesn't fade.

Sam slides closer, her shoulder pressing against mine. Her hand finds my wrist, thumb brushing over my pulse like she's trying to convince my body to calm down. "It's done, Lo. You did it. You were steady. You said what needed to be said."

I stare out the window at Montauk Highway rushing past—gas stations, diners, a pawn shop with its neon sign buzzing half-dead. Everything looks ordinary, as if the world hasn't caved in. "They didn't hear me," I murmur. "They didn't want to."

From the front seat, Jenna exhales sharply. "Of course they didn't. Reporters don't want truth—they want blood. You gave them what we needed. On record. On tape. That's what matters."

I meet her gaze in the rearview mirror. "They asked if I was jealous. If I covered for him. Like I..." My voice fractures. "Like I invited any of this."

Jenna's eyes don't waver. "They'll spin it. The Grace/Constance detail will be tomorrow's headline—mark my words. 'She didn't know who her brother's girlfriend really was.' It makes you look naive, not complicit. That's survivable."

Naive. The word lands heavy in my gut. I don't feel naive. I feel gutted—flayed open for their consumption.

Sam squeezes my hand, glaring at Jenna. "She's not a client on trial. She's a human being."

Jenna doesn't flinch. "She's both. If she forgets that, they'll eat her alive."

The hum of tires on pavement fills the silence. I press my forehead to the cool glass, watching the bay flicker through gaps in the buildings—slate gray and restless beneath the bruised sky.

Alive, I remind myself. The water was alive. I am still alive.

As the car speeds toward home, the truth hardens in my chest: being alive means they'll keep coming. The press. The town. The whispers at the bagel shop. I'll be the story until they find a new one.

All I have is this fragile, borrowed mask of steadiness, held in place by Sam's trembling hands and Jenna's relentless strategy.

For now, it has to be enough.

Chapter Fifty-Three

The correctional facility rose out of the landscape like a wound—a gray, square mass that didn't belong to the world around it. Beyond the razor wire and guard towers, there was nothing soft, nothing forgiving. Even the sky seemed to flatten above it, washed out and stale.

I parked in the visitor's lot and sat for a few long seconds while the engine ticked as it cooled. My palms were slick on the steering wheel, my chest buzzing with the same nervous electricity I felt before walking into courtrooms or hospitals. I didn't want to be here, but I had to be. This was the only way to stitch something shut, to stop the bleeding inside me.

When I finally stepped out, the chill hit hard—raw and biting. The path to the main entrance was lined with patches of brown grass trying and failing to grow. The heavy doors opened with a groan, and I was met with metal detectors, a conveyor belt, and the bored eyes of a guard who waved me forward. My shoes squeaked on scuffed tile. The air smelled like bleach, sweat, and something metallic I couldn't name.

"ID."

I handed it over with trembling fingers. The guard studied it, then studied me, then buzzed me through.

Every door that opened behind me locked with a clang. The sound landed in my stomach like lead. A reminder: once you're inside, you're inside.

The visitation room wasn't like in the movies. No long tables, no families sitting together in half-hearted reunions. Just a row of booths divided by thick, scratched glass. Phones bolted to the wall, chairs bolted to the floor. Fluorescent lights hummed overhead, casting a sickly pallor across everyone's skin.

Then I saw him.

Paxton.

My brother.

The orange jumpsuit hung loose on his frame, like he'd deflated inside it. His shoulders curved inward. His hair was longer than I'd ever seen it, dark curls brushing the nape of his neck. He looked up the moment I walked in, and his face shifted—relief, pain, something close to shame.

I sat across from him. The glass between us warped his face slightly, as if even here the truth couldn't come through clean.

He picked up the handset first. His hand shook. I forced myself to lift mine, throat tight, pulse hammering in my ears.

"Lo," he said, his voice raw through the crackling line.

I swallowed. "Tell me."

For a moment, he just stared at me. His eyes were the same deep brown they'd always been—the same ones that used to look out for me when we were kids. Now they were rimmed red, exhausted, hollow.

"I didn't know," he whispered. "Not then. I swear to God. To me, she was Grace. That's the name she gave me. That's all I knew. Her real name—Constance Keller—her life with John...I didn't learn any of it until after she was gone. When I saw her face on the news, I realized. And by then it was too late."

My breath snagged. He must have seen the flicker of doubt in my eyes, because he leaned forward, desperate.

"I need you to believe me. I never meant for any of this. I never meant for her to die."

The handset was heavy in my hand, cold against my cheek. "So what happened?" I asked, though part of me already knew—had already guessed.

He closed his eyes. When he opened them again, something in him gave way.

"She was cheating on me," he said, voice trembling. "I found the messages. The dinners she couldn't explain. The way she pulled away, like I'd stopped mattering. It ate at me, Lo. It burned me alive. That morning, when we went hiking...I couldn't hold it in anymore. I thought if I confronted her, she'd admit it—maybe even beg me to stay. I thought I could force the truth out of her."

He pressed his palm to the glass. His eyes shimmered. "We were on the Manorville trail. It was quiet—just us and the trees. I asked her, straight out. She laughed. Said I was being paranoid. That laugh—sharp, cutting—made me feel small. Like a joke. She told me to stop ruining the day. Then she turned her back and walked ahead like I was nothing."

His voice cracked. "Something in me snapped. I grabbed her arm to make her face me. She yanked back, and I shoved. Just a push. Just anger in my hands. But the ground—it sloped. I didn't see it. She stumbled. Slipped. Then she was gone, tumbling down the hill."

He broke then, choking on sobs, but forced himself to keep talking. "I chased after her. I thought I could catch her. But she hit a rock. Her head—" His eyes darted away. "The sound was loud. Wrong. I'll hear it for the rest of my life."

Bile rose in my throat. My knuckles whitened around the phone.

"I ran to her," he whispered. "Blood was everywhere. She tried to make a sound, but it was faint—and then it stopped. I shook her, screamed her name. Grace. Grace. But she didn't move. She didn't breathe. I killed her without meaning to."

Silence swallowed the booth. Just the hum of the lights and the faint buzz of the intercom.

"I panicked," he went on. "I thought if anyone found her, they'd know it was me. I couldn't think straight. I scattered her things, her phone—tried to make it look like a robbery gone bad. I covered her with leaves like a goddamn child hiding a broken toy. My mouth kept saying sorry, but my hands kept moving. I couldn't stop."

His shoulders shook as he cried. His voice sounded torn open. "I didn't know she was Constance until later. When I saw her face on TV, everything in me collapsed. Grace was Constance. She wasn't some chick who lied to me, who betrayed me—she was John's..." He swallowed hard. "She was his whole other life. And I destroyed it. I destroyed everything."

I pressed my hand to the glass. My palm stung.

Paxton's face crumpled as he shook his head, the handset trembling in his grip.

"It wasn't supposed to happen like that," he whispered. "John figured it out at the memorial. I asked him—stupid, I know—I asked him why he was cheating on you. Why he would risk his marriage to you for someone like her. And he just... looked at me. Really looked. Then he asked me what I was doing there. At her memorial."

His breath hitched, words spilling faster now, like he couldn't stop them. "That's when it clicked for him. He realized I was the guy she'd been seeing. He kept pressing me, asking if I had killed her. Swore he would tell someone—that he couldn't live with it. He kept saying it over and over, face twisted with rage and grief."

Paxton's eyes brimmed. His voice cracked. "I panicked, Lo. I wasn't thinking straight. Everything inside me was screaming. I begged him to stop, to shut up, but he wouldn't. He wouldn't stop." His throat worked. "Then I pushed him. Just to shut him up. Just to make it end."

He dropped his head into his hand, sobbing into the phone. "He fell so fast. Then he didn't move. I didn't mean for either of them to die. But one mistake kept bleeding into the next, and before I knew it, everything was gone."

The world tilted around me. John's face flashed in my memory—his laugh, his touch, the betrayal, the love—then the table at the funeral home. My stomach lurched.

"You destroyed everything," I whispered, my voice fraying at the edges. "You'll never know how much I wish I didn't believe you."

Paxton looked like a child again—small and broken behind the glass, tears cutting clean paths down his face as he pressed his palm flat against it. "I needed to tell someone," he said. "I couldn't die with it inside me. And you... you're the only one I ever loved enough to trust with it."

The guard's shadow stretched across the floor between us. "Time."

Paxton's mouth formed my name. I didn't hear it. The line went dead with a dull click, and suddenly the handset weighed a thousand pounds in my hand. My fingers locked around it, useless—as if letting go would make it real.

The room tilted.

My heartbeat stuttered, then raced—loud and erratic, thudding in my ears until it drowned out everything else. I tried to inhale and it caught halfway in, sharp and painful. I tried again. Nothing. My chest tightened, muscles seizing like they'd forgotten what they were meant to do.

No. No, no, no.

A sound escaped me before I could stop it—thin at first, then louder, breaking apart as it left my throat. I tasted metal. My vision narrowed, edges darkening, and for a terrifying second I was sure I might pass out right here—crumple onto the cold floor in front of the glass where he could still see me.

Hands closed around my elbow. The guard was talking, but his words blurred into meaningless noise. I let myself be guided because I didn't trust my legs to do it on their own. Each step felt delayed, like my body was moving through water.

The doors clanged shut behind me one by one. Each metallic slam reverberated too loudly, echoing inside my skull, sealing the truth deeper into my bones. My hands shook violently now, fingers numb and uncooperative. I couldn't stop it.

By the time the final gate opened to the parking lot, my lungs burned from shallow, uneven breaths. Cold air crashed into me—shocking and brutal—ripping a gasp from my chest. I staggered forward, barely making it to my car before my knees threatened to give.

I braced myself against the hood, metal biting into my palms, and then it all came loose. The sob that tore out of me was loud, animal, unrecognizable. My body folded in on itself as grief and horror collided—wave after relentless wave. I cried until my chest ached, until my throat burned, until there was nothing left to hold the sound back.

The sky above me was wide and empty. The parking lot was silent.

For the first time since he said it—since the truth left his mouth and shattered everything it touched—I understood that nothing, *nothing*, would ever be the same again.

CHAPTER FIFTY-FOUR

Arriving home, I'm relieved to find that although reporters still hover on the sidewalk, there are fewer of them now—only a couple of stragglers with long lenses and tired faces. I keep my head down, shoulders tight, moving fast enough that I don't have to look at anyone's eyes. I don't know what I'd see there. Curiosity. Judgment. Hunger.

The front door clicks shut behind me, and the sudden quiet hits like pressure equalizing. I sag against the wood, forehead resting there, breathing in the silence like oxygen, like maybe if I stay still long enough my body will remember how to function.

Inside, everything is exactly as I left it. The couch. The stack of unread mail on the counter. The faint scent of John's aftershave still clinging to the walls like a ghost that refuses eviction. The normalcy feels aggressive, almost mocking—proof that the world didn't stop just because mine did.

I lower myself onto the couch and sit there, elbows braced on my knees, staring at the floor as if it might open up and swallow me whole.

Paxton's words loop in my head, relentless. His face behind the glass. The way his voice broke when he said he hadn't meant for either of them to die, like intention mattered once blood was already spilled. I press the heels of my palms to my eyes, hard enough to see sparks, but it doesn't help. The images slip through anyway.

John at the memorial.

Pax's panic.

Constance's body in the dirt.

They don't arrive in order. They never do. My brain keeps stitching them together wrong, like if I rearrange the sequence enough times, I'll land on a version where this doesn't end with everyone dead and me still breathing.

My phone buzzes against the coffee table. The vibration is sharp, invasive, like something crawling under my skin. I flinch, then glance down and see Damien's name lighting up the screen.

For a moment, I consider letting it ring. Letting it disappear into voicemail like everything else I don't know how to face. But guilt curls tight in my chest when I remember how clipped I'd been with him earlier, how I snapped like a cornered animal. He didn't deserve that. None of this is his fault—yet my body is treating every voice like a threat.

I swipe to answer. "Hey."

There's a pause, just long enough for me to brace, then his voice—low, careful, like he's stepping onto thin ice. "Hi. I wasn't sure you'd pick up."

"I almost didn't," I admit, sinking back into the cushions. My bones feel hollow, like they've been scooped clean. "Sorry about earlier. I... wasn't myself."

That feels like the understatement of the century. I don't know who myself even is right now.

"I figured," he says gently. "You don't owe me an explanation, Lo. I just wanted to check in. Make sure you're okay."

The word okay lands wrong. It scrapes. A laugh escapes me before I can stop it—sharp, brittle, unfamiliar even to my own ears. "Okay? That word doesn't even exist in my vocabulary right now. I went to see Paxton today."

Saying it out loud makes my stomach drop all over again.

Another pause. I picture him sitting wherever he is, absorbing that, adjusting his mental image of me. "Wow," Damien says softly. "How was that?"

"Awful. Necessary, but awful." I drag a hand down my face, my skin still buzzing like it's been shocked. "He told me everything. About Constance. About John. Hearing it out loud from his mouth was like having my whole world ripped open all over again. I keep replaying it. Every word. Every look on his face."

I don't tell him how my brain keeps insisting that if I replay it enough times, I'll find the moment where I could've stopped it. Like this is some twisted puzzle and not a catastrophe.

He exhales slowly, the sound grounding in a way I didn't realize I needed. "You must feel so heavy. Like you're carrying all of it at once."

"I do," I whisper, surprised by how quickly the tears rise. "It's crushing. He looked broken, Damien. Completely undone." My voice wobbles. "He's my brother, and I love him, but I don't know how to reconcile who he is with what he's done. I don't know how to hold both without tearing myself in half."

I swallow hard, my throat burning. "And then there's John. God, I don't even know how to mourn him properly. Half of me still hates him for betraying me, and the other half—" My voice catches, splits. "The other half still remembers he was my husband. My partner. For ten years."

Ten years doesn't vanish just because the ending is ugly.

There's a long stretch of silence, but it doesn't feel empty. I can hear his breathing on the other end—steady, patient. It reminds me that time is still moving, whether I'm ready or not.

Finally, he says, "It makes sense to feel both. To hate him and grieve him. To love your brother and still be horrified by what he did. None of it is clean. It's all tangled. And you're in the middle of it."

The words hit somewhere deep. Tears spill before I can stop them, hot and angry. I swipe at them with the back of my hand, irritated by my own body's insistence on feeling everything at once. "Sometimes I feel like I'm losing my mind. Like maybe I should have seen it coming. Or stopped it. Or done *something*."

Because if I missed it, if I was blind, then what does that say about me?

"You're not losing your mind," Damien says firmly, no hesitation. "You're surviving something that would have destroyed most people. And blaming yourself is the last thing you need to do."

I want to believe him. I really do. But guilt has a way of sounding like logic when it's loud enough.

I let out a shaky breath. "You always know what to say, don't you?"

He chuckles softly. "Not really. I just care about you. And I can't stand the thought of you sitting in that house alone, tearing yourself apart, thinking you've got to figure this out by yourself."

His words land right in my chest, tender and bruised. I squeeze my eyes shut, letting them sink in, even as another part of me resists them—afraid that leaning on someone will only make the fall worse later.

"Why are you being so nice to me?" I ask quietly. The question surprises even me.

"Because I want to be," he says simply. "No strings. No expectations. I'm just here, Lo. A hundred percent. If you need anything—middle of the night, middle of the day—I'm not going anywhere."

Something in me finally gives way. I curl my legs under me on the couch, clutching the phone like it's a lifeline, like his voice can keep the walls from closing in. "I don't know what comes next," I admit.

"Everything feels unstable. Like the ground could drop out again at any second. But hearing you say that... it matters more than you know."

"Good," he says gently. "Then let me keep saying it, as many times as you need."

A small laugh slips through my tears, fragile but real. "You're too good for me."

"No," Damien replies, steady and sure. "I'm in your corner. Always."

We sit in the quiet for a while, neither of us rushing to hang up. The sound of his breathing steadies mine, anchoring me just enough that the silence in the house loosens its grip.

For the first time since everything detonated, the quiet doesn't feel like it's trying to kill me.

***

The bay is rougher than usual tonight.

Waves slam against the rocks like they're trying to break free of themselves, the water gray and furious beneath a sky sagging with clouds. I shove my hands deep into my coat pockets, but the wind still slices through me, needles through fabric, through skin, through whatever defenses I thought I had left. It whips my hair into my face, stings my cheeks until they burn.

I don't know why I came here. Only that I couldn't stay inside anymore.

The house had turned on me—too quiet, too heavy, every room holding echoes I couldn't escape. The couch still smelled faintly of John's cologne, stubborn and intimate, like a hand on my back that refused to let go. Every time I closed my eyes, Paxton was there too, his face warped by scratched glass, his voice breaking as he told me the truth. Love and horror braided so tightly I couldn't separate them.

So I drove until the road ended.

I grip the cold railing at the end of the pier and lean forward, letting the salt spray hit me full on. It coats my lips, seeps into my lashes. My body feels hollow, scraped clean. Like if the wind pushes hard enough, I might just lift and disappear.

Then the memory comes anyway.

John and me, years ago, at the ocean. One of those endless summer evenings when the light stayed golden long past when it should have faded. He carried me into the surf, my arms locked around his neck, laughing and screaming for him not to drop me. He didn't. Of course he didn't. He held me like the world could never pry us apart. Salt on our lips. Sand sticking to our skin. His mouth at my ear, whispering forever like it was a promise and not a hope.

Forever.

The sound that tears out of me is ugly. Animal. I fold over the railing and sob, burying my face against my arm as my whole body shakes. I cry for John—for who he was and who he wasn't. For Paxton—for the brother I loved and the man I no longer recognize. For Constance, caught in the wreckage of other people's secrets. For myself. For the woman I was just weeks ago, walking through her days believing her life was solid, that love and family were anchors instead of fault lines.

The ocean doesn't answer gently.

It roars back at me, relentless and unmoved, waves crashing like a warning: *move or drown.*

I straighten slowly, throat shredded, face numb and wet with tears and wind. The water is still violent. Still unforgiving. Nothing has softened.

But I'm still standing.

"I'm still here," I whisper, the words ripped away instantly by the wind.

Alive. Utterly shattered, but alive.

The gusts howl harder, tugging at my coat like they want to claim me too. I tighten my grip on the railing, cold biting into my palms, chest heaving as the sobs finally loosen their grip. For weeks—maybe longer—I've been holding my breath without knowing it. Living braced for the next blow. The next secret. The next betrayal. Every cell in my body waiting for the other shoe to drop.

And now... it has.

Everything is out. Ugly. Brutal. *Final.*

The bay crashes below me, steady and merciless, and I let myself stand in it—inside the noise, inside the loss—until my body finally loosens, until my lungs pull in air that doesn't hurt quite as much. One long, trembling exhale leaves me, carrying something with it. Not the pain. That stays. But the waiting.

The sound is small against the roar of the water, but it's mine.

It's finished.

As impossible as it feels to believe, there's nothing left to uncover. No more wondering. No more waiting for the knife I can't see coming.

There's a strange power in that. A quiet, uncelebrated peace.

The waves keep raging, indifferent to my survival. I stay anyway—breathing, shaking, upright—carrying the weight of everything I've lost and the hard, steady truth that nothing else can be taken from me now.

This is what's left. For tonight, it's enough.

EPILOGUE
NINE MONTHS LATER

The sun here feels different. It doesn't just shine, it spills golden and alive over everything it touches. It glints off car windows, climbs the pastel-painted houses stacked along the hills, and makes even the cracked sidewalks glow warm and forgiving. Through the wide front windows of the cafe-bookstore, I watch the life on the street outside: a couple strolling hand in hand with paper cups of coffee, a jogger with her earbuds in and a golden retriever trotting faithfully at her side, two kids chasing each other with ice cream cones already dripping down their wrists.

Inside, the air smells of espresso and old books, wood floors creaking under every step, shelves stretching toward skylights where the late-morning light filters in. It's the kind of place that feels timeless, like you could get lost in the pages of someone else's life and forget your own for a while.

It still feels unreal that this is my life now. San Francisco.

I never thought I would leave New York, but in the end I had no choice. Shady Oaks was unbearable. Every hallway, every door on that campus, carried ghosts I could not live with. John's office, the quad where whispers followed me like shadows, the way students and colleagues looked at me with pity or suspicion. The house we lived in together was worse. Every room was heavy with lies and grief. I knew if I stayed, I would keep unraveling.

Sam felt the same. Long Island carried too many scars for her as well, too many memories that left her raw and restless. She wanted to return to her California roots, to be closer to her sister Serenity, to finally breathe again. When she told me she was going, I didn't hesitate. I couldn't. I sold the house, collected John's life insurance, and we walked away.

It has been a month since we landed here and set our boxes down in the three bedroom condo off Union Street. The place still smells like paint and possibility. Sunlight fills every corner, spilling through windows that look out over a city that does not know me, does not know my story. Here, I am not Halo Roberts, the professor with the cheating husband and the murderous brother. I am just Lo.

For now, I write. I read. I sit with my thoughts instead of drowning them in noise. I have the privilege of pausing, of not needing to work yet because of the house sale and John's insurance money. It feels indulgent, but necessary. For the first time in years, survival isn't clawing at my throat.

My phone buzzes against the table, breaking me from the drift of my thoughts. Damien's name lights the screen. I feel myself smiling before I even swipe to answer. That is what it has been like with him lately. Easy. Anticipated. A thread of steady warmth I didn't know I could still have.

"Hey," I say, leaning back into my chair, the corners of my mouth tugging higher.

"Hey, Lo." His voice is warm and steady, a sound that feels like it belongs here in this cafe with the sun slanting through the glass. "Soooo... I booked a flight."

A laugh escapes me, light and surprised. "A flight? Should I be flattered?"

"To see you," he says, and I can hear the grin in his words. "Next month. Your boy is coming to San Francisco."

For a moment I just sit there with the phone pressed to my ear, watching strangers pass by outside, their lives moving as easily as the breeze rolling through the street. Anticipation swells inside me, sharp but not frightening. It feels different than anything I've carried before.

"That's a long flight just for me," I tease, tracing the rim of my coffee cup with one finger.

He doesn't hesitate. "For you, I wouldn't mind traveling to the end of the world." He says it simply, like it's a fact, not a performance. Like there was never another answer.

I glance around the cafe, at the shelves lined with books, at the light that makes the dust motes glow, and something inside me loosens. For so long every relationship in my life has been knotted with lies, secrets, guilt. But Damien has never tried to fix me, never rushed me, never filled the silence with words I didn't need. He simply shows up, again and again, steady and patient.

"When exactly next month?" I ask, smiling into the receiver.

"The second week. I'll text you the flight details once I have them. I didn't want to wait to tell you. I wanted you to know you've got me in person soon."

I close my eyes and let the words sink in, the sound of him filling a part of me I thought had gone silent for good.

"I'm glad," I whisper, my voice steady now. "I'm really glad."

There's a pause, soft and warm, then his laughter, easy and sure. "Me too."

When the call ends, I set the phone down beside my coffee, fingers lingering against the wood of the table. Outside, the street is alive with color and sound, people moving forward with their lives. For the first time in a long time, I feel myself moving too.

It hits me then, how far I've come. Nine months ago, I was living in a house that reeked of betrayal, suffocated by whispers, drowning in grief so heavy I could barely breathe. Every day felt like a punishment. Every breath was borrowed. The weight of John's death, of Constance, of Pax's confession—it all pressed on me until I thought it might break me for good.

And yet, somehow, here I am. Sitting in a sunlit cafe with a mug of coffee cooling between my hands, watching strangers laugh and chase their children down sidewalks that slope toward the bay.

I think of Sam, unpacking boxes in the condo, humming to herself as she arranges books on the shelves. She's steadier here too. Calmer. We left New York together, carrying our ghosts in boxes, but here they seem to lose their shape a little. Maybe that's what this place offers—space to lay them down without everyone watching. Without everyone naming them for you.

I think of Serenity, who hugged me like a sister when I arrived, and how Sam's smile was wider than I'd seen in years standing in her family's kitchen. I think of Damien's voice in my ear, steady and patient, a reminder that not everyone vanishes when the storm hits.

There are scars I'll always carry. John's absence is a hole that can't be filled, no matter how much I wish otherwise. Some days it still feels like I'm reaching for him out of habit, only to remember there's nothing there to touch anymore.

And Pax... loving him now is its own kind of grief. My brother exists in fragments: the boy who used to protect me, the man who sat across from me behind glass and told me the truth, the person who made one choice in a moment of rage that rerouted every life it touched. I know

now how thin that line is. How a single second, a single push of emotion without pause, can split a life cleanly in two. Before and after. Who you were, and who you can never stop being once it's done.

I carry all of him at once. The love, the rage, the sorrow, the unbearable knowledge that I can miss him and still never forgive what he's done. Sometimes the sound of his voice in that room comes back to me—raw, shaking—and my chest tightens like I'm standing there all over again, watching a lifetime collapse into a split second that couldn't be taken back.

The losses won't vanish. They don't soften with time the way people like to promise. But here, they don't feel like anchors dragging me under. They feel like markers—etched into me, yes, but no longer holding me in place. Proof that I lived through what should have finished me.

I pick up my phone again and scroll aimlessly for a moment, stopping at the blank document I'd opened earlier. The cursor blinks, waiting. I haven't written anything worth saving since everything collapsed, but something in me wants to now. Not for publication, not for anyone else—only to mark this day. This moment.

I type: *Nine months later, the sun feels different. And so do I.*

The words sit on the screen, small and unpolished, but they're mine. A beginning hidden inside an ending.

I lift my face toward the window, let the light spill over me, and draw in one long breath. This time, when I exhale, it's not jagged or heavy. It's steady. Real.

Outside, the city hums. Inside, for the first time in months, I feel ready.

Not free. Not finished.

But finally, undeniably, *alive.*

AUTHOR'S NOTE

Dear Reader,

If you're reading this, thank you for spending your time with Things We Shouldn't Do. Truly. Finishing a book is one thing; having it land in the hands of a reader willing to go along for the ride is something else entirely.

If this story moved you, unsettled you, surprised you, or stayed with you after the final page, I would be incredibly grateful if you'd consider leaving a review. Reviews may seem small, but they make a very real difference for authors. They help books get discovered, signal to algorithms that a story is worth sharing, and allow independent authors like me to keep doing this work.

Even a few sentences helps more than you know.

Thank you again for reading, for supporting my work, and for being part of this story's journey. I'm so glad you're here!

With endless gratitude,

Lindsey

Acknowledgements

This book asked a lot of me, but this story—and the completion of this book, gave me so much. For starters, this book sat at around 27,000 words for about two years while I got my bearings and fought for the safety and custody of my son. So picking this story back up and finishing it in 2025 reminded me that I am still an author.

This book reminded me that I can still write, even when life is imperfect. It required a willingness to sit with discomfort and keep going anyway. While the story may be fiction, the process of bringing it to life was deeply real, and I didn't do it alone.

First, to my readers: thank you for trusting me with your time, your attention, and your hearts. Every message, review, and quiet moment spent with my words matters more than you know. This book exists because you continue to show up and read.

To my beta readers and early reviewers: your thoughtful feedback, sharp eyes, and genuine enthusiasm helped shape this story into what it became. Thank you for reading an unfinished version, asking hard questions, and believing in the vision even when it was still finding its footing. A special shoutout to Delissa, La Reina, and Kate for sticking with me throughout the beta phase.

To my editors and creative collaborators: thank you for pushing me to go deeper, darker, and more honest. For seeing what this story could be and helping me get it there with clarity and care.

To my writing community: fellow authors, creatives, and friends (especially Debra!) who remind me that the work is worth doing even on the days it feels impossible—thank you for the encouragement, the craft talks, the voice notes, and the reminders to keep my ass in the chair.

To my sons, Zakaria and Kalvin: thank you for your patience, your love, and the grace you give me as I chase this dream. You are my why in more ways than I can ever put into words.

To Kelvin, for cheering me on even though you couldn't fathom ever writing this many words, even in a lifetime—thank you for being a support and a source of love through my return to writing and back to peace.

Finally, to myself: for returning to the page after stepping away. For trusting the pull back to storytelling. For finishing what I started. For choosing to stay with the work, even when it would have been easier not to.

This book holds pieces of all of you. Thank you for being part of it :)